Sweet Emily

Thomas J. Nichols

Thomas Nichols
Aug., 2012

© 2012 Thomas J. Nichols
All Rights Reserved.

No part of this publication may be reproduced, stored in a retrieval system, or transmitted, in any form or by any means, electronic, mechanical, photocopying, recording, or otherwise, without the written permission of the author.

First published by Dog Ear Publishing
4010 W. 86th Street, Ste H
Indianapolis, IN 46268
www.dogearpublishing.net

ISBN: 978-1-4575-1054-0

This book is printed on acid-free paper.

This book is a work of fiction. Places, events, and situations in this book are purely fictional and any resemblance to actual persons, living or dead, is coincidental.

Printed in the United States of America

Other Books

by

Thomas J. Nichols

*

Color of the Prism

The Third Dawn

Voices in the Fog

Noble Generation II – A Memoir

*

See the author's website at

www.thomasjnichols.com

Prologue

THE ROAD TO PERDITION IS a magnificent highway that flows through the majestic splendor of the nation: across vast prairies of the heartland; through blistering deserts; over tiny brooks and mighty rivers; through soft green swales and the rolling fields of grain; and into mountain passes where the snowcapped peaks reach to the heavens. It flows like a ribbon blowing in the wind above the cliffs where land and the deep-sea collide, and where crashing waves cascade on the rocks below.

A traveler can join it anytime of their choosing. The joy and pleasure of the journey satisfies the desires of all those who seek it. But, the Road to Perdition ends in a most ignominious manner.

*

Andre Ilin tilted the seat back as the Airbus climbed away from the Danish coast. The tall, angular, fiftyish Russian accepted the vodka from the flight steward, sipped it politely for a moment, and then returned to his brusque lifestyle and swallowed the remainder in one gulp. He threw an icy stare at the steward, handed the glass back, and commanded, *choba, choba*. Loquaciousness was not his strongpoint.

The Russians, Chechens, and certainly the Americans, had used his deadly skills over the years, but now he was a liability; everyone wanted to put on a new face – in public at least, so the market for his talents evaporated. He enjoyed his work too much and brought undue attention to the supposed problems he solved only to create another one.

He accepted another Beluga Vodka, eyed it carefully and thoughtfully, then swirled it into a slow and methodical flow. His old life was behind him, but he would start anew. He recalled the tale from his grandmother many years ago as they suffered through a bitter Russian winter. It was a fairytale about the father of a poor family who was reborn as a swan with golden feathers. If the family plucked only one feather at a time, they would always have enough to live on; they wouldn't be hungry again. Sadly, the greedy mother plucked too many feathers and the swan died – and the family died in the frigid Siberian cold.

Andre shrugged. He would never make the same mistake again. He turned his eyes back to the fading skyline of Copenhagen. The trip, so far, was pleasant and uneventful. The high-speed Sapsan train from Moscow's Leningradsky Station to the Mosklosky Station in St. Petersburg was covered in just over four hours. From there, a pleasant three hundred-twenty kilometer motor trip on the Lux Motor Express to Tallinn, Estonia. Then, a relaxing overnight Tallink ferry into Copenhagen.

A fresh start in America would enable him to utilize his lethal skills while enjoying the liberty and pleasure of his new home. Indeed, he looked forward to the life with its rewards of money, adventure, and most assuredly, the pleasures of the flesh.

*

Emily Morgan lay on the masseuse's table at *Bon Petite Salon* atop the Winchester Hotel across the street from the infamous Texas School Book Depository and the equally infamous "grassy knoll."

She enjoyed the final minutes of her day at the spa – a pedicure, facial, haircut and color, and finally with the practiced fingers of Dominic soothing the muscles of her graceful, well-tanned arms and legs. It was a day of majestic splendor. She smiled inwardly; she deserved it.

Her mind free floated. Single, thirty-five years old, financially secure, smart, maybe even brilliant, and most of all, she had a plan. Life was good, but was going to become even better. She knew what she wanted and was going to do it. It had begun in the not too distant past in Central America and she was determined to see it through. Her newly minted future was beyond exciting. It's possible for a woman to have everything and still have more. That's what life is all about.

*

Detective Mike Palotti tucked little Samanta into her car seat. He steadied her for a moment while her eyes slowly closed, then snapped the seat belt securely. He held a finger to his lips with a soft, "Shush," as Annalisa eased the front door shut. They were at the end of a long, hot, fun-filled day at the amusement park, and were ready to go home. Mike slipped behind the wheel, leaned over to give a light kiss to Annalisa, and then started the car.

"Great day," Annalisa said as she looked back to their little sleeping angel. Mike smiled a silent reply, backed out of the parking spot, then eased the car out of the parking lot – thirty minutes and they would be home. They'd enjoyed his three-day weekend without any callout . . . a unique and pleasant reward for the long hours he worked.

Mike leaned to his right and whispered to Annalisa, "Best weekend in a long time."

Annalisa smiled back and nodded. "It was wonderful," she commented. Mike eased their car onto the open road – onto the Road to Perdition.

***

Chapter One

THE WIND DASHED THROUGH THE dark alley. The glow of the yellow streetlights muted the stark edges of the dumpsters and rubbish that floated whimsically in the crisp air. A lone figure stood patiently in the shadows and looked up at the fourth floor window, exhilarated by the stalk as much as by what would follow. The killer's homework was finished.

Sara wouldn't be long now. She was a predictable creature of habit. She worked late every Tuesday. That ordinary work routine assured her death.

#

Sara Lynn McComb looked out her office window at the gathering darkness. A bag lady scurried with her heavily laden shopping cart across the street and disappeared into an empty storefront. Sara shivered. The nightscape was cold and uninviting, so unlike the Chamber of Commerce pictures of the lighted skyline in the glow of a Texas moon. She pushed back from her desk, adjusted her shirt, and glanced around the office. The cubicles were dark and deserted. Only the sound of the wind as it ebbed down the hallway broke the deathly quiet of the building. Everybody was gone.

She leaned down and pulled her backpack from beneath the desk, kicked off her heels, stretched, then wiggled her toes. It felt good. She stuffed her dress shoes into the pack and slipped into her Nikes. She closed her eyes, took a deep breath, leaned back in her chair and exhaled slowly. The tension flowed from her neck and shoulders. It was as though she were a new human being. Another day was done.

"Baby girl," she said to herself, "you're going to make it. We'll do fine without him." It was time for her and the kids – just the three of them. What a breath of fresh air they could be … their laughs and giggles, and the funny faces they made. She smiled and was totally refreshed. They made the work and long hours worthwhile. It would be nice if their daddy lived at home, but sometimes things just don't work out. He could still see them whenever he wanted, and he was steady with his monthly checks. Things could be a lot worse.

The muffled steps of her jogging shoes were barely audible as she walked past the quiet workplaces, their computers silent and asleep, then past the empty receptionist desk to the hall. She stopped to take one last look before she set the alarm and turned the lights off, then pushed open the exit door to the garage. Her trusty little Passat seemed to smile at her when she stepped toward it. She loved that little car. It fit her personality, and most certainly her budget. After all, it was paid for. She hit the automatic door lock and slipped in behind the wheel.

Sara backed out of her space in the parking garage, turned and twisted down from the upper decks, slipped her Reddy-Pay card in the slot, patiently watched the gate roll back, and headed for home. The long day was over. She glanced at her watch. It was seven o'clock and the kids were still at the babysitter's. It would be eight o'clock before she picked them up, stopped by O'Leary's Cow for hamburgers, and got home to feed them.

She merged into the last of the outbound traffic. Minutes later she found herself in the northbound lanes of the North Dallas Tollway, far from the hectic pace of the law firm and ready to enjoy what was left of a night with the kids. Traffic remained heavy until she passed the LBJ Freeway, then slackened. She sat back and relaxed.

She exited at the Spring Valley turnoff, made a right turn, and stopped at the traffic signal. It was only about five more minutes before she would see Molly and Mandy. Traffic diminished to almost nothing. She signaled for a right turn and started to go, but stopped abruptly when a black Mercedes screeched to a halt beside her. The driver gave a short toot of the horn, lowered the passenger side window and pointed toward the back of her car.

Sara lowered her window and glanced toward her rear tire.

A shotgun extended through the open window of the Mercedes. An explosion ripped through the air. Sara's body lifted out of the driver's seat and slammed toward the passenger side. The seat belt and shoulder strap went taut. Her body jerked back like a rag doll and crashed into the driver's door. Her matted, bloodied hair sprayed across the headliner with a final touch of artistic irony. Sara Lynn McComb, a thirty-five-year-old single mother of six-year-old twins drew her final breath.

#

Detective Mike Palotti leaned back in his chair, put his feet on the desk and yawned. His eyes burned. Long hours on the computer took a toll on him. His neck and shoulders ached, his lower back cramped along his belt line, and his brain was a fog of names, dates, places and weapons until it became an unintelligible mass of information. He reached for the mail atop his in-basket, took a deep breath and exhaled slowly, then tossed it back. He was done for the night.

Today was his birthday of sorts – five years in the Dallas Police Department Cold Case Squad, a group of detectives whose task was to solve some of the most vicious cases that eluded other detectives, some for years; murders, rapes and robberies.

"Dreaming, big guy?"

Mike looked over his shoulder. It was Maureen O'Conner, the trim and shapely red head DNA specialist from the crime lab.

"Hey, if it isn't Miss Goodwrench," he joked. "What brings you around this time of night?"

Maureen stood behind his chair, draped her arms over his shoulders and looked down at him. "Tell me, Michael, what's a big, good-looking guy like you doing sitting around a joint like this hours after you're supposed to be home?"

He took her hands in his and looked up to catch her gaze. Her lips were soft and delicate; her hair fell sensually over her forehead. "Well, I'd like to say I was waiting for some gorgeous woman to come find me, but that would be a lie. Of course, if it was true, I'd sure like it to be you." He cracked a smile. "No, I've just about worn myself out on these cases. It's time to call it a day."

"I'd say it's past time." She stepped back, turned away and dropped the strap from her shoulder bag. She pulled out a standard business-size brown envelope and handed it to him. "I promised your sergeant I'd have these reports for him by the time he gets here in the morning. Mind giving them to him for me?"

Mike took the envelope and stuffed it in his in-basket. "At least you found something I can do."

"Give yourself a break. You're one of the best detectives in the department. Otherwise, you wouldn't be working cold case homicides." She leaned forward and blew a kiss on his cheek. "Nite, Mikey."

He watched her walk back toward the door. When it closed

behind her, he swung back around in his chair. "Yeah, but what an ass she's got," he mumbled as he picked up the stack of cases from his desk.

"Too damn much for one guy," he muttered. The most recent was four months old, a seemingly wanton murder of a woman going home from work – Sara Lynn McComb. But there were others dating back nearly eighteen months. He was stuck. Every case had been reviewed; witnesses re-interviewed; every shred of evidence delivered to the crime lab where they were luminoled, x-rayed, and DNA'ed, but they still came up empty-handed. The backgrounds of the victims were scrutinized with a magnifying glass. Each case was submitted to the FBI's Violent Criminal Apprehension Program where they were meticulously analyzed. The ViCAP, as it was known, submitted every known bit of information on the victims, business and personal relationships, the weapon, the day and time of day, location, full moon, no moon, weather, or any strange tidbit of information that might shed a ray of light on the suspect. More so, the ViCAP analyzed similar cases elsewhere in the country and tried to link them together through common denominators.

Mike laid the cases on his desk like a game of solitaire. He had looked at them so many times. He felt his spirit slipping away with each beat of his heart. He was dying a slow death of failure. If this was a card game, he'd played his cards and lost with these victims:

Sara Lynn McComb, a legal secretary in a car by herself – a shotgun slug to her head.

Allison Reynolds, a dentist jogging in the park – multiple stab wounds.

Leonard Throckmorton, a news photographer taking pictures along the Trinity River – multiple small caliber gunshots.

Landa Lopez, a freelance artist – garroted with a wire in a mall parking lot.

Andrew Maines, a retired plumber – beaten with a club in a bowling alley parking lot.

Denton Ryan, a high school teacher – throat slit while walking his dog.

\#

"Hi Mike, what're you doing here this time of night?"

He laughed inwardly. Twice in one night. He looked back and saw Willie Mae, the custodian who'd cleaned the squad room for more years than anyone could remember. She put her arms around his neck and gave him a squeeze.

"Hi, Willie, how are you?"

"Just fine, honey. You were supposed to be out of here hours ago. What's the matter? Something got you troubled?" She looked at the case folders on his desk. "Sweet thing, you need to just put that bad stuff away for the night and go home. You do have a home, don't you?"

"Yes, I have a home, but I can't get these off my mind. I'm stumped, Willie Mae. For the first time in a long time, I'm totally stumped."

"Well, it looks to me like you're playing a game. Dallas is what you have there. What's that supposed to mean?"

Mike screwed his face. "Dallas? What do you mean?"

"Look, honey." She pointed to the case folders. "Aren't those the names of those dead people?"

"Yeah, sure," he replied. "But you're losing me. Dallas?"

"Mike, my boy. You're serious, aren't you? Get your tired old butt out of that chair and stand back. Look at your cases right there where you have them. Don't touch a thing."

The detective scooted his chair back and stood up. His forty-three-year-old body wrapped in a six-foot, two-hundred pound, body-builder frame towered over the tiny Willie Mae. She stepped around him, and with her scrawny little fingers pointed out the first name of each of the murder victims. "See what I'm saying? Denton, Andrew, Landa, Leonard, Allison, and Sara. See that?" she exclaimed. "D-A-L-L-A-S. Dallas."

"Oh my God," Mike rubbed his forehead and pushed his graying hair back from his brow. "Willie, what have you stumbled on? Go on. Tell me what else you see."

"Sugar, sometimes you boys work too hard and get so close you can't tell one thing from the other. Maybe, just maybe, somebody is telling you something. He might be playing a game with your head, but he's killing folks while he's doing it."

"You mean they were killed to spell out the name Dallas?"

"Now listen here, Mister Detective Michael Palotti, I ain't telling no such thing. I'm just telling you what jumped out at me when I came to empty your trashcan. Nothing more. Don't get this thing all spooky on me, ya hear me, young man?"

"Do you think some nut actually might be killing people in some sort of game?"

"Hmm, might be. Might not be. Say, did I ever tell you how my sister over in Tyler plays the lottery?"

"No, but I think I'm going to find out."

"Chicken shit. That's how she does it. Every Friday night she puts the newspaper in the floor of the chicken coop, and when she gets up in the morning she goes out and sees what pages the chickens shit on the most. The six pages with the most shit on them she plays in the lottery." Willie Mae laughed, then continued. "And there's more. She only bets one dollar a week. That's fifty-two dollars a year. She has a lot of fun and wins about eighty, maybe a hundred dollars a year."

The diminutive-sized cleaning lady smiled and nodded her head. "And it's all chicken shit. So that's what I'm telling you, Mister Detective. You might just be dealing with some chicken shit chance, or ...," she paused, "... or you might be dealing with the devil himself."

"Okay, stay with me a minute more on this thing. If, and that's a big 'if,' this really is some nut case doing this, then what do you think? The killer spelled Dallas, so is he – or maybe she, done? Might there be more? What else could he spell? Maybe the Cowboys? The Stars? How about the Mavericks? Or, maybe even Texas. What do you think he'll do?"

"Hmmm." Willie Mae stared at the folders. She rubbed her pointy little chin and continued to look at the names of the murder victims. "It couldn't be the Cowboys, because they're actually not in Dallas. But, the Stars or the Mavs? Yes sir, I think you need to be real careful 'cause I reckon someone might going to be murdered. But who? Honey, I don't have the slightest idea, and there's no way you can run out of here and save everyone. No sir," she said wistfully, "ain't no way." She looked up at the clock, then to Mike. "Young man, it's late. Get home to your wife and little girl."

Mike looked at their pictures on his desk. Annalisa – her dark shoulder-length hair and innocent smile; Samanta astride a pony at the petting zoo. "You're right, Willie Mae. There're better things to do besides hanging around here."

He watched Willie Mae roll her trash barrel around the corner dragging her dust mop behind her. Mike picked up Annalisa's picture, looked at it, and thought about when they met – their first date, the first kiss, the day he asked her to marry him, for Miss Annalisa Trocchio to become Mrs. Michael Palotti. It was all so distant, yet as fresh in his mind as if it was yesterday.

SWEET EMILY

"Baby girl, I love you," he said. He kissed her picture and put it back on his desk. Eleven years of marriage and she was as beautiful as ever, maybe even more so. The olive complexion of her skin bespoke her Sicilian heritage. Her curly long black hair was always meticulously groomed; the softness of her lips; the grace of her shape; the sexiness of her long legs … his wife, best friend, and his little girl's mom. What else could he ever want?

He shoved his chair up to his desk. "Babe, here I come."

#

Mike started his morning going through the last four years of Dallas telephone books. He made notes, then shuffled each one aside until his desk was a clutter of frayed pages and turned-up corners. It was mid-morning when he sat back and crossed his arms across his chest. Success!

Up to the time of their murders, each of the victims was listed in one phone book or another. He put the stack aside, pushed away from his desk, went to the receptionist's desk, picked up a stack of current and old city directories and carried them back to his desk. A quick charge of energy zipped through his body. He focused his mind; he had a target. Would they each be here, too?

He looked at the clock as he slapped the last book shut. It was exactly noon. The slightest smile creased his face. All of them were listed in the directory with their home address, phone number and occupation. He felt a new sense of confidence. Little by little, he was finding what each of the murder victims had in common with each other. It was not a lot to go on, but for the first time, there was a link. It was small, but nevertheless, a link. He felt a spring in his step when he walked back to the receptionist with her city directories.

A good-humored voice rang out from across the room. "Hey, Dapper Mike, what the hell are you so happy about? Haven't seen you so chipper in a long time." It was Rickey Gonzales, Mike's cubicle mate in the crowded work area they called the squad room. Rickey spun around on his swivel seat, leaned back, and looked at his fellow detective. "*Que paso, amigo*? Get laid last night?" he laughed.

"I'll never tell," Mike replied. "Anyhow, I think I got a break on these murders. I'm grabbing a car and heading out for a while. Got some places to check out. Want to go for a ride?"

"No, *gracias*, got my own cases to chase. Good luck. See you later." Rickey spun back around to his desk and poured himself back into his own work.

Mike looked at his watch. It took twenty minutes to drive to Sara's apartment in a gated community. Unfortunately, like many other so-called gated communities, the gates were open most of the time. He drove his aging and weary unmarked police car through the circuitous drive until he found apartment E-28, the former home of Sara McComb. He made a few notes to himself – single-story apartment; open carport facing the driveway; upscale, but not extravagant; trash cans kept in the carport.

He kept the cases in reverse chronological order. Next was Allison Reynolds, the dentist. She lived roughly three miles from Sara, but like Sara lived in a gated community. He wasn't surprised to find the gate open and drove directly to her apartment. Doctor Reynolds and her husband of thirty-eight years lived in an elegant, two-story townhouse at the rear of the property. Mike noticed two cars parked in the carport – once again facing directly out onto the driveway. He would check their registrations later, but with one a Cadillac and the other a Lexus, he assumed they belonged to the doctor and her husband.

The detective zipped through traffic, found imaginative ways around construction projects, stopped for a Starbucks on Preston Road, but eventually scouted out each of the victim's homes.

Leonard Throckmorton – two-story apartment on the low end of an upper middle-class apartment house. It was nothing fancy, but a nice place in a relatively modest neighborhood.

Landa Lopez – an old but meticulously maintained first floor apartment house in an area that was seeing a steady rate of re-development and higher home prices.

Andrew Maines – another apartment, this one just off Lower Greenville and close to the Southern Methodist campus in a high-priced rental area that catered to students and young professionals.

Denton Ryan – a quaint duplex in a neighborhood of comparable homes and duplexes. Nevertheless, it was a luxurious but older neighborhood with lots of gingerbread trim on the houses, well-groomed flower beds, and potted plants.

#

Rush hour traffic started to build by the time Mike pulled back into the police parking lot. A sense of satisfaction pumped through his veins. Minutes later, he sat across the desk from Lieutenant Molina. The squad sergeant, Pat Covey, sat next to him.

"I'm on to something," Mike said. "It's not great, but it's the best link we've come up with so far." He pulled his notebook from his jacket pocket, flipped the pages until he found the six pages with the notes from his checks at the murder victim's homes, then began a simple recitation of what he'd found – what amounted to the slim lead that tied together the six previously considered random murders. The issues were simple, easy to understand, and if the people were not murdered, would be no more than pure coincidence.

"Let the facts speak for themselves," he said. He pointed to his notes and continued. "D-A-L-L-A-S for starters. There were no children or elderly victims. They ranged in age from twenty-eight to sixty-one years old. Each of them lived in apartments, duplexes, or townhouses, and had carports that could be seen from the driveway or the street. All of them were listed in the phone book and the city directory. Each one was squeaky clean in their personal and business lives. All the murders occurred in a public place and in the open where they would be found almost immediately, yet there were no eye witnesses. There was no effort to hide the bodies; and, last but not least, no two of them were killed in exactly the same manner." Mike looked up from his notes and gave a sheepish grin. "Of course, they died violently."

Sergeant Covey interjected, "Lieutenant, tomorrow morning we'll put together another ViCAP package and get it analyzed again."

Molina nodded his head in approval. "Good going, Mike. I don't know if we'll ever clear these cases, but right now I'd say you're looking good. Hang in there and let's see where it goes."

#

The lieutenant and sergeant knew it would be a couple weeks before the FBI finished their work and sent the packet of information back to the Cold Case Squad. "Mike, you've got vacation time stacked on top of comp time. Why don't you get out of here for a while?" Covey remarked.

The detective nodded and tossed a friendly glance at Covey. "Thanks, not a bad idea." Mike didn't waste any time. He called Annalisa. "Sugar, the boss told me to use up some of this vacation time I've got on the books. What do you think?"

"You're reading my mind. I went to the bank this morning, got our bills paid, and just finished the laundry." She chuckled softly into the telephone. "ESP or something, but I can be out of here in a couple hours after you get home. We're cleaned, ironed and all but packed."

"How about going up to Colorado for fly-fishing and hiking?"

"I'm ready, cowboy. Let's get it on."

"A good night's sleep and we can hit the road early and beat the traffic out of town." He paused, then spoke softly, "Love you, baby girl."

"I love you, too. Hurry home."

#

After dinner, they packed the car, showered, and were in bed by eleven o'clock. It wouldn't be just a jaunt in the park, but a two-day drive to their favorite fly-fishing streams in southern Colorado – Elk Creek, the Conejos River, and a handful of lesser known streams – rivulets that flowed like silver ribbons in the sunlight, cut through eons of rock to form deep pools, and spread out on the high meadows near the Continental Divide. If there was ever a place a millennium away from the cruel murders in Dallas, this was it.

They hired pack mules to haul them and their gear up the trail in the San Juan Wilderness to Second Meadow just below the tree line. The air was pure and thin; the sky a crystal blue, dotted with puffy clouds that floated over the distant ridges.

"Look, Daddy," Samanta squealed. Twenty-five-inch rainbows darted out from the overhanging grass when she walked to the edge of the stream. Annalisa and Mike strolled hand-in-hand from their tent to the stream. Mike scooped Samanta into his arms and set her on his shoulder. "Hey, big girl, you have to stay with us and not go exploring by yourself. I don't want you to catch more fish than me," he joked. He carried her back to the tent, let her down, and gave a peck on Annalisa's cheek.

"It's time to put a fly in the water." He popped the tube open, pulled out his rod, and minutes later waded upstream. He stepped into the fast-flowing water, adjusted his grip, and moved carefully toward a calm pool thirty yards away. A trout darted from beneath a grass overhang and disappeared into the glare of the afternoon sun. Mike moved silently, casting and hauling his line until he reached the edge of the pool. He was unrestrained, as free as the clouds and the birds in the sky. He breathed deeply and was replenished by the cool mountain air. He focused his aim, and with a smooth motion put the fly exactly on the spot between the flat water and the ripples at the edge of the grass. Mike learned this lesson a long time ago – flies are not "cast" into the water. They are "presented." Cast flies chase away the fish. "Presented" flies offer the trout a meal not to be denied.

There was a quick snap of his line and just as suddenly, a release of the tension. He realized he'd lost his fish. Twice more they caught him unprepared for the power and speed when they hit the fly. On the forth presentation, he got his rhythm back.

"Yes!" he bellowed. The trout slipped unseen in the ripples and blinding glare of the afternoon sun. Mike was unaware of it being there until he heard a "pop" when the line went taut and his rod bent sharply toward the water. There was a splash when the fish broke the surface. It danced on its tail and dove to the shelter of the rocks on the bottom. Mike worked his way upstream, stepping carefully on the slippery rocks and mud in the streambed, all the while maintaining a high tip on his rod to keep the fish from freeing itself.

He slowly started hauling the line in, and bit-by-bit could feel the trout losing its strength. Finally, it was there. Just below him. He slipped the net beneath the now exhausted fish and scooped it up.

"Dinner's on," he shouted.

The next several days did not vary much from each other: a campfire for morning coffee and eggs followed by a hike up the mountainside where they could sit on a ledge and watch two bald eagles in their nest or floating effortlessly in the high mountain air. Later in the afternoon he chased the all-elusive trout with a variety of dry flies and nymphs, but the late night was the best of all times. They would lay quietly on their bedrolls spread out on the grass, count the millions of stars and listen to the noise of the night – crickets, owls, trout feeding on the surface, and some creatures that made a lot of strange sounds unknown to Mike or Annalisa.

They put Sam between them where she could curl in close to ward off the night air, and together they would make up stories about the stars and the angels. Samanta's breathing became shallow, and she fell asleep looking like a little princess in her mountain kingdom.

It was a vacation like no other. No newspapers or twenty-four-hour news channels, and no pager or cell phone; in fact, not one other human being for the entire week. Twice during the time on the mountain, Mike hiked up to a rocky overhang where he was completely alone, to a place where he looked down on the stream and across the valley to the next ridgeline. It was absolute bliss. He was at peace with himself. No headaches. No neck aches. Nevertheless, he knew if he ever had to run from the demons, whatever or whoever they might be, this is where he'd come. It would always be safe here – so far away, so secluded, so alone with the truth.

"Why," he thought, *"do I have this feeling? I don't know, but it's true. This is where I'll come."*

Finally, on the eighth day, their wrangler and mules came up the trail to load them up and head back down the mountain. Back to the uncivilized world of civilization.

Annalisa was the keeper of the money. By the time they loaded the Suburban with their gear, she pronounced that they were not yet broke. "Can't go home with money in our pockets," she proclaimed. She looked at Mike when he slipped behind the wheel.

"Over the mountain?" he asked.

"To Santa Fe," she replied. "I need some clean clothes, a shower, and some hot fry bread with honey on it." She tilted her head back and let the wind tousle her silky black hair. "Love you, Mikey," she said.

She laid her head on his shoulder and looked back at Samanta in the back seat, already sound asleep. Annalisa closed her eyes and dozed while Mike guided the Suburban up over the La Manga Pass and on to Santa Fe.

The afternoon sun slipped behind the mountaintops before they found a motel. They stashed their suitcases and backpacks in the room and walked to the square where, just as Annalisa wanted, she found the Navajo women making fry bread and covering it with honey and powdered sugar.

"I'm a fulfilled woman," she joked.

The next two days were a complete contrast to the quiet majesty of the high country wilderness, but also were a perfect fit to round out their vacation. They hopped from art gallery to art gallery; from sidewalk café to sidewalk café; from pueblo to pueblo, and store to store – new hiking boots for Mike; a bracelet and earrings for Sam; a skirt and blouse for Annalisa. She was frugal with every penny, but at last declared it time to go home.

They sat in the dining room at the La Fonda Hotel for their last dinner. Samanta wore her delicate turquoise and silver bracelet and earrings that stood out in contrast against her olive complexion and dark hair. She was only five years old and just a child, but a mirror image of her mother. Long ago she'd mastered the art of wrapping Mike around her little finger, and he loved it. He and Annalisa swore they would never spoil her, and they didn't, but nevertheless, she was his little angel.

Annalisa and Mike toasted their wine along with Samanta's glass of apple juice to themselves and the fun they'd enjoyed on their trip.

SWEET EMILY

"Here's to Daddy's fishing," Sam said when she clinked her glass against theirs.

"And to the way you could hike in those mountains," Annalisa added.

"And to the ladies of my life," Mike said. They glanced at each other, tapped their glasses again and sipped their drinks.

They ate key lime pie for dessert, had a last cup of coffee, and strolled the long way around to the park in the square, savoring every minute of the mountain air before going to their motel. Tomorrow would be a long drive.

#

Mike grabbed a cup of coffee and went into the squad room.

"In here." Sergeant Covey motioned for Mike to go with him and the others to the back of the squad bay.

"Surprise! The FBI got ahead of schedule. Your packet came yesterday, but we left it for you," Molina commented. Covey, Molina, Mike and Rickey gathered around the meeting room table and sorted through the papers until at last they came to the meat of the documents.

"Here we go," Covey said. He laid the papers out where each of them could scan down the column of information entitled: **SUSPECT TENDENCIES**.

If the detectives hoped for some quick identifier to give them the name and address of their serial murderer, they would have been sadly disappointed. Of course, they didn't look for anything quite that simple. What they found was as much as they could hope for. The report read:

SUSPECT TENDENCIES
1. ANGLO MALE;
2. LONER;
3. 30 – 45 YEARS OF AGE;
4. RIGHT-HANDED
4. COLLEGE GRADUATE OR EXTREMELY FOCUSED SELF-TAUGHT PERSON;
5. WELL VERSED IN VICTIMS' DAILY ROUTINE;
6. INTRICATE SURVEILLANCE OF VICTIMS INDICATES ABILITY TO MOVE EASILY AND NOT ATTRACT ATTENTION IN UPPER MIDDLE-CLASS NEIGHBORHOODS;

7. AVOIDS LOWER INCOME AND HANDICAPED PERSONS;
8. AVOIDS CHILDREN AND ELDERLY;
9. IDENTIFIES PERSONS WHO ARE UNSUSPECTING;
10. MAY HAVE A PERCEIVED NEED TO TEASE INVESTIGATORS;
11. MAY HAVE A VENDETTA TOWARD CITY OF DALLAS;
12. WANTS VICTIMS TO BE LOCATED SOON AFTER THE COMMISSION OF THE CRIME.

The ViCAP summary included the analyst's general observation and summary. Sergeant Covey leaned back in the chair and read aloud:

"These offenses are probably committed by one person working alone. He is an extremely thorough planner. Due to the nature of these offenses, he follows a pre-set pattern of victim selection, but does not place time constraints on his activity, thereby allowing himself to commit the crime in a public place, but leaving sufficient opportunity to escape unimpeded.

"There is a strong likelihood the suspect's innocent appearance allows him to approach the victims without arousing their suspicion.

"All of the physical evidence indicates that the wounds on the victims, whether from the front or from behind, are a result of the suspect utilizing his right hand as the dominant hand to inflict the injuries.

"The suspect may have a strong dislike for the City of Dallas based on an unpleasant personal or professional experience with local government. Your attention may be directed toward a disgruntled current or former employee, elected official, or a private citizen who has unsuccessfully challenged local government on an issue such as zoning, codes administration or taxation.

"The pattern of offenses does not correlate with any other offenses under investigation by this office."

Covey was unceremonious. He tossed the report on the desk and grunted. "Well, at least they think about the same as we do, but where the hell does that take us? Got any ideas who might be pissed at our fair city? Damn, I can come up with a thousand names right now. What about you?" He looked at Mike.

"Same. Hell, it could be some cop who got fired and is screwing us over. Could be that guy they call Crazy Eddie that runs for City Council every election and gets the crap beat out of him. You know, last election he got so crazy in one of those public forums they had to haul him off in a straightjacket. They kept him under observation for a week or two, at least until after the election, then they let him out."

"Yeah," Rickey responded, "but it can't be him 'cause your killer is a sharp s.o.b. and Crazy Eddie doesn't even know his left foot from his right."

Covey cut in. "We're beating a dead horse. Who the hell has the slightest idea who this nut is? It could be one of thousands of people." He looked at Mike. "I hope you're wrong about it being some ex-cop who got the axe from this place. That would be bad. Very bad," he emphasized.

Mike knew Covey was getting close to retirement. His whole adult life had been given to the Dallas PD and he'd seen more than his share of troubles, and didn't need another. His first partner in a two-man car accidentally ran over a teenage runaway who was sleeping under the trash in an alley; another time he was on a stakeout at a drug store when some teenagers tried to rob it, and when he moved in to be close to the door when they left, the kid saw him and in a panic, turned and shot the clerk in the head; there was the night he was on patrol downtown and caught an off-duty sergeant slipping out the back door of city hall with the next promotional exam tucked under his arm; and, the worst of all, the time he served a warrant and arrested an old cop, one who was a friend who also was nearing retirement but ran a child porn business out of his garage. Covey did not need to deal with another police scandal. He wasn't sure his psyche could handle it. He was getting too old for that.

Mike gathered the papers together and shoved them in a folder. "Let's just say our prayers that this nut is done with Dallas." He started to leave, then chuckled to himself and turned to the others. "Maybe he'll go down to Waxahachie. Now that would be real trouble."

#

The sun had long ago slipped beneath the horizon when Mike got behind the wheel of his car to go home. He promised Annalisa he would get off on time so they could go out for dinner. They would get a babysitter for Samanta and have a quiet night – just the two of them.

"Hi, lover," he shouted when he stepped through the door. The house was dark but for a lone candle flickering on the coffee table in the living room.

"Sam?" he called. No one answered.

Mike walked slowly down the hallway toward the back of the house. The soft sound of music floated in the air. He stopped and listened. It was a George Winston song,

"Give Me Your Hand," a song he and Annalisa had made love to many times.

"Annalisa," he called.

"Mike, I'm in the tub. Come talk to me."

He loosened his tie and eased the bathroom door open. The room glowed with the flickering light of a half-dozen candles. Annalisa was deep in the tub, buried in a duvet of soapsuds.

"Mom's keeping Samanta tonight," she said.

A bottle of Merlot was perched on the edge of the tub along with two long-stemmed wine glasses. "Pour for us?"

Mike sat of the edge of the tub, leaned back against the wall and looked at her. "You make my day. You don't have any idea how badly I want you tonight."

"Oh, I think I do," she responded coyly. Mike uncorked the Merlot, poured a small portion in a glass and handed it to her. Annalisa's hand rose through the bubbles and took the glass. She spun it carefully and watched the legs form on the inside of the glass. She tilted it to her nose, inhaled deeply, then sipped a taste of the wine – a slight taste, no more. She cast her eyes to Mike and smiled.

"Perfect. Absolutely perfect," she whispered.

"So are you, lover girl," Mike replied. He loosened his tie and bent forward. They kissed.

#

Mike and Rickey divided up the work. What the old-time cops called shoe leather and flat feet had evolved into a new generation of work hazards and carpal tunnel syndrome – hours at the computer pounding the keyboard. It was a nearly endless task of searching city records for the last three years looking at city council minutes. They reviewed codes administration records, matched zoning requests applications, and delved into personnel records. Somewhere in the nearly endless pages of hearings, elections, firings, zoning rejections, and run-of-the-mill politics was the answer – someone chagrined enough to decide to take on the city, to have a final say-so and leave the bureaucrats at city hall looking like fools.

Mike's fingers were numb by the end of the week. He'd reviewed every rejected application for the police department and then turned to the National Crime Information Center and ran the names. He looked for anyone who failed the DPD entry process and ran into legal trouble somewhere else. Only one name looked suspect – Roger James Garfield. He'd failed the polygraph test for new employees almost three years ago. Before he left the personnel department, he took time to go to the director's office.

Mary Dale Ford, the director at that time, remembered him vividly. He'd walked brusquely passed the receptionist, barged into her office, and in a tirade of expletives told her what he thought of her and the whole damn city. However, it was his departing comments that she recalled so well. "You people will get your comeuppance someday. Just wait and see." With that, he turned and stormed out of the office.

A surge of adrenalin darted through Mike's veins. Three months after the incident at the personnel department, Garfield was arrested in Houston for killing his girlfriend. Charges were filed, but dismissed later when the Criminal District Attorney found sufficient evidence that he'd acted in self-defense when she came at him with a baseball bat.

Mike read on through the files. The adrenalin dissipated. He read the last entry aloud. "Garfield was pronounced dead when his body was recovered in Possum Kingdom Lake, the victim of a water skiing accident." He was dead when the last two murders occurred.

Time crawled while the two detectives sat at their terminals scouring records, looking for anything that might lead them to the killer. Finally, Rickey found a good candidate in the zoning records. A Romanian gypsy immigrant, Tasmine Ulrecht, applied for a business permit and was denied. Like Garfield, he threw a temper tantrum, cursed the board members, and stormed out of the zoning hearing. Three days later, the chairman of the zoning commission reported a prowler at his house in the middle of the night. The uniformed officers who responded found the gypsy hiding under a car a couple of doors away. They arrested him on misdemeanor charges. He pleaded guilty, paid a one-hundred dollar fine and was released.

The next week he was found walking the halls at City Hall with a butcher knife tucked in his belt. Once again, he was arrested. This time, though, he was committed for a mental evaluation and was sent to the State Hospital for treatment.

"He looks like he could have the potential and more or less meet the ViCap profile," Rickey commented as he shoved the packet of reports over to Mike. "Maybe we're on to something. We'll just have to check him out."

The two detectives divided up the calendar and started backtracking everything they could find on Ulrecht for the last two years – where he lived, when and where he worked, traffic tickets, anything they could find that would document him being in the Dallas area during the time of the murders.

Rickey identified one unique thing about him that was unlike most gypsies. "Take a look at this," he said when he passed his notes to Mike. "He always lives alone, not like other gypsies we've worked. They always hang together. Not this guy. He's a loner." Rickey tossed a confident smile at Mike. "This guy is different, even for a gypsy."

The two detectives spent the afternoon compiling their notes on Ulrecht. Things started adding up against him – his temper, willingness to carry a concealed weapon, stalking the zoning commissioner, living in Dallas at the time of the murders, and his anger at the City of Dallas.

"Any vibes?" Mike asked.

"Let's play our cards and see where it takes us. I've got a friend at IRS. Let me have him scout this guy out and see what else we can come up with. It's about time we had some good luck. Let's hope this guy is alive and kicking somewhere around town."

#

The two detectives were cleaning off their desks when Rickey's phone rang. Mike stood by to listen to one side of the conversation.

"Okay, Dave. You're sure now, aren't you? I mean, this guy is a big fish to us, so you're confident about this?" There was a long pause. Mike watched Rickey nod his head, silently absorbing the information from the IRS agent, his body melting with every word from the caller. It couldn't be good news.

Rickey eased the phone back on the cradle and looked at Mike. "For sure, he was on an oil rig in Alaska when Maines was killed. He couldn't have done it. Plus, Dave ran some Medicaid records – files you and I can't have access to. Guess what? He was in Parkland Hospital with gallstones the night of the McComb murder. He's not our guy."

#

Mike sat at the breakfast bar sipping a cup of coffee and scanning the *Dallas Morning News*. "What the hell?" he clamored. There it was on the lead page for the Metro section.

Cops Close in on Serial Murderer

He zipped through the article; his temper soared with each word. Everyone knew the mayor was taking a public whipping for high taxes, labor problems in the Sanitation Department, street crime in Deep Ellum and along Lower Greenville, but this was unacceptable. In her effort to deflect criticism, she needed good news to dole out to the editorial board, and this was it. Detective Mike Palotti was hot on the trail of a serial killer who'd struck at least a half-dozen citizens in the last two years. The mayor was pleased in the police department's unwavering efforts, and was confident "the men and women in blue" were making progress helping Dallas to become a place in which the citizens can feel safe and at ease.

A quick kiss on Annalisa's cheek and he was out of the house and on his way downtown. Traffic was miserable and it only served to make him more stressed than he already was. He finally shoved his car into a space in the parking lot and made his way to the elevator and into the squad room. Molina looked up from his desk and threw a sarcastic grin toward Palotti.

"Lucky boy, Mike. This is the day you've waited all your life for." He nodded his head toward the meeting room. "Got someone waiting for you – approved by the Chief."

"What the hell is going on?" Mike asked.

"PR, my good man. Simple enough. The mayor and chief are in deep crap for some good publicity and you're it." He paused and gave a sidelong glance. "Give it hell, and good luck."

Mike walked to the meeting room and swung the door open. His heart fluttered. Surely, one of the most beautiful women on the face of the earth was seated at the far end of the conference table. He paused for a second to focus on calming his anger. Cindy Crawford, he thought, has nothing on this woman. He took full measure of her in the few seconds that he gave himself: thirty-five years old; 5'8", 130 pounds; long brunette hair flowing over her shoulders to the top of her breasts; a white open-neck blouse and navy skirt; but, no birthmark at the edge of her lip. In spite of his anger, he smiled inwardly to himself – just good police work.

"Good morning," he said. The door shut behind him.

"Good morning, I'm Emily Morgan." She rose and extended her hand in a greeting. "I know you're not expecting me, and to be honest with you, I wasn't expecting that big spread in the morning paper."

"I wasn't either, but there's nothing I can do about it. What can I do for you?" Nevertheless, his words belied his true thoughts. He worked hard and had no time for the public relations game that some idiot, Chief or not, dreamed up. He knew the rules and would do what he had to do, but that didn't soften his frustration. This was pure politics to make the mayor happy and he knew it. He managed a polite smile. "Besides, what does the morning paper have to do with you?"

"My former husband, bless his soul, was a college friend of Mayor Coolidge. In a way, I might be responsible for the mess in the paper. You see, I've been a policy researcher for the last few years. I did all of the legwork, so to speak, for my husband. You might be familiar with his work. He wrote seventeen books and another dozen professional articles in public policy manuals."

"No, guess not," Mike replied.

Emily took her seat, and Mike pulled out a chair and sat beside her. "Be that as it may, what can I do for you? I'm a cop, not a public policy type of guy. Maybe you need to see someone else." He allowed a hint of his feelings to seep into the conversation, but at the same time maintained a semblance of professional decorum.

"I apologize for the abruptness of my intrusion into your work. Of course, I recognize how important it is for you to devote all your energy to it." She smiled, and whether he wanted it or not, he felt the slightest touch of her disarming personality.

"I give you my solemn promise," she said, "I'll work with you and not against you. You'll catch your killer and I'll never get in your way. That's very important," she emphasized, "but also of importance is that my research, along with your work, may help others in the future to catch madmen before they kill over and over again. That's what this is really all about. Do you understand? Will you help me?"

Mike nodded. "I'm not sure I'm following where this is going, but yeah, I'll help if I can. Just keep in mind my priority is to catch this nut case, and if in the process I can help you write your book and help some other cops, that's great."

Emily brushed her hair back from her forehead and with a flick of her head tossed it over her shoulder. Nothing escaped Palotti's attention. Everything about her was sensual. The way she spoke, the glimmer in her eyes, and the way she held herself. She was as perfect as a woman could appear.

"That's fair, and I wouldn't ask for any more than that. So, let me tell you a little about me, and we'll see where we go from there. When my husband died four years ago, I was more or less stranded, professionally, that is. I do research, but don't have much of a writing background. My husband left me financially secure, but I didn't have any real goals for my research. I was lost." Emily shifted her chair around, modestly crossed her legs, and faced Mike. He glanced at her legs, then back to her eyes. A warm glow flowed through his body.

"I've traveled and done a bit of freelance stuff, but I'm trying to settle in on a major project. That's what brings me to you. I'm researching a book on homicides, tough homicides, not the Saturday night street shootings. It's not the crimes themselves. I'm doing an in-depth look at the procedures police departments use in solving the unsolvable. What makes you tick?" She pointed her finger at Mike. "What drives you? How do you get there – there being in front of the Grand Jury and walking out with an indictment? How do the rules fit what you do? What rules do you have to make up on the run? How does the bureaucracy serve you? Or, does it?"

Mike grinned. "You're serious, aren't you?"

"Very. I want to write the most revealing book ever done on successful police procedures. I want to make my own mark, not just be Edgar Morgan's widow. Anyhow, I pulled a few strings and sat down with the mayor last week, and wallah. Here I am. Sorry, though, about the morning paper. That was her highness on her own. I would never do that to you. In fact, I don't want to know anything specific about your cases, because it might distract or bias me in what I'm trying to learn. All of it should be pure research. The details of what you're finding would probably upset me. I'm not used to the macabre."

She smiled at him and crossed her legs the other way. "I'm from academia, and my work doesn't blend with the things you have to deal with. On the other side of that same coin, I ask that you not inquire about what I'm compiling in my research, where I'm getting it, and to whom I am speaking." She tossed a hint of a smile and continued, "That kind of thing. For both of us, this has to be pure research. I cannot and will not impose on your work, and your day-to-day investigation can't be hampered by my research."

She extended her hand to him. "Deal?"

Mike shook her hand politely. "To be completely honest with you, I don't like having to take time out from my work, but I'm willing to cut you a little time once in a while if it doesn't interfere with my primary business." He looked at her with all the seriousness he could muster. "Remember, my job is to put killers in prison, not to do somebody's public relations work. I'll work with you on a 'time available' status," he said when he formed the quotation marks with his fingers.

"Okay. A deal is a deal. I won't be asking you where else you're digging things up, and you don't push me for those things that in the business we call 'evidentiary value,'" he said while he once again formed the quotation marks with his fingers. "So, where do you want to start? But let's keep it short. I've got a pretty full schedule for today."

"I want to learn how the system and how the administration serves you. What do they do to help you solve your cases? But also, what do they do to fuck you up?"

Mike looked at her. That one word caught him off guard. She was too perfect to talk like that.

"Fuck me up?" He paused for a second and continued. "They don't. I do my job and they do theirs. It's as simple as that," he exclaimed.

"Good answer. That was what I was hoping for. You answered the way I wanted you to. Good start. See? You gave an excellent response. You think fast on your feet. You're flexible, like a boxer. You bob and weave, and come back. That just might be the key to successful investigations. It starts with personnel administration. Evaluate. Select. Train. It all starts with getting the right people to do the job."

"You don't have to write a book to figure that out. That's common sense."

"Sure. Common sense." She laughed. "Common sense is probably the least common thing we find in public policy. But you? You have common sense and that's why you're successful."

Mike relaxed. She was professional, to say nothing of beautiful. His mind roamed while she was talking. *What a job*, he thought. *Sitting here with Miss World right in front of me and I'm complaining. Most guys would give their right arm to work with this ...* he paused. *This what? Lady or big pain in the butt? Only time will tell, but I'll make the most of it.* He caught himself.

"I'm sorry. I've got so many things on my mind right now. What was it you were saying?"

Emily smiled. "I know you've got to get back to work, and I don't want to detract from your job, so I'd like to schedule a few short meetings over the next several weeks. Let me have a little time to pick your brain. I won't get into any specifics on your cases. They really are not what I am interested in. It's what you do and how you do it. What in the system helps and what hinders? How do you respond to the quirks in the system? Or, do you not respond at all? Do you plan ahead and work around them? That's what I want to know. It'll just take a little time to compile, but it's there. I know it is. I'll dissect the system, analyze it, draw conclusions, and make suggestions of how law enforcement can improve how they go about solving cases. Or, to quote our friend the mayor, 'how to make our city a safe place in which to live.'"

Emily got up to leave. "Married, right?"

"Yep. Wife and kid."

"Saturday night I'm having a little party at my house. Just a few people you probably don't know, but that's okay. It'll give me a chance to get to see the other side of you. The human. Not the cop."

"What if they're one and the same? You might be surprised. Not all cops are the same. Bet you didn't guess we go to the symphony and the art museum." He chuckled. "We even went to New York and saw 'Phantom of the Opera.'"

"All right, you got me. My mistake." Emily handed her card to him. "Eight o'clock? Bring your wife. Casual. A few cocktails and laughs, that's all."

Chapter Two

THE WEEK SLIPPED AWAY LIKE the weeks before it. Find a computer that worked; scan, sort, download, compile, refresh, names and then more names, add a few and delete a few, but nothing bore fruit. Mike knew a serial killer was roaming the streets, but there wasn't much of a trail. In fact, there was no trail at all. No footprints, no fingerprints, no hair samples, no cigarette butts ... nothing.

The mayor raised the stakes with news releases and press conferences. The detectives knew it was a matter of time before she started tightening the screws. Mike looked across the room at Rickey. "We've got to come up with something pretty soon. The Chief is going to raise hell, and that's a fact. We've got to get some leads and find this crazy son-of-a-bitch."

He rubbed his temples. His neck muscles ached day and night. He ate aspirin like it was candy to get rid of his headaches. His appetite had long ago disappeared, but on the bright side, he thought, he was losing a few pounds. He was glad to see the weekend come around. Not only to get away from the office, but also for a chance to visit with Emily. There was something special about her. Maybe the way she talked. The way she exuded self-confidence. Whatever it was, it felt good. Plus, he'd like Annalisa to meet her. They might find they have something in common and become friends.

#

Mike and Annalisa were politely thirty minutes late getting to the party. Emily's house was a realtor's dream: an elegant home in Highland Park with beautiful lawns of deep green fescue caught the fading rays of the setting sun, an array of colorful flowers lining the sidewalks, trees leaning out with an umbrella of branches and leaves to shield the street from the scorching Texas sun, and the rush of traffic, though nearby, was subdued by the flora, fauna, and elegant edifices of the upscale homes.

"Honey, she's got money and lots of it," Annalisa commented as they stepped onto the front porch.

The door swung open before they could ring the bell. "Hi, welcome. Please come in." Emily's vibrant smile and the genuine appeal of her voice swept over Mike like a warm sheet. She wore a strapless black dress with a string of pearls draped around her neck, hanging snugly between her well-tanned breasts.

After introductions and a few moments of polite conversation, she led them through the living room and into the formal dining room, past the tuxedoed gentleman playing the piano. A white-coated bartender took their order. On the back patio, a harpist wove a gentle harmony of soft strings, soothing the sound of people's voices. An ice sculpture, the centerpiece on a table of finger foods, reflected the colors of the prism from a halogen light that shone on it from the heights of a magnolia tree.

Mike and Annalisa took a sampling of cheese, crackers and fresh salmon, then found their way to a bench beside a fountain. They were balancing the drink and food when Emily came and sat with them. She sat erect, almost majestically, but was warm, friendly, and down-to-earth.

"I see you found the goodies. Aren't they scrumptious?"

"Elegant," Annalisa responded. "Your home is so beautiful, and the food is superb." She handed her empty plate to a server, then turned her attention back to Emily. "Mike tells me you're going to be working with him on his cases, but you'll focus on administrative issues." She tossed a sidelong glance at Mike. "Or, who he has to work around to get things done."

"In a nutshell, you're right. My basic theory is all of the knowledge, skills and abilities are there, along with the appropriate technology, for the police to perform admirably. The question to be resolved, and which I hope to address, is the system itself serves to work counter to the achievement of stated goals." Emily laughed and leaned forward, looking directly at Annalisa.

Mike listened closely to her words, but his gaze was pulled like a magnet to the cleavage between her breasts. She was more than beautiful.

Emily continued. "What I'll research is the depth and scope, if any, of how the bureaucracy impedes otherwise competent and capable police. If it is there, I'll find it. Then, and only then, can I make recommendations – in my book, of course – as to how chiefs and other criminal justice administrators can modify their stance so as to support rather than undercut their staff." She turned and patted Mike on the shoulder. "I think you've got a major league detective here. I'll be able to learn a lot from him." She stood up and shook hands with Annalisa. "It's been so nice to meet you, and I appreciate you coming tonight. Now, if you'll excuse me, I'll see about my other guests."

The evening was elegant. The food and drinks were perfect. The setting and company were relaxing and, all in all, the evening was everything Mike hoped for. Plus, he enjoyed the added excitement of seeing a living goddess.

#

"Glad we went," he said on the drive home.

"Me, too. I was a little skeptical how we might fit in, but I've got to give her credit. She was an excellent hostess and has some interesting friends. They seemed so genuine. I thought we might run into some plastic, veneer types, but I was impressed with how cordial they were." She leaned over and kissed Mike on his neck. "It was fun and I'm glad we went."

Mike paid the babysitter, walked her home, and was back in ten minutes. By the time he returned, Annalisa was dressed in her nightgown and sitting on the couch with a glass of wine.

He reached out, took her hands, and helped her to her feet. He wrapped his arms around her waist and they swayed to the silent sound of music in their hearts.

#

The following week was a near replica of the previous week: one step forward; one step back. Every time they started to focus on a potential suspect, something came up to eliminate them – in jail in Fort Worth; in a barroom brawl on Galveston Island; on an iron work job in Kansas City; and it never failed, those who looked the most promising turned up dead or in jail when one of the murders happened.

There was no reprieve. Regular briefings with the division commander, sending email messages to the Public Information Office to try to quench the press's insatiable appetite, and last but not least, meeting with the survivors – a semi-formal gathering of parents, spouses and other relatives to give them as little information as possible while still holding out the carrot of hope that "their" murderer would be caught. Of all the things he did, this was the hardest. The survivors thrived on false hope – the hope that he was going to tell them it was over; he had their killer. But that was not to be, and each time they left in tears. Tomorrow, they would say. Maybe tomorrow.

After they left, Mike escaped from the office to find someplace where he could be alone for at least a few minutes – maybe the library, a walk to Dealey Plaza, anyplace where he didn't feel the crowd closing in on him, a few minutes by himself so he could breath. They were killing him – the survivors, the press, the self-inflicted pressure. All of it strangled him. It was one of those things a person must internalize and not let loose to infect others.

Ten days slipped away since the party. It was Tuesday of the following week before Emily called. "Busy?" she asked.

"Like Don Quixote slaying the windmills. What about you?"

"I'm not Sancho Panza, so I won't help you with your monsters, but I need to dig in and pick your brain. What about lunch?"

Mike looked at his watch, scooted some scratch pads aside and looked at his desk calendar. "Meeting with the Deputy Chief at three o'clock. What about noon?"

"Sure," she replied. There was a pause. "Downtown places are so crowded. I'm afraid we would find it rather difficult to discuss some of these issues. What about my place?"

Mike caught himself smiling inwardly. "Sure, sounds good. I'll check out a car and see you. Can I bring some deli sandwiches?"

Emily gave a soft laugh. "No. Lunch is on me. See you at noon."

Traffic was light and Mike found time to reflect. Just one other time had he slipped, if you can call it that. It was five years ago. Della Manriquez. She was an ace detective, but going through a dirty divorce. He and Annalisa were having some major disagreements over money. She wrote checks without balancing the checkbook and he was called into the Captain's office after a complaint was made to Internal Affairs. He was angry; Della was hell bent on vengeance; so they took out their frustrations in bed and felt better about it, at least for the time being. They knew what they were doing, but did it anyway. Not just once, but twice.

Della got her divorce, a new husband, a new job in Chicago, and it was over. Gone, but not forgotten. It still bothered him. Damn, he was mad at himself. He wouldn't mess up like that again, not even if he had a chance, which he wouldn't. Not with Emily Morgan. Not in a million years.

Mike timed his drive perfectly. It was noon when he parked at the curb. He was getting out when he saw the front door open and she stepped out into the sunlight. Her presence swept over him like the scent of magnolia blossoms. She didn't do anything special to attract his attention, but nevertheless, he stopped halfway out of the car and looked at her. The hem of her skirt swayed in the breeze across her thighs; a white blouse, loose at the collar; her long hair pulled back into a ponytail. She was tall, slender, beautiful and intelligent – everything a woman could be. A trained detective eye, he said to reassure himself that he really did not have a wandering eye.

They exchanged pleasantries on their way into the house and walked to the nook overlooking the patio and fountain. "Beats the heck out of Denny's," she said when she pointed out a chair for him.

Mike laughed. "It does do that." He looked at the plate she had prepared for him – half a tuna sandwich, a cup of soup, and a glass of ice tea. Emily caught him staring at the plate.

"Hey, I'll feed you. There's cake, ice cream, and a cup of fresh ground coffee for dessert."

"You're all right, Emily. For a second I thought you were going to starve me." They both laughed.

Lunch passed quickly, interspersed with business talk. She was interested in learning more about how the police accessed local and other databases, and how much they exchanged information with other departments; the fate of her favorite team, the Dallas Stars; and just a general chance to become better acquainted with each other.

It turned out to be more learning for him than for her. Mike had never heard of the Gilder Effect – a paradigm – the vision of the future of technology; the freedom of bandwidth; the displacement of current communication technology with yet-to-be invented new systems; the unseen future that will change the world. So, between dessert and coffee, she gave him a primer on the Internet, and its actual and potential impact on the exchange of data between people, companies, and organizations, including police departments that posed far-reaching and still untouched resources to develop extraordinary results.

"The Internet," she said as she shifted around in her chair and crossed her legs, offering him a glimpse of her thighs, "is really less than twenty years old. It's a teenager. A mere child, but when it's fully developed into adulthood, its impact on society will be beyond our belief."

He glanced at his watch. The time had gotten away from him. Lunch hour had turned into almost two hours, but he'd enjoyed every minute of it.

Emily walked him to the door, opened it, but blocked him with her arm. "Thanks Mike," she said. She stood directly in front of him for a second and looked into his eyes.

A seductive thrust of passion took his breath, but before he could respond, she stepped outside. "I'll call after I compose my notes and we can go at it again."

"My privilege." He smiled and stepped off the porch, a slight bounce to his gait.

"Wait a minute," she shouted. Mike turned and saw her running down the steps toward him, her ponytail flying in the wind.

"I just remembered. I'm going to be out of town for a few days. Can I call you next week?"

"Going anywhere special?"

"Business. Boring. I'll get back Sunday night and give you a call at the office on Monday. What about lunch a week from today? Hey, what about Annalisa? Do you think she would go to lunch with me? Just girls. You can't come."

Mike smiled. "Sure. Why don't you give her a call at home?"

"I'll do it. Maybe tonight and set something up." She leaned forward and kissed him on the cheek. "Bye-bye," she said.

#

Mike finished his meeting with the top brass and Sergeant Covey. They knew, just as he did, that he was doing a lot of work, but was not making headway. Or, as the Captain described it, "a lot of activity, but not much productivity."

Mike realized his lack of progress. He had not developed a single "solvability factor" since he'd linked the cases together. All they possessed was the theory of a serial murderer. Otherwise, they were high-centered. It had reached the point they were stretching their creative skills to come up with something positive to give to the Mayor and the press. They eliminated a lot of potential suspects, but realistically, they were no closer to a solution today than they were a month ago. Nevertheless, he realized there was a moral obligation to do something. He couldn't simply give up.

"Somewhere out there ..." His thoughts faded. "Yeah, somewhere, somebody. But who?"

Mike leaned back in his chair, propped his feet on the desk, and began sorting the mail in his in-basket. His eye quickly caught a letter with a return address from the FBI Behavioral Sciences Unit in Quantico, Virginia. He slit it open, pulled the single sheet out and froze. He could not believe his eyes. The serial killer was at work in Tulsa, Oklahoma.

Detective John Baldwin had submitted a ViCAP request on three apparently unrelated murders spread over a twelve-month period. Like the Dallas cases, the victims had no apparent relationship with each other; each was killed and found in an area in which there was a substantial likelihood they would be found within minutes of their death; each died as a result of injuries similar to the Dallas cases – a jogger in a public park stabbed and his throat slit; a librarian on her way home from work was found dead in her car at an intersection, shot in the head with double-aught shotgun pellets; and an artist was garroted while she loaded her work in the trunk of her car following a show at the art museum.

Their names followed the pattern of the Dallas cases. The first was a lab technician, Thomas Parker. Four months later, the librarian, Uballe Valdez. The third, Lea Featherstone, a local artist.

T-U-L, the start of Tulsa? The work of another serial killer? The same one who stalked the streets of Dallas? Or, could it raise the possibility of a cohort, possibly a cult that traveled the country carrying out some unimaginable scheme of murdering innocent and helpless people?

Mike copied the letter, called Rickey and Covey together, and laid it out in front of them.

"Damn it to hell," Covey said. He sat back and looked at the two detectives. "This is the weirdest thing I've seen in my life." He took a deep breath and looked at the clock. "Okay Mike, get on the phone, call Tulsa PD and I'll get your travel orders done. I want you on the road tomorrow. Get out of here early and you can be there by noon. Have all your cases together and see what you can do." He turned to Rickey and tossed him a set of keys. "That's the key to my unmarked car. Get it gassed and ready to go. Mike, why don't you head home and get ready? We'll drop the car off at your place and you can go straight from there. We've got our work cut out for us. Let's roll."

#

Morning traffic out of Dallas was everything it could be: a total mess. They called it the Central Expressway, but there was nothing express about it on days like this – an overturned trailer truck backed up traffic for miles. Mike eventually worked his way across two lanes and found an exit, dove into the creeping side street traffic, and an hour later found himself leaving the Dallas city limits.

"So much for a good start," he thought. He flicked off the police radio, found his favorite FM jazz station and sat back. His mind drifted back and forth – Annalisa making love to him; Emily sitting in the nook, sipping coffee, her legs crossed, and her foot dangling back and forth. Two exceptional women. Both of them were a relief to him – a relief from his serial killer and a relief from T-U-L. Who would be next? he wondered. He laughed to himself, his mind always working. Should it be "who" will be next? Or, "whom" will be next? He shook his head. Nine dead people and he was trying to settle on proper grammar.

It was afternoon by the time Mike found the police department. He checked in and was escorted to the Crimes Against Persons Bullpen. He chuckled to himself. Not even in Texas would they call it a bullpen, but this wasn't Texas. This was Oklahoma. To each his own.

Baldwin was waiting at his desk – a jumble of note pads, crime reports, napkins and a dingy coffee cup. Funny, Mike thought, how you visualize a person over the phone and then see them in person. It was uncanny, just as he was pictured to be; early 30's; slicked-back dark hair; even the smile. A huge grin that made him easy to like; a grin you could hear in his voice. The two detectives exchanged introductions, looked at each other's credentials, swapped business cards and got down to business. Baldwin scooped up his three murder cases.

"We can spread this out if we go to the briefing room," he said.

Mike followed him through a maze of cubicles and cluttered workstations, or more appropriately, bullpens, until they came out on the opposite side of the offices. Baldwin laughed. "That's the entrance exam to make detective – make it across the room in ninety seconds. If you can find your way through that mess, then you can find anybody or anything."

The two detectives spread their work out and covered most of the conference room table that was used during roll call, meetings and training sessions. They started by comparing their ViCAP reports; one almost a carbon copy of the other.

Mike looked over the FBI report.

SUSPECT TENDENCIES
1. MALE WHITE
2. WITHDRAWN

3. MIDDLE-AGE
4. RIGHT-HANDED
5. VERY INTELLIGENT
6. BLENDS IN WITHOUT ATTRACTING ATTENTION TO SELF
7. CONDUCTED LONG-TERM SURVEILLANCE OF VICTIMS
8. AVOIDS SOCIOECOMICALLY AND/OR PHYSCIALLY CHALLANGED PERSONS
9. IDENTIFIES UNSUSPECTING VICTIMS
10. ENJOYS TEASING INVESTIGATORS
11. MAY HAVE A VENDETTA AGAINST THE CITY OF TULSA
12. HAS STRONG DESIRE FOR VICTIMS TO BE FOUND ALMOST IMMEDIATELY AFTER COMMISSION OF THE CRIME
13. MAY BE ASSOCIATED WITH SIMILAR CRIMES IN DALLAS, TEXAS.

"Screw me," Baldwin said.

"Yeah, me too," Mike replied. He popped open his briefcase and retrieved a bottle of water. He sucked it dry in one gulp. "Partner," he paused and looked at Baldwin – his new colleague, two men committing themselves to each other, "I think we've got one hell of a problem on our hands."

Baldwin's eyes locked onto Palotti's. He nodded his head in silence, moistened his lips and took a deep breath. "Partner," he whispered as he again extended his hand in a handshake. "We'll do it."

They spent the rest of the afternoon developing a reasonable system to lay out and analyze the information they would compare and contrast. Ultimately, their goal was to find a common denominator. There must be one somewhere. Something deep in the background of the suspect, not the victims, that would bring the killer to the forefront. They agreed their madman had a system and a vendetta, but what? That was the key. Find out what, and the rest would fall into place.

Of course, it was necessary to make some assumptions they could alter later, but it was necessary to establish a starting point. Their assumption was that this was a single killer, not a cult or a copycat. Later, if the information did not come together to support their hypothesis, they would go back to ground zero and start all over. Otherwise, they had so much information they would get lost in the maze of facts and theories.

It was after dark before they were ready to quit for the day. Mike had put in a long drive, missed lunch, and buried his whole being into nine murders. Enough for one day.

"What about dinner?" Baldwin asked.

"Go on home and I'll take care of myself. Just point me in the direction of a decent motel and restaurant, and I'll be fine," Mike replied.

"No, seriously. Look, I'm single. My wife, Lisa, died of cancer last year and I have a two-year-old. Little Jonah. He's staying with my mom tonight. I figured this might be a long day. I told her we'd probably work late, so she's going to take him to McDonalds. C'mon, let's get something to eat."

After dinner, Mike checked into the Sleep Inn, took a quick shower, buried his head into the pillow and fell asleep.

He climbed slowly out of bed when the alarm clock whined at six o'clock, shaved, ate breakfast, reviewed yesterday's notes, and was in the bullpen by eight o'clock.

The two detectives followed their plan and laid out everything they had, starting with the day of the crime.

Sunday	-	Lea Featherstone
Monday	-	Denton Ryan and Thomas Parker
Tuesday	-	Sara McComb
Wednesday	-	Uballe Valdez
Thursday	-	Leonard Throckmorton
Friday		Andrew Maines and Allison Reynolds
Saturday	-	Landa Lopez

Not much of a start. From there, they went to the time of day – scattered between two o'clock in the afternoon until midnight without a pattern. Next they looked at the month, but did not find any unexpected surprise. All the crimes happened between April and the end of October. Nothing spectacular, since that would be a reasonable time to find people out of their house. After all, no one spends much time outside during an ice storm.

Religion? Four Baptists, two Catholics, two Methodists, and one with no religious affiliation.

Credit cards? Everyone had a MasterCard or Visa; Parker and Reynolds also had an American Express. Landa had a Phillips 66 gas card. Reynolds had half-a-dozen department store cards ranging from JC Penney to Saks Fifth Avenue.

Family? All but two were married for several years at the time of their deaths. Ryan was a bachelor, but was engaged. Sara was a divorcee. Her husband checked out and was clean. The divorce was neat and dignified – just two people who drifted apart. He paid his child support, visited the kids regularly, and maintained a good relationship with Sara. He remarried and lived in Seattle.

Credit ratings? All of them came out smelling like a rose. Featherstone was behind on her car payment last year, but took out a loan and paid it off; no credit problems since then. Apparently, all of them lived according to their means.

Gambling or other vices? None apparent.

Tulsa and Dallas connection? Nothing in their business or family relationships.

Criminal history? Another zero. They were squeaky clean – that, and the spelling of their names, appeared to be the only common denominator that linked them together.

"Not quite," Mike commented. He looked back over his notes and then compared them with Baldwin's. "They were all listed in the phone book and city directory. All of them had lived at the same address for at least three years, and all of them lived in a house or apartment situated in a locale that was easy to see without having to use much sneak and peek stuff. Let's face it, they were selected because of their name and the fact they lived somewhere that was easy for our killer to blend in. From there on, it was just a matter of time."

"What a shame," John replied. He shrugged his shoulders and shook his head. "They all died because they were solid, normal, pay-your-bills kind of people. They didn't do anything wrong. For that, they were the bait for some madman."

The two detectives whittled away the hours of the day, stopping only for lunch in the cafeteria. It was nearly five o'clock when Sergeant Jack Shay came into the room.

"Got some news for you guys, but it's not good." He shook his head and continued, "Around noon a woman named Sandra Tully was found dead in her car. She was parked at Oak Hills Mall. The homicide detectives think she'd been shopping, gotten her hair done, and was putting a sack in the trunk of her car. Of course, the autopsy hasn't been done yet, but at first appearance, someone jabbed a knife or ice pick right at the base of her skull. Killed her instantly, and then shoved her in the trunk. The only thing that tipped mall security was some citizen found her keys in the parking lot and turned them in. The off-duty officers working the mall ran a registration check and found the car in the parking lot. They didn't see anything in the seats, but it scared the crud out of them when they opened the trunk." He paused for a moment. "Son-of-a-bitch, that would scare it out of anybody to open a trunk and find a corpse in there." He handed a copy of his notes to Baldwin – black female, sixty years old, retired teacher, widow for less than one year, lived in a townhouse a couple blocks from Oral Roberts University.

"Think that's the 'S' your killer was looking for?" he asked.

"Afraid so," Baldwin replied. They sat in silence, each with their own thoughts for a few seconds before Mike spoke.

"Any ideas who's next? Who is going to be the 'A'"?

#

The detectives sweated through the week without making any progress. They compared names, ages, religion, credit cards, professions, illnesses, banks, and the list went on and on. They were stuck. They were no closer now than when they started. The only common denominator was that the victims were clean cut, hard-working, good people – and all listed in the city directory and telephone book. And, of course, the letters of their first names spelled the names of the respective cities where they lived.

It was near sunset on Friday. The two investigators sat in the bullpen and ate fried chicken, compliments of Baldwin's mother. They were too tired to continue.

"I've had it," Mike said. He wiped his fingers on a paper napkin and shoved back from the desk. "I'm out of clean clothes, damned near broke, and I'm two hundred and fifty miles from home." He tossed his chicken bones and napkin in the trash. "I'm out of here. I hate to be the eternal pessimist, but give me a call when 'A' bites the dust. As for me, I'm heading to Texas."

#

Mike was glad to be back in his own office. It was old and tired, but a new police station was under construction. What he had and what he was going to have was a damn sight better than the bullpen.

He kept his appointment and rang Emily's doorbell precisely at noon. She answered, looking as beautiful as ever – maybe even more so – her beautiful lips, the delicate touches of makeup she wore. They enjoyed a pleasant conversation over their soup and salad, talking about her lunch with Annalisa and the teddy bear she gave to Samanta. Mike talked about his frustrating work that was not making life any happier, his headaches and neck aches, and the exasperation of "activity without productivity" as the Deputy Chief referred to it.

"Sorry, Emily, but I'm just not in the mood to talk anymore about crime. Enough is enough," he said. He got up and walked to the living room sofa.

"Then let's change the subject. Let's talk about you." She went to the bar and poured two after-dinner drinks.

"No, really. I can't," Mike said.

She sat down in front of him. "Bullshit. You're working yourself to death. Take a few minutes and relax. You deserve it." She handed an Amarillo Martini to him, took the knot of his tie in her fingers and loosened it. "There," she said. "Relax. Take a deep breath. Close your eyes and let the tension flow out your fingertips and toes. Let it go."

Mike followed her directions like a child. He took the drink from her hand, aware of how she paused when their fingers touched. She sat on the footstool in front of him and scooted herself up close to his legs. He felt a momentary exhilaration course through his body. He tasted the liqueur, then tilted his head back and drank it. Emily smiled, took the glass from his hand and returned to the bar. He watched the feminine delicacy of her movements as she returned to the footstool. He took the glass from her, but this time took the almost unnoticeable effort to allow his fingers to rub slightly against hers. He sipped the liqueur slowly. The strong beverage rushed to his brain.

"Good for you," she whispered. "It's eighty proof."

Mike smiled coyly. "Yeah, it rang my bell, so to speak. Not something I usually do for lunch."

"Sometimes you just have to give yourself a break. You work under so much pressure I don't see how you handle it." She smiled at him and continued. "We'll do well together – you and me. We can help one another."

Emily stepped behind him, slipped her fingers beneath his shirt collar, and with gentle swirls, massaged his neck and shoulders.

He took slow, deep breaths. He shivered as he inhaled the scent of her perfume and felt the light, silky touch of her fingers. He relaxed. The weight of the world lifted from his shoulders. Her fingers stroked his temples, then drifted to the corners of his mouth and flowed like feathers across his lips. Her fingers crept down his throat with only the slightest touch until she reached the buttons of his shirt. He opened his eyes to see her lean down to him and their lips touched. It was a gentle kiss, the mere brushing of her lips to his, nothing more.

She unbuttoned his shirt. His eyes were transfixed. He stared at the exquisite beauty of her face. Her fingernails moved slowly across his bare chest. He shuddered and felt the goose bumps tingle down his arms and legs.

"I can't," he whispered. His brow was covered in perspiration. "I have to go back to work. I need to go."

Emily moved closer to him. She kissed him. Her lips were as soft as the touch of the wings of a butterfly. Then she slid down and put her lips to his chest.

"I have to go." His voice was dry, not much more than a murmur.

Emily stood up and looked down at him. He sat like a wilted rag doll in the chair. She smiled and offered an innocent, mischievous giggle. "I said you needed to relax, and you did. See? I can help you when you get uptight." She took his hand in hers and kissed his fingers.

"C'mon cowboy. You've got some murders to solve."

Mike lifted his tie from the floor and stuffed it in his pocket.

"No, no," she said. "You can't go back to the office looking too relaxed or they'll think something inappropriate." She took his hand and led him through her bedroom and to the bathroom.

"Use the mirror to fix your tie and you can freshen up a bit," she said.

Mike adjusted his shirt, tie and hair, all the while taking in the surroundings of her bathroom and bedroom – half a dozen candles bathed the room in a soft display of yellow and orange colors. Three vases of fresh flowers filled the room with the sweet fragrance of roses, baby's breath, irises and daffodils. A king-size bed, a Jacuzzi bath, and a shower large enough for two people completed her boudoir.

Emily stood beside him at the sink and freshened her lipstick. He looked at the two of them in the mirror. A burst of gratification streamed through his body, a sensation unlike anything he'd experienced in years. Annalisa was his wife, a great lover, the mother of his daughter. Nonetheless, he could not extinguish the surge of electricity that shot though every centimeter of his flesh. He willed it to stay – to hold onto this moment. He wet his comb under the faucet and patted down his hair. "I've got to get back to the office," he said as he slipped the comb back into his pocket.

Emily walked him to the door. "I've got to meet some deadlines for my editor pretty quickly. Do you think you could stop by on Friday? We could do lunch, but get some real business done. I promise not to distract you too much."

"Hmm, Friday isn't good for me. I'm taking the day off and driving Annalisa and Sam to the airport around eleven in the morning. They're going to Albuquerque for a long weekend to see her sister. I figure they'll probably head up to Santa Fe and spend a few bucks up there, too." He paused and looked down at his shoes. "I need to get some yard work done. Damn, I'm so far behind with my personal life because of all of these murders that I don't know if I'll ever get caught up. Naw, I better skip Friday."

He looked into her eyes. "I'm married, Emily. I really need to be careful."

"I know that, and I wouldn't do anything to jeopardize your marriage. Besides, I think Annalisa and I are going to be good friends, so I need to be careful, too." She took his hand. "Look, how about this? We both enjoy each other's company, but we also understand that each of us has our business needs and that's our priority. Right?"

Mike nodded his approval. "Right."

"Okay, how about this? Get them to the airport and come by here. You have to eat and we'll get a ton of work done. Look," she emphasized, "I have the money. I'll have my yardman do your yard while we're working here. It's simple. We get two jobs done at the same time – your yard and my research."

"Oh, I can't let you do that," he replied.

"Nonsense. You're letting your manly self-esteem get in the way of a rational decision. By the time you get home Friday, your grass will be cut and trimmed, your flower beds will be cleaned out, and I'll have picked your brain on how you detectives really work."

Mike thought about it for a moment. "Hmm, I'm not too sure about the flower beds. That's not something I do much of. I just cut, trim and get the hell out of the heat. I don't want Annalisa to get spoiled with the yard work, especially if I didn't do it."

#

Mike's headaches and neck aches returned on Thursday. Sweat dotted his brow and he chased aspirin with even more aspirin. He was miserable and knew the source of his discomfort. He tried to focus on his investigations, but kept drifting to thoughts of Emily. It was easy to rationalize. She did not have a sexual attraction to him, but rather was truly interested in her research while, at the same time, she was able to help him relax and get his mind off the murders he faced every day.

He sat at his computer and entered what they called "search zones." In the zones, he entered the date and time of the homicides; a scan on all burglaries, prowlers, robberies, assaults, and sexual assaults within a six-block radius and within two hours prior to or after the murders. Along with that, he entered the name of every person that he, Rickey and Baldwin had researched as possible suspects. Somewhere, he thought, it would pop up – a suspect in the right place at the right time. From there, he would link them to a murder.

He entered data until mid-afternoon, punched the commands for "calculation," and sat back. Two minutes later he had his answer – "NO MATCHES FOUND."

#

After the September 11th assaults on the country, a trip to the airport lost whatever fun it used to be. They unloaded at the curb. He gave a quick hug and squeeze to each of them, and they were gone.

Mike took his time escaping the airport traffic and getting on to Mockingbird Lane. His mind raced. He and Emily were doing business, just business. He must concentrate on that and not make more out of it than what it was. Sure, she was gorgeous, but she had her job to do and he could help her. Plus, if it worked out like she said it could, he would have a hand in helping other detectives sometime in the future. And, whatever help she gave him was a plus. So what if he enjoyed her company? He felt good, and if he felt good then he was better able to do his job. It was that simple, and not a rationalization at all. There was no need to feel guilty. Besides, Annalisa was his wife. He loved her more than anything in the world and wouldn't do anything to jeopardize their marriage.

#

Emily greeted him at the door with a handshake and welcomed him into the house. He didn't anticipate what she might wear, but was still a little surprised how casually she was dressed – a blouse, shorts and bare feet.

Mike sat at the nook and watched while she stood at the drain board and mixed their salad. The conversation was polite chit-chat while she worked. To Mike, it was a time to enjoy looking at her beauty without her being conscious of being stared at. Her long, slender legs flowed with the grace of a dancer when she moved about the kitchen. She poured tea over the ice cubes in the tumblers and handed one to Mike. His mouth was dry. He sipped it down, all the while watching while she finished the preparations for their meal.

If he may have thought otherwise, he was wrong. Lunch was pure business. Emily sat with a note pad on the table, rapidly firing questions at him. She wanted to know the criminal justice policy on internet access and protocols for making contact with law enforcement agencies at the local, state and federal level. Then she wanted the legal requirements to transfer and exchange information between those agencies.

Mike stumbled through them, then went on to the Dallas Police Department policy for collection, storage and dissemination of criminal information versus intelligence information, and then to the crime analysis sources for local, interstate and intrastate crimes.

She was like a sponge soaking up his responses as quickly as he spoke. She flicked page after page on her notepad until at last she tossed her pencil into the remnants of a few pieces of lettuce in the bottom of the salad bowl.

"Time out," she uttered. She slid down in her chair and put her feet in his lap. "You've worn me out for the time being. How about a break?" She blew her hair from her brow and smiled at him. "You're a good guy, Mike. We're a dynamic duo. Right now, you have more staying power than me. I need to cool it for a few minutes. My fingers are worn out."

Mike looked at her feet, then took her toes in his fingers and began to massage them slowly, one at a time. Gentle, tender strokes up the bottom of the toes, slipping his finger between them, bending them ever so slightly backward, and then moving on to the next toe. Neither spoke until after he massaged each toe.

"Oh, Detective Palotti, where have you been all my life? I never knew a man who could massage my feet. It feels heavenly." She stretched her legs further into his lap. He rubbed the soles of her feet slowly. Her eyes closed to mere slits. Her breathing became shallow. She slipped further down into her chair until she was nearly asleep.

She roused herself with a wiggle of her shoulders and a long stretch, her feet firmly planted on his lap and her arms extended over her head. She gave a soft yawn, then tossed a quick smile to him. "Let's sit on the couch," she said. She took his hand and led him to the living room. They sat beside each other in silence for a few moments, still holding hands. She turned and looked at him, cupped his face in her hands and kissed him. Lightly at first, then passionately.

"You're special, Mike. You're the most unique person I've ever met. There's something about you – a magnetism. I'm drawn to you wherever you are. Did you ever play with magnets and see how they jump out and grab each other?"

"Um hum. I know exactly what you mean. I feel the same thing. Like a chemistry. It's something more than just an attraction. There's a bit to it I can't explain." He stopped speaking and looked at her. "You're special, Emily. So very special." He kissed her again and again.

She leaned back, crossed her arms and lifted her blouse. Mike looked at her and bathed himself in the indescribable beauty of her breasts. He touched her with his lips.

"Take off your clothes," she whispered.

Mike stood beside the couch and loosened his buckle, slipped his badge, gun and holster from his belt, and placed them carefully on the coffee table. He tossed her a quick smile and chortle. "Always on duty, you know."

He cuddled in beside her. They kissed and then made love.

#

A surge of guilt raced through his mind as he dressed, but just as quickly he cast it aside. He reminded himself that he truly loved Annalisa. She was his wife and this was not anything to be confused with real love. He loved Emily, but it was different. Annalisa was his soul mate. Emily was his lover. Some people may have a hard time understanding that, but he didn't. You have to live it to understand it. Love is not the type of thing you can explain to someone else. Emily understood him. She cared for him. At the same time, she loved and cared for Annalisa and Samanta. She was a friend to all of them.

#

Mike sat on his back porch the next day and admired the well-trimmed yard. He sipped his coffee and read the morning paper. It was a perfect day. He could not ask for anything better. He tossed the paper down, crossed his legs and listened to the birds.

He reminisced how much he loved Annalisa and Samanta. Annalisa's little quirks that were special – his toothbrush always blue and hers red. The way she poured his coffee in the old mug he'd used before they were married, but hers in a fragile little cup she guarded as though it was gold. He thought of the way she sat on the bed with cotton balls between her toes when she did her toenails, then the way she picked out the tie for him to wear to work. The list went on and on.

He loved it – all the little things she did without even thinking about it. She was cute the way she went about her little daily routines – more than cute – precious; the apple of his eye.

Emily was different. Maybe the most unique woman he'd ever met. She was brilliant, classy, rich, caring, beautiful and fun to be with. She was everything a woman could be, but not his wife. They held a special relationship with each other, and they understood it. He'd spent most of last night making love to her. They sat in her Jacuzzi until two o'clock in the morning talking about their relationship. She understood her role in his life, and he understood his role in hers. She made it clear. Annalisa was his wife – his soul mate, and Emily was happy just knowing she held a special place in his heart. Even more, she explained, she possessed a strong feeling for Annalisa and Samanta. She wanted to be their friend and to have them as her friends. She didn't have any doubt the four of them could have a wonderful relationship; it was just that she and Mike would always have a special magnetism and it would not die. Never.

#

He thought about last night, not just the passion, but the words they shared. "Tell me about yourself," Mike asked while they soaked in the warm bubbles of her Jacuzzi.

Emily had slipped into the crook of his arms and laid her head on his shoulder. Her eyes sparkled in the candlelight. Her words were soft and distant, yet filled with the depth of love. "I'm an only child. I grew up in Connecticut and went to Columbia. My folks divorced when I was away at school and it really hurt me. I love both of them, but they simply drifted apart, not anyone's fault really. It just happened. Anyhow, I was working on my Masters degree and met Edgar." She laughed.

"Hey, that's what his folks called him, so who was I to change it to Ed or Eddie or something like that? He was finishing his doctorate in Organizational Management. We were inseparable – day and night. We lived together for six months before we married."

She looked up at Mike, smiled, kissed his cheek and snuggled in closer to him. "I've never talked to a man quite like this." She smiled and again kissed his cheek. "Anyway, we had a small wedding ceremony in upstate New York. It was just our families and a handful of friends. We only went about an hour's drive to Niagara Falls for our honeymoon, but that was all right. We really loved each other and had a great life. I did the research. He wrote, delivered presentations and made a lot of money. Plus, his dad was a major investor in several big businesses, so the cash flow was never an issue for us. The only problem was Edgar's asthma. We were in Guatemala doing research on ancient civilizations for a project he was writing a book on and he got sick – terribly sick."

A solitary tear slipped from her eye. She wiped it with her finger and continued, "By the time we got to the airport and caught the first plane out for the U.S. he was in terrible condition. I got him to a hospital in Miami, but he didn't make it. I didn't know a person could die so fast from such an ordinary illness, and I have to admit it devastated me. We were married five years and were talking about starting our family."

Emily looked at Mike, caught her breath, and allowed the tears to pour from her eyes.

"Mike, I loved him so much. I never felt like that for anyone until I met you. I promise, I never would have, or could have, planned to meet anyone like you. You're so special. I can't describe it. It defies understanding. When I see you my heart melts, but I'll always understand who you are and to whom you're married. I commit myself to you and Annalisa. I'll respect you both, and I'll respect the fact the two of us have a special relationship, but it's just that – a relationship and nothing more."

Unfortunately, he would have the rest of the weekend to himself. Annalisa and Sam would be home Monday, and Emily was scheduled to go to New York to meet with her publisher. "Crap," he mumbled. What a weekend this could have been, but business is business and he always had to keep that in mind. Emily was flying out today and would be gone until Tuesday.

#

Mike sat at his desk talking about nothing in particular with Rickey. Why did the Stars make those idiotic trades? Could the Cowboys ever come back to their glory days? What about that new mayor and her promises to the police association?

He felt almost normal. He would zip out to the airport in a couple of hours and get Sam and Annalisa, have lunch with them somewhere before they went home, and then get back to the grind. Who knows? Maybe today would be the day two plus two actually equaled four. Today they might figure out who the killer was.

His telephone rang – John Baldwin from Tulsa.

"Yeah, John. What's up?"

"I'll tell you what's up. 'A' is what's up. Amanda Weathers. It happened Sunday morning – out jogging before she went to work. Another jogger found her in the park, dead as dead can be. She was shot at close range by a small caliber gun in her left eye. Hell, she was dead before she hit the ground."

John went over the details. Miss Weathers lived in an apartment in an upscale neighborhood; her name was in the phone book and city directory. Like the others, she'd lived at the same address for five years. Again, like the other victims, she did not have a criminal or traffic record. She was a department manager in a discount store with Monday and Tuesday off. Like the others, she followed a routine – she jogged every morning about five o'clock before she went to work. That was her innocent, fatal error. And, that was the only difference from the others – 5:00 a.m. – not an afternoon or evening killing. Nevertheless, everything else added up.

#

Samanta sat in her car seat and rambled on about the plane ride. She proudly wore a set of pilot wings on her sweater. "And all the Coke I could drink," she giggled.

"Oh yes," Annalisa said. "All the Coke she could drink, and three trips to the potty. In one end and out the other."

They laughed. Mike reached over and put his arm around Annalisa's shoulder and pulled her to him. She reached up and kissed him. "Um, glad to be home." She looked at the back seat. Sam's head was nodding and her eyes were half shut. She fought against it, but dropped her head and dozed off.

She was sound asleep when they got home, so Annalisa put her down on the bed. Mike and Annalisa walked back into the living room and sat on the couch.

"Son-of-a-bitch," he exclaimed. "I look at that innocent little thing and then I think about what I do for a living." He grimaced. "Annalisa, I can't figure this out and it's about to kill me. On one hand, I have that precious little angel in there that depends on me, and on the other hand …" He paused to catch his breath.

"On the other hand, I've got some crazy nut killing people just to drive us crazy. Eleven. Count'em. Eleven people dead between here and Tulsa, and we don't have the foggiest idea who the hell is doing it." He looked at Annalisa. His eyes were pleading. "Annalisa, what if I'm dealing with the devil himself? I mean it. What if this really is him? Then there's nothing Baldwin or I can do to stop him. Nothing at all."

"Come on, honey," she replied. Annalisa led him to the bedroom where they lay on top of the duvet. Their time together was nothing sexual, but deep compassion that reached from her heart to his, from a wife to a husband. Theirs was love to the depth of their souls, as deep as love between a man and a woman can be. Tears welled in Mike's eyes.

"It scares me, babe. It really scares me."

Annalisa slipped her arm beneath his head and pulled him close to her. He laid his head on her shoulder and within minutes was asleep. His every emotion was spent.

She allowed him to have a short catnap and then woke him with a gentle tease. "Hey, big guy. Your little nappy time is about to eat up the whole afternoon. You better get back to the office before somebody thinks something is up." She laughed and grabbed his crotch. "Nope, but maybe they'll think you got so horny that we were spending the day making love."

Mike laughed and rolled off the side of the bed. "Catch you about six or so," he said.

Annalisa watched him go out the door, then lay back on her pillow. "My God," she prayed, "how I love him. He's so good and kind, so faithful. Thank you for bringing him into my life. I'll cherish him forever. I can never deserve such a decent and loving man. Nothing or nobody can ever take my love from him."

Chapter Three

BALDWIN AND PALOTTI DEVELOPED A new strategy. Each of them submitted the date, time and location of their respective murders to their department's Crime Analysis Units. The goal was to have those units match the crime locations with every known video camera within one-half mile of the crime; videos from ATM's, business parking lots, convenience stores, anywhere. From that, they would pull the videotapes and DVDs – if they still existed – and start looking for matches – any kind of match: a vehicle, a person, any single thing that was peculiar to more than one death. It could be a delivery truck, a jogger, a preacher handing out bibles; it could be anything or anybody. Somewhere, it had to be – there must be – that one common denominator that would lead them to the killer.

A week went by before Mike got an answer. They had a "hit." Crime Analysis found one common identifier on the Lopez and Maines murders. Each of them came up with a 1998 Saturn with a Texas license plate – Lopez's on a mall security camera; Maines' at an ATM camera where the car could be seen in the background. The car was registered to Antonio Rosas. He ran a quick records check in the state driver's license file – no tickets, but now they had his photograph and date of birth. Another computer check ran him through Texas and FBI files without any hits. He was never arrested, served in the military, or had any job that required the employer to make a background check on him.

While Mike worked the computer, Rickey made a call to the city business license office on the hope they could find their suspect with some type of a license. Indeed, they scored a hit. Antonio Rosas was a self-employed piano tuner and personal physical fitness trainer.

That was too good a lead to pass up – two leads, in fact; a piano tuner meant he had piano wire that could be used in the Lopez murder. Covey and Rickey hit the phones. Did any of the victims or their families use him for one or the other of his specialties? It took the rest of the day to run down the survivors, but the answer was a disappointing "no."

Mike put in a call to Tulsa, but they had also come up dry so far. He gave them Rosas' name, hoping against hope that they would come up with something on him.

"I'll be back to you after we run him," Baldwin said.

#

Rosas was the best thing, in fact the only, investigative lead they had. Mike, Rickey, Covey and Martinez gathered around the conference table to lay out their plan – what there was of it. They would start with around-the-clock surveillance. A check with public utilities came up with him living in a middle-class neighborhood. He had one car registered in his name and that was the same one they saw in the videos.

They began the surveillance the next morning. While the surveillance team set up on the perimeter around the house, Mike hit the telephones again. His task was to check Rosas' credit history and search for school records from any one of a dozen regional school districts. Of course, that assumed he grew up in the Dallas area. Then the search expanded to try and find out if he was married or single, and to look for him in coaches associations, fitness clubs and music clubs. Essentially, search every place a person might have a record of any type, and from that start putting him together so they could get to know him; try to understand him. If they could do that, they might anticipate his next move. Then they would be there when he was ready to strike again.

At least Mike knew more at the end of the first day than he did when they'd started. Antonio Rosas was thirty-eight years old. He graduated with honors from Dallas public schools and went to the University of North Texas on a music scholarship where he played in the jazz band, but did not graduate. That would take a little work to find out why he dropped out, because he had good grades. Apparently, something happened. But what? That might be the clue that would give them some insight into the real Antonio Rosas.

After leaving college, he worked as a substitute music teacher in Dallas schools, but did not work there over the last six years. He obtained a business license five years ago to run a personal business, Caribbean Music and Training Services.

Mike laughed. "Now that is one hell of a combination, stretch and tune, stretch and tune. Hmm, to each his own, I guess." He looked at Rickey who'd just returned from the first surveillance tour. "Well?"

"Well shit," Rickey replied. "Dumb turkey must have forgotten to lock the door when he left. When I knocked on it a little later to see if anybody was home the door accidentally opened all by itself. Of course, being a good cop, I made sure nobody was home and maybe sick or injured, so I did a little walk through. You know, just make sure everything was safe." He shrugged his shoulders and sat down. "I don't know, Mike. I think he's a bachelor. Place was clean. No porn or stuff like that. No crazy satanic stuff. The guy's clean so far."

Rickey went on to describe what the surveillance team did, or better yet, what they didn't do. Rosas left his house about eight-thirty and went to Strong's Gym. He was there about two hours, then went to Rhythm Music Store and stayed there for an hour. He had lunch at Pepito's on Central Expressway, and then things turned sour. The surveillance team lost him in the construction work when he pulled out of the parking lot, so they drove back and set up on his house until he got home about an hour ago. Now, the evening shift was setting up on him.

That was the way it went for more than a week. They watched him go to the gym, go to three different music stores, go to the library a couple of times, eat his lunch at a different place every day, get home between five and six in the evening, and on two nights, go to people's homes after dinner. When he went to a house, the surveillance team slipped someone in close to try to be sure he was doing everything legitimate, not killing some poor slob while the cops waited outside.

They decided he was a multi-talented man. They could see through the window of the first house he went to and was working on the piano. The second house that night, he was working with a middle-aged woman with her exercise. The cops watched with interest to be sure that he didn't give her more than what she bargained for, and apparently she got just what she wanted. He screwed her on the back porch.

#

Mike worked nine days without a day off before Covey ordered him to take off for a couple of days, and the timing could not have been better. He took his surveillance tour on Friday and followed Rosas to the gym, the library, and on to lunch at Pepito's. Pure ho-hum. Mike was ready to scream for something – anything – to happen. A couple of days away from the funny farm was what he needed, even though he knew something could break and they would arrest the killer without him being there, but that was a chance he would have to take.

Besides, Emily had two tickets from her publisher for the children's exhibit at the Kimball Art Museum in Fort Worth for Saturday. She gave them to Annalisa to take Samanta to see the exhibit. They would be gone all day and he would have the day by himself where he could lay around, have a beer and not do anything, and that was exactly what he wanted, nothing but peace and quiet.

He saw them off at mid-morning, jumped in his car and went to the hardware store for some things he needed, grabbed a cup of Starbucks coffee and headed home. He was gone less than an hour and was surprised to find Emily's Mercedes parked at the curb in front of the house.

He stepped into the living room. "Emily?" She was not in there or in the dining room. He walked down the hall calling her name..

"Mike?" She was in the bathroom. "Mike, I've been waiting for you. Come in here."

He opened the door slowly, not knowing what he would find. His police persona took over – trained to respond to the unexpected. His pulse quickened. Whatever was about to happen was out of the ordinary and he couldn't anticipate what was going on in her mind?

"Emily, what the hell are you doing?" he bellowed. She was in the tub. Bubbles covered her all the way to her chin. She lifted her leg up and put her foot out to him.

"I couldn't wait," she said coyly. "You're just like every other good citizen and put a key under the doormat, so I let myself in." She flicked her fingers and splashed bubbles in his face and laughed. "Remember when you told me how you and Annalisa made love in the tub?"

"Emily, have you lost your mind? What are you doing?"

"Hey, calm down. They'll be gone until late this afternoon and I couldn't stand being without you. Here," she said as she wiggled her foot at him. "Rub my feet. Please?"

"This is too risky. I don't like it at all. Damn, what if they came home and caught you here?"

Emily laughed. "Big brave policeman. Come on, the risk is what makes it so much fun."

She pulled her foot back into the tub and stood up. The soapsuds slid slowly down her body – over her breasts, over her flat tummy, down her thighs.

Mike's skin tingled. His heart pounded. He moistened his lips.

Emily pulled a towel off the rack and handed it to him. "Please?" She stepped out of the tub and turned her back. Mike rubbed the towel over her shoulders, down her back, over her hips and down her legs.

"Kiss me," she whispered as she turned around. He stood and they kissed lightly, then she stepped back. Her beach bag was on the countertop. She pulled it to her and walked to Mike and Annalisa's bedroom.

"What're you doing?" he asked.

"Watch." She pulled the bedspread off, tossed it on the floor, and with a strong sweep of her hand pulled the sheets off and put them on top of the spread.

"Damn it. Are you crazy? We can't do this," Mike implored.

Emily laughed. "Sure we can. Look." She lifted her bag up to the chest of drawers and pulled out a silk sheet.

"You going to help?" she asked when she began to tuck the sheet down on the bed. Mike hesitated, then stepped to the other side and tucked it in. They finished, and he realized his entire body was quivering. She wet her lips and lay down on Annalisa's side of the bed. Mike sat on the edge of the bed. She reached up and pulled him to her. She kissed him and then enveloped him.

"Tell me you love me," she said between kisses.

"I do. I promise I do. I love you so very much. I want you forever."

She put her hands on his chest and lifted him up a few inches. "Call me Annalisa. I know it sounds crazy, but just for these few minutes, let me be your wife."

He paused for a long moment, then whispered, "Annalisa, I love you." They made love, curled together on top of her silk sheet to rest, and made love again. Only when he got up did he notice the little teddy bear she had given to Samanta was on the bed. She pulled it to her and held it.

"Howard. Remember? I named him when I gave him to Sam." She sat up and held Howard in her lap. "Mike, this is as close as I'll ever be to being your wife. That's why I wanted Howard in bed with us. Every time you see this little guy, you can think of me. He's our baby. Yours and mine."

Mike shook his head. "No, Emily. We're going too far. Remember when we talked about our relationship? Remember? Don't ever do this again."

"I promise, honey. I promise." She got up while Mike scooped up his clothes.

"Wait for me in the other room, please," she said. "I have one more little thing I want to show you and then I'll leave. Okay?"

Mike looked at her and smiled. He was putty in her hands. "Okay, but be fast. It's getting late." He was in the kitchen buttoning his shirt when Emily came in.

"Oh, my God," he exclaimed. Emily was dressed in Annalisa's favorite dress – a seductive, light blue, off-the-shoulder Versace she'd won in the silent auction at the symphony.

"Look, we're the same size."

"Damn it, Emily. Are you crazy? You're carrying this too far. Get out of that and hang it up. You've got to get the hell out of here."

Emily stepped across the room and kissed him. "I know it, but I want you always to remember me. I could be your wife. I know that. I love you; you love me, but …" Her voice trailed off. "I know it, Mike. But, please remember today."

Mike's heart pounded. "For damned sure, I'll never forget today. Now, get the hell out of here and make sure you get everything back where it came from."

#

Monday morning found Mike at his desk. His head was spinning. Son-of-a-bitch, he thought. He'd never experienced anything like it before. What a weekend. Emily left about an hour before Samanta and Annalisa returned. There was barely enough time to clean up the bathroom and the bed before they came dancing into the house with their stories about the museum. To make matters worse, almost beyond belief, Annalisa had arranged a babysitter for the night and wanted Mike take her to the Chaparral Club for dinner – wearing her Versace.

He didn't enjoy dinner. Not the service, the food, nor the music. Nothing pleased him, and he knew why.

#

Mike sat at his desk and doodled on his note pad. Emily was smart and beautiful, but was too much of a risk taker. She was pressing the envelope. There was a limit to what a person could do. Making love in their bed was bad enough, but when she put on

Annalisa's dress, that was beyond playing around and having fun. That was damned near diabolic.

He caught himself in mid-thought. That was twice in the last few days he'd thought like that, a diabolic killer and a diabolic lover. He shook his head and quickly convinced himself he was making more out of it than it was. A diabolic killer? Absolutely. A diabolic lover? Not just no, but hell no. She was a lover and a master at games. Nevertheless, he was off base tagging her as diabolic.

Rickey interrupted Mike's thoughts. "*Que paso, ese?*" Rickey pulled up a chair and looked quizzically at his partner. They had worked together for the last two years, and Rickey proved to be the best friend Mike ever had in the department. He wasn't much bigger than Willie Mae, but was a fabulous detective and a good friend. He knew when to talk and when to keep quiet, but the best thing about him was his intuition. He didn't need to have something drawn out for him. He could put things together from the abstract and come to a solid, logical conclusion. He and his wife, Nina, had been married about as long as Mike and Annalisa, and had two kids in school. Nina packed his lunch every day and at least a couple times a week she slipped a little love note in it. Once, a few months ago, Mike caught Rickey giving an embarrassed laugh as he hurriedly put something back into his sack. Rickey was fast, but not fast enough. It was a picture of Nina posing in the nude. Rickey had glanced at Mike and together they had a little laugh. They were good friends and Mike could keep a secret.

"Shit, my friend, you looked a million miles away. Anything wrong?"

Mike smiled. "Eleven dead people and you ask if anything is wrong?"

"Hey, man, you know what I mean. You look like crap. Is everything at home okay?"

"Yeah, sure," Mike replied. "Couldn't be better."

"Yeah, sure. Couldn't be better," Rickey mimicked. "You're full of it. What's up? We're buddies. Let me help you out. Is it Annalisa? Is she sick or something?"

"No. Nothing like that. It's just – I don't know." He looked at Rickey and shrugged his shoulders. "Ever bite off more than you could chew?"

"You mean money wise? Or something a little more, hmm, well, intimate?"

"Yeah, well no. Not exactly." Mike shook his head. "Look, let's just forget it, okay? We've got a killer to catch."

SWEET EMILY

"If you don't have your head on straight, we're not going to catch anybody. I'm not stupid. I know you've been 'interviewing' a bunch with that woman," he emphasized.

Mike got up from his desk. "Let's get out of here for a while and have some coffee."

The two detectives walked to the deli in the next block and got a booth. They sat in silence until they ordered and the waitress brought their drinks to them. Mike was sipping his coffee when Rickey blurted out, "You banging her?"

Mike choked and spit the mouthful of coffee out on the table. He sopped it up with his napkin and took time to think before he responded.

"Does it show?"

Rickey smiled and cocked his head. "To me it does. I don't think anybody else knows, but yeah. I figured it out a couple weeks ago. Are you doing it here, or is she slipping up to Tulsa and banging your dick up there?"

"C'mon, have a heart. No, she doesn't go to Tulsa. It's nothing like that at all. It's just that she is so into her work, and I'm so into mine that we seem to be able to help each other relax and get our focus back on our work." He shook his head and continued. "It's nothing serious between us. We have a good understanding of each other, and she has struck up a good friendship with Annalisa. They've turned out to be pretty good buddies and ..."

Rickey interrupted. "Bullshit, good buddies. She's screwing her good buddy's husband and you call her your wife's friend? Give me a break."

"I hear what you're saying, but it's true. She means nothing to me. I mean that. At the same time, all of these killings have about driven me to the Employee Assistance Group to see the shrink, and Emily has been there for me. I'm not kidding. She has a way with words. She helps me get the stress out of my system."

"Get the stress out of your system?" Rickey asked. "Sure, and she has a way with words. Do you realize how stupid you sound? What you are really saying is that she has a way with her body and screws you 'til you can't go another minute. If that doesn't take the wind out of your sails for a while, then nothing will. Now, that may sound lousy to you, but it's the truth. You're bullshitting yourself. She bangs you. It feels good, and it's that simple, so cut the crap about how she can talk to you and make you feel good."

Mike looked sheepish, but responded, "It's different. That's all I can say. Emily has a way about her. After we've been together I've got a clear mind. I focus, and when I focus then I know I'm going to get this crazy killing son-of-a-bitch if it's the last thing I do."

"*Amigo*," Rickey said as he paid the check, "if Annalisa gets wise to you, she'll clean your plow – big time. She says she loves you now, but if she catches you screwing Emily, you're one dead duck. She'll wipe you out."

"Well, let's keep this little conversation to ourselves," Mike said on the walk back to the office.

"My lips are sealed, but I have to warn you. You're my friend. Keep this up and you'll regret it. You'll never be able to go back and undo it. What's done is done. I'm not saying you're ahead, but you can still stop before you get in any deeper. Just keep these two thoughts in your mind – your family and your job."

They were coming to the station door when Rickey spoke again. "One last comment – the next time you see that good-looking broad and get a big stiff joint, take a deep breath and think about Annalisa, Sam, and your career. Then if you want to bang your balls off, have at it."

#

"Mike, phone for you." It was Anna, the receptionist.

Mike hooked the phone in the crook of his shoulder. "This is Detective Palotti, may I help you?"

"Other way around, Mike." It was Chief Les Cates from the University of North Texas Police Department, Mike's partner when they rode a two-man patrol car ten years ago in Oak Cliff.

"Hey, Les, ol' buddy. Got some answers for me?" He did not wait for the Chief's response. "You going to clear up these murders for me and let me get a good night's sleep?"

"Sorry to ruin your day, but the answer is no. Hell no. Your guy Rosas was clean as a whistle when he was here in school. I've talked to his professors and checked his records. The guy is free and clear. Nothing. Zip. He left school when the fellowship he was on expired and he didn't have enough money to stay around, so he dropped out."

The chief paused. The line was silent for a moment. "Sorry Mike, but this guy looks good from here. He just ran out of money and left school like thousands do every year on every campus. If he's a killer, it doesn't show up in his background."

"Hey Les, they never said life would be easy, but thanks for your help."

"No sweat. Hey, when you're ready to retire from Big D give me a call. This is a whole different life. Guess what?" He paused, and then continued, "The biggest crime we handled this semester is when some shithead broke into a dean's office and stole her grade book."

They laughed and hung up. Mike was still stumped. Rosas was all they had and they were not going to let him off the hook. Not yet anyway. They would stay with him until they were able to prove he was the killer, or prove that he wasn't. One way or the other, they would live with him day and night until they figured it out.

Mike swung back from day shift and went on the evening shift surveillance team. They picked up Rosas when he left the house about ten o'clock, something he'd never done before. They followed him up Northwest Highway until he pulled into the Yellow Rose, a urine-stenched strip joint famous to the beat cops for a weekly stabbing, half a dozen fist fights, and a couple of parking lot robberies – a class joint.

The detectives were surprised. Rosas had led a mundane existence in the weeks they watched him, so this was a sharp change in his behavior. Mike parked his car in the parking lot while the others set up surveillance on the perimeter. He got out, worked his way through the group of lecherous old men hanging around the door, and found a stool at the bar. The bartender brought him a beer while Mike looked in the mirror. The room was crowded, smoky, and smelled of spilled beer and vomit.

Two over-weight dancers were strutting on the bar, swinging their buxom breasts in front of the patrons and hoping for a dollar or two to be slipped into their thongs. Mike looked between the legs of one who called herself Candy. In the mirror, he saw Rosas sitting at a table by himself. He was sucking on a beer, watching Candy pump her hips and swing her gigantic tits in Mike's face.

She gave up on getting a few bucks from Mike, so moved on down the bar to another paying customer who was only too happy to pay her to shove it in his face.

Rosas got up and walked to the pay phone next to the bathroom door. Mike instantly left the bar and headed for the men's room. He noticed Rosas turned his back to the crowd and cupped his hand over his other ear to shut out the music and chatter from the bar. The detective took advantage of Rosas' position and paused next to the door. He was only about three feet behind Rosas.

He shoved a handful of coins in the cigarette machine and pulled out a pack of Marlboros – what he smoked when he fed the habit a pack a day. He took his time and opened the pack, all the while straining to listen to this end of the conversation.

"Yeah, yeah," Rosas said. There was more muffled conversation, but the bump and grind of the music and cheering crowd drowned it out. Mike stepped closer, having decided that Rosas was so intent that he was not paying attention to anyone in the bar.

"*Seguro que si*, you bet your ass I'm going to get her tonight. She's strung me on long enough, and tonight is payday. Why don't you come along and get into the act yourself?"

Mike tensed. Was tonight the night? Was he going to do it? If he tried, he would pay the price. They had him.

"Okay," Rosas said. "I'll get her by myself, but I'll give you a call tomorrow and let you know how it went."

Mike turned toward the exit when Rosas hung up the receiver. He went out to his undercover car and grabbed the microphone. "It's on. He was talking to someone on the phone and said that he was going to get a woman tonight. No further details."

Sergeant Covey came on the air. "Mike, we've got it covered any way he goes. Get out of there just in case he sees you when he comes out. You can follow along a couple blocks behind. We'll stay with him wherever he goes and tail him on foot when he gets out of the car."

There was a pause while the sergeant gathered his thoughts. "When he parks, the first car will drive by and give us a report on his exact location and what he's doing. Whoever is in the second and third cars will park and get up there pronto and tail him on foot. Okay guys, this may be it. Don't let him get away and whatever you do, don't let him make physical contact with anyone."

The radio went quiet. Ten minutes passed before Covey came back on the air. "Okay troops, he's getting in his car. Let's do it."

Mike watched from the dark alley where he took refuge, and saw Rosas leave the parking lot and turn toward the Stemmons Freeway. He turned left, went up on the freeway and headed toward downtown. They took turns keeping in close behind him, rotating cars often enough that he would not become aware of any one car staying behind him. He exited the freeway, turned into a side street, made a "U" turn, and finally made his way into the West End, a popular tourist and adolescent area of bars, loud music and restaurants. He swung into a pay parking lot, locked his car, and made his way into the crowded sidewalk. The cops blended into the crowd and stayed close to him. Rosas went to the door of Mug's Bar, paid his five-dollar cover fee, and went inside. Covey and Detective Joe

Rizzo followed him inside. Mike kept surveillance on the car just in case Rosas lost their tail and went back to it. Detectives Mary Roche and Freddy Joe Crawford hung out with the street musicians and teenage panhandlers, waiting for their turn to take the "eyeball" if he came outside, or if necessary, to go inside and relieve Covey and Rizzo.

Mike parked his car in a "no parking" zone and settled in for what he assumed could be a boring wait, which is what most surveillance details turn out to be. To kill time, he flicked on his penlight and went through the old surveillance notes going back to the first day they began to watch the suspected killer. He casually flipped the pages. Suddenly, it jumped out at him. On the thirteenth day, he went to the Yellow Rose at lunchtime. So tonight was not his first time there. And there it was again – on the twenty-eighth day – at lunchtime again.

Tonight was the first time in the evening, but it definitely was not his first time to go to the queen of the gentlemen's clubs along the strip of cafés, bars and video joints. Mike thought of Emily and her incessant hammering away that government organization, and cops in particular, do not communicate. What a hell of an example, fifteen cops working three shifts, each keeping notes that were reviewed each day. Now he understood how they could miss the obvious, how they could work with their eyes wide shut. They'd breezed over the routine – they were so busy looking for the "kill" that they had missed the mundane. He thought of Willie Mae: *you get so close you can't see what you're looking at.* Of course, the big question was who did Rosas talk to and what was he going to do in the West End? Mike ran through the possibilities. Kill someone? Meet some distant relative who mooched money off him? Pick up some woman he was doling out money to and it was time for her to pay him back with money or sex? Collect a past due debt from someone who used his legitimate service? Only time would tell.

Plus, what was the purpose of the Yellow Rose? Was it a contact point for a cult of killers to plan and swap information? Was it no more than a cheap thrill to stoke his manly fire before he met a date and got a little loving? Who knows? Maybe he had a long-lost cousin named Candy who danced for a living. Mike laughed at his self-depreciating humor. He did not have the slightest idea what Rosas was up to, but they had nothing better to work on, so he was it until he proved otherwise. One thing was certain. He wouldn't kill anybody tonight.

Chapter Four

THE ALPHABET KILLER STOOD IN front of the mirror and smiled contentedly. It was soothing to know no one had the slightest idea the identity of the greatest serial killer in America. What a sense of humor. How ingenious. The perfect crime! In fact, the perfect series of crimes, and it was absolutely guaranteed they would never be solved. There never would be an arrest or trial, no conviction, no date with the green needle behind the brick walls of Huntsville or Oklahoma's death chamber in McAlester.

The key was perfect planning and perfect execution. How Freudian – perfect timing and perfect teasing – not too subtle, but not too timid – communicate to the cops that they are totally incompetent and lost.

The killer remembered an old Jackie Gleason show on late-night television and one of the comedian's masterful quips, "How sweet it is."

There was nothing against those who died. It was simply a question of could it be done? Yes, it could. Was it possible for one person working alone to outsmart all of the genius within police and the FBI? Yes, without a doubt. Was there anything to be gained by killing them? Certainly there was. It would be a long-term return on investment, but yes, there was a short-turn payback – personal satisfaction.

The killer stood in front of the full-length mirror and admired the power and grace of every muscle as it was flexed; biceps, triceps, stomach, thighs, calves – all in perfect condition. All ready to strike out and kill.

Appropriate clothing for this particular murder was laid on the bed with military precision as though ready for an inspection. A dark sweat suit, dark socks and jogging shoes, a black t-shirt and baseball cap, and a pair of dark leather gloves.

The assassin opened the closet door, shuffled a stack of shoeboxes aside, and opened the door to the control panel embedded behind the wall. Moments like this were forever. A flick of the finger and the video camera was on, taping everything inside the house, memorializing the murderer's waltz of death.

The lone murderer dressed slowly, almost as if undergoing a metaphysical transformation. First the pants, then the shirt, followed by the socks and shoes. It was a dance – a practiced and perfect ritual to the sounds of silent harmony. A killer ready to take an innocent life.

No need to drive tonight. It was only four blocks to the strip shopping center – an easy jaunt, plus it meant there was no need for the extra precautions a car always required. Going on foot was so simple. Just slip in, do it and leave. It would be over and done within mere seconds.

The clock in the living room chimed nine forty-five. Fifteen minutes – no more and no less. Tommy would be on time. He always was and tonight would be no different than any of the others. He would come out the back door, stop and lock the dead bolt and the door lock, and turn and walk the sixteen steps to his car in the dark parking lot. He would walk past the row of trees that separated the building from the parking lot, but not reach his car. Not tonight or any other night.

The alphabet killer picked up the axe handle that lay across the foot of the bed, rubbed it with a delicate, loving touch, and went out into the dark night. The motion was practiced dozens of times. Just like a homerun hitter, swing for the left field fence – hard, directly toward the Adam's apple. Never swing "at" a target; always swing "through" it for maximum effect. The crushing blow should knock Tommy down instantly. He would fall backwards, and in all likelihood be unconscious or at least too stunned to react. Then, the coup de grace: put the axe handle to his throat and press it down with all the weight that can be mustered. Death would come in seconds. The night watchman should find him in ten or fifteen minutes when he made his usual door check and would call the police. Just like all the others, the cops would be baffled – no robbery, no burglary, no evidence, no nothing. It would be another perfect crime.

#

Tommy Lee James sat in the cramped office at the rear of his shoe store. Mildred, his wife of thirty years, had died and left him three years ago. It took so much time, but now he was almost there. The grief was less each day. The store was running almost as smoothly as the days they'd worked side-by-side. Life was good once again. He felt the warmth in his heart. Life goes on. A person has to grieve and cope with it, and he did. He looked in the mirror behind his desk. He was older and the years showed. Nevertheless, he smiled and winked at himself.

"Goin' to make it, you old cuss," he cracked. "Many more days like today and I might even think about retiring."

The day was superb. He ran a special sale, the first since being widowed. He gave away two pair of socks with every pair of shoes and nearly ran out of socks by closing time at nine o'clock. It was the best day in a long time, and he was already thinking about another sale next month.

He put the day's receipts in the cash box, opened the floor safe and tucked it away for the night. One last walk through the store, shut off the lights, set the thermostat, and call it a day. He would have just enough time to pick up a couple of tacos and get home to watch the end of the Mavericks game. He was tired, but today was worth it. She would be proud of him.

He left through the back door, stopped to double lock it, and stepped into the shadows of the night. He saw a sudden motion directly in front of him when he passed the elm trees that lined the parking lot. It happened too fast to react – like a bolt of lightning out of the darkness. There was an explosion in his head. He couldn't breathe. His legs crumpled with the impact to his throat. He was aware of something horrifying happening to him, but it was so fast he was helpless. The ground reached up and pulled him down hard. The back of his head smacked onto the concrete sidewalk. He tried to focus his eyes, only to make out a dark figure straddling his body. He saw the axe handle come down against his throat, and then a person put their knees on it and pressed it against him. He gagged and felt his tongue swell in his mouth. He gasped futilely. His aged hands and arms flailed weakly to grasp whatever was choking him. Then he died.

With professional efficiency, the killer stepped away from the lifeless man. A quick glance over the shoulder, an assurance of accomplishment, and it was over.

For now at least, because tonight was going to be exceptional. It would be the first time for a double-header. Tommy Lee James, the

Dallas shoe store owner, and Oscar Luna, the Tulsa convenience store manager.

Only five minutes after Tommy's murder, he was already gone and forgotten to the killer. Other tasks were at hand. In contrast to the ceremony of donning the garb for Tommy's death, the killer tossed off the clothes, ran to the basement, put them in the washing machine, dumped in a cup of powder, and turned on the washer to clean away any shred of evidence.

The assassin was driving north from the Dallas city limits only an hour after leaving the house to go to the shoe store. It would take about four hours to get to Tulsa, but that would leave plenty of time to go to the apartment, select the proper attire, change clothes, and walk through the act mentally. It would be a dry run, so to speak, but necessary to help prepare and be in the proper frame of mind.

Oscar would be a bit more complicated than Tommy, because it was necessary to park a couple blocks away and slip into position to catch him after he parked his car. Nevertheless, it wouldn't be a problem. There were plenty of apartments and parking lots, so the Suburban would fit in anonymously anywhere.

Oscar was boring. He always parked his tired old Ford along the north side of the store, unlocked the front door, and went inside to turn on the lights and the gas pumps. He returned outside to pick up the stack of morning papers, then went back inside for another day's business.

It was so easy it was almost laughable. He was another helpless little being in the world in which his life would pass unnoticed, except for the fifteen minutes of fame he would receive for being the "O" in Oklahoma.

The killer laughed. *Hey, there's a Miss Oklahoma, so why can't little Oscar be Mr. Oklahoma? He deserves it. He has a place in history. He is part of one the greatest serial murders in American history, and his case will go unsolved. Well, not really unsolved, but unsolved in a unique sort of way.*

It was three o'clock in the morning when the assassin parked in the garage, unlocked the apartment door and went inside. Renting this apartment was an absolute stroke of genius in more ways than one. The apartment had most of the conveniences of home, and was a clean and simple home away from home. It was a place to get away from the hustle and bustle of Dallas, and to rest in a maze of apartments in which no one knows their neighbor. Best of all, it provided a place to plan. Hide in plain sight – that was the genius of this plan. There was no great effort to be concealed. In fact, it was just the contrary. Be out front, be open, be friends, be whatever. Most important though, don't hide in the netherworld of crime because the police are creatures of habit. They will scour the netherworld of drugs, organized crime, hit men, cults, and revolutionaries. A masterful killer knows those are the logical places for the perfect criminal to avoid.

It was so simple it was a joke. Between the FBI, and the Tulsa and Dallas police departments, they did not have the slightest idea who or what was behind these serial murders. Their day of reckoning would come, and that would be the down payment on this long-term investment of time and talent.

The murders would amount to the perfect crimes. They would be solved, but not solved at the same time. Total perfection no one else had ever before accomplished. What a great feat. What brilliance. It would be something to be remembered forever.

The killer allowed for plenty of time. It was a twenty-minute drive from the apartment to the store. It was necessary to add on another ten minutes to have ample time to park in a nearby twenty-four hour Wal-Mart parking lot and walk through the alley to come to Oscar's store. There would be a good place of concealment next to the telephone booth that was two or three steps from where the newspapers were always stacked.

Just like clockwork, Oscar parked his car on the north side of the building opposite from where his assassin lay in wait. He unlocked the door and went in, flicked on the interior lights and came back outside. He leaned over to pick up the papers just as the silent killer slipped out from behind the phone booth, placed the petite .22 pistol to the back of his head and fired. His lifeless body catapulted forward, rolled over the stack of morning papers and landed face up. His unseeing eyes stared at the first crack of dawn on the eastern horizon. The double-header was complete; no runs, no hits, and no errors. It was a perfect series.

Within the hour, the anonymous killer was sitting at the breakfast bar in the apartment, sipping orange juice and eating a bagel. It was a hard and fast night, but went off just as planned – perfectly. Now for a good hot shower, catch a few hours' sleep on the waterbed, and be home for dinner.

#

It was after midnight before Covey came back on the radio and spoke in quick spurts. "Listen up. He's leaving with one of the barmaids. He's been flirting with her since he got here. They seem to know each other. Not so sure this is it."

Mike watched them go to the car. Rosas was a perfect gentleman. He opened the door for her and closed it behind her, then walked around to his side of the car. The surveillance team took up positions, ready to fall in behind him when he left, but were surprised when the headlights never came on. The minutes passed.

"Somebody get up," Covey commanded.

"Got it," Rizzo responded.

From where he was parked, Mike saw Rizzo walking between cars heading toward Rosas'. Rizzo slowed, went back around another car, and came back toward Rosas' from a different direction.

Rizzo put a couple of cars between him and Rosas before he spoke into his portable radio. "He's ...," there was a pause while Rizzo re-thought what he almost said, "well, they're copulating."

The detectives stayed with Rosas and watched him walk the girl back to the bar and return to his car. Twenty minutes later they watched when he turned off his bedroom light and went to bed.

Covey's voice came on the radio. "Not tonight, and I'm not sure of any other night. Any thoughts?"

Mike picked up his radio, took a deep breath, and responded. "I'm thinking about the chicken stuff on the newspaper."

Covey responded, "10-4, let's call it a day."

#

Mike went back to the day shift. It was time to start from scratch again. It was there; he simply must keep looking and it would be there. The common denominator was there all the time, but somehow slipped through. Mike commanded himself to think, to look at the individual trees and not be overwhelmed by the forest. He would find it if it was the last thing he did.

In the corner of his eye he caught sight of the Lieutenant coming into the squad room. Molina signaled to Mike and Rickey to follow him to the conference room.

"What's up?" Rickey asked as they pulled up the chairs.

Lieutenant Molina waved his notebook in front of them. "While you guys were watching the horny piano man, your killer was having a ball." He cleared his throat. "No, let me correct that. Your killer was having two good balls. Two. Get it?"

He tossed the crime report of Tommy Lee James in front of them. "And, your good buddy in Tulsa called before you got here this morning. This demonic killing machine was up there spelling Oklahoma, and he's running around here spelling Texas and laughing at us every inch of the way.

"Okay, here's what we know so far. James got whacked after he closed up around ten o'clock." He looked at Mike. "You've made the Tulsa drive. What's it take you, four or five hours?"

"Yeah," Mike responded.

"This guy Oscar Luna bought the farm around six o'clock when he got to work. The same person had plenty of time to do James, then hit the road and do Luna. Right?"

Rickey shook his head. "No, not so fast, Lieutenant. What if we're dealing with more than one person and they're starting to screw around with us? The same thing never happened twice in the same night, and no one was killed at his or her own home or business, so this is a major league change in their modus operandi. Plus, there's been enough of this stuff in the paper that maybe some copycat put two and two together and is playing their own game."

Molina cut in, "Listen to me. Now, the news hawks have even given this killing machine a name – The Creature. Some dipshit at the newspaper drew an editorial cartoon of some weird monster. They're making it like some science fiction monster bullshit. The Creature From the Black Lagoon. Remember that?"

"With all respect, Lieutenant, have you lost your friggin' mind? What the hell are you talking about?" Rickey asked.

"The morning paper," Molina barked. "They ran this cartoon and editorial about some fifty-year-old movie with an Amazon creature that was coming out of the swamps. It was one of those B-grade horror movies, and was filmed up around Lake Dallas or somewhere around here. Anyhow, they did a spinoff of that and then went ahead with their own imagination and called our guy, 'The Creature.' So now they've got something to play with, but I'm telling you guys ..."

He paused to catch his breath and then pointed his finger in Mike's face. "This is no game. It's your ass is what it is, so you guys better get humping. Look at this." He pointed to the duty roster. "I gave you fifteen cops from this unit and from the Tactical Squad to chase a piano tuner, and all we got out of it was we can verify he gets an occasional piece of ass."

Rickey jumped up from his chair. His temper flared. "Screw your organizational bureaucracy. Screw your duty roster. Screw your rank. Screw the whole damned mess. We've been doing the best we can, and if you think somebody can do it better, then just get their little ass over here and let's get it on."

He sat back down, shook his head, and choked out a nervous

laugh. "What the hell, I feel better anyway."

"Whatever," Molina responded. "Nevertheless, the stakes are getting too high." He looked at Mike. "You guys have got to get this solved. The mayor is getting clobbered. The chief is getting clobbered. You know how stuff runs downhill, so you and I aren't too far away from it. Understand?"

"Yes sir, I do. I'm going back to ground zero and starting all over. Something is there. You know it and I know it. The lab has looked at everything. The bureau has taken it twice. We've talked to every little piss ant who might have anything to do with the victims, and everything has come up sterile." He slouched in his chair and rubbed his temples. He was dying with a headache, but continued.

"Rickey, humor me, but we're going to start this mess like we never saw it before. You're going to start with the victim's minutia. I remember a few years back we finally solved a serial rapist by backtracking. We found all of the women had bought shoes from the same shoe store within two months of their rape and paid with a check. I want you to make up a list – the grocery store, drug store, car repair – anywhere you can think of and get talking to their families. We have to know every little tidbit that seems so trivial that nobody ever thought about it, that's going to be our common denominator."

He laughed. "You know what? When we figure it out, we'll sit back, slap our foreheads, and say 'duh.' I tell you, it's going to be that obvious. In fact, you know where you might start? Run down their checking accounts and see where the banks get the checks. Wouldn't it be something if all they had in common was that their banks got the checks printed from the same place? Some turkey might have picked them out at random, winnowed them down, and selected his victim."

"I can handle that, but what about you? Where are you headed?" Rickey replied.

"The evidence. What little there is of it. I'm going to go back and see what we missed." He shrugged his shoulders and looked wistfully at them. "Actually, I don't have the slightest idea what we'll find, but we sure as hell aren't going to surrender." He shook his head. "This isn't a grade-B flick. This is real life and we're going to catch that shithead if it's the last thing we ever do."

Mike sat at his desk and began laying out a list of victims and the methodology of their murders:

Denton Ryan	- throat slit with a smooth bladed, extremely sharp knife; no evidence of more than one slicing motion; no hack-sawing; cutting motion from the victim's left front with depth of cut indicating a right-handed assault; no metal traces of knife blade found; no footprints of suspect found in victim's blood.
Andrew Maines	- two blows to the head with an unidentified solid instrument; baseball bat or axe handle? both blows of sufficient impact to cause death; coroner's notes imply that the first blow was from the right rear at the base of the skull, and the second blow was administered after the victim was face down on the ground; no footprints found in victim's blood; microscopic trace of oak found embedded in victim's hair; oak untraceable to any brand or manufacturer.
Landa Lopez	- thin but strong object, such as piano wire, used to apply garrote from behind; marks on throat and neck indicate the object was thrown quickly in one smooth action over her head from behind and powerful force was used to cut through her neck, nearly decapitating her; injury was so swift that bleeding was minimal; destruction of breathing passages and arteries were each sufficient to cause death; no defensive injury indicated complete surprise; marks on victim's neck indicate the wire was attached on both ends to a solid object, such as wood or metal, because bruise on the neck is from where the solid objects were the leverage point to apply the required energy to facilitate the assault.
Leonard Throckmorton	- shot twice from behind; lack of gunpowder residue indicates the shots were fired from more than seven feet away; both shots impacted the victim's head, which indicated they were fired in quick succession before he could fall over; the .22 caliber spent slugs

were recovered; the slugs do not match the marks and grooves of any other evidence compiled in the data bank.

<u>Allison Reynolds</u> - a long-bladed, serrated knife of at least five inches in length was the instrument of death; four stab wounds to the upper back and neck; the angle of impact imply the victim may have been leaning over the water fountain alongside the jogging path when the assault occurred; the wound to the right of the spine on the neck caused minimal damage and was deflected by the spinal column; the other three wounds ranged from two inches to five inches in depth, implying an assailant of significant strength and coordination to inflict the damage; only the deepest cut was significant enough to cause death by itself; blood smears around the body indicate the assailant stepped in the blood, but used an unidentified paper or cloth to wipe away any distinguishing points of shoe style or size.

<u>Sara McComb</u> - a twelve-gauge shotgun slug struck the victim at the hairline directly above the bridge of her nose; the angle of impact and the spatter of blood and tissue indicate her head was outside the car, turned slightly to her left, and looking down at the time of the shot; the upper half of the head was completely removed and disintegrated by the slug.

<u>Tommy Lee James</u> - two points of impact to the throat; a crushing blow between the Adam's apple and the central depression on the throat; sufficient damage would cause death by strangulation; heavy tissue damage, but no external bleeding; bruising to the left side of the throat and neck; crushing damage to the larynx and artery sufficient to cause near instant death. Evidence tends to indicate the Adam's apple injury was from a

strong, quick blow by a blunt object; the bruise and crushing injuries appear to be the result of a sustained application of force by a blunt object; no evidence of the blunt object was found.

#

It was after five o'clock before Mike finished. He was to the point of a mental meltdown. He went the entire day without a break, too intense to be able to stop for lunch. He pushed back from his chair, yawned, stretched, and put his feet up on his desk. He was too tired to give it another ounce of his strength. He looked at the clock on the wall and sat captivated while he watched the second hand sweep in a never-ending circle. It went around and around, going nowhere but never stopping. How analogous, he thought. It was like his own job, going around and around and getting nowhere; always ending up right back where he started. Except his was different – every time the clock on the wall ticked away another minute meant they were one minute closer to the next person dying. Who would it be? he wondered.

He spelled it out in his mind while he wadded up bits of paper and tossed them into the trash basket. D-A-L-L-A-S, one piece of insignificant paper for every innocent person whose life was thrown away for the creature's sick enjoyment. Now they were in T-E-X-A-S. Tommy was dead. Who will be the "E?"

He pulled the phone book off the desk and opened it to random page. He did some quick and dirty calculating. There was an average of 270 names per page times the number of pages. He counted the number of people per page whose name started with an "E." The next step was some quick multiplication and percentages. He came up with 24,894 first names that started with an "E." Which one would be next?

It exploded in his mind. "Emily." She fit the perfect profile for the creature. She jogged every Monday, Wednesday and Friday at six in the morning. She went to her yoga class at seven o'clock every Tuesday evening and lived in an easy traffic flow neighborhood. Although she had a garage and not a carport, her house was nearly in the geographic center of where the murders occurred. She shopped in the Galleria Center and parked her car in the parking garage; and, of course she was cursed with the "E." He must tell her, warn her.

Mike called Annalisa and said that he would be late. He didn't tell her exactly why or what he would be doing other than something came up on the cases, so don't hold dinner for him. In his mind, he knew what he must do: go to Emily and talk to her. She answered on the seventh ring. Her voice was groggy. "Mike, I was taking a nap. I've been in New York with my editor and took the red eye out of LaGuardia. I'm pooped out and trying to catch up with my sleep."

"We have to talk," he commanded.

"Is there a problem?" she asked.

"More than you could ever expect. I'll be there in thirty minutes." He didn't pause.

#

Emily heard the connection break. This was very unlike him. She bit her lip and frowned, unsure of what or why he'd called. What did he know? What was he afraid of? She looked at the clock. He would be there in a half hour. If she hurried, her attire would be appropriate for whatever might develop. She looked through her closets for something special, something he'd never seen her wear, and certainly not something similar to the clothes in Annalisa's closet. She found it hanging regally in her bathroom closet – a beaded nightgown and robe. Feminine, delicate, sensual but not overly sexual; something to tease him; something to cause him to melt like warm butter.

#

She answered his knock with a timid peek around the door. He looked at her bright smile and felt the comfort of her allure.

"Come in here." She stepped back and opened the door. "You've scared the pooh-pooh out of me with your phone call. What's up?"

Mike stepped inside and closed the door behind him. His heart pounded in his chest. "I'm afraid for you," he said as he reached his arms around her waist and pulled her to him. He tasted the softness of her lips and inhaled the delicate scent of her perfume, the caressing aroma of his lover. His heart leapt with the tenderness of her breasts against him. "I love you," he uttered. They kissed passionately again and again. Finally, she leaned back and allowed his strong hands around her waist to hold her. She smiled and wiped the lipstick from his lips.

"Okay, now you've got my attention," she panted. "What's the big mystery?"

Mike led her to the couch and sat next to her. He never took his eyes from her beautiful face. He held her hands cupped in his.

"I'm afraid for you ..." He went on to lay out for her the complete mystery of Dallas, Tulsa, and now the newest killings of Oscar Luna and Tommy Lee James. The killing would continue. She had to know the truth to protect herself. He was not violating any secrets. He was saving her life. As much as he was lawfully bound to solve the murders, he was equally bound to protect life. In this case, he was legally obligated to protect Emily, the "E" in T-E-X-A-S.

"Mike, listen to me," she commanded. She kissed his hands. "I love you, and I know you're only doing this to protect me, but we have to look at this realistically. Look at the numbers. You calculated them yourself. What? Twenty-five thousand 'E's', and I'm just one of them? Yes, I'm in the phone book and city directory. Okay, you're right to tell me, but please don't worry. Please. Promise me you won't worry about me."

"I don't know if I can," he responded.

"You don't have any idea who's behind these murders, but the other side of the coin is there's no reason to suspect he's target me, is there?"

"Not factually, no there isn't. It's just that I can't get my mind off what that crazy prick is doing, and then I think of you. My heart sinks when I think how helpless you are. My God, Emily, you mean so much to me. It scares me to consider the thought of him touching you."

She tickled him and laughed. "C'mon, mister policeman, I'm a big girl and can take care of myself. You don't know. Maybe I would just whip his little butt if he tried anything with me."

"Emily, I love you with all my heart. I'd die if something happened to you, especially if I could've prevented it."

She rose from the couch and took his hand. "Dance with me," she whispered into his ear.

The sounds of the stereo floated through the house from another room. She wrapped her arms around him, kissed him, then stepped back and slipped her silk robe from her shoulders.

"Dance with me," he said. His lips touched hers and they swayed to the melodies of love. She kissed him back.

Chapter Five

THE MOST NOTORIOUS SERIAL KILLER in America's heartland lay propped up in bed and looked at the morning paper, disgruntled with the publicity. Certainly such perfection and the sterile, clueless crimes scenes left behind were deserving of a more worthy nickname than "The Creature." Anyone with any sense of movie history knew the "Creature From the Black Lagoon" was a slimy, web-footed, sophomoric re-incarnation of a fifteen-million-year-old Amazon half man, half amphibian – a monster. Even the clumsy Inspector Clouseau would acknowledge these murders as the work of a master criminal, not the efforts of an ugly helmeted toad.

The bastards can't recognize perfection. Well, there is a way to prove it to them. A way to make them pay for their own degenerate reporting – the stuff they call "journalism." They will have a first-hand look at the hand of death as it sweeps them into the hell in which they surely will spend eternity. Indeed, they will pay for their crime and their inability to recognize a perfectionist at work.

The Creature tossed aside the morning paper, sipped the lukewarm coffee sitting on the bedside table, and sorted through the pile of old newspaper articles, books and magazines that were spread across the foot of the bed.

David Berkowitz, the Son of Sam;
Albert DeSalvo, the alleged Boston Strangler who very possibly was innocent of the crimes;
Ted Bundy, the handsome lady-killer;
Albert Fish, the model Hannibal Lector;
Eddie Gein, the real-life Psycho;
Richard Ramirez, the Night Stalker and a real-life Freddy Kruger;
Angel Resendez, the Railroad Killer;

The Zodiac Killer, a class act who sent confessions to the news media and police;

William Bonin, the Freeway Killer;

Kenneth Bianchi and Angelo Buono, the Hillside Stranglers – a unique case that involved the police turning to a psychic for help;

Henry Lee Lucas and Ottis Toole; the vagabond Highway 87 killers;

Dayton Rogers, Portland's "Steve the Gambler" murderer;

Charles Schmid, The Pied Piper of Tucson;

Carl Panzram, the remorseless killer considered too evil to live.

The list continued. Macabre murder after macabre murder, insane predators and sex fiends who were little more than wild beasts. Yet the unfairness of it all was so obvious. They were nothing more than crude killing machines, but at least were recognized with a title that acknowledged their work. Creature? What an insult. What a failure to recognize quality.

The closest anyone came to matching The Creature was The Zodiac Killer. He was never caught in spite of his notoriety, and teasing the police and press with his confessions. Nevertheless, a big difference between them was that the Zodiac was a slob. He killed people and left everything a mess – blood, guts, fingerprints and footprints – "a garbage man," the Dallas killer dubbed him. Give him his due, with all the evidence he left behind he was never caught.

Nevertheless, there was something to learn from each of them. They killed without remorse and went on with their work. However, the lesson to be learned, whether a person is robbing banks or killing people, is this – don't be greedy. Stop when you are ahead. It's the greedy ones who end up on death row. Henry Lee Lucas was a prime example. He could have killed a few people and stopped and no one would ever have been wise to him, but no. He kept up in his cross-country journeys until he was apprehended. Then his lack of discipline mixed with his self-adulation brought forth the accusations of hundreds of murders. Maybe he did them and maybe he didn't. If he practiced self-control and discipline, he could have experienced a few moments of enjoyment while his victims sucked their last breath. Then he could go on about his business. No one would be the wiser.

That was the moral to beating the system. Plan, execute and go. Enjoy the entire process, but have an exit plan. When the goal is achieved, call it quits and move on to better things.

The Creature was resolved – only two more murders and it would be complete. Provide the world with a perfect performance and exit, stage left. The play is over. The curtain is dropped and the house lights turned on. Audience, you may leave.

The killer cleared the clutter from the bed and made it – sheets pulled tight and tucked in, pillows neatly fluffed against the headboard, the bedspread straight and smoothed.

The barefooted perfectionist murderer padded lightly to the kitchen. A scoop of fresh coffee in the pot, a glass of orange juice and a bagel provided a perfect breakfast. It was a little something to sooth the hard feelings caused by the yellow journalism in the morning paper.

The serial killer leaned against the kitchen counter and opened the window. The music of the songbirds was soothing. The Magnolia tree provided a perfect home for nature's little musicians. Clearly, it was their favorite nesting place with its alligator skin trunk and branches. They reached out over the eaves of the house to give the beautiful choir ample shade and protection from the obnoxious blue jays. The birds provided a natural sonata with their chirps and calls intermingled with the soft rush of the wind that flowed through the trees. Yes, it was a beautiful morning, a good day to die. But, wasn't every day?

It took only a few minutes to clean the kitchen before The Creature walked the length of the hall and opened the door to the basement. The wonderful musty scent drifted up the stairs when the door creaked opened. The killer inhaled deeply and held it to the point of bursting. What a wonderful dichotomy. The sweet smells of nature in the yard and the exhilarating odor from beneath the house.

The basement was clean and well kept, but between the age of the house, the humidity and the closeness of the lower level, it always maintained that certain odor. Not that it was unpleasant, just different from the main floor.

The killer flipped on the lights and descended the staircase, flicked another switch and turned to the left down the hallway. Near the end of the hall and to the right was a well-stocked wet bar, television set, a surround sound system and a pool table. The killer went beyond the game room entryway and continued to the end of the hall. Unless a trained eye was looking for it, a person would not notice the notch at the lower right at the dead end of the hall. The hand that took so many lives reached down and pressed the lever in the notch and stood back. The wall opened and revealed a long, narrow room that ran parallel to the game room. A touch on the light switch revealed The Creature's tools of the trade. Each was neatly hung by an individual clip on the wall. To the mass murderer it was nirvana:

A box cutter – an incredibly sharp, sturdy, curved 3½-inch blade that folded into its own handle;

An ice pick – a long, thin, pointed metallic blade set in a wooden handle;

Two garrotes, each twenty-four inches long, one of piano wire, the other of clothesline rope, with each end secured to a blunt one-inch by one-inch by four-inch wooden handle that served as the leverage for the killer's hands;

An axe handle;

A Louisville slugger baseball bat;

Five butcher knives with blades ranging from three inches to five inches in length, each knife of the finest quality German steel which held the sharp edge and was unlikely to break on impact with a bone;

Two Katana swords, favorites of the Samurai warriors, hung cross-bladed over each other;

A variety of handguns ranging from a .22 caliber Saturday Night Special to a six-inch barrel .44 Magnum revolver;

A selection of long-guns for every occasion – a Winchester .22 rifle, a Remington .243 rifle and scope, and at the far end of the chamber of death hung two 12-gauge Browning shotguns.

The killer walked with slow deliberation the length of the narrow room, pausing to touch and examine each instrument before moving on to the next. At the far end of the room, the killer turned and looked back at the tools. A smile swept across the face of Satan personified.

"It is good. All we accomplished together was good, but there is still more to be done before we rest. My children, our time has come. We shall have a complete victory and then we will rest forever. When our task is complete, we will never again walk this journey together. Each of you has done your job well, and I thank you."

The killer closed the chamber, went to the far end of the hall and unlocked the door to another room. It was little more than a closet. This was the master equipment room from which all of the audio and video systems throughout the house were controlled. It took only a couple of minutes to twist the knobs and flick the switches to assure everything was in good working order. Each room and the backyard were adequately covered with the lenses set to infinity.

The close-up and long-range microphones were properly adjusted. Everything was as it should be. Every word, every whisper, and every movement was recorded for posterity.

It was a standard routine each week to check the equipment. A person can never be too safe, and these digital audio and video recordings were insurance of a sort. In the not-too-distant future, they would provide the last scene before the final curtain call. Only then would the play be complete.

#

Thirty-nine-year-old Xavier Dominguez started the last day of his life as he had each workday for the last seven years, the time since he and Regina were married. He was about to join the ranks of the select few. Xavier would fulfill the last letter of the abbreviation for Texas. His death would bring to an end the Lone Star State's contribution to the perfect serial murders. By his own misfortune, he would allow the killer to strike at the very heart of the morning paper – the biased, lying piece of trash who called the killer a creature. They refused to acknowledge perfection, but now they would learn from the error of their ways. Why was it they couldn't at least acknowledge the killer was a master criminal, too brilliant and too elusive to be caught?

The Creature had made fools of every law enforcement agency that tried to make what would be a major headline arrest, but each fell short. They fell so short as to be laughable. They were idiotic stumblebums. The great Detective Palotti, heralded as the genius who would catch the killer was at the head of the class – a total jerk.

Xavier shut off the alarm clock when it chimed three o'clock. He rolled over and put his lips to Regina's cheek. She was sound asleep. He put his arm over her and scooted in to her side and held her close to him. He inhaled the sweet scent of her hair and felt the warmth and softness of her body. He paused for a moment and filled his heart with her love. He loved her more than he could ever describe. His hand slid across her silk gown and brushed her breast. He held it for a moment, then rolled back to his own side of the bed, got up, and pulled the sheet up over her shoulders. She could sleep another three hours before she got up and went to school for another day with her first-grade students.

He turned on the teapot, caught a quick shower and shave, and headed to the kitchen. He was almost there when Regina caught him by the arm. He swung around and looked at her. She wrapped her arms around him before he could say anything. They kissed and she led him back to bed.

"Fuck me, Xavier." She took off her gown and tossed it on the floor. She lay back on the bed, wrapped her legs around his waist and pulled him to her.

"You're all I ever want," he said. He looked into her eyes and smiled. "My little Regina, I love you. And I love it when you talk like that."

"Then quit talking and fuck me," she whispered. "Give me our baby."

An hour passed before Xavier got dressed and left. He'd missed his Fruity-Tooties and tea, but the taste of his lover would stay with him all day. It was going to be a first-class day.

He drove his Volkswagen into the parking lot and found his assigned parking slot. He'd had it for a year. It was a prestige spot close to the building and among the five that were reserved for the editorial board members. Their daily meeting always started at six o'clock, but he would use the time to scan the overnight newswires to see if there were any major surprises. Who knows, maybe another mid-east crisis, another plane crash somewhere, maybe another anything? Otherwise, they would evaluate their positions on the mayor's achievements since the election. One of them would put it in a rough draft before ten and submit it to the other board members by noon. It would be a full morning, as it was each day.

#

The killer stayed up all night. It's always appropriate to make a last dry run past the target. Things probably are unchanged from what they were in the last few weeks. Nevertheless, it was critical to make a mental note of the locations of the surveillance cameras that swept the lot. Any difference could completely change the game from the way it was planned.

Even a murderer can feel the pressure of the work. The Creature gave a sigh of relief. They were the same as they were on every other surveillance of the place. Now it was time to go home and change vehicles to drive the escape route. This was an important protocol. It was vital to keep in mind there may be another business or intersection under video surveillance that was not detected. It's all part of the planning process. Too many passes by with the same vehicle would attract attention from the cops, even the stupid ones. All that was necessary now to complete the plan was to make a quick sweep past the parking garage where the getaway car would be parked. From there, it would be over. Xavier would be dead. The killer could go home to the comfort of the basement.

The killer stood in the midst of the array of weapons and carried on one last mental debate about the ultimate weapon. It would have to be one that would shriek to the media fools about how they and the police were nothing less than stupid, self-centered egotists.

This was the one part of the process that was always the most difficult, but also the most pleasing. There was a little poem – something about for every season there is a reason or something like that.

So, too, was there a little poem for murder:

> *Death*
> *Is a gift from afar.*
> *It is your flight on a thousand winds.*
> *It is my gift to you.*
> *But,*
> *I will not stand on your grave and weep.*

It always helped to recite the poem during this part of the preparation. It was soothing, almost hypnotic. It became a waltz unto itself as the tools of death were touched and kissed. Each was held and measured for their balance. Every one was special in its own way. Some were more intense than others. They allowed the killer to be up close to the victim and able to say something to the person as they gasped their last breath. Others allowed the killer to stay in the shadows and enjoy the anonymity of watching the person die without having the slightest idea of who killed them or why.

In their own way, each technique allowed The Creature a degree of pleasure. It allowed the killer to decide who should die, when and where they should die, and the best part of all – how they should die. This was the ultimate power; the ultimate act of perfection; the decision of life and death.

Xavier Dominguez. How should he die? What would deliver the most sensational message to those stuffed shirts? They were no more than cigar sucking, fat sons-of-bitches in their stuffy offices. How would fear taunt them? How much would they acknowledge it to each other? They would crap in their britches, but pretend they'd continue undaunted by the death of their colleague. No fear in these brave souls. Not one bit.

The killer smiled. Oh yes, they would be scared. More scared than they've ever been in the lives. They would be afraid to go home and afraid to go to work. They would fear every shadow for the rest of their lives. Bastards, they deserved it.

#

The killer's decision was reached, and thus began the ritual dress and dance. It began at three o'clock precisely. There was no music, only the deafening roar of silence. The killer allowed a self-admiring look in the mirror – a perfect body, trim, powerful, muscular and capable.

Substantial planning and effort went into the selection of each weapon and the clothing. The objects were purchased separately with cash over the past several years even though there was no idea when or if they would be used. Everything was untraceable.

The clothing selected for this special event was out of the ordinary, even a bit humorous. No other death was carried out with such elaborate effort. Xavier would never know how special he was. The attire for this special occasion would be unlike any others. He would be killed by a Ninja.

Each item of clothing was put on with the utmost of deliberate care and motion. No underclothing was worn as a matter of habit. This bit of personal pleasure added to the sensuality of watching a person die.

The assassin slipped into the black pants, followed by the long-sleeved shirt. The high-top Tabbi shoes were next. The last item, the ultimate item, was a silk black hood and mask to cover the face. Xavier would never see the face of the killer when The Creature reached out to snare his life.

The Katana sword was in its scabbard and hung across the shoulder of the murderer. Its handle protruded up over the killer's left shoulder for a quick and smooth withdrawal.

#

The assassin parked in an abandoned parking garage two blocks from the rear of the newspaper parking lot. The vehicle was left in the inky blackness. The alphabet killer moved quietly through the shadows of the empty street to the chain-link fence that surrounded the employee's parking lot.

"So much for employee safety," the killer mumbled.

Seconds later, the killer climbed over the fence directly beneath a surveillance camera and safely out of its view. Like a snake, The Creature slithered beneath the parked cars and trucks in the lot, protected from the roving eyes of the cameras. The last car was parked just to the left of the door Xavier would enter. The killer scooted beneath it and waited.

Xavier's parking slot was the first one to the right of the entryway. When he got out of his car, he would be within striking distance of the author of the sadistic poem of death.

#

Xavier flicked off the headlights, grabbed his briefcase out of the backseat, and got out. He paused to shut and lock the door. He turned toward the entryway, a mere seven or eight steps away, and started toward it.

Something black suddenly appeared before him. His mind went into slow motion while at the same time processing the events in milliseconds. A "thing" of some sort was directly in front of him and moving forward. There were no sounds other than a "swoosh" of something slashing through the humid morning air. It was a sword.

The black-clothed killer struck from beneath the car like a cobra striking an innocent child. It was over in seconds. The killer leapt from beneath the car. A steady but swift spin with the Katana overhead allowed the centrifugal force to carry the weight of the killer's body and sword forward. The sharp edge struck Xavier directly below his left ear. With only the slightest slowing of the blade, it completely severed his head.

Blood spewed from the still pumping heart when the lifeless body fell like a sack of rags to the asphalt. The head bobbled and rolled toward the door and came to a halt. Its sightless eyes stared into the face of the phantom murderer.

The killer paused for a moment to look at the artistry of the scene and then ran toward the fence, no longer concerned with the surveillance cameras. Thirty minutes later the Ninja outfit was in the washing machine, and the sword was rinsed in the tub and ready for an acid wash. All was well with the world.

#

The morning television news was interrupted for a News Alert. The television journalist choked back his own emotions as he offered a "live-eye," up-to-the-minute briefing of the gruesome murder of a prominent member of the local media. Viewers could see the flashing lights of police cruisers and an ambulance in the background. A police commander was interviewed. His comments added fuel to what was already a terrifying scenario – a black-clothed killer murdered a prominent executive.

"Was the victim the latest target of The Creature?" the reporter asked.

"We can't jump to conclusions," the cop answered. He looked back over his shoulder at the headless body beneath the yellow plastic blanket, then looked back at the camera.

"But, I can tell you this. No one in this department will rest until we see this creature from hell on the gurney in the death chamber. I'll be honored to start the flow of poison into him myself."

Indeed, the smug media elite and the ignorant cops were shattered. The killer smiled. It was a masterpiece.

#

Officer Juan Medina and Sergeant Bobby Lee Stafford parked at the curb in front of Xavier's home, an old building updated into loft apartments. Juan looked at the sergeant. "Okay, if we have to speak Spanish, I'll do it. Otherwise, it's yours."

"Fair enough," Stafford responded.

Juan reached for the radio. "1-K-80," he said.

"1-K-80," the dispatcher replied.

"We'll be at 3013 Bucknell Drive for an emergency message."

"10-4 at zero-five-four-eight hours."

The two cops started to get out when the rain hit. First, just a few heavy drops that smacked against the hood and windshield. They paused for a second, then the wind and downpour hit with its full fury. They grabbed their hats, slammed the doors behind them, and ran to the cover of the canopy over the front door of the apartment. It offered little shelter, but enough to protect them from the full force of the storm.

"Not a good start," Juan said. He wiped the rain from his face and hands.

Stafford looked at him and frowned. "Let's do it."

#

Xavier and Regina's loft was on the second floor with a walkup stairway from the street. She was awake, but still in bed. The alarm would ring in a few minutes, but she was savoring the love she shared with Xavier. The buzz startled her. She reached for the clock before she realized it was the doorbell. She glanced at it – ten minutes 'til six. She jumped up, put on her robe and ran to the window. She looked down through the rain-streaked glass and saw the police car, but couldn't see who was under the canopy. She pulled her robe tightly around her neck. Her heart raced. Her hands trembled. Xavier had been a reporter for enough years that she understood what a police car in front of your house meant – there was a problem.

The doorbell buzzed again. She took a deep breath to calm her nerves before she descended the stairs. She stopped at the foot of the stairs to compose herself, then opened the door.

Sergeant Stafford spoke. "Mrs. Dominguez?"

"Yes," she replied. "What can I do for you?"

The rain increased and pounded at the three of them standing in the open doorway. Thunder rumbled down the empty street.

"I'm sorry, won't you come in?" she said. She stepped back and led them up the stairs. "Come in, please." She motioned for them to be seated as she took a seat on the sofa. Regina moistened her lips and nodded at the sergeant. Stafford sat beside her and Medina sat on a chair off to the side.

"Mrs. Dominguez, on behalf of the Dallas Police Department …"

Regina held her hand up abruptly to stop him. "Is he in the hospital? Was it a car wreck on the freeway?"

Stafford put his hat on the floor, gathered his thoughts and looked into her eyes. "I'm sorry, Mrs. Dominguez. Your husband is dead." He reached out and took her hands in his. "Can we call someone for you, ma'am?"

She stared at him without a hint of emotion, and then began to shake her head slowly. "Oh no, you've come to the wrong place. I know. My husband's at work right now, so you better leave. Look here, mister …" She pulled her hands free and groped her stomach. "Oh God, please make me pregnant. Sweet virgin, pray for me that I can have his child." She began to wail. "Holy Mother of God, Our Lady of Guadalupe, help me. Oh my God, make me pregnant. Give me his child," she screamed. She gathered her arms around her waist and looked at Juan. "*Tango meido, senor.*" Her eyes rolled back and she fainted.

Regina Dominguez was a widow at the age of thirty-four. She was pregnant.

#

Mike sat at the breakfast bar and sipped a cup of coffee. The morning paper was spread out on the counter. Annalisa gave him a peck on the cheek, walked to the far end of the counter and turned on the morning news. They were giving the Sky Eye Morning Update on traffic when the picture flashed in bold red letters: **NEWS ALERT.**

Mike looked over the top edge of the paper while Annalisa

shifted aside, poured herself a cup of coffee, and looked back at the television set. The reporter's face was nearly ashen. His voice trembled.

Mike put his paper down and leaned toward the television, almost willing himself to be at the crime scene.

The reporter stumbled over the scant bit of information the police supervisor provided to him, but there was little detail of the actual crime. Nothing more than a prominent member of the paper's upper echelon was murdered at the employees' entrance to the building. An unarmed security guard who was watching the video cameras that surrounded the parking lot and entrances saw the entire murder. The police were not more forthcoming on any information until they were assured of the notification of next of kin.

Nevertheless, the barest details of the crime were overwhelming. A man was killed at the door to his building in full view of the security cameras and the murderer escaped into the early morning darkness.

Mike listened while the uniform police spokesman responded to the reporter that it was much too premature to link this death with those of the serial killer known as The Creature.

Annalisa looked at Mike. "Why would they make that quantum jump?"

"Beats the crud out of me," he responded. "I think I'll hustle on down to the station. I need to head this off before they dump it on me. Even if the guy's name starts with an 'E', it doesn't necessarily link it to the ones I'm working." He shook his head as he started to the bedroom to get dressed. "All I need is for my guy to pull this crap. Annalisa, this guy's going to be the death of me yet."

"Mike, wait," Annalisa blurted out. She ran toward him and caught him at the bedroom. "Please Mike, don't let this get to you. You're the best they have and you'll catch him." She put her arms around his neck and kissed him. "Detective Palotti, you'll get your man, but listen to me." She stepped back an arm's length and spoke like she was talking to Samanta. "If you let this get to you, then you'll fall into the trap this crazy killer is betting on. Keep your cool. Step back from it, if only for a moment, and take a deep breath. You're the best there is, but if you let him rattle you then he'll win. Mike, we can't let that happen. You're the best detective in the whole damn department and you'll get him. You know it and I know it. Tell that bastard that his ass is grass and you're a lawn mower. Tell him it's only a matter of time and you'll have him behind bars. Tell that bastard he's screwing around with my hus-

SWEET EMILY

band, and if he isn't careful he'll have me to deal with."

Mike chuckled. "Baby girl, you're the best." He nodded his head. "You're right. I won't let him get to me. I think I know what kind of game he's up to. If, and that's a big 'if,' this is our guy, then he really changed his method of operation. It's as though he's screaming, 'catch me if you can.' Well, all I can say is, you crazy bastard, here we come. We'll catch you and hang you by your balls. We'll make you regret the day you were born."

Mike strapped his Glock .40 caliber and badge on his belt, slipped his cell phone into his shirt pocket and kissed Annalisa good-bye. He was pulling out of the driveway when his cell phone buzzed. It was Sgt. Covey.

"Morning, Mike. Are you on your way in?"

"Sure. Be there in about thirty minutes," Mike responded. There was a pause. Only the static of the cellular phone buzzed in his ear. Mike took a deep breath. "Go ahead, Sarge. Whip it on me. It's our guy, isn't it?"

"Looks that way. An editor named Xavier Dominguez. There was no other reason at face value that we can see why somebody would whack him. Mike, my guess is our killer just took a shortcut. Xavier. He abbreviated Texas. The bastard blindsided us." Covey laughed to himself. "Blindsided us, bullshit. He's blindsided us all along. Anyhow, I'll see you in a few minutes. Come in the conference room, but be ready. It's pretty disgusting. The prick chopped his head off with one swing."

Mike shoved the cell phone in his pocket and reached for the windshield wipers. Last night's weather report called for thundershowers overnight and into the morning, and the forecast was right. A first-class deluge plowed into them. The wipers on Mike's car were almost useless against the onslaught of wind and rain. Traffic slowed to a crawl when he moved into the downtown area, and his thirty-minute drive turned into an hour through flooded streets and stalled cars.

#

Detective Palotti grabbed a cup of coffee and went to the conference room. He pulled up a chair and sat next to Covey and Lieutenant Molina. "Sorry guys, but when it rains it pours," he said.

"No sweat," Molina responded. "It's got the whole place screwed up, plus it's totally screwed up our crime scene, but we'll talk about that later."

Chip Gillespie, the bureau's technology whiz kid, stuck the disc in the player and turned it on. The camera viewpoint was from above the door, projecting its focus to the immediate area of the door and the several yards leading up to it. On the one side, they could see Xavier pull into his parking slot. Several seconds ticked away before he got out. He turned his back to the camera while he locked his car. In the same instant he turned away from the car, a black image appeared from beneath the car at the other side of the entryway. The figure took a quick step forward while at the same time swinging a sword upward. In one smooth motion, the killer did a pirouette and lifted the sword an arm's length. As the killer came around, the sword continued in a forward arc, and went completely through the man's neck and severed his head.

The timer at the bottom on the screen displayed 1.8 seconds from the time the person appeared until the time the victim fell to the ground. Using cop lingo, "it was over before it started." Xavier was helpless to comprehend and respond to the fate that befell him.

Molina spoke up. "Can anybody tell us anything about this crazy son-of-a-bitch? Age? Size? Weight? Sex? Anything at all?"

Covey responded. "Dr. Kempe in the Crime Lab gave it a quick and dirty guess, but he doesn't want to be held to it yet. Anyhow, his tentative guess is this weirdo is a small-boned male, maybe five feet, eight inches tall or thereabouts, svelte, give or take around 140 pounds. He's athletic, well trained in the martial arts, and that's about it for starters." He laughed a sick chuckle. "He's a real live Ninja creep straight out of the movies."

Molina stuck his notepad back into his breast pocket and looked down at his feet. He was dejected. "Plus, our crime scene got washed out – totally. By the time the crime scene technicians were ready to get started, the weather hit. Damn it," he exclaimed. He banged his fist down on the table.

"Damn this shit. Our entire crime scene got washed out. We were hoping we'd find some trace evidence beneath the cars or on the top edge of the fence, but it was all rained clean. The whole parking lot drained down through there. It was under a couple inches of water. It's all gone now. Everything. I thought we might come up with something, but to tell you the truth, nothing is working in our favor."

He looked at Mike. "Homicide will handle it for now, but we're pretty sure things will shift around and you'll get it in a couple weeks. Let them work any leads, but there isn't much right now. Then, it'll be in your hands. You've got to make this son-of-a-bitch.

You're all we have."

#

The recent double-header and the beheading of the newspaper executive were almost too much for the assassin; even someone as hideous as that had limits. Maybe it had been reached. The killer cleaned up the "tools of the trade" as they were thought of, took a long hot shower, and spent the rest of the day in bed. Sleep did not come easily. Rain slapped against the windows. The tree branches scraped against the roof. The thunder was deafening; definitely not a good day to sleep. It was only after taking two Tylenol PM tablets that the pillow and mattress rose up and pulled the evil monster into a deep, blissful interlude from the havoc of the morning.

Chapter Six

IT WAS LATE MORNING WHEN Covey called Mike and Rickey to the conference room. The detectives pulled up chairs and sat across the table from the sergeant. Mike quickly sized him up. Something was wrong. The usual perfectly tied tie hung loosely around his neck. His normal neatly combed-back dark hair was mussed around his forehead and ears, a button was missing on the cuff of his shirt. The sergeant's professional demeanor was replaced by one of exasperation. His lips were pursed and a frown creased his brow.

"Molina just got shit-canned," Covey blurted.

"Whoa, not so fast," Mike interjected. "What's going on?"

"The Deputy Chief re-assigned him, effective immediately. He's packing up his office as we speak." The Sergeant pushed back and crossed his legs. "Maybe it's better for him. At least he's out of the pressure cooker. Not that he deserved to get tossed out, but that's the way shit runs downhill. He's transferred to Support Services – tow trucks, parking enforcement, and fleet management." Covey shook his head. "What a screwing."

"So, who're we getting? Or, is that too much to ask?" Rickey asked.

"Somebody I've never met, but hear he's a real go-getter. Some guy who is supposed to be a favored son of some of the top brass. My guess is he may want to re-do things around here."

"What kind of changes?" Mike retorted.

Covey walked to the window. He was silent. He stared stoically at the hum-drum of pedestrians and cars cramming themselves into the confines of downtown Dallas. It was jam-packed and wasn't going to get any better. They were like mice scurrying around the maze looking for the piece of cheese. "Do you really think anybody gives a crap about this mess – that is, besides the families?"

"Let's not get too philosophical," Mike responded.

Covey's voice was soft and distant, a reflection of helplessness. "I have a feeling we're in for a surprise, whatever it might be. Maybe he'll want the desk facing another way. Maybe he'll want to reassign cars. Who knows? Anyhow, I've got a feeling he'll stake out his kingdom to make a show – might even shuffle people."

"Does that mean us?" Rickey asked.

"Don't know," Covey shrugged. "We'll just have to wait and see. He should be here any minute."

Mike leaned back in his chair, crossed his arms over his chest and spoke to Covey. "You know what? I don't give a rat's ass. You know it and we know it. We've done everything possible to catch this crazy squirrel. If they think they've got somebody sharp enough to pull it off, then just let'em have at it." He laughed a sick chortle. "Besides, we have our association, so what the hell can they do to us? Put us back in uniform? That doesn't sound too bad to me. I can take a regular eight-hour shift; regular days off; no weird hour callouts from home. Yeah, if they want to punish me, just give me a job like that."

The door behind him opened. Mike turned to see their new boss when he entered the conference room. He made his judgment before the man could utter a word – forty years old, neat, clean and college educated. Plus, he had a resume a mile long with a pedigree equally long. Mike chuckled to himself. The guy was probably a part-time actor for a toothpaste advertisement – Mr. Clean Hygiene himself and a total asshole.

"Good day, gentlemen," he said while he went to each of them and introduced himself. "I'm Lieutenant Steven Hauk, your new unit commander." He pulled up a chair at the head of the table, a gesture no one missed. "I know y'all ..."

He paused to draw out his Texas accent – to show he's one of the boys, Mike thought.

"Y'all have worked hard for Lt. Molina, but frankly, he wasn't providing the type of leadership required for this level of investigation."

He cast a glance at each of them with calculated, measured movements. He was careful to make eye contact and adequately express himself as their commander, not one to be jacked around. He continued, "I've been given complete authority to assume responsibility for your work. Frankly, my personal opinion is that each of you is a highly-skilled and qualified investigator. However, you have not received the administrative guidance required for the work you are capable of producing." He offered a condescending smile before he continued his monologue. "I was given a unique opportunity to work on the sidelines while you were spinning your wheels running around here, and back and forth to Tulsa. I appreciate all you've done, but let's face it; you're no closer today to clearing these cases than when you started. That is unacceptable. Nevertheless, the big brass was kind enough to hear me out. I presented them with an alternative investigative technique they allowed me to do while you were beating your brains out to catch this so-called 'creature.' I hope it comes as no surprise to you that he isn't a creature at all, but an otherwise worthy tax-paying citizen of our fair community." He paused for effect, and then continued, "Except of course, he's a crazed killer. We'll not backtrack over everything you've done since I'm well aware of it, so I'll come directly to the point."

Hauk pushed back from the table and opened the door. "Malcolm, you can come in now."

Mike stretched his neck and saw a frail little man get up from the waiting room sofa and come in. As was his habit, Mike sized him up – early thirties, a PhD, or at least a genius, someone who knew the name and location of every planet in the solar system, a computer freak, and a nerd who was never laid or in a fight. Of course, "fight" doesn't count if you ignore all the times when he was in high school and got shoved around.

"Gentlemen, allow me to introduce you to Mr. Malcolm Buford. Malcolm is a civilian employee of the FBI and has been on loan to this project for a few weeks."

"How do you do, sir," Malcolm repeated as he went around the room to shake everyone's hand. He pulled up a chair and seated himself next to Covey.

"Let me explain this to you," Hauk said. "One of the most apparent weaknesses of how we investigate crimes is that we work on what has served us well in the past, with the assumption it will continue to serve us in the future." He looked at the detectives. "That is not to say what you were doing was without merit, but the bottom line is that yesterday's practices, if you will, have their limitations." He cleared his throat and prepared to lay out his technique of creating solvability factors that can be applied to the serial murderer.

"About forty years ago someone in academia developed a theory that almost everyone can be linked to anyone else within six links. The basic theory is that any two people can be connected to each other in no more than six human connections, and very possibly in as few as four." He smiled. "Quite a theory, is it not? So, if we take your murder victims and apply this theory, it should direct us to what you," he nodded at Mike, "have mentioned in your reports as the common denominator. You looked high and low, but did not sufficiently expand your horizons to find it, did you?"

"Guess not," Mike smirked.

"Guessing is not in our lexicon. Cold, hard facts, though, are what we deal in – not guess work." He glanced at Malcolm. "Go ahead."

"Yes, thank you." Malcolm reached for his briefcase, but halted. "Excuse me Lieutenant, but there is something I need to explain to these gentlemen before we get into this too deep."

"Have at it," Hauk replied coarsely.

"Sergeant, detectives, I have an idea of what is zipping around in your minds right now, and believe me, I understand it." He looked at Mike. "Sir, you are tall, dark and handsome to say nothing about very athletic looking. But, look at me. I know you did, and what did you see? A dork, I believe, is what I have been called all my life. I can hear it, but will never get used to it and will never like it. Nevertheless, I know people and how they think. 'Here comes that dried up little shit,' they will say. Gentlemen, there is nothing I can do about my size." He laughed. "Runt of the litter, as they say. Maybe you were the homecoming king or something like that while I was relegated to washing jock straps or some such chore. Nevertheless, that does not detract from my ability. I'm smart and not ashamed of it, and I love my work every bit as much as you love yours. It's different, that's all. But, believe me, if we work together we will catch this crazed fiend." He flexed his muscles like a weight lifter. "Not much in the gym, but I can carry my weight in catching malefactors of all sorts and putting them away."

Covey smiled and shook hands again with Malcolm. "Welcome on board. We're glad to have you."

"Thank you, sir. Now, if I may, I will give you what I have deduced from your victims, and hopefully will show you a road map to *our* killer," he emphasized. He opened his briefcase and unfolded a single piece of butcher paper that stretched the length of the conference table. "Don't let size scare you," he said.

The detectives looked at the lines, circles, triangles, squares and names that ran the length of the table.

"An analysis flow chart, but much too cumbersome to walk through right now, so let me summarize it for you." He handed each of them a single sheet of paper with a list of the victims' names and what he identified as points of a common denominator. "The lieutenant was correct when he said your horizon was not quite broad enough. Remember, if we assume that any two people can be linked in no more than six connections, then we are allowed, in fact commanded, to pick up our heads and look a little further." He looked at Mike and Rickey. "I saw where you were very thorough in your efforts to link the victims through a link analysis, but it didn't work. Well, what I did was spread it out. I gave myself the whole arena to work in – six layers. In a nutshell, here is what I found by looking at the victims, plus everyone in their nuclear family and each of their financial transactions over the previous five years that were done by check or credit card." He shook his head and wiped dots of perspiration from his brow. "What it required was for me to develop computer files that documented every transaction all of those people conducted in five years. Literally, it was thousands, but I found it. Your common denominator."

"I'm impressed," Mike replied, his tone a mixture of sarcasm and sincerity. He was skeptical; but nevertheless open to hear Malcolm's thoughts.

Malcolm continued. "Steinfeld Jewelers. That was and is the common link between each of your victims. Even of more interest is the fact that in this process, the effort is to identify the link, or connection, within six degrees. Therefore, a connection with a value of one is the closest, and a connection of six is the most distant. The theory provides for levels of expectations, and in most cases it will lie between four and six degrees. Links between three and four degrees are considered to be quite strong; two to three are exceptional; and anything less than two is considered to be an extremely close linkage. Gentlemen, I offer you the fact that each of your murder victims has a link with Steinfeld Jewelers in Dallas at an average link of 2.336. This is not a mere chance encounter. Your connection will be found at the jewelry store."

Covey smiled and leaned his elbows on the table. "This is what we needed. Thanks."

"Ah, but there is more," Malcolm replied. "I went ahead since I was really getting into it and enjoying myself. I contacted a friend in the bureau who contacted a friend at the IRS to get us a word or two on tax returns." He laughed. "Thank God for computers or we would still be struggling with this. Of course, the IRS is not supposed to share that kind of information, but," he joked, "it was a connection of only two degrees."

A few chuckles filled the room. "Go ahead," Hauk barked. He was irritated at Malcolm's effort to become the center of attention.

"Don't rush me," Malcolm said acerbically. "Let me enjoy my

moment. Okay guys. Get this. The store is co-owned by David Steinfeld, but he is about sixty-five years old; probably not your killer. His son, Donald, is the other co-owner. I did a bit more slapping the keys on my keyboard and here is what I came up with: Donald is a tri-athlete; a very athletic man. I ran him through the newspaper archives and found him there a dozen or so times – running, swimming, biking, tennis. He is very involved in sports of all kinds, including the Dallas County Gun Club. He shoots trap and skeet that I know of, and who knows what else? And, there is more. He sat on the Board of Directors of the Dallas Arts League at the same time as Dr. Reynolds. They knew each other."

"Good grief, I can't believe all the stuff you found on this guy. I'm really impressed," Rickey said.

"Thank you. Now here's the frosting on the cake. He's a black belt in karate; a good one. Three years ago he won the state title for his weight class. Let's see," he said while he thumbed through his notes. "Yes, here it is. He weighed in at one-hundred forty-eight pounds." He looked at the lieutenant. "Isn't that the approximate weight of your Ninja guy?"

"I've got to ask," Mike said. "Anything about Tulsa?"

"I'm sorry, but you got ahead of me. Yes, to answer your question." He flipped a couple more note pages. "Yes, yes, here it is. Broken Arrow, Oklahoma, a few miles outside of Tulsa. They have a store there, too. They've owned them both for a little more than eight years."

Covey nodded his head. "This looks good. Maybe too good to be true, but we need to roll on it. Mike, get the troops together and get on this pronto," he commanded.

"I'll have it set up for an afternoon shift, then we'll take him around the clock," Mike responded. He got up from his chair and moved toward the door, but stopped and looked back over his shoulder. "Mr. Buford, do you ever go to Tyler?"

"No, why do you ask?"

"Oh, it's nothing, just a thought. Forget it," Mike replied.

Rickey followed and shut the door behind him. "Hey, what the hell was that all about? You came across as a smart ass in there," he said as he pointed back to the conference room. "That lieutenant isn't going to take a shine to you or your shit. Keep it up, partner, and you'll find yourself taking family fight calls in Northwest Division."

Mike flicked his ballpoint pen at his desk in an act of frustration. "I don't have a good feel for the way Molina got dumped, or about

Hauk and his sneaking around doing his own investigation behind our backs. Plus, I sure as hell don't buy into Buford's linking theory. Damn it, I can accept the general concept that we can all be linked within so many interpersonal connections, but that doesn't do squat for me in establishing a solid connection for murder. So what if somebody's mom and somebody else's kid bought some cheap trinket at the same store two years apart. What about this? What if they both had breakfast at Denny's? Yeah, how about that? Do we start chasing the cook or the waiter?"

He shook his head and bit his lip. His face was red. Anger seethed in every part of his body. "No, it isn't there. They're looking for something too simple, too clear cut, too absolute. Our killer isn't going to fall into some clean and neat little pigeonhole of orthodox standards; not at all. You just wait and see. We'll catch this son-of-a-bitch, and it won't end up being anything like we've ever thought about. It's going to be something totally new to us."

"New to us?" Rickey frowned. "That scares the crap out of me. New to us? We've seen just about everything, and if it's something that hasn't come down the pike by this time, then it really is going to be weird. That isn't cool." He smiled to himself and mumbled under his breath. "Creature From the Black Lagoon?"

"I've got some things to get done and some errands to run," Mike said. "I'll be back later and see where we go from here."

"Got an interview?" Rickey asked. His voice reflected his cynicism.

"No," Mike shot back. "How about the credit union, plus I'm going to get the hell out of here for a couple of hours to catch my breath. I'll get back after lunch, get my thoughts together and get in gear."

Mike walked the two blocks to the deli, sat at the counter, and had a corn beef on rye and dill pickle. He washed it down with a glass of milk, and then killed time with a cup of coffee while he enjoyed his solitude in the midst of the lunchtime crowd of civilians who could care less who he was or what was on his mind. It was nice to have a little time away from the frustration and pressure of work. He caught himself rubbing the back of his neck and temples. He had another headache. On a whim, he pulled his cell phone from his pocket and called Emily. She answered on the second ring. "I'm going crazy in the bureaucracy," he said.

"Isn't that one of things I asked you about the first time we talked? The bureaucracy and how they serve you? Or, do they hinder you? Remember that?"

"Oh yes, I remember it very clearly. That's why I'm calling you. Do you have a little time to talk this afternoon? I really need you – badly. They're about to drive me up the wall."

"What about now?" she asked. "We could have lunch. Come on over."

"I've already eaten, but need to run by the credit union to pay my car loan. What about an hour of so?" He paused and took a deep breath. "Emily, can we just talk?"

"See you in an hour," she responded.

#

Mike made a quick dash to the credit union, and thirty minutes later was knocking on her door. She answered wearing an ankle-length white terrycloth robe and a towel wrapped around her hair.

"Didn't we say an hour, cowboy?" She stepped back from the door and motioned him inside. "I was getting out of the shower when you knocked. I wasn't quite ready. Hope you don't mind. Hang on a second. I need to shut my alarm off – forty seconds, that's what they give. If it isn't reset by then, they call the cops." She looked at him and smiled. "We wouldn't want that, would we?"

Mike stood behind her when she opened the closet door and pecked her four digits into the alarm pad. He smiled inwardly. He would never lose his trained eye; zero-two-seven-four. She turned back and he kissed her ear.

"You're beautiful any way you dress," he said.

"Mike, you look like shit, if you will pardon my abruptness. Come in the kitchen while I make some tea." He followed and sat at the breakfast nook while she put the teakettle on the burner.

"I'm really not a tea drinker," he said sheepishly.

She looked over her shoulder at him and smiled. "You're in my house and I'm the doctor. Green tea, that's what you need. Green tea and a little time to yourself, with me of course, to let it all out. Scream if you want. I don't care." She adjusted the fire under the tea pot and turned toward him. "Give me your hand," she commanded as though speaking to a child. Mike extended his hand when she stepped forward. She stood over him, looked deeply into his eyes and kissed his fingers. She held him to her lips. Their eyes pierced into each other's innermost being, reading every thought and emotion. They didn't speak; there was no need. Finally, the tea pot whistle broke their trance. Emily poured the steaming water into their cups over the packets of tea.

"Three minutes," she said. "That's how much time it needs to steep."

She sat on his lap, put her arms around his neck and kissed him. "Talk to me. Tell me what happened."

The tea was drunk, and the cups and saucers rinsed and put away by the time Mike finished his tale of the day's events – Molina transferred; Hauk and Buford; the six link connection; the jewelry store; and his own smart aleck comments. He didn't leave anything out.

Emily smiled and shook her head. "Mike, I think you've fallen in with a couple of semi-smart people who think they're brilliant, and that's what makes them dangerous. Not just to you, but to their bosses and the public they're supposed to serve. It's fine to be smart, but to be a half-wit and think you're a genius, and to be in charge is very dangerous. I know the concept Buford is talking about. There used to be a game. I think it was called the Six Degrees of Kevin Bacon. Yes, I'm sure that was it. We played it a long time ago. The idea was to link any actor with Kevin Bacon in six links or less. It was a trivia type game – lot of fun, especially if you've had a couple drinks." She laughed. "Or a few hits off a good marijuana pipe. There was even a movie and play about it." She nodded her head. "I have no doubt what Buford said is true, but you could say the same thing about almost anyone else. That's what I mean. A little knowledge is dangerous. The fact he linked all of the killings through two or three degrees of separation doesn't mean a thing. Not a damned thing."

"What about me? What the heck do I do about it? I think they're wrong, but Hauk is calling the shots. Do I waste my time and let the real killer get away, or do I call his bluff and do what I think needs to be done?"

"Do you really think it's a bluff? Do you think he's holding two pairs and you've got a full house? Are you that confident?"

Mike shrugged his shoulders. "Nope. I don't have a damned thing. Neither does he, but his lieutenant bar say he's the boss."

Emily looked at the clock. "You need to get back. Just fall in like a good trooper for now, and we'll think about this and come up with some ideas. What about right now? How are you going to get started and keep your lieutenant happy?"

Mike thought for a few moments, and then described how Covey would set up three surveillance teams, *deja vu* the wasted time with the piano tuner. They walked to the door and kissed good-bye.

Emily spoke. "I'll give it some thought and get with you in a day or two. You'll keep that simpleton happy, and at the same time we'll fashion some thoughts into a plan of action for you to put the real killer behind bars."

#

Two weeks crept by while Mike, Rickey and Covey each led a surveillance team on Donald Steinfeld. All the while, Mike and Emily talked on the telephone swapping ideas. They knew Hauk was wrong, but couldn't come up with a better solution to their problem. How would they ever get Hauk to change his mind? He was confident they were following the killer, so it was only a matter of time. Eventually, they would either catch him in the act, or would find enough tidbits of information to put together a search warrant and raid his house. Hauk said it almost every day: "We'll get inside there and find all of it; the guns and knives, the ropes and wires, the Ninja crap. All of it. Y'all just stick with him. You're getting close, and when he slips, you'll have him. Mark my words. He's the killer."

Donald was unaware of the surveillance. Otherwise, he would have taken some drastic measures to adjust his lifestyle: making love three different times to men in the restroom at White Rock Park; throwing his love machine to the valet at the Town House Inn, Dallas' center for the elite homosexual crowd; and buying his coke and marijuana from Wesley Ashcroft, one of the narcotic officer's favorite snitches who would turn him in when the time was right. Mike mumbled under his breath, but it wasn't anything the others weren't saying to themselves. They were chasing a rich, dope smoking homosexual, but not a murderer.

The detectives watched while Donald's bedroom lights were turned off. He was home and in bed – alone. Mike swung his car around and headed to the station to get his own car. It was nearly midnight. He stretched back in the seat and yawned. It was another worthless surveillance. The pager on his belt vibrated. He pulled it up to the light from the dashboard and read the phone number. It was Emily. He called her on his cell phone.

"What are you doing up at this time of night?" he asked.

"Thinking about you. Is that a crime?" she replied.

Mike smiled and felt a sense of jubilation run through his body. "No ma'am, no crime. What can I do for you?"

"I'll come right to the point, Mike. I want to make love to you, and I want to help you get this mess behind you. Can you come over?"

"No. Not tonight. Annalisa knows I'm getting off at midnight, so she's waiting up for me."

"Can't you call her and tell her a little fib? You know, something's working and you can't get away."

Mike shook his head. "No, really, I can't. Emily, she's my wife."

"I'm your lover. Doesn't that count?"

"You'll never know how sorry I am, but I've got to get home. I owe her."

"Owe? You owe yourself a break. Come on, make love to me."

Mike slowed and pulled to the curb. He started to make a U-turn, then stopped. "Rain check? Please?" he pleaded.

"Mike, be honest. Is she better than me?"

"Never. We've made love so many times, nothing is new anymore. Just the same ol' same ol', but I'm married to her. What can I say? I'd take you in a second, but I know I can't do that and neither can you."

"Good night then." Her voice was pouting. "You'll never know what you missed. Something special I was planning."

Chapter Seven

MIKE AND EMILY DIDN'T TALK for a week. He stayed busy wasting his time on surveillance, but accomplished nothing. Hauk finally conceded the personnel costs were exorbitant, too exorbitant to maintain twenty-four hours a day. He allowed them to eliminate the midnight shift and to cut back the day shift when Donald went to the jewelry store. Covey and the others knew exactly what was running through the lieutenant's mind: they were wasting their time. Nevertheless, they acknowledged one point. As long as they followed him, no one was murdered. They lived with him for three weeks, and the alphabet killer did not strike. Coincidence? Only time could tell.

The phone on Mike's desk rang. "This is Detective Palotti."

It was Emily. "Hi, Mike. I've missed you. What about lunch today? Can you come over?"

"I've missed you, too." He took a deep breath and tossed a casual glance at Rickey. The young detective was buried in his own work – a serial rapist who raped and robbed prostitutes in the Deep Ellum neighborhood.

"Why not? We just keep wasting our time. Got any ideas for me?"

"That's why I want to see you. I think I might have something. Can you take the afternoon off?"

Mike looked at the calendar. "Sure, I've got more comp time on the books than they'll ever be able to pay me. See you in an hour. Does it look good?"

Emily giggled. "Detective Palotti, you always look good, but yes, I have a thought for tracking down your killer. See you for lunch."

It had been a couple weeks since they were together intimately. Mike refused to allow himself to plan on it, but still felt a rush thinking about her. Would they make love? He bit his lip. He was infuriated with himself. It wasn't good for either of them, or for his relationship with Annalisa, to even think like that. He got in his car and headed toward Highland Park. He forced himself to think about work. That's what he had to concentrate on – solving the most shocking serial killer ever to hit Dallas. That was his goal. Emily? She was the most unique person in his life, but also a professional associate who worked with him and for him. Anything else was a natural magnetism that happened – nothing more and nothing less. She would never detract him from his love for Annalisa and Samanta. He was obligated to them.

"Chemistry, damn it," he bellowed to himself. His mind was torn – the killer, his wife, his child, his job, and of course, Hauk and Malcolm. What he needed was some time to relax. He smiled. Who better than Emily knew how to help him relax? He fidgeted with the buttons on the radio until he found a station playing an old Dizzy Gillespie tune. He turned the mirror where he could look directly at himself.

"Yeah, I love her. If I wasn't already married, I'd run off with her right now, but I *am* married," he emphasized. In his mind, he pictured Annalisa walking down the aisle wearing her flowing, white wedding gown. "I love you, Annalisa. I'm just a screwed-up mess. She's good for me. So good that ..." His voice trailed off. "You're a damned liar, Michael Palotti. Rickey was right, but I don't give a damn. She's good for me, and in the long run, good for Annalisa. I'll get through this crap and Annalisa and I will be better and stronger than ever before."

He gave a sick laugh. "Sure, and we'll live happily ever after."

Twenty minutes later he was getting out of his car at Emily's. She met him on the front porch with a casual kiss to his cheek. "Good time, Detective Palotti. Did you have to speed to get here so fast?"

Mike laughed. "Sure. Hell, I could win at Texas Motor Speedway if I knew you were at the finish line." He took her hand and went inside. As he did so many times before, Mike went toward the breakfast nook.

"No," Emily interjected. "This way." She took his arm and led him to the dining room. "Look, a new dining room suite. Isn't it extraordinary? I wanted you to see it the other night. You know, wine, candles, that sort of thing." She gestured toward the furniture. It was a heavy, dark wood table surrounded by eight leather-bound, high-back chairs.

"Italian Renaissance. You don't know how long I've worked on getting these pieces, but it was worth the effort and the money. God

Almighty, you would think I was buying it from the pope himself." She laughed and hugged Mike. "It's like you, Detective Palotti, rugged and handsome, but worth every penny. And, look at those," she said. She pointed out two candelabra centered on the table, each with four flickering candles. Soft shades of yellow and orange flames danced through the otherwise darkened room. "This was a labor of love. I bought these through a dealer on one of my New York trips. Aren't they beautiful?" She didn't give Mike time to respond before she continued, "They're 17th century French – very rare."

She turned her attention to Mike and put her arms around his waist. "Hungry, honey?" It was something unique, something loving when she called him that. "I want this to be a special meal for us – very special. Here," she said. She pulled the chair back from the head of the table and motioned for him to be seated. Mike took her hands in his and kissed her cheek.

"You smell good." He sat down and pulled the chair up. "And, what may I ask, is for lunch?"

"A glass of wine and conversation for starters," she replied. Suddenly, her loving aura evaporated; her lips pursed; her eyes focused; her expression became intense. "Mike, we need to talk for a few minutes, because I've thought about what they have you doing. Maybe we, I mean you, can go them one better."

She started toward the kitchen, speaking while she looked back over her shoulder. "You're going to catch your killer, Mike. I guarantee it."

She was gone before he could respond. He sat at the table in silence, taking in the elegant serenity in which he found himself.

Emily turned on the surround sound system. Soft music floated from speakers. Several minutes passed before she came back to the dining room. She was carrying a bottle of wine and two glasses.

"I had trouble with the cork, but finally got it." She sat the glasses in front of him and passed the bottle to him. "Pour?"

A quick grimace shot across his face. "Emily, I don't know. I'm supposed to be at work. I don't want Annalisa to get any ideas."

"Nonsense," she replied. "You have all afternoon, and it'll be long gone from your breath by the time you get home. Pour. Besides, does she treat you like this when you come home?"

He paused, captured by his own internal conflict, then poured the two glasses of wine. "A toast?"

"Absolutely," she said. They lifted their glasses and clinked them together. "To Detective Michael Palotti, the man who will solve the serial murder cases." They took a sip and looked at each other for a moment with their own thoughts – Mike, silent in his passion for her; Emily, silent in more than just passion. She had a plan.

#

She rolled her glass between the palms of her hands. She was doing mental gymnastics on how she could best approach him. She had planned and found it to be very simple. Nevertheless, she had to get Mike past Hauk. He was the court jester, but still was Mike's boss. Somehow, Mike would have to convince Hauk to listen to someone besides himself and Malcolm. Her lover would have one chance. It was all or nothing. Well, not quite, but she wouldn't explain that now. It would just confuse the issue. She placed her glass gently on the table, leaned forward on her elbows, and looked directly into Mike's eyes. Her mannerisms were not a casual act, but a well-considered movement to establish her knowledge and authority. She knew the term "command presence," a time-honored phenomenon in the military and semi-military organizations like police departments.

"Mike, I said in the beginning I didn't want to get into the details of your work. I had no idea then that I would fall in love with you, but I have. So, I broke my own rule and got to work digging up all the old newspaper files on this so-called creature. Who, by the way, is no creature or madman at all. I think your killer is an extremely dedicated person who has some strange agenda that is beyond the average person's imagination. Nevertheless, this creature has eluded capture so far, and Hauk is keeping you away from the real killer. Donald Steinfeld isn't the killer."

"I know that," Mike interjected.

"I know you do, but hear me out. I've done a time analysis of these cases – here and Tulsa."

"We have, too," he said.

"Then you need to get behind what I'm going to say. Listen, Mike, your killer struck as often as twice in about six hours, and as long as four months between killings. I calculated the mean, median and mode. Then I did the standard deviation – pretty basic statistics. Anyhow, my calculations say this person will strike within the next two weeks at the longest; maybe as soon as tonight. Mike, you must convince your idiot boss to go back full time on little Donald, the happy jeweler. He isn't your man. The hard part, though, will be to make sure Hauk figures it out himself. That way, the around-the-clock surveillance is his idea, not yours."

Mike shook his head and put down his glass. "I know it isn't him, so why should we hit him full time?"

"Simple. As long as Hauk thinks he's the murderer, and if one happens when you guys are not following him, Hauk will think you dropped the ball. Mike, it'll be your head. You're the lead investigator." She smiled and poured herself another glass of wine. "So, the logic is this. At this very moment you don't have any idea who the killer is, right?"

"Absolutely."

"Okay, so if my numbers are right, you and your buddies will be all over Donald twenty-four hours a day when the real killer strikes. I don't like to sound cold hearted, 'cause I'm not, but that'll prove how wrong Hauk is, and how right you are. Then, you'll be able to get out from under his umbrella and get to work finding the real person – whoever it is. And Hauk?" She smiled at her own satisfaction. "Maybe he'll be chasing paperwork for some Assistant Chief. He deserves it. He's an ass.

"Anyhow," she continued, "go over the statistical breakdown and projections with him. Let it be his genius that it's time to get on Steinfeld full time. Of course, you're just a good little trooper, so you do as you're told. Get your guys lined up and get on him. Stick to him like glue." She chuckled and nodded her head. "Mike, the numbers don't lie. While Hauk has you watching this homosexual creep, the real killer will hit, in Tulsa of course; some poor slob whose name starts with a 'K.' I'm sorry for whoever it is, but at least it'll get you clear from Hauk, and then you and your friends in Oklahoma can get after the real killer."

She reached across the table and took his hands. "Mike, I know it like I know my own name. Steinfeld may be all sorts of things, but he's not your murderer. It's unfortunate someone else will die while Hauk is so focused on him, but that's how it's going to have to be."

"Yeah, but how can we let some innocent person die just to prove the lieutenant wrong?"

"Remember, you don't have any idea, and neither does Tulsa about who is doing this. At least you can positively eliminate little Donald."

Their hands were clasped together. He looked into her eyes, then lifted her hands and kissed her fingers, slowly and with gentle passion..

"Damn, this is horrible," he whispered. "I hate my job. I hate everything about it." He paused and took a deep breath. "However, it brought us together."

Emily got up, stood over him, and they kissed. "I'll get our lunch. You just sit here and mellow out for a few minutes. I'll be right back."

Mike sipped his wine and listened to her working in the kitchen. His mind faded back and forth – Annalisa; the killer; Hauk; and, of course, Emily. "Shit," he mumbled. He loved it and hated it. Two women who loved him; two women who would give their whole being to him; two women who meant so much to him. Of course, there are two sides to the coin – more than two sides, if that is possible. Annalisa was his wife; Dallas PD was his job; people were dying; Emily was his lover, plus, she was his silent partner in the case. *What a mess*, he thought.

He looked up to see Emily come back to the dining room. She was more gorgeous than ever. She wore a negligee, and what he had learned to call her CFM shoes. She left little to his imagination. His muscles tensed. He offered a sheepish smile and wet his lips.

"Hey, big boy, not yet. You need your nutrition." She presented him with a plate of cold cuts arraigned in a symmetrical pattern surrounded by an assortment of cheeses, celery sticks, tomato wedges and crackers. "A healthy meal for a growing boy," she wisecracked.

"I think I'm already grown."

"Good, then you need to eat to keep up your stamina – or whatever." She sat along the side of the table while he remained seated at the head. They were close enough so their knees touched. She placed the plate between them so they could pick and choose as they desired. Mike poured each of them another glass of wine. They sat in silence, taking advantage of the setting to enjoy the passion of each other's presence, the mood of the room, and the music to set the tone for what surely would follow.

Emily slipped off her shoes and caressed his leg with her toes, teasing him as he tried to nibble the bits of meat and vegetables. He choked and nearly spit out a mouthful, but got it down before she broke into laughter.

"Michael, Michael. Didn't your mother tell you to take small bites and to chew before you swallow?"

"Yes, she did, but I never had a Greek goddess rubbing her foot all the way up my leg to … to there," he gestured with a slight nod. He sipped the last of the wine from his glass and pushed back from the table. "Delicious," he exclaimed.

"Good, I'm glad you enjoyed it." She lifted the tray and excused herself. "Be back in a minute with your dessert."

Mike could not take his eyes off her when she went to the kitchen, then returned to the dining room. She paused in the doorway.

"Want something sweet?" She didn't wait for his response before she began taking slow and deliberate steps toward him. She stopped alongside the table, took the candelabras, and placed them at the far end.

"This is all for you, Michael; all of it. Everything about me is for you."

Mike got up and reached for her. His hands trembled.

"Not yet," she said. "Not yet. Want me. Need me. I want every fiber of your body to be filled with passion for me."

"I do," he said. "I want you so much my heart is ready to jump out of my skin."

"I love you, Michael Palotti. I'm your Annalisa – your wife." She leaned back, lifted herself onto the table and dangled her legs in front of him. She leaned back on her elbows.

The music filled the room with sounds of birds and flutes. There was no place on earth that was ever filled with more passion than Emily's dining room at that very moment.

He inhaled her beauty.

#

Mike called the office to check-in with the secretary. No new messages. Good. He had things to do. He tapped in the numbers on his cell phone.

"Crime Analysis, Miss Larkins speaking."

"Sally, Mike Palotti here. Got time for me to swing by for a few minutes?"

"Michael, my boy, I was just getting ready to call you. You bet I've got time. I've got something for you."

Twenty minutes later Mike strolled into the Crime Analysis Division. He was as happy as a lark: Emily helped him relax. Together, they developed a plan to dump on Mr. Clean Jeans himself, get rid of him, and get back to finding the real killer. Things couldn't be better.

"Mike," Sally said, "pull up a chair. I was winding up some odds and ends and was going to give you a buzz. I don't have all the answers, but if we can pull this crap together one little bit at a time, then we'll get your s.o.b. killing machine."

She laid out two city maps – one of Dallas, the other of Tulsa. Red pins marked the spot of each of the murders. Next, she laid out her computerized printouts of the murders; the classifications of the victims: age; sex; occupation; cause and nature of death; time, day and date of death; and last of all, their activity at time of death.

The next printout was a matrix of street names, locations of the murders, and mileage charts. The third printout was, to the untrained eye, a maze of colored lines laid out over a computerized city map.

"Looks like chaos to me, but go ahead. What is it?" Mike asked.

"Geographic profile," Sally responded. She cocked her head and looked back and forth to Mike and to the printouts and maps. "Here's what we have so far. Keep in mind, Mike, this isn't an exact science, but it's going to lead you in the right direction. What I'm telling you is you can probably eliminate suspects who live and or work outside of the boundaries I'm going to give you."

She pointed with her bright red fingernail to the map. "There, Mike. Give or take a half mile or so in any direction, and that's where you'll find your killer."

Mike leaned forward and squinted down at the map. The tip of her fingernail was exactly on the intersection of Hillcrest Road and Walnut Hill Lane.

He looked at her quizzically. "You telling me this nut lives between the Tollway and Central Expressway, and between Royal Lane and Northwest Highway? That's a pretty high rent area." He shook his head. "Don't usually find crazy killers living high on the hog like that."

"Mikey, my boy, you're not looking for a regular nut. You're after somebody who's really weird. Something you've never seen before." Sally pulled out a chair and sat down. A thin smile creased her lips. "There's more. I worked with a Captain Daniels in Tulsa, and he did the same type of analysis I did."

She nodded her head to confirm what she was about to say. "We both came to the same conclusion. Your killer lives in Dallas, not in Tulsa. Their murders are all over the place – no pattern; very scattered. Ours, I mean yours, are all centered in the mid-city area. But, he keeps it in Dallas. He never goes into Highland Park, University Park, Plano, or Richardson.

"Mike, you've got a pretty sharp killer and he lives right here, not in Oklahoma. He hits Central Expressway to go north, does his deed, and then heads home. Or, if he's going to murder someone here, he stays pretty close to the Tollway and North Central, or he gets east and west on Royal, Walnut Hill, or Northwest Highway. He lives more or less in the center of the action. He doesn't head far from home when he kills someone. As the saying goes, the nut doesn't fall far from the tree.

She continued. "Now, I'll even go it one better, but this is just my guess, so don't take it to the bank. Your killer, this so-called 'Creature', is totally out of the norm for a serial killer; wealthy, well-healed, well educated, social. Everything just the opposite of what we normally see in a serial anything – murderer, rapist, whatever. Nothing like what your FBI profile says."

Mike sat back and folded his arms across his chest – defiant. "Gotcha. You made one mistake. Just one, but it's a big one. Listen to what you just said. 'Everything just the opposite of what we normally see in a serial anything,' right? Isn't that what you said?"

"Yeah, but I don't see any mistake."

Mike smiled. "Oh yeah, a big one. One we never thought of until right now. Everything the opposite?"

"Where are you taking this, Mike?"

"It's not a guy. It's a girl. A woman. Everything the opposite? Then it's not a man."

"Son of a gun. You might just have something there. We've got that one video at the newspaper." Sally nodded her head slowly and acknowledged Mike's insight. She smiled a wicked smile. "A woman, but not a lady."

"Okay," he said, "but I've got another question for you. Talk to me about our killer's timeframe. Have you thought about that?"

Sally chuckled, reached out her hand, and rubbed Mike's head. "Hey, big guy, you're on a roll today, aren't you?" She didn't give him time to reply.

"Yep, Daniels and I went pretty hard at it. We both realize what you guys are up against, so we've been going rapid fire to learn whatever we can to help you out." She shuffled through the computerized charts and graphs until she found the one she was looking for.

"Here it is." She laid it out in front of Mike. "You can have that, but I'll give you a summary." She took a deep breath and let it out slowly. She was casting her dice for all the marbles. She threw a mournful glance at the detective.

"Mike, it's time. Not here. We think this nut case has proven his point in Dallas, but he …" Sally paused. "She's due any time now. She'll do it in Tulsa and it'll be some person whose first name starts with a 'K'. Daniels and I have already scoured everything we could get our hands on to try to get a step ahead of this creep."

She shrugged her shoulders – exasperated. "We can't find any public figure like Xavier in Tulsa that might come up on our radar as a likely target. We looked at elected officials, fat cats, you name it. Nothing. *Nada*. We can't help you. We don't have the slightest idea who's going to get killed, but ..." She took a long pause. "She's due anytime now. In fact, she might have missed her period, 'cause the way we figure it is she should have hit within the last week or so."

"Baldwin got all this information, too?"

"Yes. Daniels and I talked on the phone early this morning just to go over this stuff. We both keep coming to the same conclusions. Our guy – I mean, our *female*," she emphasized, "lives here, but has her sights turned on some unsuspecting person in Oklahoma this very moment. It could be some young mama taking her kids to kindergarten; a widow taking a walk; could be anybody. Anybody, that is, whose name starts with the letter 'K.'"

Mike was silent. He smiled inwardly. Steinfeld lived in Irving, miles from where Sally was pinpointing the logical area where she though The Creature might live. If she was anywhere close to being right, Hauk would eat it.

#

Mike sat across the desk from the Lieutenant. "That's what she says, and the Captain in Tulsa agrees with her. Now, personally, I've got a guess or ..."

Hauk cut him off. "How many times do I have to tell you? We don't play that game. Guessing is for TV game shows. This isn't a game. This is life and death, and damn it, it's time for you to quit your guessing game and get to work." Hauk sat back in his chair and folded his arms. "You're a good detective, Mike, but you've got a lot to learn. You need to start by unlearning some of your bad habits. It's a new world, and if you don't get on, you'll get left behind."

"Yes, sir. My apologies."

"Accepted. Now, here's my plan. Get your crews lined up again. We're going to get that dirty son-of-a-bitch. Cling to him like stink on a skunk. Don't let him out of your sights, and when he's ready to do it we'll wrap him up. If he heads up the highway toward Tulsa, stay with him."

He tossed a condescending smile to Mike. "I read you like an open book. I know what you're going to say before the words can get out of your mouth. Sure, call your Tulsa buddy and let 'em know we're coming. However, I want our people, Dallas PD, in on the act. These are our cases. It's our brains. It's our murderer, and we'll tie that son-of-a-bitch in a knot. Sure, they'll get to put him on trial, but everybody'll know we did the work." He wagged his finger back and forth. "Me and you. We did it. Those stinking Okies are just along for the ride."

#

Mike sat at his desk. There was just one phone call to make before he told Covey and Rickey about what they were going to do. But first, Emily.

"We did it, lover girl. He bit ... hook, line and sinker. He took the bait and we're going to set up on Steinfeld this afternoon."

"I knew you could pull it off, honey." She paused. "Mike, I love you. I want you so badly I can taste it. I want you to get your killer. I want you to have the world. I want everything good to happen to you."

He heard her crying softly.

"Oh, Mike. I love you. I'm so proud of you. I knew you could pull it off. Now you'll get your real killer. You're my hero, Detective Palotti, my real American hero."

"I love you, too," he whispered.

"Honey, tell me. Do they have any idea who might be next?" she asked.

"Not the foggiest notion. Who knows? Got any ideas?"

"No. You're the detective, not me. I don't have any idea. Just somebody in Tulsa, and their first initial is a 'K'. I miss you so much. Can you come over for a celebratory glass of wine?"

Mike looked down at the notepad on his desk. Like a little boy, he drew a heart with her initials in it. "You know I'd love to do that, but no. I'm going to get with Sergeant Covey and we'll set up on Steinfeld. I'll be busy for the next however many days it takes. What about you? What'll you be doing?"

"I'm going to New York the day after tomorrow, but will swing around and catch the red-eye home. It's just a quickie trip to finish some financial contracts with my editor. Maybe see you next week? In fact, I haven't seen Annalisa in a while. I'm going to call her as soon as we hang up. Maybe she, Samanta, and I can have lunch together tomorrow." There was a long pause. "Mike, you've got a beautiful wife and little girl. I know my place. I hope you don't mind me being friends with them."

"Not at all," he replied. "Go ahead and call her. Have fun. She likes being with you, and Sam loves you. She sleeps with that little teddy bear every night."

"Does it make you think of me?"

Mike's heart quickened. "Every time I see her cuddle up with that little guy, I think of you on our bed with it."

#

Mike, Rickey, and Sgt. Covey, each in separate cars, took up positions outside Steinfeld Jewelers. Rickey took the eyeball across the parking lot. He parked facing away from David's Volvo, adjusted his mirror, and settled back to wait. Covey took a position a block north; Mike set up a block south. Either way he went, one of them would fall in behind and the others would follow. They did it enough times that it was like a playbook to them – no more than two minutes on the tail, then fall off for the next car to pick him up.

"Okay, here he comes," Rickey said over the radio. "He's pulling out to the north."

"Got him," Covey responded. Mike swung around and within three blocks had a position two car lengths behind the sergeant. He looked in his mirror to see Rickey swinging into traffic a block behind him. The surveillance was underway. The trio followed him through traffic and onto McKinney. The Volvo made a U-turn and swung into a parking slot at the Busy Baker, an upscale but casual watering hole and café. Steinfeld locked his car and went inside.

"I've got him," Covey said over the radio. The sergeant parked across the street from the café, darted between oncoming cars, and went inside. Rickey and Mike took positions down the block where they could see the Volvo.

They had just enough time to get comfortable and have a good view of the café and Volvo when Steinfeld returned to his car carrying a "to-go" bag of food.

"Crap, here he comes already," Rickey barked over the radio. They watched him back into traffic, make another U-turn, swing around the corner, and disappear out of sight.

"Get him, damn it," Mike snapped. Out of the corner of his eye he saw Rickey jumping his car over the curb, go against traffic, and make the turn. "I've got the eyeball," came the soothing words over the radio. "Just about a block ahead of me. I'm cool. He never saw my little maneuver."

Mike pulled onto the street just in time to see Covey getting back into his car. "You guys got the tail?" Covey asked.

"10-4," came the terse response. "It looks like he's heading home."

The detectives slipped back into their routine. Thirty minutes later, they watched when he parked on the street in front of his house. They took up positions where they were confident they would see him if he left, and he didn't. An hour after he carried his dinner inside, he came back out with his gardening tools and worked in his yard until dark. He went back inside, and at eleven-thirty turned off his lights.

"Hang on a bit longer," Covey directed.

Mike screwed his worn-out body down in his seat where he could be reasonably comfortable and still see the back of Steinfeld's house. It was after midnight when Covey came back on the radio. "Any action?"

"Negative here," Rickey said.

"Same here," Mike reported.

"Okay. Midnight shift is here to take up the watch, so let's call it a night."

"10-4, see you tomorrow," Covey directed.

#

Annalisa and Emily sat in the booth. They sipped their soft drinks while Samanta gulped hers down, ran out the door, and joined half-a-dozen other kids in the McDonald's playground.

"I don't know for sure, but I have a good feeling your husband is going to break this case of his," Emily said.

"Gosh, I hope you're right. This is hard on both of us." She shrugged her shoulders. "All three of us really. He's hardly had a minute for Sam. When he's home, he just wants to drop in front of the TV and zone out." Her voice cracked. She dabbed a tear that dropped from her eye. "It's not fair how much pressure they're putting on him, but he seems to have a special reserve he can call on and pep him back up. Sometimes when he leaves in the morning, I don't know if he'll make it through the day. He's so tense."

She smiled and looked at Emily. "Then he comes marching through the front door at night full of vim and vigor like a new guy. I love him that way. Unfortunately, those days are few and far between. Anyway, if I knew for sure what it was that picked him up, I'd encourage him to do it every day." She took a deep breath. "Emily, I just have to let it out. I have to vent."

"Go ahead. That's what friends are for."

"I can't believe I'm saying this, but … but for a while I thought he was seeing a girlfriend. He did that once when we were having some trouble. We worked through it and everything came out great.

Really great, that is, until these murders started happening. Then one night I got my nerve up and asked him." She took a tissue and wiped her eyes.

"It was after midnight. I couldn't sleep and I don't think he could either, but he was faking it. So, I rolled over and said, 'Mike, what's her name?' He shot up like a bullet and denied everything, and I believed him. 'Hauk,' he said. 'The jerk is killing me.' Well, I believed him then, and I believe him now."

"No idea what he does or who he's with when he comes home like that?" Emily asked.

"No. He doesn't talk much about the job, and that's fine with me. Anyhow, I don't want Sam to hear it."

Annalisa looked around, then leaned forward to share her secret. "Emily, please don't repeat a word of this, but I think he's seeing the department psychologist. You know, to talk it out. He gets it out of his system and it works. What a joy when he comes home like that. It's just like the old days. We laugh and have a good time. He plays with Sam and fiddles in the yard."

She played with the straw in her cup and then looked at Emily. "Yeah, just like the old days, and he's a great lover, too. Really great. I'm so glad I found him. He's the best husband a woman could have – if this job doesn't kill him."

"Annalisa, I've interviewed him several times, and now that you mention it, yeah, I can see the difference in him." She smiled and looked outside to watch Samanta. "I think I know what you mean. He was always a little up tight when we interviewed, but after a while he understood I wasn't out to do some reporter's hatchet job on him. He became a bit more relaxed, but yes, the last time or two he's seemed extra tense. It's that guy, Hauk. I think he's the problem. I don't know, maybe just intuition, but I think Hauk is a short timer. He won't last. Then you'll get back the neat guy you married."

She reached out and took Annalisa's hand. " I bet he'll be the best lover in the world."

Annalisa looked at her watch, brushed the hair from her forehead and smiled. "It's great to have a friend to talk to. Thanks. Now we've got to get going so I can get groceries." She laughed. "Mother Hubbard's cupboard is bare."

The two women walked arm-in-arm to the playground, got Samanta from the top of the slide and walked to the parking lot. Emily reached down and hugged Sam, then turned and kissed Annalisa on the cheek. "I love you guys. See you later." She watched as they got in their car and pulled away. Samanta turned and looked out the rear window, caught Emily's eye, and waved goodbye.

Emily checked her watch and mumbled to herself, "Damn it, I need to hurry."

#

The serial killer loaded the Mercedes, and ten minutes later was northbound on the Central Expressway – Highway 75 toward Tulsa – all the way to the final curtain call. The dashboard clock clicked over at 6:00 p.m. Eight hours to go. Eight hours for Kelly "The Bull" O'Brien to live.

Give him his due. He is one tough guy. Tough, that is, if you are a wrestling fan. More a dance and clown show than real wrestling, but the people ate it up and paid through the nose to watch. So, what the hell? If they'll pay, he could just as well get their money as someone else.

Nevertheless, he was a "creature" of habit. *Freudian, is it not?* the killer thought. He'll fight on the main event tonight, meet his drinking buddies at Mambo's for a late night dinner and drinks, and get home and in bed – never before 2:00 a.m.; never later than three. Every fight night was the same. There would only be one exception – tonight would be his last fight.

The murderer cruised past the Tulsa Convention Center Arena. The parking lot was packed, but the crowd was starting to leave. The Friday Night Fights were over – forever for Kelly "The Bull" O'Brien. His death would be the most difficult, but also the most rewarding; a murder no one would ever forget.

The Creature parked at the apartment, carried a violin case inside, and five minutes later was brewing a cup of espresso. It was just what the doctor ordered – a good caffeine surge for a long, hard night.

The Bull was the most difficult to plan. It was full of challenges, but nothing was too much of an obstacle to be overcome by America's greatest serial killer. Kelly, "The Bull." What a way to close the play. There would be a standing ovation. It took more than two months of dry runs, but it was worth the effort. No one would ever match this.

The killer laid out the appropriate attire for the night. The sword would strike again, and there would be no doubt in anyone's mind that one person had done all of them. One person outsmarted every cop in the country, including the country bumpkin, Michael Palotti.

The killer slowly hummed the poem:

Death
Is a gift from afar.
It is your flight on a thousand winds.
It is my gift to you.
But,
I will not stand on your grave and weep.

Chapter Eight

THE COLD-HEARTED MURDERER GAVE ONE last inspection to the clothing and sword. The Ninja outfit served a variety of purposes for Xavier; the newspaper parking lot was under video surveillance, so a disguise of some sort had to be worn, otherwise even the stumble-bum cops would see the killer "up close and personal." There was some intimate satisfaction in wearing it – it was fun, and it also was very practical because of the need to climb the fence and crawl under the cars.

Tonight would be quite different. The cold, sharp steel of the sword would deliver the message. There was no need for any melodrama, just some plain and simple jeans, hiking boots, a long-sleeve shirt, and a pair of latex gloves. That would do it.

Besides, the "fun" part was there each and every time. To choose the time, place and manner of a person's death is the ultimate reward a person can ever have. The murderous hands opened the violin case, removed the sword and placed it gently on the bedspread. It reflected the overhead light back into the killer's eye.

"You're winking at me, aren't you? You want to go to work? Good boy. One last time, then we'll call it quits. But, tonight is your night to shine – cute, huh?"

The murderer wiped the blade to a sheen, slipped it back in the scabbard, and put it back in the violin case. A self-satisfying smile crossed the killer's face. The cold, heartless eyes took one last look around the room, then walked out the door, casual as anyone going out for a late-night jam session at a bar or coffee house. Not a worry in the world.

It was one-fifteen in the morning. The time was perfect. The Mercedes slipped silently into the darkness of a lover's lane no more than four hundred yards from Kelly's house. Not wanting to turn on the overhead light when the door opened, the killer rolled down the window and climbed out, a la NASCAR. More fun. The sword and scabbard were slung over the left shoulder.

The Creature blended into the dark shadows of night and jogged effortlessly back down the lane, across the paved street and into the utility right-of-way behind the row of upscale houses where Kelly lived. The killer reached the third house from the end – the home of Kelly O'Brien, the millionaire wrestler – the man who would become the hallmark of serial murderer victims.

The Creature found a foothold in the vines that covered the patio wall and within seconds was over the top and in the backyard. The swimming pool lights reflected waves of blue and silver across the yard, bathing the Angel of Death in a soft effect as the killer padded silently across the yard.

Kelly was too tough, too self-assured. He was an icon of a rags-to-riches Americana type of guy. He gloated in his fame and glory. He never used an alarm system. He seldom locked his doors. Nevertheless, to be on the safe side, the killer carried a KwikPik lock pick device.

Kelly feared no one, and with little wonder. People worshiped him. He was almost a god to the crazed fans of the wrestling world. They loved him and he loved them.

Of course, not everyone loved him – not The Creature.

The killer stood at the sliding glass door from the patio that led into the bar. A few lights were on. The house was quiet. The mere touch of a gloved hand and the door slid open. As expected, he didn't lock it. The assassin took a deep breath. This was it. This was the final act. After tonight, it would be over. Then, the real fun would begin.

The lone figure moved silently across the floor, up the stairs, and into Kelly's bedroom. There were three closets: one for shoes; one for winter clothes; one for spring and summer clothes. The killer took one last look around the room. Everything as it should be. The king-size bed in the center; bedside tables, each with a lamp turned on, but dimmed to cast a soft glow across the room; a love seat and overstuffed chair against the wall; a floor-to-ceiling window to give him a view of the city while he lay in bed; the bathroom door ajar; and a nightlight above the sink. Everything as it was on the last two forays into "The Bull's" inner-sanctum.

The killer stood beside the bed and waited. The bedside clock clicked 2:15 when a car slowed in front of the house, then turned into the driveway. He was home.

Quiet as a snake slithering across moist warm grass, the killer opened the closet door and went in. The room was inky black and stuffy – very stuffy. The killer felt along the sweaters and overcoats until coming to the back wall, then slipped in behind the last garments. Now, it was just a matter of time.

The sound of a door closing echoed up the stairs. Moments later, footsteps clomped across the floor. The lights were turned up; their rays crept beneath the closet door. More light. The bathroom. Water ran – a long time. It didn't sound like the shower. Apparently, he was washing his face; maybe shaving or brushing his teeth. The water was turned off. He burped; ugly, very ugly. Then the sound of the toilet seat being raised followed by the sounds of Kelly taking his last voluntary pee.

He would do it again soon. All dead people do.

The bed gave a creak when he sat on it. He was undressing. His shoes dropped on the floor; the smooth "*ziiip*" of his trousers when he slipped out of them. It sounded like he walked barefooted across the room and threw his clothes on the chair. He walked back to the bed, burped, and whipped back the bedspread and sheet. He turned off the lights, burped again and passed gas. Then the killer listened to the sounds of him getting into bed, fluffing the pillow, and adjusting the sheet.

The closet was stifling. The alphabet killer waited for what seemed like eternity, but it didn't matter. Time wasn't important. It was almost over. The "K," and that would be the end.

The luminous hands of the wristwatch were almost impossible to see, but it looked like Kelly in bed for at least an hour. The killer shuffled silently past the heavy clothes, grasped the doorknob, gave it a slow twist, and eased it open. The only illumination came from the city lights in the distance.

The Creature stood silent for a minute. The cool air was exhilarating. As the seconds ticked away, the murderer's eyes adjusted to the dim light. Everything in the room came into focus – the chairs and lamps, the bed, Kelly. All was in perfect order. Better than that. He was asleep on top of the sheet – his muscular, heavy-weight body, the ripples of his muscles. He was almost too perfect, but that was what made him so ideal for tonight. His naked body stretched out on his stomach was no match for what was about to befall him. His immense strength and power were nothing. He was helpless against the greatest serial killer of all time.

The assassin eased the sword from the sheath, strode across the room, danced a swift pirouette, and drove the edge of the sword through the back of his neck.

Kelly didn't move for a moment. Suddenly, his central nervous system responded. He began to quiver and tremble. His hands and feet fluttered from his autonomic nervous system. His body twisted away from his head. As quickly as he started, he stopped and gave his last involuntary urination.

The final act was complete. The first play was finished. The actor would go home. The stage was set for the best play of all time – coming soon to a theater near you.

#

The drive back to Texas was a joy. The play was a resounding success; the audience spellbound; the cast was superb.

All the clothes from the night were dumped in the washing machine, spun dry, folded, and put back in the dresser drawers. The sword was cleaned meticulously; the sheath cleaned with a combination of alcohol and battery acid – hard on the sheath, but that was the price of doing things right. It was nothing more than a business expense.

It was a bright and glorious day by the time The Creature found time to immerse that wicked body into a tub of hot water, sip a glass of wine, and allow the soft music from the Bose to massage an otherwise cold and heartless mind and body to sleep.

The empty wine glass slipped free from the hand that only hours earlier had slain an innocent sleeping man. It tumbled softly on the rug. The killer's head lay back against the tub pillow. Soothing, peaceful, and blissful sleep.

Even sound asleep and deep in the succor of the warm water, the killer's face managed a faint smile. Complete success without any help, any advice, any financial support from anyone, especially from a man. It was complete satisfaction. And still, the best was yet to come. The encore.

Chapter Nine

EMILY ROUSED HERSELF FROM HER bed, stood in front of the mirror and combed her hair. It was the very same mirror she'd shared so long ago with Detective Michael Palotti.

Little Mikey Boy, Little Johnny Boy, she thought, *your time is coming. Now, let's see how tough you are. Let's see how moral and professional you can be. Let's see how two great detectives can deal with it when they are slapped in the face; when it knocks them down only to pick them up and knock them down again. I'll do both of you at the same time just to give you a sporting chance. You guys talk about police communication. You're a couple of idiots.*

She recalled hearing Baldwin make a comment when he'd spent the night at her Tulsa apartment. They were watching the ten o'clock news and saw where a grocer had shot and killed a hoodlum in a bungled robbery. John had pulled her naked body against him in bed and laughed. "SLA. That's what we say when somebody smokes a shithead. SLA. So long asshole," he laughed.

#

Emily combed her hair and smiled. "So long asshole." She took her cell phone, the one she bought in Tulsa, and dialed the number.

"Detective Baldwin speaking." John adjusted the receiver in the crook of his neck, freeing up his right hand to take notes from whoever was calling.

"Good morning, Detective," Emily said seductively.

"Hey, sweet thing, good to hear from you." He looked at his caller ID. "I see you're in town. What're you up to?"

"I saw a potential client. Got in late yesterday and we had dinner together."

"You spent the night here without calling me?"

Emily laughed. "My client is a woman, so no, I'm not messing around on you. We ate dinner with her family and discussed some things they want me to do for them." She paused. "But, I thought about you when I went to bed. It's so big and empty without you to keep me warm. I dreamt about us – just the two of us."

"I love you, Emily. You know that, don't you?"

"I love you, too." She blew a kiss over the telephone. "I've got to get going. I'm heading out right away. I've got some business with my editor back in Dallas." She paused again. "John, there's something I've got to tell you. I've been working on something I haven't told you about. It's something big. I know I promised when we started working on our projects that I'd stay out of your business, but I have a confession to make."

She paused again to give it time to sink in. "Johnny, I love you so much I just couldn't watch helplessly while you and that guy in Texas were busting your butts on this madman. So, anyhow, I broke my promise and did some research on the computer. I think I've got a lead for you. If you can go to Dallas this Friday, I'll have it all together. You're going to be surprised, honey. Really surprised at what I've come up with."

"Yeah, sure I can go down there. Mom will keep Jonah. Where should I meet you?"

"My house, but we won't be able to make love. Not this time, because I'm going to invite Detective Palotti also. I've read about him in the paper and feel almost like I know him. In fact, I called and introduced myself. Gave him a bit of a phony story to peak his interest, and he'll be there." She laughed softly. "He doesn't know about us, and we can keep it that way. You never mentioned me to him, did you?"

"Not just no, but hell no."

"Good. Anyhow, I told him I do criminal justice research and was working on those cases with some crime analysis tools – just enough to rouse his cop curiosity, and he said he'll be there. Seven o'clock."

"I'll be there."

"Love you, honey. I miss you so much I can taste it. It's been weeks since you spent the night in my bed."

"You can count on me – you know that."

"Call me Lisa. I love it when you do that. I love it when you make love to me and call me her name. Johnny, I want to be your wife. I know I can't replace her. It's much too soon for that, but let me be her for a night."

John took a deep breath and closed his eyes. "I love you, Lisa. With all my heart, I love you and want you with me right now – right this minute."

"Will you make love to me in my bed and call me Lisa?"

"I'll love you. You're my soul mate."

"Oh, you sweet thing," she murmured. "Hey, how's Jonah? Does he still have the little teddy bear I gave him? Little Howard?"

"Oh yeah, doing great, and they sleep together every night."

"Give him a kiss for me. Well, I need to get on the road. Love you, and see you Friday."

Emily clicked the off button on her cell phone, turned off the tape recorder, and made her second call.

#

Mike answered on the first ring. "This is Mike Palotti."

"Hello, Detective Palotti," Emily whispered into the telephone.

Mike leaned back in his chair and smiled. "Hey, lover girl, how'd you know I was thinking about you?"

"ESP, I guess. Mike, you know you're always on my mind. I just couldn't get in a good mood without talking to you. I need to hear your voice, to hear you tell me you love me."

Mike leaned forward on his desk and whispered into the telephone. "I love you as much as a man can love a woman, and I want you always to know that – to know what you mean to me." He paused and cleared his throat. "But, also what you mean to Annalisa and Sam. They think you're something special."

"How is that precious little Sam? Is she still sleeping with Howard?" Before Mike could answer, she continued, "Do you think of me in your bed when you see Howard?"

Mike gave a soft chortle. "How could I ever forget?"

"Call me Annalisa."

Mike looked around the room, then spoke softly. "Annalisa, I want you. I want to hold you close to me – to kiss you."

"Michael, oh Michael, I love you so much, but I'll always be mindful of my place in your life. I miss it when we're apart." She paused for a moment. "Honey, any chance you could work late Friday night and come over. I think I'll have a surprise for you?"

"What kind of surprise?"

Emily laughed. "Well, I'll have to think about it, but maybe I can give you a night to remember."

A grin swept across Mike's face. "Something to remember? Sounds intriguing. I was scheduled to be off Friday, but I'll tell

Annalisa I have to pull an extra shift. She'll understand – wives always do. I'll be there. Can I bring anything?"

"Just that hunk of a body of yours. See you at seven. Mike, one other thing. I kind of broke my promise to you – the one where I said I wouldn't get too involved in your work. Remember?"

"Sure, but what are you leading up to?"

"You know I'm a research geek, so I've buried myself into a crash course on crime analysis. Now, don't jump the gun and get mad, but I called that guy in Tulsa and talked to him. I told him a little about my interest in these cases and told him I found something important, something really big that both of you missed. I think I've really hit on something.

"Of course, he doesn't know anything about us. Personally, you know. Anyhow, I told him I was inviting the two of you over for a light dinner and business meeting to discuss what I've found. I'm serious, Mike. I found something too big not to be the common denominator you've talked about."

"I'm impressed. Sure, I'll be there. Is he coming?"

"Oh yes. I poked around a bit and found out he lost his wife not too long ago, so I invited him to Big D. He jumped at it. Anyhow, he's eager to get away for a day or two, so he'll be here.

"Mike, after he goes, will you stay with me for a while? I want you. Every inch of you. I want us to make love again."

"Seven o'clock. See you then."

Emily hung up the phone and turned her tape recorder off again.

#

Friday evening traffic was snarled. Mike arrived twenty minutes late to find John's shiny new red PT Cruiser already there. He liked John, but smiled inwardly with an air of cockiness. His colleague was a top-notch investigator, but in some ways he was still a kid. A PT Cruiser – not a very big item with most macho cops.

Mike got out and closed his door, but paused to enjoy the elegance of Highland Park – the rows of colonial mansions, each a monument of power and wealth. The full moon hovered in the evening sky. Its soft blue glow slipped through the leaves of the elm trees and painted the neighborhood with an aura of peace and tranquility. The sweet scent of freshly-cut grass wafted on the evening breeze. He inhaled deeply and held it. It was too good a moment to allow it to escape. Maybe the end was near.

Emily answered on his first ring. She was enchanting. Her dark hair flowed as though every hair was groomed individually, each one in its place; a dark navy business suit with a high, white-collared blouse; hose and low heels; very professional; very beautiful. Somewhat out of place, her lipstick bore the slightest hint of a smear – quite unlike her usual perfection.

"Detective Palotti, how nice of you to come." She extended a handshake and gave a courteous nod of her head. "Come in, please. Detective Baldwin got here a few minutes ago. We were just having a glass of wine. Won't you join us?"

"Mike, how are you doing?" Baldwin said as he approached from the dining room.

"Well, you know each other, so Detective Baldwin, if you could show him the bar, I'll get some food from the 'fridge." She looked at Mike. "Will you have a drink with us? Wine? Or, something stronger if you wish."

"Thanks, yes. Scotch and water will be fine."

"C'mon, Mike. I'll pour while Mrs. Morgan is getting things ready." The two detectives walked toward the bar. Baldwin was the first to speak. "Any idea what she's got?"

Mike shook his head. "Not the slightest. I've talked to her on the phone, but when she said she might have something big for me – I mean, for us, then sure. I said I'd be here. What about you? What do you think?"

John took the silver tongs from the top of the ice bucket and held them up to the light. "Well, she does things first class." He removed the top from the bucket and put three cubes in Mike's glass.

Mike looked at her well-stocked bar – Chivas Regal, Catto's, Cutty Sark, Pinwinnie, Whyte and MacKay, Glenfiddich, and Balmore – a collection of fine Scotch. He privately questioned why he'd never browsed her liquor selection. Nevertheless, he selected a bottle of Glenfiddich. "Might just as well drink the lady's good stuff." He poured the glass half-full, and then gave it a squirt of water. He laughed. "Don't want to mess up good Scotch."

John topped off his glass of wine. They walked toward the dining room where Emily was laying out the refreshments. Mike did a quick calculation. He'd seen it before on this same table – a tray of fresh vegetables, cheese, and crackers. Even the two candelabras. He paused. It was the same music floating softly from the sound system. Everything was the same. His mind wandered. Would it be the same after Baldwin left?

"Gentlemen, be seated, please," she said.

John quickly stepped around the table and pulled out a chair for Emily. She smiled and gave him a quick glance. "Thank you – a real gentleman." She gestured to the chairs. "Make yourselves comfortable, and please eat some of my goodies so I don't have leftovers to eat by myself tomorrow."

Mike took his place, the same place where he was seated on that glorious day.

She scooted the tray in a position where each of them could comfortably reach it, then passed them crystal plates. "Let's eat," she said as she helped herself to a slice of tenderloin and a cracker.

The detectives filled their plates, but their attention was on Emily. "So, Mrs. Morgan, what is it you've found that appears to be a critical link in our cases?" Mike asked.

She smiled and tilted her head. "Detective, can I call you Mike?" She didn't wait for a response. "Let's enjoy ourselves for a moment or two before we get too deep into this thing, but I can ease my way into it while we stifle our appetites." She tossed a quick look to Baldwin, then to Palotti. "Let me start this way ..."

Over the next thirty minutes, she covered the story Mike heard so long ago – Edgar's death; her research; his writing; her desire to establish herself as a criminal justice expert.

She took the last bit of pork tenderloin, placed it on a cracker and slipped it into her mouth. "Why don't you move to the front room while I get our coffee?"

The detectives pushed back from the table and went to the living room. Soft lights threw gentle shadows across the room. A bouquet of roses in a clear bowl filled with lemon slices was positioned in the center of a coffee table. The aroma of the flowers provided a relaxing and sumptuous setting. Everything was perfect, as only Emily could do it. Mike's mind wandered to what might come to pass later. His muscles trembled.

The two detectives found comfortable chairs with an end table separating them. Mike noticed two television sets in opposite corners of the room. They hadn't been there before.

Emily returned with a pot of coffee and three cups on a tray, served the men, and then seated herself majestically on a high-back chair across from them. She crossed her legs and allowed a shoe to slip from her foot.

"From the beginning ..." She paused, adjusted her skirt, and flipped her hair back. "Gentlemen, I undertook this endeavor to provide assistance to the criminal justice system. So, the very beginning was to look at you as human beings – very nice human beings at that," she smiled. "I've done a little work without sharing with you, but all with an honorable intent to improve the criminal justice system. What I quickly learned was that in both of your departments, you are considered to be of the utmost in investigative ability, trust, and for lack of better terminology, you have stick-to-it-ivness. I spoke confidentially with your supervisors," she lied. "They think a great deal of you. You know the systems and how they work, and you know how to take appropriate detours when you find the system restricting your otherwise lawful investigative techniques."

Mike tossed a quick glance at John who was nodding his head in agreement, but whose eyes were more interested in her shoeless, dangling foot.

Emily continued. "Furthermore, I found you to be similar inasmuch as your bosses identify both of you as being very solid, well trained, and trustworthy people – officers who are willing to put in many more hours than you will ever be paid for." She looked at Mike, then slowly to John. She moistened her lips. "And, perhaps most important in the personnel process is that your departments found men who loved their families; men who idolized their wives and children; men who would give their lives not only for their family, but for their profession. Your loyalty runs deep through your veins. Your blood runs red, white, and blue."

She looked to John. "You have a child?"

Mike noticed his expression. His lips were pursed, his brow furrowed. He was leaning forward, on edge. "Yes," he replied. "A son. Jonah. He's two."

"And you were recently widowed?"

John bit his lip. "I'm not sure where this is going. Do you have a point?"

"Yes, yes," she replied. Emily turned to Mike, who leaned back and crossed his legs. He was comfortable and ready. She would have to play the game in front of John, but she already knew about Annalisa, Samanta and him.

"Mike?"

"Yes, I'm married and have a little girl. Her name is Samanta, but we call her Sam."

Emily cast her glance to John, then back to Mike. "Fair to say each of you loves your family more than anything, and your profession is second to that. Correct?"

"Yeah, that's about it," John said.

Mike nodded in agreement.

Emily got up, kicked off her other shoe, and took the coffee pot from the serving tray. "More?" she asked as she stood over John. He lifted his cup. Their eyes met for a moment, but Mike caught it – a sudden and unplanned moment that expressed something between them, then she filled his cup. She turned to Mike, who put his hand over his cup.

"Night time. No more coffee, thanks."

Emily returned to her seat and scooted her feet beneath the chair. She sat more erect than previously. Mike understood her body language. She was center stage and showing her command presence.

"My primary point was to examine your communications process, and gentlemen," she paused and with a caustic smile, looking back and forth between them, "you failed miserably."

Mike sat forward. Where was she going with this? What was she doing? He looked at John, whose face was blank. He was expressionless.

"Both of you have spoken to the killer. I'm positive of that, and I'm equally positive that neither of you ever communicated to the other with any degree of precision who you were talking to."

"Hang on a minute," John interjected. "We communicated like crazy. So did the FBI. I don't know where you're going with this, but if you think we *both*," he emphasized, "talked to this killer, then you've really missed the boat."

Mike joined in. "Mrs. Morgan, I have to agree with Detective Baldwin. One of us talked to the killer? That might be possible. Both? Not one chance in a million. In fact, our crime analysis units go over every report and identify any of what I'm sure you know we call those common denominators."

"Ah, Detective," she fired back, "but you're wrong. Dead wrong."

Mike felt a rush. He was surprised, seeing a side of her he had never seen before. He wasn't prepared for her. He had a twinge of emptiness in his chest. He couldn't think fast enough to keep up with her, much less get ahead and anticipate where she was going. She was beating him at his own game.

"Gentlemen, you might want a drink before we go any further."

"Yeah," Mike replied as the detectives got up, swapped quick glances at each other, went to the bar, and poured another drink. Scotch for Mike, this time without water. John refilled his wine glass.

He whispered to Mike. "What's up?"

Mike shook his head. "Let's go see."

Chapter Ten

THE DETECTIVES SAT DOWN ACROSS from Emily. She wasn't smiling. There was nothing sexy about her. Her lips were pursed; her eyes glared; her demeanor was robotic. Mike didn't know her. She was a stranger, filled with hate.

"Enjoy your drink, and if you need to refresh it, just help yourself. Now, let me come to the point. Each of you loves your child. Mike, you love your wife." She looked to John. "And you still deeply love Lisa. Am I correct?" She did not wait for a reply. "Now I can tell you with one hundred percent accuracy that both of you spoke to the killer, but don't be impatient," she chided. "First things first. I'm certain the one person who bears sole responsibility for the deaths of those people has also so inoculated themselves that even when you learn who it is, you will be helpless ..."

"Damn it to hell," John shouted. He stood up, his muscles rigid and taut. "I don't know what kind of crap you're tossing out here, but I'm not going to sit here and take it." He slammed his glass down and started toward the door.

"Just a minute, Little Johnny Boy," Emily snarled. "Sit your royal ass down right here and shut up. You might be surprised. You'll learn something."

"What?" John fired back. His voice was pitched with anger. He reached out to backhand her across her face, but froze under her icy stare.

Mike's heart pounded. His head throbbed – another headache. He put a hand on John's shoulder. "Cool it. Let's see what she's got. If she's full of it, we get the hell out of here and go have a drink."

"Good idea," Emily shot back. She pointed to the chair. John crouched his neck into his shoulders and sat down.

"Gentleman, I'll offer definitive proof of the identity of the person you're looking for." She threw a condescending smile at Mike, then turned to John, "And more so, unequivocal testimony that the killing is over." She shook her head. "There won't be anymore."

Mike started to speak, but she held her hand up.

"Hold it, Mike. Your time will come, but hear me out. Lastly, and of great surprise to you, is the fact you know who the person is. Nevertheless, by your own volition, not only will you resist any effort to arrest the perpetrator, you'll commit yourself to protecting this person the newspaper so cruelly called "The Creature."

Mike rose from his chair and walked toward the bar. "With all due respect, Mrs. Morgan, what you're saying is totally impossible."

John smirked. "I think he's being pretty damn polite. I think you're playing a game, or have lost your ever-loving mind."

"How's Howard?" she asked.

"Fine," Mike responded. "Sam sleeps with him every night."

John froze. "Howard?" He looked at Mike, then to Emily.

"Yes, how is the bear? Is Jonah still sleeping with him?"

Mike turned and stared at them as they glared at each other. He was right. There was something between them. "What the hell is going on?" he asked.

Neither Baldwin nor Emily surrendered their stare. "She gave Jonah a little bear. She called him Howard," John replied.

Mike's skin crawled. He looked at Emily. "She gave one to Sam, too." His voice was cold as ice.

"Thank you one and all," Emily said as she lifted the remote control from the floor by her chair. "Arrest your killer, and lose your family; lose your job; lose everything you hold dear. You'll be ruined beyond redemption. There'll be no turning back. You and your families will be totally destroyed – and now, let's see the feature film."

She flicked the remote. The television came on. Mike's mouth went dry. Goose bumps covered every inch of his skin. His head ached like never before. He was shaking, but couldn't move. They were full screen in sound and color. They were making love in his bed calling her Annalisa while she held the little teddy bear; drying and kissing her in the bath tub; Emily in his wife's clothes; and, their adventure on the dining room table. She'd recorded every tryst in living color; every syllable of lust and pillow talk. Nothing was omitted.

Emily spun and flicked the remote again. John stood up slowly. Mike saw his shirt was soaked with sweat. His lips quivered. His face was red. He was filled with rage. They were making love on the floor with little Jonah asleep in his bed beside them; John standing in his underwear in front of her and telling sex jokes; and worst of all, a late-night in the bullpen being very indiscreet with their intimacy.

John's eyes watered, but he stopped short of crying. Mike stepped to him, put an arm over his shoulder and held him, but his eyes never left Emily. "Okay, bitch," Mike said, "what's next? Besides the fact we might kill you right now."

Emily laughed and flicked off the televisions. "I don't think so. Beside, this very moment is being recorded." She flicked the remote again. They were on both TV sets. "Sit down, we have business to discuss, unless you need another drink," she laughed.

Mike guided John into his chair, filled his own drink a third time, and returned to his chair. "This better be good, you filthy whore."

"Michael, it's wonderful. Now tuck away your macho little wee-wee and let's talk real police business. Hear me out, then if you want to kill me, go right ahead. But, I should tell you that everything you've seen, plus tonight, is loaded on a server and even I don't know where it is. I have to go to New York City to do it on a specific terminal. All I know is the code. Every thirty days I punch in the code and the system resets for another month. If I don't do it, it'll send everything to your Chiefs, AP, UPI, and Reuters. You'll be ruined. Tomorrow is the twenty-fifth day. If I miss, you can kiss your families and you careers *adios* because both of you are two dead dicks," she emphasized. "And, no! Don't even think about it. You can't torture me for the code. It's different every time. I filled out a twenty-three page questionnaire. It's loaded into the program and each time I re-load it, I have to give multiple responses. If I goof, it'll give me a second chance. If I miss again, it's sent.

"Now, let's talk about your killer – me. I'm your lady and you can't touch me."

"Prove it," John demanded. His face was red. His dark eyes pierced to the depths of her soul.

"Oh, John, don't be so angry. My goodness, just an hour ago I gave you a little oral sex and you professed your unending love for me. Do you want me to fast-forward so you can see it? You men, how small-minded you are with your love affairs."

"Shut your mouth and talk about the proof," Mike interjected.

"Okay, I'll offer plenty of proof. Sometime in the next few weeks your Chiefs will receive some information that can come only from the real killer, not some spurious liar trying to get publicity. On top of that, I'll guarantee the killing is over. In fact, it is. I'm done. I proved my point."

"What exactly is your point?" Mike asked.

Emily laughed. "Well, I won't tell them about the great lovemaking we did, if you're worried about that. However, I completed my research. I'll distort the documentation sufficiently, but will show how even with the best of intentions, and all the money of two cities plus the FBI, you missed out on the basics of it all, inter-organizational communication. You missed a serial killer, and you'll never catch HIM," she again emphasized.

Mike looked down at the glass in his hands. Condensation dripped from the sides and onto his shoes. He took a deep breath. A surge of confidence, however small, crept into his chest. *"No doubt, she got the best of us, but tomorrow will be another day,"* he thought. He looked up at her. "So tell us, how did you get the videos every place you did it with us?"

"Simple enough, but obviously too intricate and complex for your pea brains." She flashed her nasty little smile to them. "The spy store. I doubt you've heard of it, but they're in the bigger cities. Every type of camera and bug you can imagine. Be right back." She got up and went to her bedroom. Seconds later, she returned with an armful of her equipment – a purse; an overnight bag; a cell phone; and a pair of sunglasses. She tossed them on the floor. "Take a look. Cameras and microphones in all of them."

She looked at Mike. "You were so horny that day in the bathroom that you could've seen the lens in the handle of the overnight bag if you gave it half a glance. Good grief. You were kissing and adoring my precious body. You were like a teenager seeing a girl for the first time. When I looked at the bag and saw the bathroom light reflected off the lens, I thought, 'Oh shit. If he sees that thing I'm a goner.' Thank goodness you get horny so easily." She laughed. "You're too easy, Mike. Then when we went to the bed I put the bag down facing the wrong way, but what the hell. You didn't see anything but me and weren't even aware when I moved the bag around to get us in the picture." She smiled at him. "Want to see it again?" she asked coyly.

"So what's the game plan now?" Baldwin asked.

"Your lives go on. Just do the work you're paid to do and don't look back. It won't do you any good. You'll get over this, but ..." she paused, "if we stop these interviews too quickly, your bosses may get curious. They'll get their letters about the killer, but we can't do anything to arouse their suspicions. Just let things play out for a while, then we can let it dry up. It's over."

"You expect us to continue doing this with you?" Mike asked.

"No, no," she laughed. "Remember, they don't know about our little games, so let's allow that dog to go to sleep. Just have a few phone conversations. Let them dwindle, then die. Life goes on, and so will yours."

"It can't end like this. You've killed so many people; you can't just walk away like nothing happened," Baldwin interjected.

Emily pursed her lips and blew a kiss to him. "Yes I can, Johnny Boy. I already did." She got up and walked toward the door, opened it, and looked back. "Good night, gentlemen."

The detectives looked at each other, then walked past her without saying a word. They heard the front door shut when they got to their cars.

"What now?" Baldwin whispered.

Mike looked at the house. Memories flooded him – that first party with Annalisa; the lunches and conversations; her friendship with his wife and daughter; the kissing and flirting that evolved into lovemaking.

How did I let it happen? he wondered. More than reflections of his deeds, the weight of his betrayal against his family and profession overwhelmed him. His head and neck ached. His temples pounded. *How could I let myself slip so badly?* he thought. The answer stung as sharply as a wasp. She was smarter than he.

He was quiet for a moment, then uttered, "We kill her."

Chapter Eleven

BALDWIN WINCED. THE SOFT GLOW of the streetlights floated through the trees and reflected in his eyes. He trembled with rage. "God Almighty," he uttered. "What's become of us?"

"Not here. Not now," Palotti fired back. He reached for his car door and looked back at Baldwin. "You know the Café Ipanema on Central?"

The young detective nodded. "I've been there a couple times with her."

"Meet me there. We need to talk."

Ten minutes later the two men sat in a corner booth. They sipped dark Brazilian coffee. Their voices were little more than a whisper.

Mike looked at Baldwin who breathed slowly and closed his eyes, trying to regain his composure. "We're in a hole, but we have to be on our toes," Mike remarked. He held his coffee cup in both hands and tilted it to his lips. He inhaled deeply and savored the scent of the steamy drink. He peered over the top of his cup and continued, "She can't walk. We can't tolerate that happening. We've got to out-fox her." His piercing dark eyes relayed his commitment.

The young detective shuffled in his seat. "I don't know, Mike. I don't think I can add to this mess by doing something like that. I wasn't brought up that way."

"Neither was I." Mike's voice was hushed, but commanding. "It's counter to everything we know and believe, but there's no other way." He looked into his cup and swirled it as though reading tea leaves. Seconds slipped away before he looked again at Baldwin. "We'll take our time and wait – just be patient. She'll relax, let her guard down, and make a mistake. Mark my words. It'll happen."

He smirked. "We did it. Both of us knew better, but we did it anyway." He shook his head. A hint of a smile cracked his lips. "Oh yeah, she'll slip up. And when she does, we'll be there." He walked to the counter and refilled his cup. He scooted back into the booth, gave a piercing stare at Baldwin, and leaned forward. His whispered voice stabbed his young colleague. "Can you kill her?"

"I can't talk about this anymore." Baldwin put his money on the table and got up. "I'll talk to you later. I need time to think." He started to walk away, then turned abruptly. "Maybe you do, too." As quickly as he said it, he was out the door.

Mike sat in the booth and watched the PT Cruiser pull out of the driveway and slip into the Express Way traffic. *Not a very macho car,* he thought.

#

Palotti looked at his watch. It was only two hours since he'd parked in front of her house, so cocky and self-assured. He looked again at his coffee as he swirled the remaining drops in the bottom of the cup. His mind raced over how he'd fallen into her trap. Her beauty beguiled him. He was foolish and reckless. He was stupid and didn't need anyone else to tell him. He was his own accuser.

Mike looked at his reflection in the window. "You got jacked, mister," he mumbled to himself. He pushed his cup away and slipped out of the booth, walked out the door and took a single step before he felt his stomach churn. He stumbled like a drunk to his car, leaned over the rear bumper and vomited.

"She ruined me. I never saw it coming," he cried. He trembled. Goosebumps raced down his arms and legs. He was cold and hot at the same time. His lips were burning. Every emotion was drained.

He dried his eyes and wiped his mouth with his handkerchief, then returned to the café. The brilliant detective, now so defeated, ignored the other patrons as he made his way past the counter and to the restroom. He locked the door behind him and leaned over the basin. Icy cold water poured from the faucet. He splashed it over his face and hair, then leaned over and scooped it into his mouth, rinsed and spit. With his hands gripping the basin, he lifted his head and looked into the mirror. Water dribbled off his chin. His hair was disheveled.

Someone twisted the knob and tapped on the door. "Okay in there?" the voice shouted.

"Yeah," Mike responded. He continued to look in the mirror and quietly uttered, "No, not at all." He reached over, unlatched the door, and stepped aside while the black clad teenager with purple hair scooted past him and stepped up to the urinal.

"Wow, mister. You look like hell if you don't mind me saying so," he said as he unzipped his trousers.

Mike laughed. "Well, I feel that way, too." He pulled out the paper towels, wiped his face, and combed his hair while the young man gave it the two obligatory taps. "Stay sober tonight, my friend," Mike said over his shoulder as he left the restroom.

"Hope I don't end up like you," the teenager called out through the closed door.

The detective chuckled. "If you only knew."

#

Mike drove slowly down the block and looked at her house. He talked to himself and chuckled. "Like whistling in the graveyard, but that's okay." He slowed nearly to a stop in front of her house. "Emily Morgan, you whore. You'll get yours. I know something you don't know about. I know your alarm code."

He gradually accelerated and turned for home.

Samanta and Annalisa were on the couch watching television when he walked in. "Daddy," Sam cried out. She jumped to her feet and ran to him. "Mamma told me I could stay up 'til you came home. Look," she said as she pointed to her bare feet. "I got a sticker today and Mamma put a band aid on it."

Mike picked her up and cradled her in his arms. He lifted her foot to his lips and kissed it. "There. A get well kiss. Now it won't hurt anymore." He held her on his hip and stepped toward the couch.

Annalisa straightened up from where she was slouched, reached out, and pulled her husband and daughter toward her. "I missed you tonight, sugar boy. We had hot dogs and chips. What about you?"

"Worked right through dinner," he replied. He put Sam in her mother's lap, then leaned over and kissed Annalisa. "You're all I want for dinner." Mike sat beside her. She turned and put her feet in his lap. He paused for a moment, then took her toes into his hands and began to massage them – slowly, one at a time. He looked up and saw her beautiful smile. He tried to speak, but the words wouldn't come out. Her toes were prettier than Emily's. They sat quietly, listening as the clock gonged the hour.

Samanta curled deeper into her mom's lap. Her eyes closed, opened, then slowly closed again.

"Let me take her," Mike whispered. He lifted his daughter into his arms and walked to her bedroom. With one arm holding her and the other pulling back the sheet, he leaned down and put her on the pillow. "Goodnight, little angel," he whispered. He kissed her cheek. Once again, the events of the night raced through his mind. He knelt beside her bed and prayed. "Forgive me, Lord, for what I have done, and please forgive me for the sin I'm going to commit."

He didn't hear the footsteps when Annalisa stepped behind him. She touched his shoulder. "Honey, what's wrong?"

Mike shuddered. The touch of her soft hand on his shoulder pierced him like a bolt of lightning. He closed his eyes for a moment, took a deep breath, and turned to look at her. She wasn't smiling.

Annalisa looked down at him. "Michael, I heard that. What did you pray for? What's going on in your life? You can't hide it from me. I've known for a long time that something was wrong. I even asked Emily about it. Talk to me! Tell me what it is."

He stood, took her hands in his and led her out of Samanta's room. They returned to the living room where he turned down the lights. Only a soft light from the hallway illuminated the room. The house was quiet.

"Sit with me, baby. I need to talk." He guided her onto the couch, sat beside her and took her hands in his. "It's these murders. I said the other day how I thought I was dealing with Satan himself, and I really believe that now more than ever. Annalisa, I've never encountered anything like this." He lifted her hands to his lips and kissed them softly. "I'm beat and I know it. I can't take it anymore. I need a break." He slid down on the couch and leaned over. His head was on her lap.

Annalisa gently stroked her fingers through his hair. "It's okay, honey," she whispered. "I love you. You're our hero. Quit. We can make it. Don't let them tear you down like this. It's not worth it." She put her lips to his ear. "I'm the luckiest woman in the world to have you. You're the most perfect and honorable man in the world, and I won't let them do this to you."

"I need time, baby – and space. I've got to think this through."

"Space?"

"I just need to get away and step back to look at things. That's all."

Annalisa's voice cracked. The tone of her voice reflected her surprise. "Is it Samanta and me? Michael, are you saying it's more than just work? It's us? Or, is it just me?" Tears flowed down her cheeks. She gasped for breath.

Mike sat up and scooted away from her. "Hell no, it's not you guys. It's me. All me, and that's the problem. I don't think about anyone but myself – me and that devil." He shook his head. "No baby, it's not you and Sam. I just need some time to myself, that's all."

"You say you need time and space. Michael, when you need that you cut us out of your life. That says we're part, maybe all, of your problem. You can't treat us like that. Why do you need to be alone? What about us? Where are we supposed to go?" Annalisa sat back. Her spine was erect; her arms folded across her chest. Mike saw her neck and face flush. Her lips were dry. The tears stopped. They had been married so many years that he could read all of her emotions. They changed in a few seconds from love and compassion to anger and disappointment. She was no longer the soothing lover, but the inquisitive wife who suspected his truthfulness.

He started to speak, but she interrupted. "Hold it right there. I don't normally drink, but I think I need one now."

Mike watched her walk toward the kitchen. The heels of her bare feet pounded into the hardwood floor. He listened as cupboard doors were opened and slammed shut. She returned in a few seconds with an empty glass and a bottle of Hiram Walker. She sat on the chair across from the couch and held up the bottle. "Best we can afford." She poured the glass half full, slammed the bottle down on the end table and put the glass to her mouth. "Here's to you, Mike." She chugged the whiskey, put the glass on the table and looked him in the eye. "Emily, right?"

"It's not what you think, damn it."

"Listen to me, you son-of-a-bitch." She poured another drink and gave a deep chortle. "I only drink an occasional glass of wine, but this one is on you, buddy boy."

"Emily," he blurted. "I mean, Annalisa. I'm sorry." He hung his head and looked at his shoes.

"I've loved you so much for so many years. How could you?" she demanded.

Mike opened his mouth to speak, but she held up her hand.

"Hear me out, Michael. Years ago I caused you a lot of trouble with the department. I screwed up our finances. I thought we were going to lose the house. My crappy bookkeeping almost cost us your job, and it was my fault. So now, as they say on the radio, here's the rest of the story.

"When all that mess was going on and I felt so terrible about what I did, one day I made lunch for you and went all the way to the station to take it to you. I even put a love note in the bag. I timed it perfectly – more perfect than I ever imagined. I walked in the north door just in time to see you and that woman detective going out the side door. I called your name, but you didn't hear me. I tried to catch you, but you were in such a hurry. I saw you go down the street, and how fitting it was. You stopped at the alley down the block and kissed her. Just like two tramps."

Tears flowed down Annalisa's cheeks. "But, I took the blame. It was my fault. I'd caused you so much trouble you just had to find some relief, someone to care for you." She shook her head and a little smile creased her lips. "I felt so guilty. You went to another woman because of what I did to you. I came home and cried. That's what I did. I accepted complete responsibility for your affair. My fault! Not yours."

Mike arose from the couch and stepped toward her.

"Stay away from me," she commanded. "Sit down and be truthful for a minute. Try telling your naïve, stupid little wife how many other women you've had. Go ahead; I'm a big girl. I can handle it."

"Her name was Della. We were both having trouble at home. We made love. That's all."

"Love? How about calling it like it was – you fucked her."

"Please, Annalisa. What I did was wrong, but I want to make everything right. I'm sorry. I promise."

"What happened tonight?"

"All I can say is it's over."

"Emily?"

"Yeah."

"My friend? My little girl's role model of a wonderful woman screwing her daddy? Yep, quite a lady." Annalisa smirked. "You know what they say, 'the lady is a tramp.'"

Annalisa picked up the whiskey bottle, looked at it and put it back down. "I can't drown my troubles. They're bigger than that, and I'm too much of a lady to try." She looked across the room at her husband and continued, "It's over, Mike. Not this time. It's not my fault. The two of you lied to me and our daughter over and over. I just can't accept that." She tucked her feet beneath her and tilted her head. "I'm curious. Did you tell her what a lousy lover I am?"

Mike began to weep softly. "No," he mumbled.

"Did she tell you how I asked her advice on how I could help you when you were down? Did she hold you in her arms and tell you how she loved you? Tell me, Mike. I need to know the truth."

He looked at her through his red, tear-filled eyes. "I hate her, Annalisa. I can't tell you how wrong I am and how wrong I've been. Please, give me a chance. I'll make it up to you, I promise."

"You did it in our bed, didn't you? Don't lie about it. Sam and I were in New Mexico when you did it. Want to know how I know? Because I'm a good detective. I learned from the best. I never put the bedspread on like that. Somebody else did, but not me. And, you didn't put the sheets on correctly when you were finished. They weren't lined up with the hem right. I knew it in my heart then, but I swallowed it. I wanted to trust you." She got up and walked across the room, put her hands on his shoulders and looked at him with her lost love. "I loved you with all my heart, but you lied. You cheated. To make it even worse, you did it in my own bed. You filthy son-of-a-bitch." She reached back and swung with all her might. Her open hand slapped across his face. "Get out of my house," she said softly. "Now! Go!"

Chapter Twelve

MIKE THREW HIS SUITCASES IN the trunk and pulled away from the curb. He didn't look back. An hour later he was in a room at America Host Inns. His bags were strewn on the bed and floor. He went to the bathroom and looked in the mirror. What he saw terrified him. Her red handprint was still emblazoned in his cheek. His hair was uncombed; his eyes red from crying; his normally dapper clothes rumpled and sweat stained like rags.

With a minimum of organization, he dumped the contents of the suitcases in the drawers, hung up the two suits he'd brought, and laid on the bed exhausted. His headache pounded. Nevertheless, his muscles gradually relaxed. His eyes grew heavy and he went to sleep with his clothes on.

Sunlight slipped through the draperies and massaged his eyes. He rolled over and looked at the clock. Nine o'clock. "Damn, I haven't slept this late in years," he uttered. He looked at the calendar on his watch. Saturday. *I've got the weekend to plan*, he thought. "Better be good," he mumbled.

He took off the clothes he'd slept in, showered and shaved, made a pot of complimentary coffee, got the newspaper from the hall by his door, and lay back on the bed.

He looked across the room at himself in the mirror – a lonesome man in an empty motel room wearing his underwear. "Pathetic," he muttered.

He whittled away the morning – coffee, television news, and the newspaper to help get his mind off his own problems, but it didn't. Finally, the time arrived. "Got to get on with it," he said to himself. Then he laughed. "I already need somebody to talk to. Just twelve hours and I'm lonesome." Tears flowed from his eyes. He choked and looked again in the mirror. "I'm sorry, babe. I really and truly am sorry."

He picked up the phone and dialed his home number. He dialed slowly, but froze when he reached the last digit. His will evaporated. "Not now. I can't do it. I won't do this to her," he said.

Once again he dialed. This time to Baldwin's home.

"Hello." John's voice was hollow.

"John, this is Mike. How are you?"

Baldwin's tone intensified. "Don't call me again." The receiver slammed in Mike's ear.

Mike bit his lip and his face flushed. He hit the redial with a vengeance.

Baldwin answered on the first ring. "I said I don't want to talk. Don't you understand English?"

"Damn it, don't hang up until you hear me out," Mike responded. "I didn't dig us into this mess any more than you did, so just calm down and listen to me. Do you understand?"

Mike waited. The phone was silent. Finally, Baldwin spoke. "Go ahead. Yeah, you're right. It's both of our mess. So what do you think?"

"We need to take our time, talk this through and use our heads. That's what I think. But, the other side of that coin is we can't just sit back and wait for her next move. What if she kills somebody else?"

"Okay, I agree with you so far. So what?"

"We need to talk. Can you take some time off? I know a good place - very private and no interference. We can spend a couple days and work through this."

"Probably," John replied. His tone was less than enthusiastic.

"I've got the perfect place in the mountains up in Colorado. Quiet and peaceful. We can work it out there."

The two detectives searched their calendars and arrived at a mutually acceptable time period - two weeks from today. They would meet in Chama, New Mexico and drive the remaining miles together to the San Juan Wilderness trailhead.

Mike paused to reflect on what they would do - hike into the mountains, absorb the peace and tranquility of the towering peaks, gather their thoughts and hopes, and refresh their spirits. Last, but not the least, they would develop a plan to bury forever their deeds of the past. "Freudian," he pondered.

#

Mike walked into his office on Monday morning as though his life was unchanged. He was neatly groomed. Well-pressed clothes, neatly combed hair, everything just as if Annalisa helped him get ready for work, something she did every day. As usual, he attended the briefing session and roll call, then went to his desk. The phone rang.

"Mike, John here. We've got a problem."

Palotti reached for his coffee cup and took a sip. It was lukewarm, but wet his mouth. He knew he needed it. "Go ahead. Give it to me."

"I got a call from Crime Analysis first thing today. She hit again. I don't have the case yet and probably won't for a few weeks when Homicide finishes up their work. Assuming they don't bust someone, it'll come to me." Mike waited patiently when Baldwin paused. "It was the 'K.' She abbreviated Oklahoma."

Mike started to interrupt. "But what about …?" John cut him off.

"It happened Wednesday night or early Thursday morning; probably thirty-six hours or more before we met with her. Cut his head off. Ring a bell with you?"

Mike leaned forward and put his elbows on the desk. His face reddened. His mouth was dry, cold coffee or not. He nodded his head. "You'll meet me?"

John's voice was resolute. "Chama. I'll be there."

Mike gave him directions where and what time to meet. In the meantime, they would carry on just like Emily had told them to do.

#

It was noon when Mike slipped into the parking lot at the Purple Coyote Café. The narrow gauge railroad across the street chugged away from the station. Smoke billowed from the stack and floated up between the tall pines of the mountain community. Early signs of fall whipped through the air – a brisk breeze, the scent of wet pine cones still evident from an early morning shower, the tourists' shorts and sandals replaced by Levis and boots.

Mike stepped onto the wooden planks of the boardwalk. He looked around. No sign of John's PT Cruiser. The lot was filled with an eclectic variety of the café's customers: Harleys, BMWs, Suburbans, a few rattle-trap pick-up trucks, plus the run-of-the-mill family cars. He walked through the swinging barroom doors and paused to let his eyes adjust to the dark interior.

He recalled Annalisa's observation about it – an elegant dive, and so it was. It never changed. Basically, it had been unchanged for one hundred years. Billy the Kid, Pat Garrett, and dozens of other lawmen and outlaws found solace in the lines and shadows of the Purple Coyote – or whatever name it was known by in frontier days. They were men with guns and were ready to use them. Times hadn't changed.

Mike worked his way through a mob of Bandido bikers, the "one percenters," and their old ladies. He called out a drink order to the bartender and found a booth next to the unisex bathroom door. He felt a twinge of relaxation and humor at the atmosphere of the place. It was a one-of-a-kind place. She was right – it was an elegant dive.

The barmaid smacked an iced mug of beer on the table. "Going to eat?" she asked. Mike looked her in the eyes. She was the ugliest thing he'd seen in a long time. He swallowed a chuckle. "Got to wait a few minutes. My buddy will be here, then we'll have something."

"Honey," she replied. "I can't let you hold down a table just to nurse a beer. I've got lots of customers to feed. You gotta eat or go."

The pleasure of the past few minutes evaporated. His face flushed. His eyes glared. His mind raced. He was not in a mood to joust with the bitch. He already had one to kill, and was in no mood to get screwed around by a slimy barmaid.

The waitress stepped back from the table. "Okay, mister. Don't get all riled up in a big sweat."

Mike looked past her. "See, no problem. He's here. Give us another beer."

John slipped through the crowd and scooted into the booth. "Nice joint you found for us." He nodded toward the bathroom door and the sound of the toilet flushing. "The ambiance is very unique. I can't recall ever being in such a fine eating and drinking establishment." He smiled at the waitress when she returned with a schooner of beer, then looked at Mike. "Just hope to hell your plan is better than your choice of restaurants." The two detectives laughed and clinked their glasses together.

"To a good end," Mike toasted.

"Okay, you got me all the way out here in the middle of the boondocks, so why are we going up in the mountains? We're already there."

"Simple. I've got a place I've been going to for years. My dad took me there as a kid. Annalisa and I honeymooned up there. I go back as often as I can. Wait until you get there. It's worth the hike. It's beautiful."

He hung his head, then looked at John. "She kicked me out." His head bowed as his vacant eyes stared into the remaining drops of beer in his glass. He swallowed hard. "She knows about Emily. Not everything, but she knows I was getting screwed." He shook his head in disbelief. "I can't believe how ignorant I was. What an ass.

"Anyhow, this is the place I need to go to and get my mind straight. We can do it together. It's where a person can get away and see things clearly." He nodded and smiled. "When we leave there, both of us will know in our hearts the right thing to do. I promise. It's the best place in the world for a person to see themselves honestly – the good and the bad, and we've got a fair share of both, wouldn't you say?"

They ordered their meals and ate in near silence, each with his mind filled with the burden that lay in wait for them: to right the wrong.

They paid their tab and worked their way once again through the crowd and out the swinging doors. Mike looked at his car. "Son-of-a-bitch," he uttered. He pointed to the back tire. "A friggin' flat. Just what I needed."

Mike opened the trunk, shuffled his packs and supplies, then pulled out the spare and jack and tossed them on the ground.

"C'mon, I'll help and we'll have it done in five minutes," John said. He pointed down the block and across the street. "There's a full service gas station. Not many of them left. We'll get it fixed and hit the road." He grabbed the jack, got on his knees and shoved it beneath the car. He leaned under the car to slip the jack into position. He rubbed his eyes and froze. "Mike, we've got a problem. Take a look."

Palotti crawled under the back bumper and scooted beneath his car. "What's up?"

John pointed to the cigarette pack size transponder and antennae affixed to the frame in front of the gas tank. "We've got company."

Mike stared at the device. She knew where they were and what they were doing. Stupid was not one of her traits.

"Don't touch it. Leave it as it is. Let's get this flat fixed and get on with our business." He paused and looked at the antennae spitting out to some satellite their precise longitude and latitude. "That bitch."

Minutes later they tossed the flat tire into the trunk. Mike looked around the parking lot. "Where's your toy?"

John gave a soft chuckle. "Maybe a little good luck for us. I told my brother-in-law I was going to the mountains for a few days." He pointed to the four-wheel-drive pick-up truck at the far end of the parking lot. "He thought I should drive a truck up here, so we swapped rides before I left town. If she put one on my car, and I assume she did, she's shit out of luck. Danny is in Wichita to see his and Lisa's mom."

The two detectives laughed. "Dumb luck, but we'll take it any way we can get it," Mike commented.

"Yep, she won't have any idea we're together. Maybe it's her turn to be so full of herself and cocky that she slips up. I don't know if you believe in omens, but this sure is a good one," Baldwin quipped.

#

The sun slipped over the craggy, snow-capped peaks as the two men passed between the boulders and reached the open grassland of Second Meadow. Less than one hundred yards upstream, a bald eagle swept with deadly precision from the treetops and snatched a trout feeding on the surface.

A soft but steady breeze sent a chill up Mike's spine. He inhaled deeply, closed his eyes, and whispered into the wind. "I love this place. I know it in my heart. We're going to come out okay." He opened his eyes, glanced around, and pointed to a grassy area between a tall pine tree and the monoliths that formed the lower side of the closest hill. "We'll pitch our tents around there. Just find yourself a flat place and let's call this home for a couple days."

The men busied themselves scraping away twigs and branches that were blown down from the trees, tossed aside a few rocks, opened the straps on their packs and spread their tents out on the grass. In a matter of minutes, their tents were pitched and a few rocks gathered together to form a fire circle.

Mike stepped back and admired their handiwork. Purple shadows reached down from the mountaintops and slipped over the campsite. He turned his collar up to ward off the now icy breeze.

"We're set, *amigo*. A good fire, a little of our dehydrated chicken and noodles, and a sip of Scotch is all we need." He reached in his pack and produced the leather-bound flask.

"Glenlivet. Why not? We've got some hard work ahead, but we've done enough for one day."

"That hike up here about did me in," Baldwin joked. "You kept saying we were almost there, but crap, my heart pounded like a jackhammer. No work for me tonight and no booze either. It'll kill me at this altitude. Speaking of altitude, I can hardly breathe. How high up are we?"

"Over ten-thousand feet."

John wiped his brow and sat down in front of his tent. "Dinner's on you. I'm sitting right here and let you fix it, then I'm crawling through this little flap and going to sleep."

#

Mike crawled out of his tent at the first chirp of the birds. The eastern horizon was brightening to a golden hue. He spotted a black bear casually loping across the meadow beyond the creek. *It's a new day*, he thought, *fresh and new, and there's no looking back.* He sipped a drink from his canteen and looked up to the rock – the point he'd rested on so many times before. It was the place where he could clear his mind and gather his thoughts. He reached into the tent, grabbed his boots and put them on. John was snoring, dead to the world.

Half an hour later he was sitting on the ledge. His feet dangled over the vast openness between him and the meadow below. He scanned the ridges across the valley. The trees swayed gently to the touch of the air as it swept down the mountain. The silver ponderosa leaves shimmered like so many mirrors catching the sunlight and throwing it back. The blue sky was painted with a broad swath of high-level clouds. He reminisced back to his days in college and his futile attempt to study meteorology. It was too much math in spite of his interest, so he changed majors to Public Administration.

Nevertheless, he loved the clouds. The high-level ones across the valley were at least 20,000 feet high. They were like a million tiny prisms reflecting the glow of the morning sun. A smile swept across his face. "I'm okay," he said to no one. He nodded in self-approval. "We'll get through this and get on with life. I'll win her back. I'll change. I'll quit the department. I'll do whatever I have to do, but I can do it."

His slowly lowered his gaze from the clouds down to the treetops and on to the meadow. The stream's current was strong but smooth. The water was flat. The world was the way God intended it to be.

The camp remained silent. John was still sleeping, but it was time to set into motion that which they came to do. Yes, they were here to find peace, but more important, to create a plan – a plan to rid the world of Emily Morgan.

The time was at hand.

Chapter Thirteen

THEY CLEANED UP THE CAMP and sealed their food and trash in zip-lock bags in their backpacks. Mike put on his pack and hung John's loosely over his elbow. He walked to the water's edge, paused a moment, then bounded over the rocks until he reached the other side. The water was no more than a couple feet deep, but was swift and cold; not a happy thought to fall into it fully dressed.

He looked back at John. "Still got my balance 'cause I sure as hell didn't want to take a dip this early in the morning," he joked. He dropped the packs on the ground and pulled a rope from the pack, then walked a few yards uphill to a grove of Aspen trees. He scanned them with a quick measure and found just the right one – sturdy and tall, but with a strong protruding branch. He ran the rope through the pack straps, then tossed it over the branch and hoisted the packs high enough to be clear of any marauding animals.

"No since tempting the bears. It's far enough out on that limb to be out of their reach," Mike commented. He looked around for a smooth rock to use as a starting point to return to the campsite. He planted his boot firmly, then hop-scotched from rock-to-rock as he made his way across the creek.

John spread his poncho on the ground and lay back, Huck Finn style, with a blade of grass between his teeth. He glanced at Mike after he'd successfully landed with a hearty thump on dry ground, then looked up to the clouds.

John's voice was shallow. It echoed his melancholy. "I didn't sleep much last night, and not because I was afraid a bear would want me for his midnight snack. It's her. I can't kill her. As much as I hate everything about her, it was a love story. She was a gift from God for my son and me." He paused and caught his breath. "I'm not a murderer. I thought about it. I prayed about it. I just can't kill someone, even a devil like her." He didn't look at Mike to see his reaction. He'd said what he wanted to say.

Mike sipped from his canteen. He looked across the meadow, but didn't look at John when he spoke. "Go ahead. What or how do you want to handle this?" He turned slowly and looked at John. "I'm starved for another answer – some solution, but I don't see it. You've got to come up with something. We simply can't let her skate. She's a mad-dog killer. She's a mean, cold, calculating bitch. What's to make us think she'll keep her promise that she's done killing? She's a damned hypocrite on top of everything else, so why should we start trusting her now?"

Baldwin responded. "Trust her? No, I don't trust her. I don't believe a word she says." He spit out the blade of grass, rolled over on his side and propped his head on his hand. "Think about this. She's a liar, right?"

"Right," Mike replied.

"She tells us to get on with life, but she sticks transponders under our cars. You know why she did that?" He continued before Mike could respond. "Because she doesn't know what we'll do. She may think she's smart, and to an extent she is, but the bottom line is she has no idea what we'll do. She's worried. She may not show it, but deep down inside she knows we're up to something and she doesn't have the slightest idea what it might be."

"Neither do we," Mike replied.

John continued, "Yeah, but she doesn't know that. So, let's take this one small step at a time." He sat up and crossed his legs. "Let's take what we know, but what she doesn't. First, the fact we're here together. It's very unlikely she knows it. Did you ever talk to her about this place?"

Mike nodded in agreement. "I love this place. Sure, I told her about it."

"So, you being here is completely in character, at least in her mind," John interjected. "She thinks you're fishing at your great escape. She figures you're thinking about the fix you're in, but she doesn't know I'm here. The bitch thinks I'm in Wichita, and she sure as hell heard me talk more than once about going up there. Oh yeah, she's sitting back right now thinking we've gone different directions, maybe have gotten pissed at each other and not even speaking." He gave a slight, self-assured chuckle. "Oh yeah, she's starting to make mistakes and it's just a matter of time. Our day will come. Plus, one other thing. You said you know her alarm code, right?"

"0-2-7-4," Mike responded.

"So that means we can get into her house and she won't know about it. There's another strike on her."

"Okay, we're on a roll," Mike responded. "It's not a great big one, but on a roll. Now you've got me thinking. I've got a buddy with Transportation Security at the airport. He can scan any airlines and get their passenger manifest – anybody, anytime. We can know when she's out of town and what her ticket shows when she's coming back." A hint of confidence was in his smile. "When she's gone, I can pick her locks, turn off her alarm, and take a good look-see through the house. It may take more than one trip, but I'll get through every inch of it. I'll find every one of her dirty little secrets. Of course, I'll have to do something with her friggin' voodoo cameras."

"Okay, let's make a mental list," John responded. "Don't put any of this in writing, even for our own sake. We can't take a chance of a scrap of paper getting caught up in a summons or being left around where somebody might find it. Let's take our time, lay out a preliminary plan, work in some logistics and take it from there. We'll have to play it slowly and carefully. We can't be in a hurry. We have to take our time, be thoughtful, and sure as hell don't get too impressed with our own self-confidence. Let's be cool, not like when we got into this mess."

"I agree. We screwed up like Hogan's goat," Mike said. "Not this time. Now it's her turn. When she lets her guard down, we'll move, whatever that means."

"Are you agreeing not to kill her? To work something else out?" John inquired.

"No," Mike replied, "I'm not ready to make that leap yet. I think we'll end up taking her out, but I'm all ears to see if there's another way." He shook his head in the negative. "It may appear I *want* to kill her," he emphasized, "but that's not the case. I want to see something else, but I think she's so evil the only way we can resolve this is to snuff her. Anyhow, I agree with you that we need to get into her house and do some intelligence gathering."

A cocky smirk creased his lips. "Know your enemy. Know more about them than they know about you. That's one of the basic rules, and frankly we don't know squat about her. She fed us such a crock and we fell for it. No wonder she thinks we're stupid."

He picked up a rock and threw it into the stream. Ripples flowed out in concentric circles growing larger and larger. A frog jumped out of the overhanging grass and into the water. "That's a metaphor," he said. "I did something by surprise and caused a ripple. The frog was caught off guard and jumped at nothing. That's what we need – to see her jump when she's caught unprepared." He paused. "When she does, we have to be ready to move, to do whatever it is we're going to do."

He stretched, got up and walked to the streambed. The sun was high in the sky and the thin mountain air was sweet and fresh. He turned and looked at John. "So what happens after we know everything about her? What do we do then?"

"Follow our own rule," John replied, "which starts with taking our time and not hurrying. Take it one step at a time. When we're satisfied we know everything there is to know, we sit down together and update our plan – just so we're playing the same game. I want us to get all the way around and land on Boardwalk, but I know every play is a throw of the dice; there's a Go to Jail, a Luxury Tax, Chances. Not every roll is perfect. There're risks. Let's just take it one roll at a time. Give it a whirl and we'll find a way."

"But if we don't, are you ready to kill her? Can you keep that in your mind?"

John exhaled strongly and looked at the ground. "No, Mike. I can't kill her, even if it cost me everything. I just can't do something like that. Look," he implored, "I'm raising a son. I go to church. I took an oath of office. I've messed up bad enough as it is, but I'm not going to add to it."

Mike responded, "Then one other thing. If we play the game like you said and it doesn't pan out – if I kill her, can you keep your mouth shut? Can you take our secret to your grave?"

"Son-of-a-bitch, Mike. Let's don't go there. It's too early. We can cross that bridge if we come to it. Right now, let's table any conversation about murder. Let's do what we have to do and see where it takes us. No more. Just that for now. Okay?"

Mike took slow, thoughtful steps away from the stream. He looked at his own feet. His hands were on his hips. Slowly, he extended his right hand. "Okay. I agree for now. We learn everything we can and put our heads together to see where it takes us. In the meantime, we don't mention popping a cap into her brain, which I can do without a moment's hesitation, but that's it for now. Deal?"

The two men shook hands. "Partner," John said softly. "Remember the first time we called each other that? We had no idea what we were getting into."

"What to know something else? We still don't," Mike replied.

"Let's change the subject a little bit. You haven't mentioned your wife. What happened? How much does she know?"

"She knows I was screwing her friend. It doesn't get much worse than that."

"When did she find out?"

Mike's eyes watered and he allowed himself to crumple on the poncho beside John. "She's suspected something for a while. That night after we left the Ipanema, I broke down right in front of her. I crashed hard. I wanted to die, and I deserved every bit of it. I threw everything away – my wife, my daughter – all for a gorgeous piece of ass."

"Did you tell her everything?"

"Not quite. Not about Emily being the killer. Thank God I didn't go that far. It was bad enough as it was. Anyhow, she slapped my face and told me to go. Both the women I loved kicked me out in a time period of an hour or two. Talk about having my ego crushed. I've never felt so empty."

"Do you have any chance to reconcile?" John asked.

"I know I'm going to try. I just pray she'll forgive me and take me back." He shrugged his shoulders. "I don't have a lot of faith she'll do it. This is twice she's caught me. Hell, I don't deserve her, but I'm sure going to try."

"You're a dichotomy, Mike. Listen to what you've said in the last couple minutes. You pray to God that Annalisa will take you back, but you also say you're ready to put a bullet in Emily's brain. Doesn't that strike you as being kind of weird? You want God to help you do one thing and you want to kill somebody."

"Maybe I'm a head case."

"Yeah, you're that, too. Both of us are." John put his hand on Mike's shoulder. "You can't go north and south at the same time. You have to make a decision, your wife and kid, or kill the bitch and live with it ... if you get away with it. It's got to be one or the other, but not both. It just doesn't fly." He pointed up the hill to Mike's ledge and pointed. "Do a lot of thinking up there?"

Mike nodded and held back his tears. His young friend and partner was giving him advice, and he was right.

"You've got the rest of the day. Why don't you take the climb?"

#

The afternoon passed slowly. John sat along the stream and watched the fish dart from place to place, and then he found a patch of soft, cool grass beneath a tree where he whiled away the day.

Mike spent the long, sunny afternoon propped against a boulder on his ledge, his feet dangling over the precipice. He watched the distant clouds sweep slowly over the mountaintop. Shadows grew long across the meadow. The storm clouds gathered over the peaks. He was running out of time. The rain was coming. The cool outflow of wind gave him his final warning. He scurried down the hillside and looked back to see his ledge bathed in the driving rain. A few large drops splashed onto their tents, portending the coming deluge. He raced the final few yards, opened the flaps to John's tent and slipped in as the storm hit.

John was the first to speak. "I saw it coming and just made it. I was wondering if you'd get back in time."

"My day was full of metaphors. The frog jumped at nothing, and our sweet little Emily will do the same thing. Then, I sat up there and watched the storm in the high country. I was hoping it would go across the valley 'cause I wanted more time to think about my alternatives." He bit his lip and looked in thought at the top of the tent. "I had an answer, but I wanted more time to think about it, to see if I was missing something. Damn, it was just like that cloud was reading my mind. It swung around and came right toward me. I tell you, John, somebody was telling me I had my answer and to get over it." He laughed. "Then, to make sure I didn't spend any more time up there, the rain came straight at me. Yeah, God or something – maybe one of your omens – anyway, here I am and I'm sticking with it. No more second guessing. I won't kill her if I can find any other way out." He bowed his head. "I've got to swallow my pride and get on with life. We'll see what we can do with her, but murder isn't in the cards now."

John draped his arm over Palotti's shoulder. "Thanks. It'll come out okay. It just has to. Don't ask me how, but it will."

#

The night was pitch black before the rain subsided. Clouds hung heavy over the meadow. John and Mike crawled out of the tent, pulling their butane stove behind them. Within minutes, they were eating their dehydrated spaghetti and meat sauce, and chasing it with fresh rainwater from the cups they left outside.

Mike looked across the faint glow of the flame. John's unshaven face was nearly obscured in the dim light. A touch of wind made the flame dance, almost go out, and then come back to life. "Were you going to marry her?" He saw the whites of John's eye as he looked at him.

"I really wanted to. We hadn't talked about it, but I loved her so much and she loved me. At least I thought so. Damn, she'd make a great mom for Jonah and a perfect wife for me. I thought I could never replace Lisa, not until I met Emily. Then I knew she was the one."

He looked into the tiny flame that reflected the tears in his eyes. "That bitch. How could anyone be so evil? She sang bedtime songs to my little boy; she talked about a woman's love for a child; and, I let the bitch screw me with my kid right there beside us."

Mike gathered a few dry sticks and put them in the fire ring, then dumped a bit of fuel on them. He lit the fire, and both of them put their hands over it to warm themselves. They were quiet for a few minutes before Mike spoke.

"I think she made another mistake. Listen and see how this sounds. I came home and found her in the bathtub, and then we made love on the bed. I didn't like it at first, but she made a little joke that I had to learn to take risks. That's what she said, 'risks make it more fun.' Did she say anything like that to you?"

"Yeah, in fact she did – twice. After she put Jonah to bed and sang to him, the next thing I knew she was undressed and lying on the floor beside him. I about croaked, but she gave that cute little laugh of hers and said something about the risk. Like a fool, I screwed her right there. Damn, I was scared, but I did it anyway. Afterward, we were getting dressed and she made a comment about how the risk made it so much more fun, and I agreed with her. On the one hand I was petrified, and on the other it was the best sex I've ever had.

"It was the same thing that night at the office. Talk about stupid, but I let her talk me into it. I admit it was one hell of a sexual experience. Son-of-a-bitch, she taped both of them." He shook his head. "I can't believe how stupid I was. I did things with her I'd never do, and I let her talk me into it. Sure, it's my fault, but I let her challenge me with the risk and I took it. I fell for her body cum laude."

"There's her mistake," Mike commanded. "She takes risks and bets they'll come through. She's a lousy gambler and likes to play it safe. No 'Hard Eights' for her. No sir, she'll bet the 'Come Line' and protect her money. That's what she did with us. She gambled and bet we'd fall in line. Like a couple of jerks, we obliged. She knew her money was pretty safe; it wasn't much of a gamble for her. That's her mistake. She wants to make us think she's a risk taker, but she's not. She was a liar and we were gullible. How'd you say that? 'Body cum laude?'"

He put another stick on the fire and poked the ashes. The flames flickered brightly. "That's her mistake. We were stupid, but she's not really a risk taker. She placed a couple pretty safe bets and we fell in like two country bumpkins. Now it's our turn. She doesn't figure two idiots like us can match her intelligence. She made us think she was the perfect risk-taker and covered her bets, but we're going to find our dear Emily is full of crap. Her self-proclaiming perfect crimes are going to eat her alive." He paused and took a deep breath. "Now all we have to do is figure it out and do it."

#

The sky was clear in the morning sun. Once again, Mike saw the black bear across the meadow slowly meandering through the grass, heading back up into the high country. A lone eagle was perched majestically on the top of a tree on the ridge behind their camp. One small, single cloud drifted in the otherwise crystal blue sky. It was a perfect start to the day. Mike felt self-assured. He was comfortable with his decision and if there were omens, the splendor of the day was a good sign.

Three hours after leaving camp they crossed the wooden foot-bridge, climbed the last incline, and found their cars covered with dew and needles from the overnight rain.

"What about the GPS?" John asked.

Mike got down on his knees and peeked beneath his car. "Still here and I'm going to leave it there. The more she thinks she knows means the less she actually knows. Let her track our cars. So long as we know it, then it can only work to our advantage."

John took a precautionary look under his truck, then tossed his camping gear into the bed. He looked at Mike as he stuffed his pack and tent into his trunk. "What are you going to do?"

Mike gave a soft chuckle, smiled his smirky little grin, and replied. "I'll get to Amarillo tonight, then hit Big D tomorrow. I'll be careful, but when the time is right, I'll get inside her place. Curiosity will be killing you, but when I have something I'll touch base. What about you?"

"I'll drive straight through and be back to work tomorrow. I'll play it day-by-day. Stay in touch."

The two men stood in the muddy parking lot, their clothes covered with the grunge of the backcountry. They were silent, looking at each other, but alone with their thoughts. The moments crawled by awkwardly. John was the first to speak. "I'll say my prayers for both of us."

"Thanks, we'll need it. I've never been much of a church guy, but I might give it a try. Anyhow, I'll keep you posted." He started toward his car door and then turned back abruptly. "There's one other thing. I know she'll keep up her game and call us. She might even drop by the office. We've just got to be cool. Let her enjoy her self-confidence, but don't let on to anything."

"What about if she asks if we've been talking?" John asked.

"Just keep it business. Sure, we talked, but not about her. Let her think she won and beat the crap out of us. We're just two jerks who'll make a big show out of trying to catch the killer. That's all. We'll acknowledge she beat us and we're going on with life, just like she told us to do."

"And if she doesn't bite?"

Mike laughed. "Hey, I'm the one for putting a bullet in her brain."

#

Mike's morning in-basket was full – mainly the bureaucratic flood of reports, acknowledgements, late notices, upcoming meetings, and the never-ending United Appeal pledge card. Buried in the mess was a "While You Were Out" call sheet. Ms. Morgan called Saturday morning, the same day he got to Chama. "Covering her bases," he muttered. She knew what the GPS showed, but she doubled back to check to be sure he wasn't in the office. The duty officer's scrawled note gave her what she wanted: "Told her you were out and be back Wednesday and would call her back."

Mike smiled confidently, folded the note and put it in his breast pocket. "Score one for the good guys," he whispered. He walked casually to the coffee pot and filled his cup. It was good this time of morning – hot, fresh and flavorful. He felt good. The phone was ringing when he got back to his desk. "Detective Palotti speaking."

"Made it back okay?" John asked.

"Sure did, and guess who called Saturday looking for me?"

Laughter filled his ear. "She called here, too. They told her I was off and would be back yesterday. I'm a little uncomfortable that we both were gone at the same time, but her GPS showed us hundreds of miles apart. I checked my car when I got it back and sure enough, there it is. Anyhow, I just got off the phone with her. Really coy. Just playing her game. I told her I took Jonah to his grandmother's house and I think she believes it. Shot the breeze just like old times, and that was it. Mike ..." There was a long pause. "I've got to tell you, it was hard talking to her. I used to work undercover and was pretty good with my bullshit. I had to dig deep to do it with her, but I did it and think it worked okay."

"Thanks for letting me know," Mike said. "I'll stay in touch."

He busied himself sorting and prioritizing his backlog. After a few minutes, Angie, the secretary, called him on the intercom. "Visitor to see you. Ms. Morgan."

Mike stopped cold. He thought he was ready, but he wasn't, not this soon or this early in the morning. "Detective Palotti, you have a visitor," Angie repeated.

He flicked the microphone button and responded. "Be right there. Give me a couple minutes." His face flushed. He walked to the bathroom and looked in the mirror. His neck and face showed his anguish. He splashed water on his face, put his hand under the faucet, took a swig and rinsed his mouth. He felt like a dog slurping in the toilet bowl. He was dry. Seconds ticked by slowly. He waited until he felt he was in control of his emotions, then walked to the door, swung it open, and saw her sitting in a straight-back chair like a patient waiting to see the doctor. She was thumbing restlessly through an old magazine. She looked up at the movement.

"Good morning, sir," she said. She stood, walked slowly across the room and extended her hand. "Thank you for seeing me. I got into a time crunch. Sorry I didn't have an opportunity to call ahead."

"No problem. I was just sorting some paperwork. Why don't we go into the conference room?" He led her to the same room where he'd met her that fateful day so long ago – or not so long. Time was jumbled.

Emily seated herself in the same chair where she was that day. She had a plan. He would just have to see where it went, but he was ready.

"I'm working, Miss Morgan. I've got a crazy killer to catch and don't have time for your phoniness, so you can just cut it out. Do you have business? If not, you can go," he commanded.

"Mike, I know you won't believe me. All I ask is that you hear me out, nothing more."

"You're right. I don't believe you, so why waste our time?"

"Because I didn't kill anyone – not one person. Never." Her faced reddened.

Mike detected resoluteness in her voice.

"Everything I've been involved in was orchestrated by John Baldwin." She paused, looked down at the floor, took a deep breath and looked him in the eyes.

He sat straight in the chair, almost statuesque. His breathing was imperceptible. He glared at her.

"Everything," she whispered. "That is, until I fell in love with you." She reached into her purse for a tissue, then dabbed a single tear that flowed over her cheek. The room fell silent, each waiting for the other. Finally, Emily continued, "I don't think he's a killer, but somehow he's mixed up in it. It's a game with him. Just like you and me. We're his pawns in a macabre chess game. When he's ready, he'll sacrifice both of us."

She rose and stood directly in front of Mike. "I can't sit here in the middle of the police station and talk like this. It's hard enough as it is." She reached in her purse, pulled out a key and placed it on the table in front of him.

"My door key. I'll wait – forever if I have to."

"You really think I'll fall for this?"

She offered a heartbreaking smile. "It's time for us to be perfectly honest with each other. Our lives depend on it." She stepped past him, stopped and looked back over her shoulder. "I love you and I trust you. The cameras are gone. He took them out. It'll just be the two of us. Talk, Mike. That's all we'll do."

He looked at the key, then reached out slowly and picked it up. He looked at her, paused for a moment's reflection, and then slipped it into his pocket.

Chapter Fourteen

IT WAS MID-AFTERNOON. HIS headache was back. He sat at his desk massaging his temples and reading summaries of some of the more notorious serial killers who struck in the last twenty years – the Lieutenant's brainstorm. He didn't know what he was looking for other than to find some insight into those sick personalities. Why did people kill so many others? What did they hope to gain?

His own mind was jumbled. She'd confessed, then turned on Baldwin and laid it at his feet. What was the truth? Did the truth matter? Did anyone really care? *Am I going crazy? It can't get any worse than this*, he thought.

"Mike, you have a visitor." It was Angie again on the intercom.

He shoved back from his desk, disgusted. He wasn't in the mood to talk to anyone. The door flung open when he hit it with his open hand. A uniformed process server sat across the room. He looked at Mike and rose from his seat. His expression was a heartless stare. He looked right through Mike. He'd done it to hundreds of other people over his career and this was no different.

"Michael Palotti?" he asked as he reached out with an envelope in his hand.

Mike took the envelope. "Can I help you?"

"No sir. Consider yourself served." The man spun on his heels and walked out.

Mike turned slowly and walked toward his desk, staring blanking at the official Dallas County summons. Rickey was coming toward his desk from the parking lot.

"You okay, *amigo*? You're white as a ghost."

Mike's lips trembled. He looked at Rickey, then turned abruptly and walked to the restroom. It wasn't necessary to open the envelope. He knew what was in it. He stood before the mirror and looked at his reflection, yet saw nothing. He was an empty shell.

Rickey came in and put his hand on Mike's shoulder. He spoke softly. "I'm your friend. What can I do for you?" He looked at Mike in the mirror. "It's shown for a while, but now I'm worried about you. Tell me about it. You can't keep going like this. You've got to have help. You need it now. What about Annalisa? Is everything okay?"

Tears flowed from Mike's eyes. His gasped for breath, leaned on the basin and cried. "I'm a mess, Rick, ol' buddy." His voice faltered. He continued. "A total mess and it's my fault. I screwed up as bad as a guy can do." He straightened up, looked again at his reflection and managed a weak smile. "Thanks for being there. I appreciate it." He took a deep breath and looked at the envelope.

Rickey's eyes followed Mike's to the notice from the court. "You guys getting a divorce?"

Mike didn't answer. He stepped across the room and sat on the bench against the wall. Rickey sat beside him and watched while Mike opened the envelope –

"You are commanded to appear in this court within twelve days after service of this summons to answer to the petition for divorce from Annalisa Palotti. Petitioner demands custody of the only child of this marriage, Samanta Palotti. Furthermore, said petitioner demands fifty percent of all assets held by either or both parties to this marriage, and demands fair and reasonable support of said child until she reaches the age of eighteen years.

The court orders defendant Michal Palotti not to go within two-hundred feet of petitioner, not to make telephone contact, nor communicate with petitioner or the child, Samanta, in any manner whatsoever."

Mike bowed his head and held the summons to his breast. "I'm so sorry, Rick. I was such a fool, a complete bastard."

"You've got to get a lawyer. Don't just fold your cards and give up, Mike. That's not you. You've got to win her back. Beg her, plead. Do something, but don't quit."

Mike walked to the basin and once again stared at himself. He didn't like what he saw. Looking at Rickey in the mirror, he spoke, though his voice was nearly inaudible. "Tell the Sarge I got sick and had to go home." He nodded his head and offered a weak smile. "It's not a lie – never was a greater truth told than that."

#

Mike walked to his car in the parking lot and as it had become a habit, he checked the undercarriage. It was still there.

He was half-way to his apartment when he remembered her key.

She couldn't have known, yet she was there when he needed her most. It was a coincidence, nothing more than that, but fortuitous nevertheless.

He exited the Stemmon's Freeway, made a U-turn and drove toward Highland Park. Fifteen minutes later, he slowed, turned onto her block and saw her stooped over, deadheading the flowers in her front yard. She didn't see him as he drove past. She looked so wholesome and All-American – flowered Capri pants, a pink t-shirt, white jogging shoes and a baseball cap with her hair pulled back into a ponytail flowing from beneath it.

He went to the corner, made another U-turn and pulled to the curb in front of her house. She turned and looked at the sound of the car. She smiled and waved, then tucked her garden tools into her apron pockets. His taut muscles relaxed. He opened the car door and his headache disappeared.

She was magic. Mike was conscious of a bona fide smile creasing his face. He was happy for the first time in a long time.

"Michael ..."she paused. Her voice kissed his ears like music. "Michael," she repeated, "I hoped you'd come." She turned toward the house. "Won't you come in?" she asked as she stepped onto the porch. He followed her to the door and stopped. She stepped inside and looked back at him. "It's okay. I promise. Everything's gone." She extended her hand and he took it, then followed her to the living room.

"Don't be afraid. It's all gone. He has everything, the cameras and listening devices. They were his and he got them all."

He noticed that only one television set remained. She caught his eye looking where the other one was located. "That was his, too. Gone! I've got my house again."

Mike lowered himself into the chair where he sat that dismal night, the night his world came to an end.

"Off duty?" she asked.

"I'm on sick leave. I needed the afternoon off after the day I've had."

"Honey," she said, "before we go any further, I've got to tell you one thing. It's more important than Baldwin, even more important than those innocent people who were murdered." She walked across the room and sat in the same chair as that auspicious night. She curled her feet beneath her, reached over and turned on a lamp. "Would you?" she asked when she pointed to the lamp beside his chair. "We don't need any mood lighting today," she joked.

Mike turned on the lamp. The room was flooded with light.

"Right. No sweet nothings today. Tell me, what is it?"

"I called Annalisa to set up a lunch date a couple weeks after Baldwin's encore here in this room. I guess I was stupid. I didn't think she knew about us. Mike, I truly love your family – and you. I never planned something like this mess we're in. Anyhow, as soon as she heard my voice ..." Emily began to cry. Her lips trembled. She bit her lower lip as she tried to calm herself. Finally, she bolted from her chair in tears.

Mike sat silently. Once again, he felt like an empty shell. Everybody he touched suffered for having known him. Minutes crawled by. The grandfather clock chimed the hour. Somewhere in the distance a siren droned. He was alone – so in love, yet so alone.

After what seemed like an eternity, Emily returned to her chair. She had discarded her cap and apron, combed her hair and freshened her lipstick. She was gorgeous.

She blurted it out. "She screamed it at me, 'You fucked my husband. You stole him from his daughter and me. You can burn in hell. Don't ever call here again.' Then she slammed the phone down. Oh Mike, I cried so hard. I felt horrible. I still do. I can't believe what I did." She paused and looked at him. Her eyes were moist, her lips pouting, her chin trembling. "Baldwin caused this whole thing, but the worst part is I fell in love with you. What a horrible sin, yet what an honor: to love a man like you."

Mike leaned forward and rested his elbows on his knees. "I don't know whether to kiss you or kill you. One side of me says you're the biggest liar in the world, and a serial murderer on top of that. The other side says we both got used by an expert and our salvation will come from our love for one another." He cocked his head. "Now to add to it, my wife served me with divorce papers today."

"I'm so sorry. Poor thing," she whispered as she rose from her chair and went to him. She sat on the floor at his feet. "Michael, I'm so sorry. What can I do?" She stroked his hands softly.

"Nothing. I'm not going to contest it. She deserves her break from me." He took her hands in his. "Whether I let Baldwin or you set me up isn't important. What I did, I did. Nobody put a gun to my head."

Emily leaned forward and kissed his hands. "Michael, I love you. I can't stand to see you in this pain. Please, let me help."

He continued. "I know lots of lawyers – been a cop for too many years not to have one or two indebted to me. I'll get through it. All I want is visitation for Sam. Otherwise, she wants half of everything.

That's fair. I can live with it. I've got an apartment and I'm getting settled in."

"Please let me help with something. You can't just stand there alone and let the world beat you up. I've got money. I can do something."

"How about a Scotch?" he joked

#

Two drinks later, Mike was still seated in the same chair. Emily was in the kitchen. He listened to the sounds of the cupboard doors opening and closing, the silverware being set out, the soft sound of water being poured. It was music to his ears – the sounds of a family at home.

"Late lunch, Detective Palotti?" she asked when she peeked around the corner of the door. Mike walked to the breakfast nook and paused, flooded by memories. She took his hand. "We'll get through this. I'll stand beside you, I promise."

The meal was nothing like the first time they'd shared food and drinks together. It was a simple lunch of sandwiches, chips and soft drinks – nothing gourmet. They ate without chit-chat, no smiles or giggles, no sensual touches or gestures. To Mike, it was one of the more awkward times of his life. He couldn't talk. Thoughts and words would not come together in a reasonable manner. That, he decided, was precisely the problem. This time with her was anything but reasonable. His emotions were divided – he hated her and loved her. He finished the last bite of his sandwich, sipped the Diet Coke she served him in the can, and pushed back from the table.

"Emily, I'm still a detective, and you're the prime suspect in these murders. We can't sit here and pretend like nothing happened. A lot happened, and you owe me one hell of an explanation." He wiped his lips on a paper napkin – no soft linen this time.

"Where do you want me to start?" she responded as she wadded her napkin and tossed it unceremoniously onto her plate.

"John," he demanded. "You said this is his – what did you call it? A macabre game?"

"Yeah, that's exactly what I said," she fired back. Her brow furrowed. Her lips pursed.

He shot back. "No need for me to read your Miranda rights to you. I think we're long beyond that point, so go ahead. I'm all ears."

Emily pushed back from the table and got up. "I'll make us some coffee. I think we'll be here for a while."

Mike watched her go to the kitchen. It was nothing like the other times. There was no silent waltz as she prepared a meal and served it with a passionate flair out of Hollywood. This was a routine part of daily life – spoon the grounds into the filter, measure the water in the pot, and carefully pour it to the exact measurement on the side of the coffee maker. It was life without any semblance of sensuality. She could pass for Maude, the truck stop waitress. She stood impatiently at the counter, taping her fingernails on the granite in a monotonous tic-tack while the coffee dripped. She ignored him.

The minutes were interminable to Mike. He wanted not just to hear her explanation, but to give her a first-class interrogation. He was primed and ready, and she was killing time – making up her story, he knew.

Finally, she brought two cups. Mike tilted it to his lips and paused to savor the fresh aroma. It was good.

She pulled up her chair, sat down and leaned her elbows on the table. "Take notes if you want. I'm not afraid. You're a cop and you think I killed some people, so take your best shot; get me in your sights and shoot. Anyway, here's what happened.

"There's a part of me you never met; I'll admit that much. However, there's a part of John Baldwin you didn't meet either. Did he ever tell you he worked undercover?"

"Yeah, he mentioned it."

"And did he tell you what he did?"

"I assumed drugs. That's what most cops do when the go UC."

Emily cocked her head and gave him a condescending smile. "Wasn't that how all this got started? Remember? I was studying how cops communicate, if they talk to each other at all?"

Mike nodded in agreement and sipped his coffee.

"The two of you didn't communicate very well, so I'll tell you what he did – undercover white-collar crime. Not narcotics. Furthermore, do you want to know where and how we met?" She didn't wait for him to answer. "He got me cold in a fraud case. It was the Oklahoma version of White Water where the Clintons got into so much deep shit. Except, of course, I didn't have the political pull of the White House, so I was going to have to take the fall." She stopped and lifted the coffee cup, then looked across the rim as she raised it to her lips.

Mike looked into her eyes. He'd seen the look before – lots of times. They all look like that, and the physical act is the same. In the interrogation room, they typically will put their elbows on the table and rest their chin in their hands, partially covering their mouth. Psychologically, they find comfort or protection by "hiding" when they lie. In Emily's case, she was hiding behind her coffee cup, but the scenario was the same – take refuge and spurt it out. She was bracing herself for a lie.

Suddenly, she put her cup down, leaned forward almost to the point of touching him, and looked directly at him.

"I made over a million dollars in a little over three years. It was like kiting checks, but I was moving acres and acres of undeveloped land from one contract to another. I was making money faster than I could spend it. Of course, I earned a lot of legal money – paid taxes and all, but I made the real money illegally. I was on top of the world. Then I got this nice-looking guy with access to more money than I could comprehend. That should have been my clue, but by that time I was greedy. He seemed to be too dumb to stay up with me. He told me he'd inherited quite a bit of old family money, plus stock in some oil wells." She laughed at herself.

"I was going to take him for a ride – going to make a chunk off him. To make a long story short, we met in my office on a Friday night and signed some contracts. It was just the two of us. Then he pulled his badge on me – Detective John Baldwin. On top of that, he had a search warrant." She looked down at the table and nodded her head as if in disbelief.

"To say he hit the jackpot was an understatement. I was looking at forty to fifty years in prison."

"What about your husband?" Mike asked.

"This was after he died, and that's what makes it even more idiotic. I had money. Not as much as I wanted, but plenty to live on. I wasn't going to starve. I had a good job in real estate. I was at the top of the market and on top the world, but wanted more. It was just so easy to do. I couldn't stop myself, so I started my own little con game. It was unbelievably simple and I let it keep growing. The cash flow was phenomenal. It was like an addiction."

"What about the office manager or the agent you worked for?"

"They were happy. I wasn't stupid, just greedy. I had enough legitimate closings and they thought I was their cute little wonder girl, especially the office manager. He was demanding from time-to-time, and I figured out what he wanted. I don't think he was ever on a date in his entire life. You don't have to be a brain surgeon to figure that out, but I was not about to go to bed with him. I let him take me to dinner at some nice places, on his arm, let him give me a good-night smooch, but nothing more than that. The little bastard. At the end of the quarter, he'd stop by my desk and asked me out to dinner. He got his kicks being seen with me and I got what I wanted.

He cooked the books, but was too dumb to catch on to all my smoke and mirrors. I don't know. He may have been doing some himself – probably was."

She paused to refill her coffee, then plopped down in the chair and continued. "Sometimes we have to accept the good with the bad, and that's what I did to get along with him. I can tell you exactly – six quarters; a year and a half. That's how long it lasted, and that's how many times I paid my debt to that creep. A little kiss from time-to-time. Nothing more. Funny thing, though. He died. Son-of-a-bitch keeled over right there in the office. Had a cerebral hemorrhage and fell over dead." She gave a caustic laugh. "I didn't have anything to do with that either. You can look it up in the obituaries: Walter C. Bumstead. Hell of a name, isn't it? He was such a strange little guy."

Mike returned her caustic smile. "I'll take you up on it and review his death certificate and autopsy report. Tell me, where did you work?"

"American Plains Realty and Trust. It's still there. None of them knew about Walter and me, and they sure didn't know about the land fraud I was working. Baldwin kept it quiet – for a price. Of course, so did I."

"What do you mean, 'for a price'?"

"He gave me a copy of his search warrant and loaded his car with boxes of documents from my office, then told me to get in. I thought we were going to jail. I started to cry."

Emily stopped and looked at Mike. Her eyes drooped at the corners, her normally perky lips looked plastic. She swirled the coffee and watched it go round and round.

"My world was crashing down. I couldn't stand it. I asked him what I could do to work this out. Was there some other way? 'Yes, Mrs. Morgan, I think there is.' Those were his exact words. So, we worked things out, if you get the drift. His wife was sick and he was down in the dumps. Their little boy was just a tike. The great Detective Baldwin was stressed to the max and there I was. I was his antidepressant and that was the trade – make love to him and stay out of jail." She offered a shallow laugh. "Doesn't take much math to figure it out, does it? Actually, we got to be pretty good friends – in fact, lovers. I really liked him and he liked me."

"That still doesn't explain the killings," Mike said as he went to the counter and poured himself another cup of coffee. He looked back at her. "More?"

Emily laughed. "I'll be up all night as it is. No thanks."

Mike returned to the table and sat down. "Go ahead. I'm listening."

"He got weird. After a few months, he wanted to do some pretty kinky things – stuff I don't do." She stopped and looked at Mike. Her expression was deathly solemn. Her voice began to quake. "This is hard for me. It's scary, but for the first time, I can tell you the truth."

Chapter Fifteen

SHE CRIED SOFTLY AS SHE spoke. "He made me rent an apartment. I leased out this house and was living up there. I already lived in an apartment, but he wanted me to get another one, so I did. That's where he liked to go to have our little trysts."

"Why there? Why not your own place?" Mike asked.

"I lived in a small gated community. He thought, and I agreed, that the neighbors would see him coming and going. It wouldn't look right – the grieving widow having a congress with a man. Since Edgar's aunt lived in the same complex, it would be totally inappropriate. It would be a case that doesn't take a brain surgeon to figure out – no lovers there." She took a deep breath and held it, then let it out slowly.

"I might have some trouble getting through this, so be patient." She reached across the table and took his hand. "I couldn't stay in this house after Edgar died, so I got out. His Aunt Emma lived in Tulsa and invited me up there. I stayed with her for a few weeks, then sub-leased the townhouse across the drive from her. It was a stylish place; two bedrooms, a Jacuzzi bath, private patio – a nice place and I could afford it. I didn't have the passion for writing, so I went to school and got my realtors' license. Emma introduced me around town and I made some excellent contacts. That's the name of the game – contacts. Well, actually there are two names to the game: contacts and location. I started out pretty well and one closing led to another, and then another. It was unbelievable, but it was real. The problem was, I got greedy. It was too easy to do and I certainly wasn't the only one doing it. Lots of people were, and that's what brought the cops, excuse me, the police into it. There was too much going on. Too many of us were raking it in and they had to do something. So, the Attorney General implemented a Task Force, and that's where John came in. They sent him to some classes in Virginia and down in Georgia. He learned a lot. In fact, more than I ever expected a cop to know about real estate and business law. Of course, I didn't know what they were doing, because I was so busy hauling in my money. I thought I'd met a rich country bumpkin Okie and he probably thought he'd run into a dizzy airhead." She laughed at herself. "Sure enough, we were made for each other – two people too smart for our own good."

She shoved back from the table. "Now, here it comes." She walked to the bar and poured a glass of wine. "Wine? Scotch?" she asked.

"No. Not now. I want a clear head. No games. Just stay focused."

Once again, she flopped very un-lady like in her chair. She sipped the wine, looked at her glass and took a deep gulp. "He tied me up on my bed and blindfolded me. That was part of the kinky stuff I didn't like. Then he taped my mouth shut. I was scared."

She shook her head. "Not scared – petrified. I thought he was going to kill me. I heard him moving around the room and doing things, but I couldn't tell what he was doing. Things went quiet for a couple minutes and I knew he'd gone to another part of the house. Then he was back. Nothing was said, but I knew he wasn't alone."

Tears began to flow down her cheeks. Her lips trembled. "It was horrible," she uttered. "They did it to me – two of them. All sorts of things." She lifted her glass, but her hand was shaking. She put the glass to her lips, but it slipped from her hand and crashed on the floor.

Mike jumped from his seat, but not before she bolted to the bathroom. He followed, but she slammed the door. He stood in her bedroom and heard the sounds of her vomiting and flushing the toilet. He walked back to the kitchen, found the broom and dustpan, took some dishtowels from the rack, and began cleaning the glass and spilled wine from the floor. He finished, poured a shot of Glenfiddich for himself and walked slowly to her bedroom. The bathroom door was still closed. He tapped lightly. "Are you okay?"

She didn't answer.

"Emily?" he called through the door.

The doorknob turned slowly and the door opened. She was wrapped in a towel; her soiled clothes were heaped on the floor by the commode. Her once beautiful pink cheeks were ashen. "I didn't make it," she whispered.

"Are you going to be okay? What can I do for you?" he asked.

"Nothing. This happens a lot. You can't believe what I've been through or what I'm going through. It's a living hell."

"I'll go. We can do this another time," he said.

"No." she snapped. "We've started it and we're going to finish it – no turning back now. We're beyond the point of no return. It's now or never. I've got to get this out of my system before I kill myself." She tilted her head toward the breakfast nook and spoke. "Wait for me while I get something on."

#

He looked at his watch. The time passed ever so slowly. He took the last sip of Scotch, then went to her bedroom door and knocked.

"Be right there," she responded. Her voice was almost musical. She sounded like her old self. Mike was walking to the bar when he heard the bedroom door open behind him. He looked over his shoulder. It was the Emily he knew – her ponytail freshly combed; her cheeks were their usual rosy self; bright red lipstick; a button-down shirt open at the neck; and a pair of shorts. She was a stunning masterpiece.

"Sorry, Mike. It happens and I can't stop it. I have to work my way through it and then I'm okay until the next time." She took his empty glass and went to the bar. "Thanks for cleaning up my mess," she said as she poured another drink for each of them. "Let's sit in the living room. It's more comfortable." He followed her and sat on the couch. She sat at the far end, then scooted sideways and faced him.

"We went through that for two months. I hated it, and had no idea who the third person was. It was sickening and terrifying. Whenever John and I were alone, I'd tell him I wanted to stop, but he'd show his handcuffs to me and make some smart-aleck remark. The bastard! One night he came over and had his briefcase. We ate dinner and were just talking. There wasn't any lovemaking. Then out of the blue he said he had some videos he wanted me to see. I never could have guessed what it was. He popped a CD into my player and turned it on. It was us. First the two of us, then there was the other person – three of us."

"Who was the other guy?" Mike asked.

"I don't know. He always had his back to the camera. He was an Anglo, not much bigger than me, but muscular, not nearly as big as you." Tears began once again to flow over her cheeks. "I told him to turn it off, but he hit me. The same guy who said he loved me back-handed me right across my mouth. He made me bleed and told me to shut up. I was horrified. I knew he was going to kill me. I sat there like a rag doll and watched all of it. He loved it. I could tell he was excited."

"Did you ever see him set up the camera?"

"Never. He had all those little ones in his whatever – briefcase, overnight bag. He had several of them, so I was never aware we were being taped until I saw the videos. It was not as though he put a camera on a tripod."

"How long did this go on?"

"From beginning to end, four years. I actually thought of myself as a rape victim at first, but then decided he was a nice guy – that is, before he got perverse. Up to that point, I thought he was sad and lonely, and a dishonest cop, but who was I to complain about that? I liked having him around. He was fun and we had some great times together. It was pretty tough when his wife died, but I helped him through it and I'm sure I was a positive force in his life. I was good for him and thought he appreciated it. Obviously, I was wrong about that.

"It was nine months after she died that we had that – what should I call it? When the two of them assaulted me. It happened three other times, then suddenly he was gone. I never asked about him and John never brought it up. I was still scared, but what could I do?"

Mike sat his glass on the coffee table. It was empty. "This is pretty hard to swallow. Bizarre, is how I would describe it. How do I know you're not just making this up?" He looked her in the eye and shook his head.

"I swear, every word of it is true," she responded.

Mike propped his feet on the table and leaned back. "Go on."

"He was the one who told me to get out of Tulsa and go home. 'Get the hell out,' he said. I thought he was feeling guilty and was I only too glad to come home, so I did. I gave notice, had one more closing, packed my things and came back to Dallas. My home. No one else's. I spent the first week in bed crying. I was a mess. I thought about going to a shrink, but talked myself out of it. I was too frightened and too ashamed. I even thought about suicide.

"He came down a couple weeks later. I didn't invite him, but he just showed up at my door late one Friday night. He was a crazy man. He walked through my house, opening and closing my drawers, the closets, looking under the bed. I asked him what he was looking for, and he just smiled and said 'Nothing.' He asked about a basement, so I took him down there – you've never seen it. I have a game room, a couple closets and a wine cellar. I showed him everything and he said, 'Perfect. It'll do.'"

"And you did nothing? You just showed him around like you were showing the house for sale?"

She pursed her lips. "Damn it, Mike, I was scared to death. You've never suffered like I have, so don't try to judge me."

"Okay, so what then?"

"He kissed me goodbye and left."

"He left?"

"As in 'gone,'" she responded sarcastically. "He got in his car and left. I didn't see or hear from him for a couple weeks, then just like the other time, he popped in on a Friday night. We didn't have sex, didn't even have anything to eat. He was like a robot. He brought in boxes, rolls of wire and cables, and all sorts of electronics – things I don't know a thing about. He wasn't interested in me at all, but told me to stay out of his way, and I did. Mike, I was scared to death. I didn't know what he was going to do. You saw the results. My house was wired top to bottom. Come on downstairs, I'll show you."

Mike followed her to the steps leading to the basement. "I call this my game room down here," she said as she flicked the light switch. "When I entertain friends on a Friday night and we're having a few drinks," she paused at the foot of the stairs and looked back at him, "or a few joints, we come down here. Come on, I'll show you."

Mike caught up to her as she turned on the light in the game room. The walls were oiled walnut paneling, the carpet a deep burgundy, and a Budweiser light hung from the ceiling over the green felt of the pool table. Television sets hung from wall mounts in opposite corners and a cd/tape player was fitted into an armoire on the far wall. Barstools were scattered along the walls.

Emily stepped across the room and pulled back a sliding door to open the wet bar. "There are lots of good memories in this room, but those are from more innocent days." She pulled up a bar stool and sat down. "Whatever innocence I had, I've lost. I'll never be the same. No more young professionals having a party on Friday night. Those days are gone forever."

"There's more," Mike said softly. "Why did we come down here? Go on with it. I need to know."

"I can't go in there. It's too painful." She pointed to the hallway. "Turn right and look down. There's a release button to the wine cellar. Look there, then I'll tell you."

He looked over his shoulder at the hallway, took a step, then hesitated. He spoke without looking back at her. "What's there? Dead bodies?"

"Go look, and then I'll explain it to you."

Mike followed her directions. He tapped the latch with the toe of his shoe and the door slipped open, releasing a contact button and turning on the light at the same time. The room was humid, but not musty. He went a few steps inside and stopped. He took quick mental measurements – five feet wide and the same length as that of the poolroom. The walls and ceiling were of oak, interspersed with corkboard. The floor, too, was a dark oak. The room itself was empty. The thought entered his mind – a prison. A person could be kept here and their screams not be heard. They could die here.

He heard footsteps. In an instant, he knew. She was going to close the door. He turned, and she was there, her hand on the doorframe. He exploded with all his might before she could move. He crashed into her midsection with his shoulder. They slammed against the wall and crumpled to the floor. He was on top her. She gasped for breath. Blood trickled from her lip.

He lifted himself slightly, then straddled her with his knee. Her eyes were watering. She started to speak, then turned her head and spit blood onto the floor.

"You bitch," he uttered as he put his hands to her throat. "I ought to kill you here."

Emily began to cry. She choked again on her blood and spit. "Go ahead. Put me out of my misery," she cried. "I haven't been in there since that day we took everything out. What the hell's wrong with you? I thought I could come back here with you – I'd be safe. I could do it with you."

He loosened his hold on her throat, but kept her pinned to the floor with his weight. "What are you talking about?"

"Here, damn it." She reached up and pushed him back. "This room. Now get off me and I'll tell you."

Mike got up, reached for her hand and pulled her to her feet. Emily stood, then leaned back against the wall and slid back to the floor. She bowed her head and began to cry, then to wail, "My God, help me. I need help. Somebody help me." She gasped for breath.

Mike sat on the floor, scooted close to her and took her in his arms. He held her tightly in his grasp. She shivered, unable to control herself. She continued to cry, then leaned over on his lap and closed her eyes. He put one hand to her hair and stroked it gently, and with the other rubbed her back. Minutes ticked by and her breathing became shallow. He continued to console her, talking softly, saying her name. The house and basement were quiet. Finally, she went to sleep.

Mike was at peace. He closed his eyes and rested. She was innocent.

Chapter Sixteen

MIKE WOKE UP AND LOOKED at his watch. One o'clock in the morning. Emily was still asleep on his lap. He twisted slightly to the side. His leg was asleep from where her weight was on it.

She stirred, opened her eyes and jumped upright. "What happened?"

Mike pulled her back against him. "You went to sleep. Everything's fine. You had a bad night, but you're okay now."

"I had a dream." She started to cry again. "Oh, Mike, how will this end? I can't go on like this."

"Just sit here for a few minutes and compose yourself. I'm here. I'll take care of you."

Emily looked at her empty wine cellar. "That was where he kept everything. He had a huge assortment of weapons – guns, knives and clubs. I don't know what all, just a variety of things. He had hooks on the wall and hung them up there." She pointed with her hand, but pulled it back when she saw how she was trembling.

"He made me watch when he put them up, but told me never to come back down here again by myself, and I didn't. He had a camera at the end of the hall." She gestured toward the opposite end of the hall away from where they were seated. "Up there in the corner. He could see anyone who came downstairs, and I damn sure didn't."

"What would you do when he came here to pick up a weapon before he killed someone?"

"I was never here. Remember all those times I told you I had to meet an editor or had a business meeting somewhere and would be out of town?"

Mike nodded. "Sure."

"It was a lie. He'd tell me when to be gone and I was – anywhere but Tulsa. I'd get out of town for a day if not two. I was never around here, but knew what was going on. He'd call; I'd go. Later, I'd read where someone was murdered. It wasn't too hard to figure that out.

"He had a door key and the alarm code. I'd get out of here as fast as my two legs would carry me – New Braunfels, Austin, Fredericksburg – anywhere I could go in a couple hours. I flew to New Orleans once. I'd go somewhere and force myself not to think of him. Or, maybe I should say *them*." She stood up, adjusted her clothes, and took his hand. "Let's go upstairs." She flicked the latch with her bare toe and watched the door close, then followed Mike back to the living room.

"Be right back. Have to rinse my mouth, thank you."

He watched her go to the bathroom and close the door. He sat in silence and waited. He heard the water running and felt guilty about smashing her into the wall. Nevertheless, it was something he had to do at the time. He brushed aside his guilt. He did it and wasn't going to second-guess himself.

A few moments later she came out and sat on the couch. There was no sign of the dry blood. Her lipstick was freshened and her hair brushed. She sat beside him. The scent of her cologne bathed him. They were going to be okay. He smiled inwardly.

"Do you think he was the one, or was it the other guy?" Mike asked.

She shook her head. "I really don't know, but something – maybe a woman's intuition – tells me it was the other man. You never saw John undressed like I did. You saw him on the videos and could see how thin he was, but they don't actually portray him very well. He's skinny. He didn't have any muscles at all. Not that he was feminine, but he didn't have any physical agility. From your description, your killer was very athletic. Svelte, I believe is how you described him – athletic and svelte."

"That's what I'm led to believe, but nobody knows for sure."

"John wasn't strong. Sure, he can slap a lady, but it doesn't take much of a man to do that. Listen to me, Mike. He and I were intimate any number of times, and when I tell you he didn't have much stamina, you just have to take my word for it. It has to be the other man. If we can get our hands on those videos, you'll know what I mean. He was just as you describe – very wiry and strong as an ox."

"What's their connection? It doesn't make any sense."

"You answered your own question. 'It doesn't make any sense.' That, Detective Palotti, is how they got away with it. They didn't fit the pattern of any serial killer. They were and are unique. To use your words, they had an exit plan. Kill however many people, play their sick game, and then stop while they're ahead. Believe me, when he told me to say I was finished killing, he was telling the truth. The game was over, except it was them, not me."

She rested her head on his shoulder, stretched and yawned. "I'm tired and have to go to bed. You can stay here if you want to. You can use the guestroom." She looked into his eyes and smiled. She was beautiful.

He thought about it for a moment before he responded. "No, I'd better go. I'll talk to you tomorrow. We need to think this through." He tilted her head to his and gave her a soft peck on the lips. "Good night. I'll call you in the morning."

He opened the door and stepped onto the porch, then looked back. She was still on the couch, but was crying – a sad and pathetic little girl.

"Michael, I'm scared," she whispered.

His mind exploded with thoughts and memories like bolts of lightning flashing from the clouds – Annalisa and Samanta; Rickey and his other friends on the department; Emily, his beautiful lover and the victim of an unspeakable criminal; or, Emily, a cold and devious murderer. In that one instant, he was torn. He turned back toward her, took a single step and paused. "You'll be alright. I'll talk to you in the morning." He spun around and closed the door behind him. There were too many unanswered questions.

#

Mike looked at his watch. The morning slipped away. He talked to Sgt. Covey and explained what he described as his "personal issue," then arranged to take a few days off. Next, he called Roger Goldberg, a cantankerous old attorney, but a good one. Even more important, he owed Mike a favor.

Mike acknowledged the errors of his ways and agreed to an amicable divorce if necessary, but first, there had to be a move toward reconciliation. Roger must push her attorney to discuss with her the consideration of marriage counseling. He'd wronged her more than once; his affairs and lies were wrong. He acknowledged them, but wanted one last effort to re-build his family. He was willing to go to any length. The terms were hers to determine. He would accept them.

However, if she did not accept his offer, all he wanted was reasonable visitation rights to Samanta. He couldn't ask for more, even though deep down inside what he wanted was to go home like the old days, a short two or three weeks ago.

Before he completed his conversation with Goldberg, he thought ahead of one good thing that might come out of this: if he could prove Emily's innocence, she would marry him.

#

There were a few more things to get done, then he would go see her. Now, though, was the time to challenge her veracity. He unplugged the telephone and hooked his modem into the telephone line. A few quick taps on the keys and he found what he was looking for – Oklahoma Real Estate Commission. Every broker and every agent – a veritable treasure trove of information. He entered the search zone for American Plains Realty – there it was: 4707 Wally Post Drive. *Okay*, he thought, *she knows the name of a real estate office. Good start, but not the end yet.*

He hit the search zone again with the scant information he knew about her: Emily Morgan. Then it dawned on him; he knew almost nothing about her. He dialed the office on his cell phone.

"Detectives. Angie speaking," came the typical pleasant voice of their secretary.

"Hi, Ang. Mike here. Can you run a records and driver's license check for me?"

"I thought you were off sick. What are you doing calling here?"

"Yeah, well, you know. Cops are never off-duty. Take this name – Emily Morgan, white female, mid-thirties. See what you get."

"Say, isn't she the woman who was doing all those interviews for a book? Don't answer," she quipped.

Mike waited and listened to the sounds of her fingers dancing on the keyboard. Seconds later, she had his answer. "This must be her – a special background check for the mayor; lives in Highland Park, right?"

"That's her. What do we have?"

"Driver's license active; no wants or warrants; date of birth March 1, 1970. Full name of Emily Anderson Morgan." There was a pause. "Need anything else?"

"Thanks, no," Mike responded dryly. He didn't know what he'd expected, but hoped for something – anything to help him find his answers. He turned back to his computer and ran her name on the Oklahoma Commission website.

The search droned. He watched the screen move slowly, so much so he thought it was frozen. Suddenly, there she was. All it showed was her name and status – Inactive. But, that was enough. So far, even though the background information was cursory, she checked out.

He searched again, this time for Wesley Bumstead. "Can't be too many with that name," he muttered as he pecked at his keyboard. First to Oklahoma newspapers, then to Tulsa, and finally to the obituaries. It was that simple. Wesley was real. Born November 6, 1955 – died suddenly February 24, 2004. Memorials suggested to the Oklahoma Realtors Scholarship Fund.

Mike sat back, satisfied. Everything she said was validated to this point – just a couple more issues to verify, then he could relax. He realized he was taking short cuts, but if anything looks sour, he'd dig deeper. He looked at his watch. He was late. He'd told her that he would see her in the morning and it already was one o'clock.

He called her from his cell phone. She answered on the first ring. "I thought you'd call this morning. I've been waiting for you."

"Sorry, but I had to see my lawyer. Got a divorce going, if you remember?"

"I'm sorry," she whispered. "Can we have lunch?"

"Give me an hour and I'll be there. Do you want to go out?" he chuckled. "How about Denny's?"

"Michael, you know I don't do that place. How about something here?"

"I'll be there," he responded.

#

Thirty minutes later he pushed back from the computer and laughed at himself. Isn't that what she was talking about in the first place? The Gilder effect? All the information that's available at your fingertips?

Edgar Morgan – born December 20, 1969; died May 23, 1999 – Survived by wife, Emily Morgan.

He leaned back in his chair and looked at his laptop, reached out with exaggerated pleasure and turned it off. She was clean. Every word out of her mouth was true.

#

He started to get in his car, then remembered he hadn't checked the GPS in a few days. It was something he'd learned to live with and didn't concern himself about. He climbed out and went to the side, ducked down and peered at the front underside of the gas tank – it was gone.

"Damn it," he muttered. He knew he should have checked every day. He'd allowed himself to be sloppy and this was the price – when was it removed?

The drive to Emily's wasn't as relaxing as he'd hoped for. He was angry with himself. How long? When? Where was I? The thoughts raced through his mind. He was too good at his job to permit such a mental gaff. He'd screwed up and couldn't undo it. It's easier if someone else does it. You can forgive them, but not when you do it yourself and have no one else to blame.

The longer he drove, the angrier he became. Cops – good cops – don't get careless and let mistakes like this happen. He bit his lip and looked at himself in the mirror. "Learn from it and get on. There's nothing I can do about it now," he muttered. He made a pledge to himself. Think. Be careful. If it's not her, then it's John and his friend. They're still out there. I can't relax.

As he considered those things, he also thought about how it might come to an end. Or, simply, would it never end? Would it have to go into the historic files of unsolved cases? He mumbled aloud to himself, "That's unthinkable. I know who did it. Am I going to have to live with this forever?"

#

She was sitting on the front step waiting for him, sipping a cold drink. He watched, mesmerized by her grace and beauty as she stood and walked slowly down from the porch toward his car. He waited until she was almost to the curb before he got out.

"I'm sorry I'm late. It took longer with the attorney than I thought." He shrugged his shoulders. "I've never been through a divorce before." He walked around the car and put his arm around her waist. "I'm glad to be here. We're going to whip this thing and we'll do it together."

She slipped her arm around his waist, led him up the steps and into the house. "Look. Clean," she gestured. "I was too upset to sleep, so I spent the night cleaning house. It's not my normal job, but it helped get my mind off these terrible things. How about lunch? I've got things ready."

They walked arm-in-arm to the nook. The table was set with linen napkins, placemats, china, and a vase of roses for the centerpiece. "For you," she said as she leaned forward and smelled the flowers.

A bottle of white wine rested in an ice bucket on the counter by her chair. She lifted it from the bucket and with the deftness of an experienced bartender, removed the cork, tipped the bottle and measured a small amount into a glass. "Do us the honors, please?" she asked.

Mike twirled the glass, tipped it slightly to observe the wine's legs form on the side, then put it to his lips. He inhaled deeply to savor the aroma and finally took a taste. "Excellent choice, madam," he teased.

Emily poured a glass for each of them, returned the bottle to the bucket and sat down. She held the glass by the stem, took a sip and then spoke. "Mike, you'll never know how I feel at this exact moment. I'm free. For the first time in years, I believe I'm getting my life back – thanks to you."

They lifted their glasses and looked at one another. Mike's heart quickened. "To our new lives," he said. The glasses clinked and they toasted themselves.

#

Lunch passed peacefully. They didn't discuss their past indiscretions, the murders, or the pain of last night, only the future – and the future started now.

"If we truly care for one another, we have to be open and honest all the time," Mike said.

She nodded in agreement and he continued, "My lawyer is going to do what he can to salvage my marriage. I told him I'd agree to counseling, but I don't have a lot of hope for it. I wronged her, and she was hurt. I don't think she'll accept, but I have to try." He bit his lip, looked down at his plate, then spoke softly. "I have a family and a responsibility. If I can save it, I must. I hope you understand."

Emily took his hand to her lips and kissed it. "Absolutely! If you do less, I'll be disappointed in you. Let there be no doubt of my love for you, but I can't take you so long as you have any hope of rebuilding what the two of us together destroyed." She leaned forward and kissed his cheek. "You're a good and honorable man, Michael Palotti. I want the best for you and if that includes me, so much the better."

Mike tipped his wine glass to her and nodded his appreciation for her words. "You are a class lady, Emily Morgan. You're one of a kind."

"Now it's my turn to be open and frank with you," she said. Her face flushed. She wet her lips and continued. "The sex we had was totally orchestrated by that evil son-of-a-bitch. Did I want to do it with you? Yes, after a while I did, but not like that. What and how we did those things was designed like a movie script. I never make love to a man like that – in his wife's bedroom with his child right there; in his office. Those things were perverse. They were totally insane. I was frightened beyond belief. That was not lovemaking. It was nothing less than cheap pornography. He designed it, then enjoyed himself looking at those videos time and time again.

"We'll make love again. I know we will, but it'll be an act of tender love – a private moment between a man and a woman. Please, don't think less of me for what he made me do with you. Then the bastard made me show those things to you when I had to do it with him." Her lips began to tremble. Tears ran from her eyes. She looked forlornly at him. "I'm so sorry."

Mike stepped around the table and took her in his arms. She stood and they kissed; first softly, then with passion. She dried her tears, and he freshened their wine. "So what happens now?" she asked.

"The divorce process will take time, assuming it happens, but within a couple months it'll be behind us. I'll see Sam regularly and have her on a few weekends – maybe even take her back up to Second Meadow next summer. I'll get back to work. Normalcy will return. It'll take time, but it will. What about you?"

"I can feel the passion again and can pursue my research and writing. I want to finish my book and begin a lecture series to criminal justice agencies. More so, we'll have time together. There cannot be any permanent commitments now, but allow our relationship to grow – allow the love for one another to blossom."

Mike leaned forward to take her hands in his. "We can't forget John and the phantom. They're the question mark. Will they fade into oblivion? Will they kill again? Will they come back to haunt us? We've got some issues ahead of us that we can't forget. Somehow, we have to learn the truth."

#

It was late afternoon when they got up from the table. The salads and sandwiches eaten; the wine was drunk; and the napkins were placed over the soiled plates. Their luncheon was complete.

Emily led them onto the patio where they scooted lawn chairs into the shade of the magnolia tree. The fountain in the backyard sprayed a soft melody of soothing water that cascaded over a decorative waterfall. The day was glorious. Mike was content and he knew she was, too.

"There was a lot we didn't cover last night," Emily commented. "We need to talk some more."

Mike nodded in agreement. "Go ahead."

"I'll be right back," she said as she got up and went into the house. She returned moments later.

His eyes froze on what she was carrying – a GPS antennae. "I was getting a lube job on my car a couple weeks ago and the mechanic came and got me out of the waiting room. He took me to the garage; my car was up on the lift. He pointed up to this thing and said, 'Look there, lady. Do you know what that is?' Of course, I've never seen one of these before, and neither had he, but he knew it didn't belong there."

"So what did you do?"

"I told him to leave it there. I had an idea what it was, so I came home and got on my computer. Told you about those things, didn't I?" She didn't wait for his response. "It took me all of five minutes to learn what it was. A GPS sending device and I knew immediately who did it and what he was up to. It was that bastard John Baldwin. He wasn't going to leave me alone – he was watching my every move, albeit from a distance.

"I didn't know what to do. I couldn't call you. I was stuck, so I did a little investigating myself and decided I'd play with his mind. I took it off my Mercedes, that's the car I usually drive, and put it on the old lady's car next door."

"You what?" Mike bellowed.

"Mrs. Dingle," Emily fired back. "She's a seventy-five-year-old widow and still drives her own car, not much, but she gets to the beauty shop and a few places." Smugly, Emily picked the device up and turned it around in her hand, examining it from every angle. She smiled in self-satisfaction. "Hope I drove him crazy. Anyway, I took it off a couple days ago and put it on a shelf in my garage. Now, I don't know what to do with it. How long is he going to stalk me?"

"I wish you'd left it on and never found it," Mike uttered. His voice was raspy. His eyebrows peaked. "Damn it, now he knows you know about it."

"How?" she responded.

"Because he put one on my car. I found it by accident, I thought, but left it there. I know why you did it, Emily," he reached out and took her hand. "You thought you were doing right, but you played into his hands. He knows you know. But, in my case – well, let's just say things aren't that clear. He found it. I didn't. I had a flat tire and he was putting the jack under the car and saw it. Or, so he says."

Mike frowned. His eyes pleaded when he looked at Emily. "He made sure I found it. That left only one person – you. The killer. You were watching me, as you said, 'safely from a distance.'"

"Wait a minute," she demanded.

Mike held his hands up in surrender. "He outfoxed me, too. He planted it there and made sure I knew it, so there was only one conclusion I could draw. It was you. Hell, you'd already confessed to the murders and all that recorded sex with both of us. What else could I believe?"

"Then he put it on my car, too. He was watching me?" she asked.

"Yes, but ..." Mike paused. "I'm not sure when, but sometime in the past couple days, he took mine off. He was watching both of us. Can't you see? He was making sure I was more than convinced about you. You killed, you blackmailed us with sex, and then you put the GPS on our cars. But," he emphasized strongly, "assuming he came to your house a day or two ago, he didn't get yours back. He knows you found it and that's not good. Remember, he's up to his neck in murder. He got you over a barrel with your white-collar scheme, then got me to believe you were the serial murderer and you had me over a barrel. He covered his bases. He did well, that bastard."

"And you didn't look under his car to see if I put one there, too?"

"No," he responded sheepishly. "He wasn't in his car then, and I never considered it later. I just assumed you did it."

"Michael," her voice pleaded, "don't you cops ever stop assuming and verify your facts?"

"Dumb. I know it. I trusted him."

Suddenly, she panicked. She put her hands to her face. "Does he know about us?" Her voice quaked. Her face flushed. She was blanketed in fear.

"I don't know. Probably not." He shrugged. "Who knows?"

Emily began to sob. Her voice was broken. "A few minutes ago I felt so safe, but now ..."

"We'll work through this, I promise." He stood and led her back into the house. "I need to use the restroom, then let's talk. It'll work out; we just have to plan and not panic. Somehow, we're going to win."

Mike was caught off-guard when his cell phone rang. He was on sick leave. Nobody should be calling – certainly not Annalisa, and there wasn't anyone else. He pulled it from his pocket and looked at the caller identification – Tulsa Police. He froze. His heart pounded, but just as quickly that automatic police response to sudden danger

SWEET EMILY

swept over him. He did as he was trained. Slow down, deliberate, be composed and maintain control.

He flicked the button and spoke calmly. "John, how're you doing?"

John spit it out, almost too fast for Mike to comprehend. "The chief got the letter from her."

"Wait a minute. Run through that again. Who got what?"

"Remember she said she would send a letter to your department and mine? She'd confess, and then say she was done."

Mike looked at Emily. She was staring at him.

"Sure. Go ahead."

"I got called into the old man's office this morning and they showed it to me. She confessed, just like she said she would. It was a typed letter – plain, cheap stationary and a plain envelope. No prints on it. Clean and sterile. Mailed in Durant, Oklahoma the day before yesterday. Did your chief get one, too?"

Mike breathed deeply and looked at Emily. She didn't move. She stood stoically, watched his body language and listened to his half of the conversation.

"If he did, I don't know anything about it. I'm on leave working through my divorce." Mike paused, then asked, "Have you heard from Emily lately? Any phone calls or stopping in to see you?"

"No, thank heavens. Maybe the bitch dropped dead. What about you?"

"No, nothing. Of course, I've been off, so if she called it'll be on my register at the office. Otherwise, not a peep out of her."

"Good. Well, I wanted to touch base. Let me know, okay?"

"Will do, and thanks for calling."

"Wait. One other thing, Mike. I'm supposed to leave here in about an hour. I'm going with a crew from the crime lab. The letter said the sword was buried in a specific location in a place called the Settler's Cemetery in Durant. The directions are very precise. I know it's there. She said she'd prove the letter wasn't from an imposter. It'll be there. I know it. She's doing exactly what she said she would do."

"John, we haven't talked about it, but what about a GPS locater on your car?"

"Yeah, it's there. At least, it was the day before yesterday. I haven't driven it and haven't looked, but it was there then. You still got yours?"

"No," Mike replied. "She took it off a few days ago. Can you take a look?"

"Sure, hang on a minute."

Mike waited, holding the phone to his ear. He and Emily stood looking at each other. She was statuesque – petrified with fear, but beautiful nevertheless. He put a finger to his lips. She must not talk or make a sound.

John came back on the phone. His voice was excited. "Mike, it's gone. When the hell did all this happen?"

"We both got sloppy. A day or two ago. Thanks for calling. Stay in touch." Mike clicked the phone off and shoved it in his pocket. "Him! Said you sent your confession and where to find that sword. Plus, you got your GPS device back."

"Mike, he's insane. What are we going to do? There never was one of those things on his car, was there?"

"Probably not." Mike turned and went into the bathroom. It was exactly as he remembered it – the soft light of candles danced off the mirrors, fresh flowers in a crystal vase filled with fresh lemon slices and water, and the sweet scent of a woman's intimate domain. He looked at himself in the mirror, déjà vu so long ago when they'd stood side-by-side refreshing themselves. This time, however, things were different. An insane murderer held them in his grip.

He examined himself and saw what he liked, the real Detective Palotti. He knew what to do – return to the basics that guided his success over the years. He remembered a song from years ago: "Dance with the girl you brought to the ball."

He knew what he would do. Be bold and go on the offense. Take calculated risks without being foolhardy. The future was not in looking back, it was in the development of strategy, tactics and timing. The timing started now.

Chapter Seventeen

MIKE WAS ONE OF THE first detectives in the office the following morning. There was a bounce to his step. He laughed quietly at himself, wondering if his co-workers might compare him to a Viagra commercial, but he couldn't help it. He felt good and it showed.

As if on cue, Covey came in the door leading from the parking garage. He took one look at Mike and chuckled. "Did you get a haircut or lose weight?"

"None of the above, but I'm ready to hit it and get some work done," Mike responded.

"We've got plenty for you. I started to call yesterday when the crap hit the fan, but thought I'd wait to see if you came in today. I'm glad you're here. Follow me." The two men walked into the sergeant's private office and closed the door. "Have a seat and look at this," Covey said as he pulled a file from the cabinet and slid it across the desk. "The original is in the crime lab checking it for prints."

Mike opened the envelope carefully. Although he knew what was in it, he felt a surge of anticipation like a little boy who knows he's getting a bike for Christmas. He wants to run down the stairs and see it standing next to the tree. There's not another feeling like it.

The detective focused his attention on the moment, pulled the letter from the envelope and readied himself for John's letter. He couldn't wait to see it. His eyes savored every syllable:

> To Whom it May Concern:
>> My work is done. Your ineptitude is untarnished. Can you believe me?
>> Yes, of course. The proof is in the instrument. At the Settler's

> Cemetery in Durant, you will find a monument to Legree Triplett. Thirty yards east of the monument is a weed patch. It measures approximately one hundred yards by eighty yards. In the center of the weeds and approximately one foot deep you will find the instrument that served in a case in your city and another case in the city with whom you cooperated in these investigations.
> You will not receive any further communication from me.

"I don't like it," Covey commented. "It's too simple. Something's wrong, but I don't have any idea what it is." He opened his desk and retrieved a pack of gum. "Want one?" he offered. "I go through a pack a day since I quit smoking." He was slow and deliberate in unwrapping the stick of gum, then plucked it in his mouth. "It's too staged. That's what I think. It might be from the real killer, but this bullshit game isn't over – not by a long shot."

"I understand Tulsa PD sent their crime lab to retrieve it. When should we expect some feedback?" Mike asked.

"You've been talking to Baldwin, haven't you? Yeah, they got it, but we're not looking for a genie to pop out of the jar. If the note is real, then I think the sword is real. Plus, we have to believe the suspect wouldn't give it to us if there was even a remote chance of it being traceable or having a fingerprint on it."

Mike nodded in agreement. "I've got an idea. Do you mind signing a travel order for me? I want to go to Durant."

"What are you going to find that we don't already know? Lieutenant Crenshaw from Tulsa filled me in on what they did. They talked to anybody and everybody who might have any information on the cemetery. Nobody saw anything. Zilch. That's what they got."

"Be a gambling man. Sign the travel order," Palotti challenged.

#

Mike left his apartment before the morning rush hour and was in Durant by ten o'clock. He pulled the map into his lap. Go west one mile on Elmont; turn left on Cheyenne and go two-thirds of a mile to Settler's Cemetery.

He guided the unmarked police car across the cattle guard and onto the cemetery property. The grounds were ragged and old, surrounded by a barbed-wire fence. The weeds along the dirt road were trimmed, but still nearly a foot high. The once green Bermuda grass had long ago died for lack of water. He slowed and watched a lone tumbleweed bounce and roll across the road in front of him. The wind was hot and dry; puffs of dust chased each other among the tombstones like little ghosts playing tag. Fifty yards into the cemetery a dozen withered Mulberry trees lined the road, casting a miser's portion of shade across the desolate burial grounds. Settler's Cemetery was left for the ages, and the years had sucked whatever life there was from these once proud and hallowed grounds.

Mike eased the car over the rutted road and followed it to the back edge of the property. A lone grave marker stood like a haggard sentinel gazing out over the lost land of the dead. The name was clear – Triplett. Mike parked and got out, taking time to look over the place where the dead were laid to rest. The cemetery itself was joining its inhabitants in returning to the dust from whence it once spouted. He pulled the notepad from his shirt pocket and made notes:

Legree Triplett   Born December 21, 1900   Died April 13, 1932

There was nothing else. Mike walked around the nearby graves looking hopefully for family members on the dozen or so scattered grave markers, but without success.

The weed patch was easy to identify, so he walked through the waist-high jungle of tumbleweeds, stunted salt cedar and buffalo burs until he found the recently turned earth. This is where it was. He poked around with the toe of his shoe, paused and looked out over the flat expanse of the land. It was so desolate. He trembled. A chill ran down his arms and legs. His nemesis previously stood in this exact spot knowing exactly what Mike would do – he would come.

I'll get you, John, if it's the last thing I do, he thought. He returned to the car, hit the accelerator and pulled out. He'd seen what he wanted. It was no more than psychological, but at this moment he knew the trail he wanted to cut into the killer's mind.

"You play too many games, you bastard, and that's going to be your downfall."

#

Mike found a brief respite from the loneliness of the graveyard when he pulled to the curb in front of the newspaper, *The Durant Express*. He chuckled softly. It was not exactly a big city newspaper. If fact, it didn't depict any more sparkle or life than the cemetery. The brick façade of the single-story building was weathered and faded, and the large front window was cracked from one end to the other. The old clock hanging precipitously over the door stopped at 8:47, but who knows how many years ago.

Not exactly a shot of encouragement, he thought as he walked through the front door. His footsteps echoed on the hardwood floor. He stopped to take in his surroundings. To say it was old was an understatement. The wrought iron, barred, teller cages marked "Advertising" and "Payments" gave testimony to the 1930's architecture. Mike decided service, if there was any at all, would be better at the "Payments" window, so he went there. He peered through the bars to see two elderly women and an even older man sitting in the back room drinking coffee; otherwise, the office was abandoned.

"Hello," he called. The trio looked up in surprise, unaccustomed to customers at the window.

"Here I come," shouted a bouncy gray-haired woman, apparently the younger of the two. "Howdy do," she said as she approached the counter. "What's a fine looking young man like you doing here this time of morning?" Her smile was soft and pleasant, even though it revealed the sad state of her ill-fitting dentures.

"Morning ma'am. I'm looking for a little help and thought I might find it here; some history, if you will."

"You can just bet your boots I will." She leaned forward and extended her hand through the cage. "I'm Cleona Bellwether, and who might you be?"

Mike shook her hand. It was soft and warm, a manifestation of her personality. Instantly, he decided to slant his story so as not to arouse too much interest in his purpose. "I'm Mike Palotti. I'm doing some family research. I live in Dallas and came up here to see if I can learn anything about a man, maybe my great-uncle, by the name of Legree Triplett. I've been out to the cemetery and found his tombstone, but I need to try to document a little of his history, if I can, for our family book. We've got a reunion coming in a couple months, so I'm trying to finish things up. Think you can help me?"

"Legree Triplett?" she paused.

"Yes ma'am. He died in 1932. Would you have any records going back that far?"

"Sure do. Go back to 1900 for a fact. More than a hundred years. 1932? What do you need?"

"Obituary would be great. I'd be glad to pay you for your time."

"Not my time – yours." she retorted. She leaned over, pulled the gate open and pointed to an old microfiche scanner. "Come in and have a seat. I'll get the records for you. Might take a minute, but make yourself comfortable."

#

It was four-thirty when he found it. He was covered from head to toe with the grime of the dusty boxes of the decades, but he knew Legree Triplett.

Mike sat back in the old chair and read the front-page article one more time. Deputy Sheriff Triplett's body was found at the side of the road, shot once in the head. Authorities suspected the infamous duo of Bonnie and Clyde committed the murder the day after they robbed the bank in Argyle, Texas. Sheriff Leonard Pitts of Bryan County, Oklahoma, reported dispatching his deputies to patrol the back roads near the state line in search of the desperados. Deputy Triplett's body was found by cowboys after they heard gunshots beyond the hill where they were branding cattle.

The Sheriff determined from the evidence at the scene of the crime that Triplett was surprised by the killers. His gun was missing and he was executed with a shot to the back of his head.

Mike's mind wandered – what type of game is Baldwin playing? This gravestone wasn't chosen by chance. It's a message, but for whom? Me? Emily? Or, is it just an extra piece of the puzzle to tease and play mind games? A dead deputy then; a dead detective now?

#

Southbound traffic was light, giving the detective ample time to relax and enjoy the rolling grasslands with cattle and horses grazing in the setting sun; pastures outlined with white split-rail fences; a tour guide's dream of the real Texas – the Lone Star State as it was meant to be. It was peaceful and he was in control of himself. He was back to his roots. He would do what he was trained to do. Now, he was closing in on "The Creature," Detective John Baldwin.

Legree Triplett, he considered, died from one of several possibilities: reckless bravado trying to capture the famed Bonnie and Clyde by himself; taken by surprise possibly while doing nothing more than stopping to relieve himself, unaware of the bandits being nearby; or, being reckless and callus about the real danger and not taking his assignment seriously. Whatever his choice, he paid the price.

"Damn," Mike muttered. He looked at himself in the mirror. "You're another Legree." He thought about his own situation. "I got too close! I was reckless and full of my own confidence, but not anymore. I know it. He gave me a message. I'm close, and if I get too close, he'll do to me just like they did to Legree seventy plus years ago."

"Thanks for the insight, John," he said aloud, as if to give himself a bit of self-assurance. "I got it, and now it's my turn."

Chapter Eighteen

MIKE, SERGEANT COVEY, AND LT. HAUK gathered in the Lieutenant's office. Mike was seated in a straight-back chair directly across the desk from Hauk. Covey was similarly seated to his left. The Lieutenant leaned back in his leather executive chair, using his massive, privately owned mahogany desk as a separation from his subordinates – physically, socially and hierarchically. He clasped his hands in front of him, his forefingers linked together across his lips.

Mike thought he looked like a praying mantis waiting for a bug to come crawling by for his next meal – a simple matter of the food chain. *It's not going to be me, you bastard*, he thought.

Hauk allowed his eyes to gaze at his ego wall decorated with diplomas and certificates – Southern Methodist University, FBI Academy, Senior Management Institute for Police, Northwestern Traffic Institute, and a half-dozen other awards and honors he'd picked up over the years. He cleared his throat.

"Gentlemen, I've done well in my career, and I intend to carry forward with that same degree of excellence until my retirement. You," he pointed at Covey, "are starting to become a thorn in my side." His voice was pitched. "You should not have signed those travel orders and sent this man off to run around some graveyard. We knew full well it served no material value to us other than what Tulsa PD already accomplished." His face reddened as he leaned forward on his elbows. He glared at Mike. "If there was a shred of evidence, we would know it without spending good government money on you running up and down the highway. Do I make myself clear?" He stared at both of them, awaiting their reply.

Mike bit his lip, but held his temper. Covey broke the silence. "Yes sir, I should have checked with you. I understand and won't do that again."

"What about you, Detective?" Hauk asked acerbically.

"Sir, I'd like to know what Tulsa told you."

"There's nothing there – noting but that samurai sword. There was no groundskeeper to interview; no readable tire marks worth a damn; and no footprints. Nothing! They'll analyze the sword and give us a written report."

Hauk continued, "Just to fill in some of our curious points, the cemetery opened in 1893 and had its last burial of record in 1941. It was county property, but there's a current court case between some Indian tribe and the county about who really owns the place. The Indians say its holy ground and belongs to them. The county says it theirs and they want to remove the bodies and convert the land to a public housing project." He glared at Mike. "You had no right second guessing my knowledge and authority. Do I make myself clear?"

"Yes, very."

Hauk's face reddened in anger; his piercing eyes glared at Mike. "Are you satisfied after wasting our time and money that your trip was worthless?"

"No, sir, I'm not. I think there's more to the cemetery than meets the eye – broaden the horizon, as you say. I assume they didn't tell you about Legree, did they?"

The Lieutenant tilted his head to the side like a mutt listening to a siren wailing in the distance. "Legree? No, they didn't."

"Legree Triplett was a Deputy Sheriff. He was murdered ..." Mike told Covey and Hauk what he'd learned from the newspaper articles and of his own concerns that they were close to the killer. Maybe too close for comfort.

Hauk sat back and relaxed as Mike spoke. The more in-depth he went, the more the Lieutenant softened. Mike knew he'd shattered the Lieutenant's veneer. He'd whipped him. The real Detective Palotti was back.

"I've taught you well, Detective," Hauk said as he clung to the last vestige of his ego. "You did indeed broaden your horizons, and I tip my hat to you." Hauk leaned across the desk and shook hands with Mike and Covey. "Good work. Keep it up. I acknowledge my error. I'm seldom wrong, but this one time I was. Please accept my regrets."

#

Covey and Mike sat at a back booth of the deli. Mike nibbled around the edges of his corn beef on rye while Covey picked the cucumbers from his chef salad and scooted them aside. He chuckled as he searched the depths of the lettuce with his fork. "You got him good, Palotti. That's for sure. I loved it." He sat back and sipped his ice tea. "So tell me, you know who it is, don't you?"

Mike shook his head. "If I knew and could prove it, I'd be at the District Attorney's office right now getting a warrant."

"I'm not saying you've got an airtight case, but in your mind you know damned good and well who the bastard is, right?"

"Maybe. Maybe not." He shook his head again. "Close only counts in hand grenades and horseshoes."

"Two of them?" Covey's voice was commanding, yet inquisitive. "Is that what you think? You hit on Bonnie and Clyde." He paused to take a bite of lettuce and tomato, then continued. "A couple killers working in tandem similar to Henry Lee Lucas and Ottis Toole?"

"Look Sarge, I'm not there yet. In fact, we might never get there. Right now I'm trying to take a huge crossword puzzle and put it together. Sometimes a piece fits, but most of the time it doesn't. Yeah, I've got an idea or two, but I can't put squat on the table. Not yet at least."

The men continued their meals with idle prattle – the Cowboys draft picks, what was happening in the NHL, and the never-ending story of the mayor and chief having it out on the front page.

#

Mike sat his desk, sorting "While You Were Out" messages. It was that time, and he dreaded it. Even the thought gave him a headache. It was time to call a meeting with the survivors. Another time to lead them on, but be as honest as possible.

Bonnie and Clyde? he thought. No. Don't go down that road. Tell them a new lead developed, but don't go into any details he didn't want to read about in the paper. Parents, siblings, kids, all waiting to invoke justice on the thief who stole their loved ones from them. Good people – all of them, yet starved for information. Nevertheless, the morning paper bled them dry to find a headline article. Whatever he discussed with them would find its way into the paper and the ten o'clock news. As they say, "If it bleeds, it leads."

He wouldn't include Legree Triplett and the sword buried in the Settler's Cemetery.

#

The voice from the intercom snapped him back to reality. "Mike, your attorney is on the phone."

Mike pulled his chair close in to his desk and nudged the receiver into the crook of his neck. He wasn't anxious for anyone else to hear his half of the conversation, whichever way it might go. "Hi, Roger. Tell me some good news."

The old curmudgeon never developed a sense of humor. "Call your mama if you want some hugs and kisses, but I'm your attorney. You sitting down?" he snarled.

Mike rolled his eyes. "Go ahead. Hit me. What do you have?"

"How about this? You lost your ass."

Mike took a deep breath. His eyes watered. It was over. Whoever said hope is eternal hadn't gone through a divorce. "Okay, give it to me."

"She gets the house and the SUV, you pay nine hundred dollars a month child support and twenty-five percent of her house payment, and you get Samanta one weekend a month plus every other Christmas – same on her birthday."

"Do I get to keep my dirty socks?" he quipped.

"I did the best I could do, my friend. I'm sorry. I truly am. You screwed up big time and she's had it. She wants out." There was a long silence on the phone. "Her attorney is a pretty decent lady and was willing to work with us, but your former wife is really pissed."

"Where do we go now?"

"Come over to my office tomorrow and sign the papers. Get it over. If we go to court, she'll wipe you out completely."

Mike dried a tear that hung on his cheek. He was empty. His voice was soft. "See you in the morning."

#

Mike slipped behind the wheel of his VW, the last material thing he owned from his marriage. It was over. He pulled out of the parking lot and eased into traffic. The moment became a metaphor. The further he drove from his attorney's office, the greater the distance he placed between his family and himself. There was no one else to blame. He pulled to the curb and cried.

#

Dave Matthews jazz floated soothingly over his wilted body. He felt like an old man slouched in his Lazy Boy – tired and worthless, wearing only his underwear and socks. It had been two days since the divorce was final, but it felt like a month.

He looked across his efficiency apartment at the kitchen counter cluttered with dirty dishes and empty cans; tomato soup, sweet corn and clam chowder. They were his favorites, and in his judgment all he needed for a healthy diet. An empty cracker box lay on the floor next to the trashcan where he threw it and missed – no sense picking it up. He would get it when he emptied the trash.

Mike's mind had wavered back and forth ever since he'd signed the final decree. He was torn between self-pity and self-righteousness. He'd caused his own problems and deserved what he got, or he was another victim of police stress who fell into the clutches of a vice – in his case, sex. It was a professional hazard. Annalisa knew it. Everybody did. It wasn't his fault. The job did it to him.

He grasped the lever and lowered the footrest, pulled himself up and looked at the clock on the mantel. It was time to call an end to it – get on with his life or check out. Lots of cops did it. They even had a term for it, one they all understood. "He ate his gun," they would say.

Mike walked to the sink and with a sweep of his arm, sent the empty cans cascading onto the floor. "Bullshit," he bellowed. "There isn't anyone who can drive me to that. No one." He grabbed the broom from the corner and twenty minutes later the kitchen was in presentable condition – trash bags tied and neatly stacked by the back door; dirty dishes feeling the blast of sudsy hot water in the dishwasher; and the stinging scent of cleanser stinging his nostrils from the now sparkling sink.

He looked at his reflection in the back door window and laughed. "You're one ugly son-of-a-bitch, but you're getting your lazy ass back in gear." He looked again at the clock on the mantel. "Eleven o'clock. That's not too late. She'll still be awake," he whispered to himself.

She answered on the third ring. "Michael, where have you been? I've been so worried and haven't heard a peep from you."

"I've been on my private little trip to hell, but I'm back. I'm ready to get on with my life."

"You poor thing," she responded. "Tomorrow is Saturday. You don't have to get up early and go to work. Want to have a drink?"

"Yeah," he responded. His voice was strong. "Yeah, I really do. Give me an hour. I've got a couple things to do and I'll be there."

"What could you possibly have to do at this time of night?"

Mike laughed aloud. "Sweet Emily, I'm a single guy. I need to empty the trash, then shower and shave. I've put in one heck of a day, but I'll be ready for a drink when I get there."

"Anything else?" Her voice was a whisper.

He stopped breathing. His heart pounded. His mouth was suddenly dry. "You! You're what I want."

"See you in an hour," she replied. Then she hung up.

#

Fifty-four minutes exactly. He laughed confidently. "Pretty damn good if I do say so." He pulled to the curb. He was back – full of confidence, self-assured and ready to take on the world.

Emily stepped onto the porch as he walked up the sidewalk. "Hey cowboy, you're fast."

Mike smiled and nodded approval. "I'd tear the world apart to get to you." He stopped at the bottom of the stairs and looked at her. She was wearing an ankle-length nightgown that flowed to her bare feet and a single strand of black pearls draped her neck, standing in contrast to her soft white skin. The indirect light from the house highlighted her shape on the otherwise dark porch. She extended her hand to him. "Come here, Michael."

#

The sun shone on Mike's face. He rolled over and looked at the clock – ten o'clock on the nose. He lay back on the pillow and looked at Emily, still asleep, curled in a little ball under the silk sheet. He smiled, confident he was regaining control of his life, and equally confident he would capture the real "creature," Detective John Baldwin.

Twenty minutes later he stepped out of the shower and opened the bedroom door. Emily was up. The heady aroma of coffee floated into the bedroom from the kitchen. He wrapped a towel around his waist and went to the kitchen. He stood silently in the doorway, watching her as she moved about, unaware of his presence. She was wearing a pink, knee-length silk wraparound. She was glorious doing what millions of other women do every day, but she was unique, a one-of-a-kind.

"Good morning," he said softly.

Emily started, taken by surprise, then looked back over her shoulder. "Good morning to you, lover boy. How about a bagel and coffee? I've got some orange juice, too. Fresh and pulpy, just the way I like it. Want some?"

Mike smiled and sat down at the table in the nook overlooking the backyard. He watched in silence as she placed their breakfast on the table. Two toasted bagels on a platter surrounded by crystal containers of cream cheese, jelly and butter. She sat the mugs of coffee on the table, then slipped into the chair beside him, kissed his cheek, and whispered into his ear, "I love you, Mike."

"I love you, too."

He sipped the coffee, returned the mug onto the coaster, and moved sideways in his chair where he faced her directly. "Emily, it's too early for this and I know it, but I want to marry you. I've never loved a woman like you. I never felt like this for a woman. I love you with every fiber of my being."

She put her finger to his lips before he could continue.

"We have to be careful and we have to be realistic. We're in love, but we have to guard against jumping-in based on our passion." She leaned forward, cupped his cheeks in her hands and kissed his lips, then nibbled his ear lobe. She whispered in his ear as she stroked her fingernails through his hair, "If we truly love each other, we'll take the time to plan our lives together. Forever. Mr. and Mrs. Michael Palotti." She shifted her weight so they were face-to-face. Once again, she put her hands to his cheeks and her lips to his. They kissed softly.

"I love you, Emily. You give me purpose in my life." He nodded his head in approval. "Give me some time to get over this divorce. Give us time to really get to know each other, and time to grow our love." He smiled and kissed her forehead as he'd done so many times to little Samanta. "Our lives will be good."

He paused and looked into her eyes. "Until death do we part!"

Chapter Nineteen

MIKE FLICKED THE PAGES OF his desk calendar. It was less than two weeks until Labor Day and there was work to be done if he wanted to get away for the long weekend. It was a shot in the dark, but something he had to do. The Lieutenant said so. It was something they should have thought of sooner, but didn't. Anyhow, it wasn't likely to amount to anything.

"*Que tal, amigo,*" Rickey asked as he pulled a chair alongside Mike. "Sarge said we've got to get something done on your cases. What is it?"

"Swat flies," Mike joked.

"Yeah, well, where there are flies there's usually a pile of crap, so let's get it on."

Mike thumbed the envelopes in his out-basket, found the one with Rickey's name, and handed it to him. "You take half and I take half. We're going to try to backtrack and go after all their personal computers. If," he shrugged, "they still exist. Tech Services and Crime Analysis will go through them and see what if anything they find in common."

"We're back to the common denominator?" Rickey asked.

"Yep. They'll look at everything." He counted them off on his fingers. "URL's, email addresses, cookies, favorites, business transactions, deleted files, the whole ball of wax. If we're lucky, they'll find something. Otherwise ...?"

"Back to ground zero," Ricky responded.

Mike tore off yesterday's calendar page, wadded it up and tossed it in the basket. He looked at Rickey. "That's another metaphor."

#

It was mid-morning Thursday before they logged the last one into the Evidence Room. Each tower stood side-by-side. Sentinels lined up on the shelf like pagan gods guarding their secrets. The dim overhead light cast a muted shadow over them like so many corpses in the cooler waiting for the autopsy in the Medical Examiner's Office.

Mike stepped back and looked at them. Would these lifeless pieces of hardware hold the key? Only time would tell.

Rickey broke the silence. "Let's get the hell out of this dungeon. It gives me allergies with all the dust in this joint. Man, it's like a graveyard for a bunch of worthless shit."

"Right behind you, my good man," Mike responded as they turned toward the exit. "I'll call Tech Services when we get to the office. Keep your fingers crossed," he lied. He shivered. What if they each had a business transaction with American Plains Realty?

#

With more time on the books than he could ever use, Mike took Friday off as a comp day. Crime Analysis promised they'd work over the weekend so he could have some results, however tentative they might be, by Monday.

It was time he put to good use. Laundry, dry cleaning, car wash and an afternoon nap on Friday; Saturday was even less exciting – vacuum, dust, fold and put away the laundry; apply for a new credit card in his own name, and last but not least, hit the Triple Bar T on Greenville Avenue for a barbeque sandwich and beer for dinner. Not overwhelming excitement, but in these times a little bit went a long way. Sunday would be a late sleep, read the paper, shine shoes, watch the NASCAR races on TV, and be in bed by ten o'clock – the fast life of a novice bachelor in Dallas – somewhere in the neighborhood of ho-hum.

#

It was mid-afternoon on Monday when the envelope arrived on his desk.

"Okay, Mister Detective, here it is," Angie said when she laid it carefully, almost religiously, in the center of his desk. She chuckled softly and tossed a quick glance over her shoulder as she turned to leave. "C.A. said you'd have a ball with this. Good luck."

He watched her walk away. She knew what she was doing, and he knew she knew what he was doing. She had a tight butt, slim waist, and walked with the elegance of a model. He'd never tried it, but if she kept it up, well, who knows? He smiled. Oh, yeah, she would.

He pulled the half-dozen sheets of paper from the envelope and scanned them quickly. Each sheet was titled in bold letters. URL Commonalities; E-mail commonalities; Cookies; Temporary Internet Files; Temporary Files; Bookmarks, Favorites, and History Files. He looked back in the envelope. There was another single sheet of paper. He pulled it out and saw it bore the heading, "Executive Summary." He read it slowly.

> To: Detective Michael Palotti,
> The Dallas Police Department, Crime Analysis Division, has completed an inspection of the computer files you logged into the Evidence Division. Working in conjunction with the Technical Services Division, and with the information you provided, we find no substantive evidence to guide further investigation based upon these computer files.
>
> None of the computers has any information pertaining to Emily Morgan, Walter Bumstead, any Oklahoma real estate company or transaction, a cross-file of the names or addresses of any of the listed homicide victims or locations of death, a reference to Bonnie and Clyde or any crimes of that era, Durant Oklahoma or any other cemetery, nor the names of any known members of the Dallas Police Department or the Tulsa Police Department.
>
> There are numerous comparisons of computer usage of Internet Service Providers such as AOL; on-line shopping such as Barnes and Noble, Amazon, and numerous other retail establishments; map and people finders; yellow pages; and the weather.
>
> By contrast, there were no findings of pornography or any X-rated websites, searches of government data-bases, nor of posting on blogs or similar websites.
>
> In conclusion, there is no identifiable linkage between these computers and the murders of the several victims identified in your report.
> Signed,
> Capt. Rae Martinez
>   Crime Analysis Division

#

Mike typed a brief memorandum to the Lieutenant and Sergeant to maintain the paper trail of this latest effort, however futile it was, attached a copy of the Crime Analysis Executive Summary, then dumped them unceremoniously into his out-basket. He leaned back, put his feet on his desk, locked his fingers behind his head and breathed a quiet sigh of relief – there was no realty business to link her to any of the victims.

Not guilty, he thought. *She didn't do it*. A confident smile creased his lips. Deep in his mind he knew there was some possibility, however remote it might be. Nevertheless, every stone he turned over didn't have her name on it or anyone else's for that matter. She must be innocent. If she truly was, that left only one other person who fit the common denominator theme – Detective John Baldwin. Not to be forgotten, though, was the second person, whoever he might be. Baldwin was the key to finding him.

#

It was nearly eight o'clock by the time he delivered the last of the computers to their rightful owners. He offered each of them the same simple explanation, but left them with a glimmer of hope – there always must be something to keep them going.

"Thanks, it was a big help," he would say. Or, "No, it didn't give us anything definitive, but at least gave us some guidance to keep us on the right path and not let us get too far astray." Then with a gentle smile and nod of affirmation, he closed, "We've had something new pop up, so there're some leads we have to check out. We'll get him; it's just a matter of time. Have faith; his day is coming. We won't give up."

It was after nine when he flopped down with a cold Foster's in his Lazy Boy. He kicked off his Cole Han loafers, flipped up the footrest and stretched out.

The ceiling fan turned slowly, circulating the warm, humid summer air. He rolled the beer can across his forehead and felt perspiration run down the side of his neck. The day was hard and he was tired. What if, just what if, her name was in any of those computers? The thought made him quiver. She was innocent. No, not just innocent. She was another victim, albeit an unreported one, but one of Baldwin's victims nonetheless.

He placed the beer can on the table, crossed his arms across his chest and closed his eyes. Sleep crept up on him and soothed the stress and concerns of the day.

#

He woke with a start, drenched in perspiration. It was a dream – a nightmare. He looked about quickly, then lowered the footrest and rubbed his eyes. He checked his watch. One o'clock. He'd slept for at least three hours, maybe four. What a horrid dream. He pulled himself up and went to the bathroom. Suddenly, it was déjà vu at the Ipanema Café.

He leaned on the countertop and looked at his reflection in the mirror. His hair was tousled; sweat ran down his forehead and off the tip of his nose. He glanced down at his fingers gripping the edge of the sink. They were shaking. He was as frightened as he'd ever been in his life.

The dream – he was in his chair. She stood over him. He didn't know what she was wearing. She pointed a gun into his face and fired. He saw the bullet coming out of the barrel; the unspent gunpowder was dark specks in the raging flame that exploded from the pistol. The bullet ripped into his nose, then into the roof of his mouth and stopped midway through his brain. He was dead, but still aware of what was happening. She was laughing – hard. Almost hysterically. He knew she was enjoying every moment of his agony the way his head crashed back against the headrest, then flopped forward and lay across his chest; the way his warm blood soaked his clothes and the chair; the mess on the wall behind him; the involuntary urination and defecation that covered his trousers.

He watched her laughing subside. She smiled her most gorgeous smile, then leaned over his lifeless body and kissed his forehead. She straightened up and he saw her mouth covered with his blood. She licked her lips, turned and left.

#

Mike stood beneath the shower and let the hot water pour over his face. His head pounded. The headaches had returned with a vengeance. He leaned against the imitation marble and allowed himself to slide down into a sitting position. The water cascaded over him. He lowered his head and wept. Their marriage was dead. Never again would Samanta run to the door to meet her daddy. There would be no more adventures going to Six Flags for the day, no squeals of delight and terror on roller coasters or water rides, and no more Saturday afternoon jaunts to Dairy Queen. Never again would he kiss Samanta's little bumps and bruises and make them well. Never again would Annalisa lay her head on his shoulder after they made love and go to sleep.

He'd killed all of it – all of them. There was no one else to blame. He was the most vicious killer of all. Emily? Maybe so. Probably not. It was Baldwin. It had to be. Tonight was just a bad night, nothing more.

He watched the water spiral down the drain into the sewer. It was a dream, not a premonition. Just a dream. That's all.

#

Mike sat at his desk. The case was done. He knew it, but nobody else did. Neither he nor Hauk, nor anyone else, would make a case against Baldwin. He was too smart and covered his tracks, and sure as hell it wasn't Emily. She was as much a victim as the people who were dead and buried. There wasn't anyone else. To hell with Baldwin's friend. They'd never identify him. Not without Baldwin, and that son-of-a-bitch would get away with it.

Mike's mind wandered. Why would anybody, especially a cop, kill so many people without any reason? It didn't make sense. There was no logic to it. Maybe that was the answer. There was no logic because he was a psychopath. He killed for the pure pleasure of murder – the joy of watching someone die.

Another question haunted Mike – was he done, or would he sometime, somewhere, strike again?

CHAPTER TWENTY

IT WAS GOING HOME TIME. The clerks and secretaries had abandoned their keyboards and telephones and left fifteen minutes ago. Covey was on vacation. Hauk's office light still shone into the hallway. The prick! He would stay just to prove a point until everyone else was gone for the day. Then he would satiate his ego that he worked longer and harder than everyone else. He would be liberated to go home to his Junior League wife and his Honor Roll second-grade brat.

Mike shoved back from his desk, flipped off his light and started down the hall past Hauk's door. He mumbled under his breath, "SLA, sir."

"What was that, Detective?" the Lieutenant called out.

"See you later, sir," Mike replied.

"Yes. Yes, Mike. See you tomorrow."

The detective laughed to himself. It was a little something good that came from Baldwin. "So long asshole."

#

Two traffic accident detours and one hour later, Mike unlocked the door to his apartment – his home. He pursed his lips and gritted his teeth. He was filled with regrets, but couldn't undo a thing. He accepted his responsibility. Now was the time to build his future and it started with her.

He stood in front of the open refrigerator and sorted through his ample supply of beer – some of it excellent, some good and some okay. He made his purchases based on the balance of his checking account that day. He shrugged. Anyhow, it gave him a pretty broad sample of tastes.

He picked a green-labeled bottle of one of the better ones – Grolsch Lager. He snapped it open and held a frosted mug over the sink while he poured the beer into it. The foam rose to the rim, balanced itself and stopped. He leaned over and dipped his upper lip into the suds, then sucked lightly to savor the smooth delicious taste.

He grabbed a second bottle from the refrigerator, found the television remote down in the cushion of the sofa, and sprawled out as he kicked off his shoes. He placed the beers on coasters on the coffee table, loosened his tie, and pulled his cell phone from his belt. He held the phone up in front of his face for a moment and studied it as a golfer takes time mentally to visualize his shot before he approaches the ball.

The phone beckoned him silently. It commanded him – call her. He hit the speed dial and leaned back. She answered on the second ring.

"Hi, cowboy. I was waiting to hear from you."

"Full day, that's for sure. Got time for dinner?"

"Can't tonight. I had a call this afternoon from Aunt Emma. Remember her?"

"Yeah, what's up?"

"She needs me up there for a few days. She had an emergency gall bladder operation, goes home tomorrow, and wants me to come up and help her." Emily paused. The phone was quiet.

"Back to Tulsa?" he asked.

"Never thought I'd do it, but yeah, I have to. I'm all she's got and she needs me."

"When will I see you again?"

"I don't know – maybe three or four days. I'm packing the car now and will drive up there in the morning."

"Can you handle it?" Mike paused. "You know what I mean. There. Him. You won't let Baldwin know you're in town will you?"

"Give me a break, Mike," she laughed. "Not just no, but hell no."

"We've got to stay ahead of him. There's no way we can let him know you're in town." He paused to gather his thoughts. "Hold on a minute, let me think about this – okay, leave your cell phone turned off. I won't call you. Only turn it on to make a call, but don't let him have access to you. He's a smart guy. We can't let him have any chance of finding you there, in his den so to speak. If you want to call me, turn it on, keep it brief, then flick it off. If he talks to you after you get back here, you can just pass it off that you're having trouble with it – and that's not much of a lie. We have so damn many connection problems with these things, he'll believe you."

"Thanks" she replied. "Good idea. Anyway, I'll keep it quick. I sure don't want to spend much time around there. I'll do a little grocery shopping for her, that kind of thing, then I'll give you a buzz when I'm heading home."

Mike looked at his phone. His mouth was dry. His voice cracked. "I'll miss you. Be careful."

"Just a few days, then let's take some time for us."

He smiled. "I love you."

"I love you, too, Detective Palotti. Bye-bye."

#

Take some time, he thought. Yeah, that's what we need to do. Have some time alone – Second Meadow. Maybe First Meadow. It's not as high and has better natural shelter. There're plenty of trees and more of a closed canyon to shelter us instead of the wide open space further up. It'll be just the two of us. We can talk, plan our future, and get some healthy reality back into our lives.

She'll be home Monday, Tuesday at the latest. If we leave Friday morning we can have the whole weekend there alone. It's too late in the year for fishermen to be up that high. We can pack light, but warm, and have a great weekend in the perfect place. A campfire; morning coffee beneath the pines; cold and crisp pure mountain air; life the way it is supposed to be. And, most of all, Emily. Sweet Emily.

Finally, life was changing for the good.

#

Mike's Thursday went smoothly. He worked a two-man team with Ricky on a search warrant of a garage looking for a red Toyota hatchback that was the suspect vehicle in a serial rapist case. Bingo. It was there. The detectives looked at each other, high-fived and called for the Crime Scene Investigators to take over and search the car for trace evidence – hair, blood, and, of course, semen.

Mike drove to a nearby Starbucks while Rickey stayed with the car and waited for the other investigators. He returned as the CSI van pulled into the lot. He followed behind and watched as two men and a woman, all dressed in their DPD blue jumpsuits, got out and began talking with Rickey. He saw Rickey nod to him, so he got out, two coffees in hand. As he approached, he recognized the taller of the men as a partner from years ago in the Patrol Division.

"Andy," he said as he handed a coffee to Rickey, then shook hands with his old friend.

"Hello, Mike. Long time, no see. How have you been doing?"

"Knockin' em dead," he joked. "Just taking it as they come. How about you?"

"Been doing this for the last two years. What'cha guys got here?"

Mike nodded to Rickey.

"This is our suspect vehicle in a serial rape case, so we need you guys to take it apart and see what you've got."

The female investigator stepped forward and spoke. Mike looked at her. Tall, blond hair pulled back under a net, just a touch of makeup, professional yet attractive in her light blue jumpsuit and military boots. "Were any of your victims in the car? Did the assault happen in it?"

"Yeah," Rickey replied. "We think this guy did four women, and we can definitely tie him to this ride. He picked one of them up in Deep Ellum and dumped her down by the Trinity River. He left her for dead, but she wasn't. That's how we got the tag number, but the suspect stowed this piece of junk in this storage garage and we couldn't find it – until today, that is. Then just a little luck and a search warrant, and we got it."

"Okay, thanks," Andy replied. The CSI detectives walked back to their van, opened the side doors and pulled their toolboxes from the truck.

Mike returned to his and Rickey's car. He slid in the passenger's seat, then got out again and called to Rickey, who was following the others into the garage.

"Hey, Rick, I'm going to call and have somebody pick me up. You don't need me here. There's nothing I can do. You guys've got it."

"Sure thing. Thanks for coming. I'll catch you Monday."

#

Mike kicked back into his Lazy Boy and watched the fading red rays of the setting sun dart through the shutters of his only window to the outside world – a view of the parking lot, a row of oak trees, and the bumper-to-bumper traffic on Desmond Lane.

His mind wandered as he sipped one his beers – one on the low end of his scale, Old Milwaukee. She should be there by now. He took a deep breath, glanced at his cell phone lying quietly on the coffee table, then closed his eyes. She wouldn't call, not this soon.

He relaxed, but still felt a surge of adrenalin flow through his veins. He knew what he had to do. This opportunity was too great to pass up. He would never forgive himself if he let it slip through his fingers. He could prove her innocence or guilt. One way or the other, he had to know. Tonight was perfect. His right hand rose slowly from the arm of the chair and touched his shirt pocket. With the slightest touch of his fingertips, he caressed the outline of her key. He exhaled, closed his eyes and lowered his head. The confidence of years past filled his mind and body. The time was now.

Chapter Twenty-One

HE THOUGHT ABOUT IT WHILE he drove casually to her house, listened to the radio and tapped his fingers on the steering wheel. There was no hurry. Whatever was there could wait for him. He could take his time, be calm and collected, be thorough and most of all, be objective. Call a spade a spade, whichever way it turns out. Tonight would put to rest any doubts.

She'd given her key to him, but never mentioned her alarm code. Not that it was a big deal. He knew it anyway and could bypass most alarms in a few seconds, but why give him one without the other? Was it a slip of the mind? Or, maybe one last shot to set him up?

He parked at the Movies 16 a few blocks from her house. His nondescript VW parked in a couple acres of otherwise non-descript cars and trucks. He tucked a pen light into his pants pocket, checked to be sure her key was in his pocket, opened the lock-pick kit one last time in case he needed it, and walked out of the lot. He crossed the thoroughfare and into her shaded street with its overhanging oaks, elms and magnolias protecting passersby from the glare of the streetlights.

He strolled the four blocks to her street, then jogged across the street when he approached her block. He wanted to be on the opposite side from her house to make a pass-by; to have one last look before he committed himself.

Michael Palotti, now a rogue detective, paused to check his watch. Eleven-fifteen. Perfect. Most of the people in her neighborhood were asleep or watching some late-night program. It was be very unlikely anyone would see him.

He walked purposefully, not wanting to draw attention from anyone who might be outside and see him. He strode the length of the block with only a casual glance at her house – no more and no less than he did the others.

The darkness and the lights and shadows reminded him of when he was a little boy and they played outside at night. It was what they called "creepy quiet." Surely, tonight was that way. No one was stirring. The shadows from the trees scurried back and forth on the sidewalk in the gentle breeze. An occasional light shone from a scattering of porch lights; soft threads of light floated from what were most likely bedroom windows. Otherwise, it was creepy quiet, just like that which scared little boys. He couldn't have ordered it any better. He continued on another block, crossed over and retraced his way back to … *What?* he thought. *Guilty or another victim?*

He stopped when he reached the front of her house, took a deep breath, pulled her key from his pocket and walked up the sidewalk. He acted as though he was home – no hurry, take your time.

He slipped the key into the lock, twisted it to the left and heard the bolt slide open. He didn't pause as he stepped inside. The house was dark. He reached out with his left hand and felt the knob on the closet door. He pulled it open with one hand as he took the pen light from his pocket and flicked it on. He knew most alarms were set to pause forty seconds after being activated before sending a coded message to the emergency office. There was plenty of time. There was no need to hurry, but no time to be lackadaisical.

The digital readout on alarm pad flashed small red letters – OPEN DOOR. He opened the dust cover and shined the light on the keypad. It was so simple. He tapped in her code, 0-2-7-4. The flashing letters stopped. The alarm was off. He was home free.

Mike shuddered. It had been too many years to count since he'd made his last clandestine entry. It sent a chill through his body. He shivered, took a deep breath and accepted what he was about to do – not exactly legal, but something that must be done.

The house was ghostly quiet. He was conscious of her absence – whether she was a maniacal killer, a crime victim or a passionate lover didn't make any difference. Nevertheless, the house seemed so empty without her. The only sound was that of his pounding heart.

He shut the closet door and shone the narrow light beam around the entryway and living room. Everything was as he expected them to be – tables, sofa, chairs, lamps, everything in place. No surprises.

He turned the light off and gave his eyes a moment to adjust to the darkness and put his mind at ease, to come to grips with who he was. Michael Palotti, the man? The detective? The lover? The man searching for the truth? He pulled up the occasional chair across from the entryway closet and sat down. He took time to adjust to the various sounds: the house; the sounds outside; to become part of the environment; but, to be careful and thorough in his search for the answer.

Time crept slowly. Perspiration ran down his brow. His back was wet with sweat. His mind focused on the moment and the task at hand. He became one within himself. After a few interminable minutes, but when he was comfortable with his surroundings, he stood up, flicked his light on and walked silently to her bedroom. If there were an answer, it would be here or in her small private office adjoining the bedroom. Nowhere else.

He felt her presence, even in the seclusion of her bedroom. The king-size bed was neatly made. Half-a-dozen throw pillows were arrayed against the headboard. The floral design bedspread was pulled tight. It hung perfectly over the sides and was tucked beneath the footboard. Everything was neat and orderly as always.

He stepped quietly to the nightstand on the right of the bed, knelt down, then leaned back on his heels and shone the light along the edges of the drawers and diagonally across the top on the nightstand. Mike, the detective, looked for any telltale signs of a trap; a single hair or thread surreptitiously planted to snare a careless – who? Who would she lay a trap for, him or John?

He caught himself holding his breath in anticipation. He exhaled and gave a congratulatory chuckle – nothing there. The nightstand was clean. No smudges or dust he might disturb. The drawer wasn't rigged. He was clear. He pulled the drawer open slowly and caught himself biting his lower lip. It was a nervous habit when he was under pressure. He stopped and brushed the sweat from his brow with the back of his hand again, then pulled the drawer out and put it on the floor. He took a moment to catalog mentally how and where things were placed, then lifted each item one-by-one. A nail file, a bottle of fingernail polish, two blank scratch pads, four pencils, two ballpoint pens, a C-cell battery, several lightly soiled tissues with smudges of makeup on them, and in the back corner a small tan leather-bound book. It was no bigger than a pack of cigarettes and appeared to have been buried there and untouched since long ago.

Mike sat back and leaned against the bed, gripped the penlight in his teeth and opened the book. It was inscribed,

To my darling Emily,

> *Happy 14th Birthday to my sweetest niece.*
> *This book of Irish poems is fitting to your*
> *Wonderful experiences as a fledgling writer.*
> *With love,*
> *Aunt Emma.*

Mike thumbed quickly through the pages. It was just that – a book of poems to a little girl. Nevertheless, it supported her assertion there was an Aunt Emma; she wasn't a figment of Emily's imagination. She was real and Emily was with her this very minute. The book wasn't evidence, per se, but it lent support that the two of them were related, and it went back for many years.

Mike carefully replaced each item exactly how and where it was, then eased the drawer shut. He put his hand on the bed and lifted himself upright, then walked around to the other nightstand. Once again, he examined it for traps, but there were none. He paused for a moment and thought about himself as a trespasser, a sneak, a thief in the night. He flicked off his light, sat on the floor and leaned back against the bed. His shirt was soaked with sweat, yet goose bumps covered his body. He bit his lip again, flicked the light back on and opened the drawer. He had a job to do, trespasser and sneak or not.

He chuckled quietly. It was her love making drawer, but for him, John, or who? Maybe herself? A bottle of almond massage oil, another labeled Natural Botanical Aromatherapy Massage Oil, and a bottle of Natural Herbal Massage Lotion. He smiled inwardly. At least she believed in "the natural."

Mike replaced the items and closed the drawer. He let out a deep breath. So far, so good. Aunt Emma was real and Emily enjoyed sex. There was nothing to implicate her as a serial murderer.

He shone the narrow beam of the light across the room to the door to her office. He took only one step away from the bed when he heard it – a voice. He froze and shut off the light. He knelt gingerly beside the bed, taking his bearings and listening to the voice, or was it voices? He waited in the darkness. His heart pounded.

He had an excuse if he needed it, but it was weak at best. Certainly she would learn he was in her house while she was gone. His mind raced. Did she plan this all along? Did she set him up?

He felt his back pocket. Every cop carries one – an off-duty gun. It was there. His little peashooter: a two-inch barrel .38 revolver loaded with five hollow-point rounds. He made his decision and moved quietly through the house in total darkness, unconcerned with bumping into furniture; he had been in her house so many times that he knew every nook and cranny like the back of his hand. He wouldn't trip over anything, but had to take the offense. He couldn't simply sit and wait. He would see who was outside and take it from there.

It would be one of two things. First, somebody saw him and called the Highland Park Police. Or, the worst case scenario – there was a real burglar breaking into the house. It was time to find out.

He walked to the front of the house, taking only the lightest breaths, moving as silently as a shadow and stopping alongside the door. The voices, more than two, were on the porch. Someone with a flashlight was shining it in the windows. He leaned back as much as he could as the beam danced along the walls and furniture, nearly scathing his face as he willed his body to melt into the wall. He lowered himself slowly to his hands and knees and crawled back into the living room.

It could only be the cops. No burglar would stand on the porch and look in the windows like that. It could only be the boys in blue from Highland Park. Someone saw him and dialed 9-1-1.

He saw beams of lights shining through the windows from the front, back and one side, all at the same time. The house was surrounded. If they came in, he would use the feeble excuse that he was the owner's fiancé and planned to house-sit while she was in Tulsa with her sick Aunt Emma. His purpose was that she has trouble with an ex-boyfriend, sort of true, so he was simply guarding her place for her – just in case.

He was glad he'd made the decision against using latex gloves. Burglars use them – boyfriends don't – and his story was weak enough without having to explain them. The cops wouldn't like his story, but he could show them her key and give them her alarm code. Hell, they could call Aunt Emma. Besides that, a cop, too – one of Dallas' finest.

They'd have their doubts about his story, but they couldn't book him. Yeah, she might find out and he'd explain it like that if he must. He'd already made up a bullshit story for her just in case – he was waiting to see if John Baldwin, the little weasel, was watching for her to be gone so he could get back in the house and start some of his sick games again. However, the best solution to this mess was that the cops would check the house, find everything secure, call it another false alarm, and go back to wherever they came from.

The roving lights gathered on the porch. He heard their voices, but was not able to distinguish what they were saying, so he again crawled back to the door. The voices were muffled, but clear enough. One of them was speaking: "... if that crazy old whack calls in another prowler, I think we should commit her at Parkland 10-96. She's crazy as a loon."

There was all-around soft laughter and the sound of footsteps moving away from the house toward the street. Mike rose carefully, moved to the edge of the window and peered outside. Two marked police cars were parked at the curb. He watched as two cops approached the car in front of the other. One cop got into the passenger side and a large rotund patrolman got in behind the wheel. A female officer, with her ponytail flowing from beneath the back of her cap, went to the other car, got in, accelerated, made a U-turn and headed out of the neighborhood. Mike watched as the two-man car sat with their dome light on while the driver was leaning over, apparently updating his activity sheet – another false alarm. A minute later, they were gone. He was alone.

The clock on the mantel chimed the time – midnight. Mike walked slowly to the kitchen, turned on the faucet, leaned down with a cupped hand and took a long drink. He was hot and dry. He looked out the back window into the darkness. It was beautiful solitude. He loved this place. Most of all, he loved Emily. A melancholy mood swept over him. He was comfortable. He had time to do what must be done and let things fall where they may. In his own heart, he knew he wouldn't find anything, but he must look through everything. Just this one time and its over – guilty or innocent. Tonight he was the prosecutor and the jury. He could present all the evidence and make a finding.

"Please, God," he uttered, "I've screwed up so many lives. Please let this come out okay. I need her, and I know now that I need you. Please."

With his eyes adjusted to the darkness, he moved carefully to her bedroom and then to her office. It wasn't big or fancy. In fact, he recalled her as describing it as utilitarian. He nodded his head in agreement; nicer than his cubicle at the department, but not an over expenditure of elegance. There was an oak desk with three drawers, the pc tower on the floor next to it, and the flat screen monitor beneath a dust cover on the desk. A matching oak five-shelf bookshelf stood alongside the desk. Each shelf was filled with books. He scanned them quickly with his light – Police Administration; Organizational Analysis; a complete set of police command books on the major divisions of most police departments – Patrol, Investigations, Traffic Enforcement; Traffic Engineering; Organized Crime – the list went on. It covered every facet of criminal justice. It was just as would be expected from someone doing research and teaching in the law enforcement field. On the opposite side of the desk was a three-drawer file cabinet.

If the answer existed, he was within an arm's reach of it. He had to find it. *Where to start?* he thought. He pulled up the steno-type chair and sat at her desk. The tiny green light of the pc was glowing. Her computer was turned on. He commanded the keys to her kingdom. He moved the mouse slightly and the screen came alive. He was into her DSL connection. He smiled to himself. It was too easy. With a glorified swing of his hand, he tossed the dust cover aside and bowed to the monitor as it came alive. "Welcome to the play," he whispered.

His hand moved the mouse up to the history icon; he clicked it and, it was there. Ten days of her Internet use. He scrolled down – *Wall Street Journal; New York Times; Discovery Channel; Google search; Internet payments; CNN weather*; her email, you4me@desdra.com; and last and least, The Horoscope Channel. He scanned the emails – all spam.

He flicked over to the cookies files – empty. Temporary Internet files – also empty. Finally he went to her "C" Drive. It was checked for errors and de-fragmented two days ago. Nearly everything was cleared out, and what little was left further served to vindicate her. He slipped the mouse back where he'd found it between her speakers, pushed back the chair and smiled. No serial murder sites here.

He moved to the file cabinet, got on his knees and opened the bottom drawer. He pulled it open and found it filled with a jumble of photographs. His heart quickened. With the disorganized clutter so much out of character for her, Mike wasn't concerned about taking them out and replacing them in any particular order. With legs crossed Indian style, he sat on the floor and removed a handful of them – old family pictures. Most of them were black and white, and even a few Polaroid shots of what probably were family pets: a mongrel dog, two kittens and a parrot.

He recognized Emily as a teenager in a couple of them. Others were of friends and family members at birthday parties, Christmas, vacation at the beach, and several class pictures in elementary school. He dumped the first handful back and took another. It was more of the same. Not much more than a junk drawer, he decided. Old photos that she couldn't part with, but not interested enough to organize and file them.

He pushed the drawer shut as the clock chimed the half-hour. It was twelve-thirty. *One more hour,* he thought. *No more than that. Don't push your luck.*

He opened the middle drawer and his eyes were drawn immediately to the tabbed folder where the light was focused – Income Tax. He smiled. This had to be the answer if there is one at all. He pulled out the file on top – last year's tax return. He opened it carefully, teasing his own curiosity of what he was going to find.

He laughed aloud. She paid $2,347.88 on her taxable income of $167,543.00. He flipped through the pages. Almost all of it came in the form of dividends on stocks and bonds, plus a rebate from a previous overpayment of taxes. He shrugged. No income from a job.

He laid the file down and pulled out the previous year. She did better. She got back $469.85 on her income of $198,318.00. Once again, most of it from dividends in the stock market, but she also had a W-2 from her real estate job in Tulsa where she'd earned $69,632.69. Mike laughed again. Sure, that's reported, but how much did she make that was never reported? Of course, that's where Baldwin got into the act.

He took a deep breath and blew it out. He wasn't proving anything, but the opposite was also true. He wasn't finding anything to tie her to the murders. Therefore, he was finding more to support her innocence. Maybe it was exactly as she told him. He nodded his head. Maybe so.

He quickly flicked to the third year back and opened the file. "Son-of-a-bitch," he mumbled. She reported income of $204,602.00. Once again, most of it in dividends, but she still reported $71,105.45 income from her real estate sales. He shook his head. She was cleaning up and got too greedy. He wondered how much more she'd made under the table. She was making a killing. No wonder the cops and feds were beating the bushes to put her and people like her in jail. Another glaring example, he thought, of white-collar criminals making a fortune and all the little Mexicans and Blacks robbing gas stations for a few bucks and going to prison. He shook his head. That's the way the game is played.

He put the tax files back and closed the drawer. He was finished. Everything he found supported her story. She was clean – well, clean as far as not being a murderer. She just let herself get greedy and along came the great Detective Baldwin, and down went the pretty little real estate queen of Oklahoma. Bim-bam, thank you ma'am. He gotcha, and gotcha good, that bastard.

One last look. The top drawer. He got up on his knees and opened it slowly. His mouth dropped open. His picture glared up at him. He leaned over and looked closely at it. His heart pounded. Suddenly, out of nowhere, his head began to ache as hard as ever. He lifted the picture out of the drawer and held it in his trembling hands. Drops of perspiration dripped from the tip of his nose. He was short of breath. It was a framed 8 x 10 in a sleek silver frame with a black mounting – just like when he last saw it on their dresser. His and Annalisa's dresser.

Mike sat back on the floor and shone the light on his picture. His mind raced; his head pounded. How? When? Why did she have it? He thought about it. This particular picture was one he never liked and he once asked Annalisa to put it away, but she liked it and left it on the dresser. *Damn it*, he thought. *When did I last see it?* He shook his head. He couldn't remember. It's just one of those things you see every day and never pay any attention to it. Somehow, it ended up in Emily's drawer. The question was a basic cop question they ask when they interview victims and witnesses – when, why and how? Detective Palotti didn't have an answer.

He laid it on the floor and peered back into the drawer. There was a like-sized box beneath where the picture was. He lifted it out, but the beam of his light shone on what was under the box.

A similar sized picture of John Baldwin stared back at him.

Chapter Twenty-Two

MIKE SAT ON THE EDGE on the bed with Baldwin's picture in one hand and the stationary-sized box in the other. His hands trembled. Did he find the answer? He laid the photograph beside him, opened the box with a slow and deliberate motion, and shone his flashlight on its contents. A small stack of newspaper clippings were on top. He unfolded them and briefly scanned their contents – four different articles, each about Baldwin. The first was an old picture and clipping of him when he arrested a man who killed his wife and two children; the second was a group picture of him and four other cops being promoted to detective; the third was an article about his former wife and him serving food at a dinner for homeless men. The fourth article, the one on the bottom, caused Mike to pause and read it a second time, then a third. Its headline was abrupt. He read it slowly:

DETECTIVE REPRIMANDED FOR ESCAPE

Detective John Baldwin received a letter of reprimand and a three-day suspension from the Chief of Police for his alleged negligence in the escape of Martin Delmonico, a sexual predator. Delmonico was left alone in an unlocked interview room in the Tulsa Police Department for what police officials report were only a few minutes before he fled undetected.

Detective Baldwin was conducting the interview of the prisoner, who was already incarcerated for several sex crimes, when the detective left the room to take a phone call. In his report, Baldwin alleged he went no more than fifteen feet from the interview room and thought he locked the door before taking the call.

Delmonico, who has eluded capture, is described as a Italian male, 5' 9" tall, weighs 155 pounds, and is described as being strong and muscular. He has dark hair and a mustache.

Anyone knowing Delmonico's whereabouts should call the Tulsa Police Department and may be eligible for a cash reward.

#

Mike looked at the date of the news clipping – four years ago. It preceded all of the Tulsa and Dallas serial murder cases, and it preceded Emily's real estate venture in Tulsa.

Could it be? he wondered. Could Delmonico and Baldwin be working in concert? Was the escape part of a greater plan? Did this one article stand in support of Emily's allegation about another man? Was he the so-called "other man" she spoke of when she was raped?

His hands trembled as he sorted the other papers in the box. "Junk," he whispered to himself – Baldwin's home and cell phone numbers; his home address and business address; his dead wife's name along with his son's name and birth date. All of it added up and made sense. She interviewed him as part of her project; she was a victim of his and maybe Delmonico's sexual deviance; she was aware of his wife's death and his little boy. Mike shook his head. The Delmonico story was an earthquake!

Suddenly, he shuddered. His breathing quickened. An explosion of electricity ripped through his body. Didn't he describe the killer to himself and to Annalisa as being demonic? Now, this name – Delmonico. Was this the link? Did this little box validate her innocence and at the same time link Baldwin and Delmonico together in these grisly crimes? It had to be.

He returned each item to its proper place in the box, then opened "his" box. Déjà vu Baldwin's box. Half-a-dozen news articles of cases he'd worked over the years before he ever heard of Emily Morgan; pages ripped from her notebook with his phone numbers when he lived at home with Annalisa; another with his apartment address and phone number; her "hen's scratch" shorthand notes from their first interview at his office; a recipe for pineapple upside cake on a 3x5 card in Annalisa's handwriting; one of the formal invitations to the party at Emily's house which he and Annalisa attended together; and just as in Baldwin's box, a note with Samanta's birthday written on it.

He wet his lips. The box was void of anything to support any thought, however remote, of her involvement in the murders. Nevertheless, she had his framed picture. How and why did she have it? He could only guess she took it when they enjoyed their tryst at his house. That must be it. But the question persisted – why? Was it her little kinky thing to steal his picture right out from under his wife's nose? At what point, he wondered, did her own pleasure take over from Baldwin's and Delmonico's direction? Or, was that even a part of their production, and then she'd kept it as she fell evermore in love with him?

He didn't know, and it didn't make any difference. That was then and this is now. He looked at his watch. Fifteen more minutes. That was all he could allow himself. It was his plan – get in; don't dally; inspect and go. Don't get greedy to find more. Most of the people in jail were there because they were greedy and didn't know when to say when. He did. Fifteen minutes and out.

He put the boxes back in the drawer and closed it. He flicked off his penlight and sat in silence on the edge of her bed, willing himself to become one with the room. If there was anything else there, it was now or never.

He listened to his own heartbeat. He waited – there was nothing. He could look all night and wouldn't find anything because there wasn't anything there. It was over. She didn't kill anyone.

#

It was two o'clock by the time Mike left the Café Ipanema. He wouldn't sleep tonight anyway, and two cups of coffee and a chocolate muffin would guarantee he had enough caffeine in his system to keep him awake for hours.

He joined the never-ending traffic barreling down the Central Expressway toward downtown, took the Lover's Lane Exit, slipped by the Southern Methodist campus and eased his way back into her neighborhood. He laughed to himself – every criminal feels the urge to return to the scene of the crime. He was no different. He guided his VW down Emily's block, but never slowed as he passed her house. Nevertheless, he looked at it out of the corner of his eye – exactly where he'd left it. Everything was the same and no one was the wiser. He breathed deeply and let it out slowly. He was finished. She was no serial killer and he was in love with her.

For the first time in a long time, he relaxed and felt good about himself – well, pretty good.

#

Mike sat in the silver-blue hue that bathed his living room. He stared blankly at the television screen with the artist's name, a short biography, and the name of the album and song that was playing from the uninterrupted, twenty-four hour music – the sounds of the season. It was soft and melodic, and soothed his troubled soul.

What did he miss? He closed his eyes, listened to the music and concentrated. He didn't miss anything because there wasn't anything else there. Whatever hunch he held that she might be involved in the murders was dispelled by the facts, and they were cold and hard. They didn't link her to the crimes. If it wasn't for that bizarre evening at her house, she would never be considered as having any knowledge of them. Was she what the police classified as an "involved party?" Absolutely. A suspect? Possibly, but was cleared by all the evidence, none of which pointed back to her.

The soft melodies penetrated his soul – love songs, and he was in love, but troubled. He asked himself the question. Was he blinded by love and passion? Did he close his eyes to the possibility of Emily being the heartless serial murderer? Where could he possibly find the answer to remove the lingering doubt she was implicated in the cases? Baldwin! He was the answer, but he would never confess – not in a million years.

Mike eased himself slowly from the Lazy Boy and walked across the room. Harry Belafonte Calypso was too much for this time of night. With a flick of his finger, Harry was gone. The room was dark and quiet. He walked to the window and stared out at the emptiness of the early morning hours. The parking lot was still and quiet. Traffic beyond the trees on Desmond Lane was nearly non-existent. A pale moon shot little glimpses through the scattered clouds. He shuddered. Michael Palotti, the husband, the dad, the detective, was as alone as he'd ever been in his life. There wasn't anyone he could talk to about his thoughts and conjecture, yet in his mind he knew there was only one other place to look for evidence – Baldwin's house. If he found anything there, it would confirm Baldwin as the prime suspect. If he found nothing, at least he would know in his own mind that he literally looked beneath every rock to determine Emily's guilt or innocence. Plus, he might find the first solid bit of evidence to tie Baldwin to the murders. However, that raised another problem. The search would be illegal, so he could not use it in a criminal case.

"What the hell," he muttered as he kicked off his shoes and flopped on the bed, "at least I'll know and screw the system."

#

Mike rolled over and looked at the clock. He'd slept longer than he thought was possible. It was nearly ten o'clock. He sat upright and looked at himself in the mirror. It wasn't a pretty picture; mussed hair, unshaven, rumpled sport shirt and trousers, and his socks hanging off the tips of his toes. It was quite a night. He looked like a washed-out drunk.

"Screw it," he muttered as he stood up and peeled off his clothes. Seconds later, he was standing in the shower. The hot water poured over his head and cleansed his body and mind. He shampooed and scrubbed until he felt like his fingertips were going to strip away his scalp, but it felt good. He was fresh and clean, and had a plan. It was high risk, but a plan nevertheless.

#

He leaned against the kitchen counter and punched the numbers into his cell phone. Three rings later, the familiar voice answered.

"Hi, Mike. Long time, no speak. What's up?"

"Just that," Mike answered. "It's been a long time and things aren't right. We need to do something about her. We can't just let her off the hook." He paused for a moment, but there was no response. "I can be there by mid-afternoon. Can I come by your house?"

Baldwin's voice was soft, nearly imperceptible. "Yeah, I guess – sure, come on if you want to, but I don't see what good it'll do."

"We can bury the hatchet for starters and see where we can go after that."

"Sure. Okay. Not a bad idea, I guess. Come on up. Do you have my address?" He didn't wait for a response. "It's 3108 Harley Drive. Think you can find it?" he asked. His voice was somber and emotionless.

"Sure," Mike replied. "I'll Google it and see you later. What about a cold beer for old time's sake?"

"See you at three o'clock," John replied as he hung up.

Mike rinsed and dried his coffee cup, placed it back in the cupboard and smiled proudly to himself. "Gotcha, you son-of-a-bitch," he uttered.

#

"Right on time," he whispered to himself. "Three cheers for the Internet. It would make Emily proud." Nevertheless, John's repulsive little PT Cruiser parked at the curb made it easier to find. He saw it from a block away. It was the ugliest car in America. Mike gritted his teeth. It was easy to abhor Baldwin; to hate him and everything about him. He was as rotten as a person could be.

Mike tucked the tail of his sport shirt in his trousers as he walked up the driveway and turned onto the sidewalk leading to the front door. He took time to notice the well-groomed grass and neatly trimmed boxwood hedge that ran the length of the house. The bastard took care of his yard, a damn sight better than his own apartment surrounded by a paved parking lot and a pitiable row of trees to separate it from the noise of the boulevard.

He paused when he reached the door to take a moment and check himself in the reflection of the glass storm door. He looked great, probably better than he really was.

The door swung open as he reached for the doorbell.

It was Emily.

Chapter Twenty-Three

MIKE TOOK HALF-A-STEP BACK and pulled the door open. His eyes buried themselves into her. She wasn't smiling, and neither was he.

She gestured with a nod of her head for him to come in. "I accidentally left my cell phone on and he called me about an hour ago," she whispered. "I don't know how, but he knew I was at Aunt Emma's." She paused as she looked down at her own feet and wiped a tear from her eye.

Mike was puzzled. A tear? What was happening?

"I guess he's been watching Aunt Emma's just in case I ever popped in there."

Mike glanced at her as he entered the living room. She was dressed as sloppily as he'd ever seen her – Levi's, jogging shoes, a faded gray sweatshirt, and her hair pulled back into a ponytail.

"How did you get here?" he demanded through his pursed lips. His voice was muted.

Emily pointed out the door. "I'm parked right across the street from you."

Mike looked out the door. He was so focused on the PT Cruiser that he didn't look at anything else. Her Mercedes sat directly across the street from his VW. "Where's John?" he asked.

She pointed toward the hall leading to the bedrooms. "There – in bed. He's dead."

"What?" Mike's voice was dry. A cold shiver shot the length of his body. He shivered. "What the hell happened?"

"Come on, I'll show you," she replied as she started down the hall. She stopped at the last door on the left – the master bedroom. "He didn't answer the doorbell, so I came in. I couldn't figure it out.

I thought maybe he'd run out for a few minutes and would be right back." She nodded with her head toward the open bedroom door. "I started walking through the house and calling his name. Then I found him."

Mike stepped to the door and peered in. Baldwin was lying on his back across the bed. His right arm hung limply over the side, his head toward the pillows and his feet near the foot of the bed. He was dressed in a t-shirt, tan denims and loafers. A revolver lay on the floor just inches from his fingertips. Blood soaked the bed and dripped onto the floor. The entry was to the right temple and exited through the left, taking the majority of his skull and brains. They were sprayed over the headboard and the wall.

"How long have you been here?"

"Just a few minutes before you got here. I didn't know what to do. I was scared. Then I heard you out front." She put her arms around him and kissed his cheek. "Thank God you came. I was terrified."

Mike took her hand and led her to the living room. He sat on the sofa and she sat on the straight-back chair across the room. "This is deep shit," he uttered. He leaned forward and buried his head in his hands. His head pounded like a sledgehammer. His voice was whispered. "Did you touch anything?"

"The door, I guess that's about it."

"Not the gun or anything in the bedroom? Where's his kid, Jonah?"

She shook her head. "I don't know. I guess maybe at his grandmother's."

"We've got to look," Mike said as he got up and returned to the hall. He quickly looked in the other two bedrooms. No one was there. He hurriedly retraced his steps to the living room. "We've got five minutes at the most," he commanded. "We've got to see if there's any evidence of the murders, then we've got to call the PD."

He turned back to the master bedroom, stepped gingerly around the pool of blood that had begun to coagulate, and opened the closet door – shoes, trousers, shirts, old sweatshirts and winter shirts on the upper shelf. Mike rummaged quickly through it. There was nothing of interest.

"What about a note?" he asked as he stepped back out of the closet.

"I didn't look, but I don't see anything obvious," she responded as she glanced around the room.

"I saw his computer in the dining room. Be careful with your fingerprints, but take a look and see if anything is open where he might have left a note." He watched her back out of the bedroom before he stepped around the mess on the floor and went into the hallway. He glanced up and saw the panel to the crawlspace above the ceiling. He pulled off his shoes, shoved a toy box from Jonah's room on the floor beneath the panel, hopped up and slid it back. Just inside the edge were three cardboard boxes. He quickly pulled them to him through the opening, got down from the toy box and opened the first one – Christmas decorations. He shoved it aside and opened the second one – more seasonal decorations. He sat it atop the first box, then opened the third one.

"Bingo," he uttered through grimaced lips. This was his goldmine. The box with all the cameras, cd roms, and microphones he'd seen on the floor of Emily's house that night – the night from hell.

"Nothing here," he heard Emily call out as she came back into the hall.

He looked over his shoulder at her and smiled as she approached him. An air of confidence filled his face. "We've got it."

"Okay," she nodded as she looked into the open box, "but what are we going to do with it."

"Put it back for now and call 9-1-1." He smiled at her, looked back at the bed at Detective John Baldwin and nodded his approval. "It's over."

#

They sat on the sofa while an Internal Affairs Lieutenant, a Detective Sergeant, and a Uniform Division Sergeant asked them questions and dutifully made entries in their notebooks.

The lieutenant pulled up a chair, the same one Emily had sat in less than an hour ago. "Okay, let me make sure I've got this straight. You two," he nodded at Mike, "were working a tag-team affair on this cold case string of homicides. And you, ma'am," he gestured toward Emily, "were working with the blessing of both our chiefs on a research project."

"That's right," Mike asserted.

Emily moistened her lips and dabbed the tears that flowed from her eyes. "Yes, I'm staying in Tulsa with my aunt while she recovers from a trip to the hospital. Detective Baldwin called me about two hours ago on my cell phone and said we needed to talk."

"About what?" the lieutenant asked.

She shook her head. "He didn't say, but we've worked on this for months, so it wasn't all that unusual for one of us to call the other. Anyhow, I waited until my aunt took a nap and drove over here. I saw his car, but when he didn't answer the doorbell, I thought maybe he'd run out somewhere with his little boy. I tried the door and it was open, so I let myself in." She shuddered and dried her tears again. "In my heart, I felt something was wrong. I didn't know what it was. I called his name and started walking through the house." She paused, dabbed her tears again, and then continued, "I found him in there."

The plainclothes sergeant reached his hand toward her. "May I see your phone?"

Emily opened her purse, retrieved it and punched in the commands. "Here, I'll find it for you." She hit the history panel and then handed it to him.

"Okay," he mumbled as he glanced at it, made his notes and handed it back to her. "One forty-four inbound from 555-1729." He got up and stepped across the room to a desk in the corner. The telephone, a note pad and a framed picture of Jonah were neatly poised on it. Once again, the detective made a note in his book. "That's the number."

"Sir, we've found this."

Mike turned as a young patrol officer entered the living room from the bedroom. His gloved hands were holding the edges of a single sheet of paper. Blood soaked the bottom edges. "It's a suicide note, sir. It was under his body," the officer said softly as he twisted his wrists around for the lieutenant to see it without having to handle it.

The cops gathered round the note while Emily scooted in close to Mike, then lay her head on his shoulder and began to cry.

Mike held her, not lovingly, but compassionately. He put his hand to the back of her head and guided her gently into the crook of his neck, then looked at the group of cops as they continued to look at the note. "Can you tell me what he said?"

The detective sergeant turned and shrugged his shoulders. "Not much. He just couldn't take the pressure anymore. Then he gave some directions about his kid." The sergeant turned away, removed a handkerchief from his pocket and wiped the tears that began to flow. He looked at Mike and offered a sick smile. "It's the job. It's a bastard." He turned away and walked outside.

The lieutenant nodded to the patrol officer, then turned toward Mike. "Detective Palotti, you called this morning and made an appointment to come up?"

"Yes." Mike quickly read the Tulsa cops' collective minds. "We were high centered and stuck. I was frustrated, and so was John." He shook his head and pursed his lips. "Totally frustrated – both of us, so I figured we would just park our butts on this sofa and rehash the whole damned mess. Somehow, we might come up with something. Or, if nothing else, we could at least say we gave it our best shot." He paused and caught himself. "Bad choice of words, but I think you get the meaning."

"Yeah, I think I do. Did you call from your cell phone?"

Mike nodded agreement, took the phone from his pocket, handed it to the lieutenant and watched as he found the screen, then the outbound number to John's house. It was the same number as the one that made the call to Emily. Everything matched up.

"Right," the detective responded. "Anyhow, we need to have both of you come downtown with us so we can test your hands – just routine, you understand."

"Yeah," Mike retorted. He looked at Emily. "A quick and painless test to make sure we didn't fire a gun."

Emily nodded her approval. "I'm ready. Can I take my own car?"

#

Mike looked at his watch as he and Emily stepped into the fresh air. He paused for a moment on the steps and glanced back at the front door of the police station. The orange glow of the sunset reflected off the double glass door. A foreboding darkness was sweeping over the city. He shuddered. A chill ran down his spine.

He turned and looked at Emily, put his hand on her arm, and gently guided her toward the parking lot and their cars. They walked in silence. A siren wailed somewhere in the distance. Its crying sound echoed off the towering canyons of downtown. Mike felt her shiver. She looked at him, started to speak, then lowered her head and pulled her keys from her purse. She unlocked her car, slipped behind the wheel and lowered the window.

Mike leaned in and spoke. "I'll take care of everything. Don't worry about it and I'll touch base with you later."

"How much later? What are we going to do?" she asked through the choking gasps as her tears again flowed over her cheeks.

"I'm not sure. Just some things I have to do."

"What about his little boy?"

"They notified his mom and she was taking care of him, so things are okay." He stepped back and shrugged. "If you can call any of this okay. Anyhow, they told me his mom said he had been depressed for a couple months, so it all fits together." He leaned back in her window and spoke softly. "You and I know the truth. Now I've got to get that stuff out of there."

#

Mike checked his watch in the glow of the moonlight. It was three o'clock and time to get it over with. He shivered, not from the cold, but from the unscrupulous life he accepted. In his mind, it wasn't something he wanted to do, but something that was demanded of him.

"This one last time," he whispered to himself as he opened the gate to Baldwin's backyard. He paused for a moment, then took eight quick steps across the small grassed area to the back door, and without pause took the lock-pick set from his hip pocket.

His stooped down and allowed his knees to touch the ground. He paused again to take time for one quick glance around. The neighborhood was dark. He was alone. Seconds later, he twisted the doorknob and let himself in the house. It was dark and silent. He waited, and as he did at Emily's, allowed himself to become one with his surroundings. It was safe. In two more minutes he would have the box and be gone. The case was closed, and to hell with whomever else may have been involved with the late former Detective John Baldwin.

Mike took his mini-flashlight from his pocket, put his finger on the switch and was about to turn it on when the lights inside the house came on. He was blinded for a moment, then recognized the Tulsa officers as the lieutenant spoke.

"Detective Palotti, we've been waiting for you." He approached Mike with his handcuffs in his hand. "You're under arrest."

Chapter Twenty-Four

MIKE WAS EXHAUSTED. IT HAD been more than twenty-four hours since he'd last slept. He stunk. His clothes were rumpled and wet with perspiration, but more than anything else he was alone. The barren walls of the thirty-square-foot interrogation room closed in on him. The recessed overhead light took its toll on his mental and physical strength. His reserves were gone and he knew it. On top of it all, he was facing a misdemeanor charge of Breaking and Entering.

He turned when the door opened. It was Lt. Hauk. He was dressed for the occasion – dark pinstripe suit, a starched white shirt, and a red and blue stripped tie – the victor. He towered over Mike like a vulture looms over carrion on the roadside.

The lieutenant stepped inside and stood nearly on top of him, intentionally invading his personal space – what there was of it. "Mr. Palotti," he emphasized, "you are relieved of duty immediately. You're on suspension until the outcome of the Dallas Police Department internal investigation is complete." With a touch of dramatics, he slowly removed a folded, legal-size document from the inside breast pocket of his suit coat and handed it to Mike. "Consider yourself served. You are in no way to identify yourself as an active member of the Dallas Police Department. You will remain on-call at the behest of Internal Affairs. You have the right to be represented by an attorney, but you are prohibited from being in contact with anyone from the department, or to go on Dallas Police property without the prior approval of Internal Affairs. Do you understand?"

Former Detective Michael Palotti took the legal paper from Hauk, opened it briefly, then re-folded it and stuffed it in his shirt pocket.

He glanced at Hauk, then looked down at the table and nodded his understanding. "Yeah, I do," he uttered.

Hauk turned to leave, then spun on his heel, leaned over Mike and whispered in his ear. "You're done, you son-of-a-bitch. You are an embarrassment to the department and to every cop who ever wore the badge. I hope you burn in hell."

Mike looked up. Their faces were only inches apart. Hauk never saw it coming. The powerful right uppercut caught him squarely on the chin. He was thrown back into the edge of the open door. Blood spurted from his mouth and nose. He slithered to the floor. Blood from the gash on the back of his head smeared the length of the doorjamb. He fell in a semi-conscious stupor partially in the interrogation room and out into the hallway.

The sound of footsteps and loud voices filled Mike's ears as he stood and towered over the mumbling and incoherent slobbering of his former boss.

"Damn it, Palotti," shouted one of the Tulsa cops. Mike turned and went back to his straight-back chair while the Tulsa officers helped the lieutenant to his feet. Mike felt the slightest twinge of satisfaction as Hauk's blood continued to flow unabated down the front of his clothes. He was a bloody mess.

"Shit, Palotti, you didn't need to do that." It was the Tulsa Detective Sergeant who spoke. He and Palotti watched as two uniform officers helped Hauk regain his balance, then go down the hall and out of sight.

"Temporary insanity," Mike replied. He looked down at the microphone on the tabletop, tapped it lightly with his finger, then looked up at the sergeant. A thin smile crossed his lips and he whispered, "Everything recorded, right?"

The sergeant returned the smile. "Yeah, he was a prick, but you shouldn't have decked him." He shrugged his shoulders and gave a soft chortle. "Who knows? Maybe you can have a civil suit against him for driving you crazy."

Mike used his handkerchief to wipe the smear of blood off his knuckles, then looked at the sergeant as he pulled up a chair on the opposite side of the table. They looked at each other in silence for a few seconds before Mike spoke. "Where do we go from here?"

The sergeant leaned forward on his elbows and spoke while he flicked invisible lint from the sleeves of his sport jacket. "We think it's a legitimate suicide. He did it himself, but the big question is why?" He stopped picking the lint and looked directly at Mike. "What the hell were you guys up to? You should have known this couldn't go on forever." He didn't wait for a response. "We saw the videos of you guys banging your balls off with her." He shook his head. "Yeah, she's a good-looking woman, but where the hell were y'all's minds?"

"You think she's the killer, don't you?" Mike responded.

The sergeant looked at Mike with dismay. He tilted his head like a dog waiting at the table's edge for a tidbit to be slipped to him. He shook his head and smiled forlornly across the table. "Yeah, she is. I heard your bullshit all night, and no way do I, or any of the other detectives here, think John had anything to do with it. Your Legree story is just a crock of shit that doesn't mean a thing. You guys got used – period. You both were a couple loose cannons, but at least John knew something was up. He went on sick leave a week ago and was seeing the department shrink."

"I didn't know," Palotti replied.

"Yeah, well there's a lot you don't know."

"Okay, but you've got the videos, so are you going to arrest her?" Mike asked.

The detective shook his head. "Not now. There're just too many loose ends." He pointed his finger at Mike. "Palotti, you're one of them. We've verified your story about when you broke into her house. Highland Park PD shows they took a prowler call that night and cleared with no evidence of criminal activity, but they validate what you said. Sure, you were there, but your own words were that you didn't find anything to tie her to the murders." The detective got up and opened the door. "How about a pee and some coffee?"

Palotti smiled and nodded his approval. "You bet," he responded as he followed the sergeant down the hall. The air was cool and refreshing, even in the bathroom. It felt good. He felt a shot of adrenalin. He was going to make it – not unscathed, but he would survive and get on with his life. Baldwin was the killer and he knew it.

He looked at himself in the mirror as he washed his hands. A lot of water had gone under the bridge since the night they left Emily's and went to the Ipanema.

The two men walked leisurely to the elevator and took it to the basement coffee shop. "I'll get the coffee. Grab us a booth," the Tulsa cop commented as he pointed to the only empty table in the room. "Want anything to eat?" he asked.

Mike retrieved his wallet from his hip pocket, took a five-dollar bill from it and handed it over. "One of those burritos and some salsa would be great. Thanks," he commented as he slipped into the booth.

Moments later the two men, albeit colleagues and to some degree, adversaries, packed the cholesterol loaded food into their empty stomachs. As he was prone to do since he was a child, Mike inhaled his food with a minimum of effort. He smiled at the detective and spoke with a full mouth. "I know you told me your name at the house, but my mind is a blank."

The detective stretched his hand across the table. "Triplett. Detective Sergeant Simon Triplett."

Mike shrunk back slowly into his seat. His gaze fixed on the sergeant's eyes. "How did I not catch that?" he commented softly.

"You've had a hard night," Triplett replied. "We all have."

"Related?" Mike asked.

Simon nodded his agreement. "He was my grandfather's brother." He took time to add sugar and cream to his coffee again, stirred it slowly, then looked Mike in the eye. "This thing is weird. Too weird and I don't like it."

Mike returned his look and replied quietly so no one could overhear their conversation. "Weird doesn't even come close to it. How about supernatural? You're related to Legree Triplett." He counted them off on his fingertips. "One of the murder weapons is buried by his grave; your own detective kills himself when things are closing in on him; that same detective may have a tie-in to a second person who is a sexual predator and is still un-accounted for this very minute; and, you still think Emily Morgan is the murderer?" He shook his head in disapproval. "No, it was Baldwin and very possibly Delmonico – no one else."

"I said there was a lot you didn't know," Simon interjected. "Why don't you try this on?" He paused, leaned back in the booth and took a deep breath before he leaned his elbows on the table. He was only inches from Mike's face. "Weird. Eerie. Call it what you want, but now let me throw another card on the table. Delmonico is dead. After he escaped, he disappeared from the face of the earth until the day before yesterday. He was found beaten to death in a rundown apartment in," he paused again, then spoke, "... in Durant."

Mike's face was ashen. He wet his lips. "Any suspects?"

Simon shook his head. "Not a one. He was working odd jobs – lawns, handyman, that kind of thing. He lived there about two months. We don't have a clue where else he was in the meantime. His landlord went to the apartment to collect the rent and found him on his bed. The guy was dead as a doornail, nude and tied spread-eagle on his bed, beaten to hell and back. His skivvies were stuffed in his mouth and half way down his throat."

"Nobody saw or heard anything, I suppose?" Mike asked.

Triplett nodded agreement as he sat back and sipped his coffee. "In that neighborhood, nobody sees or hears squat."

Mike spoke in a soft tone as he leaned across the table. "John's note. What'd he say – exactly?"

Simon reached in his shirt pocket and unceremoniously pulled out a copy of the letter, unfolded it, and scooted it gently across the table.

Mike spread it out on the table and read it slowly:

Jonah, Mom,

I'm so sorry. I'm sorry, but the time has come that I must pay for my evil. I have been living death for I don't know how long. Now, I can find peace and sleep. I can have peace in death.

Pray for me. Please pray. I'm so sorry, but now I'm going home. Forgive me. I love you.

John and Dad

Mike pushed the paper back across the table, leaned back in his seat and allowed the tears to flow. He lowered his head into his hands and felt Simon's hand on his shoulder.

"Hang tough, Palotti. We all feel that way, but at least he's found peace 'cause he sure as hell couldn't get it here. It was just too rough on him, what with his wife's death, being a single dad, the job, and then her. Emily Morgan."

Mike looked up, dried his tears with the back off his hand and offered a weak chortle. "So what other surprises do you have for me?"

Simon shrugged. "Let's go back upstairs and finish this off – if you're up to it."

Mike slid out of the booth as Triplett got up. "Yeah, reckon I am. I don't think it can get much worse than what it is already."

The Tulsa detective looked over his shoulder as they entered the elevator. "You'll see."

Chapter Twenty-Five

THE TWO MEN SAT ACROSS from each other in the sergeant's office. It was a typical government-issue faux walnut desk, a straight-back chair for visitors, and an imitation leather executive chair for the sergeant. Mike took a quick glance around. It was nothing like Hauk's throne. This was a working cop's office. No honor roll kid's pictures or certificates for doing the Lord's work displayed on the walls. Besides, it was too small for much of anything.

Mike made himself as comfortable as his tired body would allow, then spoke. "Okay, you've got my attention. What's next?"

Simon leaned forward and rested his elbows on his desk. "Well," he said in his strong Oklahoma accent, "we're not going to press charges against you for starters."

Mike smiled and nodded his appreciation. "Thanks. Right now any news short of cutting my balls off is good news. Anything else?"

Simon closed his eyes, lowered his head and gave a soft exhale. "I'm tired. It's been a long day and night, but we've got to plow through this mess." He opened his eyes and looked across the table at Mike. "All of us think you had nothing to do with these murders – here or in Dallas." He smirked as he continued. "You were blind with passion. That's dumb, but it's not criminal. You got used. So did John. Both of you, but at least he recognized it and tried to get help. It was just too late, poor bastard, and it got him killed."

"I thought you said it was suicide?" Mike fired back.

"Yeah, it was, but he was murdered by that bitch just as much as if she did it herself. She drove him to it. In fact, it's my guess that she stood right there and pressured him into suicide." Simon shook his head and pursed his lips. His brow was furrowed; his eyes red from lack of sleep. "He couldn't handle it anymore, so he did what she knew he'd do. He blew his brains out." Triplett leaned back in his chair, crossed his arms over his chest and stared at Baldwin. His voice was soft. "And, you're next."

"What the hell are you talking about? Next? Who me?"

"Yeah, you. If you'd quit thinking with your dick and started using your brain, you'd see what the rest of us see. Let me spell it out for you. First, there's John. You know about that, so let's move on. Alexander Delmonico. Yeah, this should catch your interest. He turns up dead in a shit-hole motel in Durant. However, did you know a convenience store surveillance camera picked up your sweet little screw gassing her car in Durant at three o'clock in the morning the same day the desk clerk found his body? Coincidence? She thought she was so smart that she didn't use a credit card, but paid cash so she couldn't be traced. Nevertheless, she botched it. Even a crappy little joint like that has a surveillance system and sure as hell, Teddy's Toot and Moo caught her on their camera."

"How did you get onto that so quick?"

"As soon as we heard about the murder we contacted the state police – the OSBI, and they did a quick check and found Teddy's system. There she was in living color." He paused, then leaned forward and looked into Mike's eyes. "For sure, you're next on her list."

Mike fired back. "I find this a lot of conjecture. You're reaching for the stars to clear your man."

Triplett shook his head. "No way! Those two have been together for we don't know how long, but this is just too cozy to be a chance time and place for her to get gas. Then, to sweeten the pot, how about Delmonico's history? Two arrests for felony assault, but no convictions. Later, he got busted for molesting a woman in a park, and that's the time he escaped from the interrogation room. From there, we lost him until he turned up dead."

"So, was he tied-in to Baldwin?"

"We didn't think so back then when he escaped. John just happened to be the on-call detective when some patrol officers caught the son-of-a-bitch. They put him in the interrogation room, turned him over to Baldwin and they left. There was a hell of a big investigation, but John had to take a hit because it was his prisoner. He just screwed up, that's all. He got a phone call right after the patrol guys left. He thought they'd locked the room, and they should've, but nevertheless he signed for him, so it was his prisoner. They no sooner left when he got the phone call. Bim-bam, the rest is history."

"So you're telling me Delmonico never had anything to do with Baldwin at all except for those few minutes? I find all of this hard to believe."

Triplett leaned back again, put his feet on his desk and continued. "This story ain't done yet, so hang on tight. Those videos of the little trysts she had with you guys?" He paused and cast a sideways glance at Mike. "I watched them three times."

"You did what?" Mike fired back.

Simon nodded and continued. "Three times. I have to admit the first one was pretty voyeuristic, but the next two were strictly investigative."

Mike leaned forward and pointed his finger in Triplett's face, but Simon fired back. "Just hold your horses and you'll see what I found."

Mike rubbed his temples and leaned back. "I've got a hell of a headache."

"I imagine you do, but hear me out, 'cause it's going to get worse." He leaned back and folded his arms across his chest before he continued. "You and your sweet little lover weren't alone most of the time when you did it. It was the same with John. I caught it midway through the second time. It was all so natural it was almost indistinguishable, but there it was." He leaned his elbows on the table and looked directly at Mike. His eyes squinted. His voice was subdued but raspy. "It's like when you're watching a movie. You don't notice the little things – something like a slight change of the camera angle, or maybe a slow and easy zoom to the action." He took a deep breath and continued. "Someone was controlling the camera on all the shots at her house. All of them! However, when you or John did it somewhere else, she used one of those little portable jobs and everything was just a straight shot. There wasn't any lens action other than where it was originally pointed when she put her bag down."

"Are you telling me Delmonico was in the house and running the cameras from somewhere in there?"

Simon nodded his agreement, then sat back, yawned and stretched his arms over his head, loosened his tie and looked back at Palotti. "There's more."

Mike rubbed his red eyes and his throbbing temples. "I'm pooped, but go ahead. I'm all ears."

Triplett offered a soft chortle. "Delmonico is an alias. We lost him after he escaped, but the feds didn't. His real name is Andre Ilin, but when we tried to run down anything on him, his paper trail just vanished into thin air."

"What do you mean? You're losing me."

Triplett continued. "We put the full-court press on to find him after he escaped, but kept running into a brick wall – literally, we were getting stonewalled. Then we figured it out. He was working for somebody big and was probably doing a little business of his own on the side. Whoever he was working for, they were a lot bigger than us. We found all our traditional sources dried up – poof, like he never existed."

"So how did you come up with his real name?" Mike asked.

Triplett smiled in self-confidence. "We ain't just a bunch of Okies, but sometimes the impossible takes a little longer. I can't say how, but take my word for it. That's his name. The person I talked to was sticking his neck out to give me that much." He nodded approval of his own statement. "Andre Ilin; a Russian. One hell of a bastard, and I'll leave it at that."

"That's it? There isn't anymore?"

"Not that we haven't tried, but nope. From the day he escaped until he was found dead, we haven't been able to find zilch on him – not one damned thing."

"So exactly how long was it from when he vaporized until he bought the farm in Durant?" Mike asked.

"Four years, five months – give or take a couple days," Triplett responded as he pushed back in his chair and got up. "It seems about that long since I saw my wife, so if you'll excuse me, I'm calling it a day and going home." He gestured toward the door. "You're free to go. Why don't you head back to Texas and try to get your head on straight?"

Mike got up, rubbed the small of his back to relieve the stress of the last twenty-four hours, then nodded in approval. "Good idea. Thanks."

The two men shook hands at the office door and turned to go in opposite directions. Mike took only two steps when Triplett called his name.

"Palotti!"

Mike looked back at the Tulsa cop. "Did you forget another horror story to give me something to think about on my ride home?"

"No. Just don't forget what I said. You're next."

#

Mike slipped into the afternoon traffic and headed south – back to Texas and his home, what there was of it. A worthless piece of crap apartment like a million others that cram the Dallas/Ft. Worth Metroplex.

There's no place like home, he thought. Judy Garland made a mint singing it, but she didn't have the slightest idea what the real story was all about. He looked at his watch as he crossed the state line; it was two-thirty exactly. The open road did wonders for him. He opened his window and let the fresh air swish through the car, bringing with it the smell of freshly-cut grass from the mowers working along the shoulders of the road. A white split-rail fence ran along the left side of the highway. Behind it, and stretching to the horizon, was the greenest grass in the world. A herd of Longhorn cattle was scattered throughout the pasture, their massive heads lowered as they grazed away in the warmth of the sun, their glorious horns stretching out for three feet on either side of their bodies.

Mike breathed deeply. It was good, and he had an idea. He would find the story of Andre Ilin, and from there he would know the truth about Emily.

Chapter Twenty-Six

MIKE'S MIND FLOATED LIKE THE afternoon breeze that swept across the prairie. The miles sped by. The tall grass swayed gently at the kiss of the wind. A red-tail hawk sailed high on the thermals, its wings spread wide to catch the slightest uplift of air. A herd of Charolais cattle stood tall beneath a grove of elms on the leeward side of a hill, their massive pale white bodies and pink muzzles in stark contrast to the deep green of the grass. Everything looked so genuine, so undisturbed, so much the way things are supposed to be.

He nodded his head and took a deep breath. Surely, that's not the way things really are. It's a world of murder and deceit, a life of catch me if you can.

"This is the world I live in," he uttered. Nevertheless, he was relaxed and focused. There was a plan, flexible of course, but every cop knows how an investigation works. Be prepared for setbacks, but never lose sight of your target. Look for the obvious, but don't overlook the tiny threads beneath the smoke and mirrors. It's in those threads where the cop will pull them together and find the complete garment – the shroud of guilt. Then he will drop the son-of-a bitch into hell.

If she is guilty, hang her. If not, clear her once and for all. Delmonico or whatever his name is? He's bought and paid for, but still has to be part of the equation. Whether he was working with or without Baldwin or Emily, he almost irrefutably was the killer. Proving it would be a different matter, but at least in his mind, Mike could find the answer. Then, he could relax. It would be over.

Mike coasted into the roadside park, slipped the cell phone into his pocket and strolled effortlessly across the well-cut and trimmed grass to a picnic table protected from the afternoon sun by an overhanging live oak tree. He smiled as he sat on the edge of the table and propped his feet up on the bench. His fingers tapped in Rickey's cell number.

"*Que te pasa, amigo?*" his long-time partner answered.

"I guess you've heard about my little mess by now?" Mike asked.

"Oh, yeah. Good news travels fast, but bad news travels really fast," he emphasized. "Where are you?"

"On my way home, but you know me. I might be down, but I'm not out. I just need a little help. Are you in?"

"We've been through a lot of before, so let's get it on," Rickey laughed.

"Edgar Morgan was Emily's husband. Supposedly, he died of asthma in a Miami hospital." Mike paused and looked at the passing traffic. Another metaphor, he thought: *The world is zipping past me and I've got to get on.*

"It's not much, but see what you can find. Did he die a natural death, or under suspicious circumstances?"

"*No problema, ese.* Can I call you back at this number when I've got something?"

Mike nodded his approval. "Thanks, my friend."

#

The sun had long ago set by the time Mike parked his VW and walked up the stairs to his apartment. It wasn't much, but at least there was a plan. That will have to do for the time being. Now, just play it out and see where things go – good or bad. One more card to play today and then take some time for himself – shower, shave, have a good meal, and last but not least, sleep.

He looked at his watch. It had been three hours since he'd talked to Rickey, so there was no sense holding his breath to wait for an answer. Things don't happen that fast. No sooner did the thought race through his mind than his cell phone beeped. He grabbed it on the second ring. "Tell me something good," he answered.

"You've got to decide whether it's good or not, but I've got something to sink your teeth into."

"Shoot. Let me have it," Mike replied. He sat on the edge of the sofa and turned a scrap of paper over to its clean side, then snapped open his ballpoint pen.

"Remember my cousin, Felipe? You met him once when he was out here on a vacation." Rickey didn't wait for a response. "Well, he's a detective with Broward County, so I gave him a call and he got right on it. Ready?"

"With baited breath."

"Okay, the official cause of death on the Death Certificate is natural causes as a result of severe asthma. The certificate was signed by Doctor Leonard Goldfarb." There was a pause. Mike's ear strained to hear the deafening silence. "Weird," Rickey continued. "Or, maybe it just was circumstantial. A week later, the good doctor bought the farm."

"What?" Mike fired back.

"Murdered. That's what," Rickey replied. "Felipe is a pretty good dick, and on his own he ran a record check on Goldfarb and hit paydirt. Doctor Goldfarb lived *mucho* upscale, as you might figure. Alone. No marriages. No evidence of homosexuality. The crime report shows it was a home invasion, beaten to death with a blunt object. The murder weapon was never recovered. The house was ransacked – stereo, jewelry, stuff like that was stolen. Whoever it was took his Lexus. They found it the next day out near a dump, burned. No evidence." Rickey paused. Mike heard him take a deep breath before he continued. "Mike, they came up cold on this guy. They were never able to tie it to any other cases. They never came up with any suspects and never recovered any of the stolen items except the car. Zilch. He bought the farm. Case closed."

"Closed?" Mike asked.

"More or less. The damn thing went through the ringer – cold case investigation, FBI lab, everything. Right now, it's parked on a shelf in the Cold Case Squad gathering dust."

"So you're telling me that Edgar died of natural causes because the good doctor said so. Then, that same doctor met up with the Grim Reaper. Does that sound about right?"

"You're saying it, not me. Anybody who meets up with that sweet little Yellow Rose of Texas ends up on a slab in the morgue."

"Thanks, Rick. I appreciate your help."

"*De nada, mi amigo.* So, what's next for you? What are you going to do?"

"First things first," Mike replied. "I'll stay in touch. Thanks again for your help."

#

SWEET EMILY

Mike popped open a beer. One of his good ones, then sat back in his Lazy Boy and put his feet on the outstretched footrest. He rolled the chilled beer bottle across his forehead and closed his eyes. The cold felt good. Somewhere deep inside he always knew she wasn't a little angel, but hoped against the odds. Now her picture was coming into focus. He was taken for a sucker. His lover was a killer – maybe not herself, but her hand was in all of them. Why? Who knows? Maybe she did it just for the fun of killing. He'd heard it before. It was Justin McIntire the day before his execution about ten years ago. He told it to a reporter. Now the words rang in Mike's head: "I did it for the joy of killing; for the pleasure of watching someone die. It was pretty damn simple."

Mike chugged the rest of his beer, placed the empty carefully on a coaster so he wouldn't put a ring on the table, and looked at his cell phone. "Magic little toy, aren't you?" he mumbled. He scrolled down the "contacts" list until he came to it. He didn't use it much – maybe only three or four times in the last couple years, but now was a time he needed to talk to him.

Mike's mind raced back in time. Eric Westbrook sat behind him in rookie school. They went different directions after the academy, but a couple years later ended up in a two-man car. They became good partners, just like it was with Mike and Rickey. Eric was trustworthy and a good cop. He knew what to do and when to do it. Conversely, he had the knack to know what not to do and when not to do it. Eventually, Mike went to the Detective Division: Eric went to the street as an undercover narc.

Mike never heard the whole story, and even when they talked later Eric never discussed it. One day he was a narc and the next he was gone. At first they talked bullshit, but nothing of substance. With time and distance, they spoke less and less. Mike figured out Eric was working for someone, probably the feds, but it was a hush-hush topic. Nevertheless, every once in a while when one or the other needed information, he could get some more-or-less under the table help – no questions asked. You pat my back and I'll pat yours. That's how the system worked.

Now Eric lived on a ranch in the Texas hill country. Maybe two-hundred acres; a couple horses; a view to kill for; and, lots of privacy. His wife, Julie, was a self-employed consultant, but the best Mike could tell is that she was almost always away on a business trip, as was Eric. Maybe so. Maybe not. He didn't inquire. If they wanted him to know, they'd tell him. *Probably in the same business,* Mike thought, *whatever that is.*

He smiled and took a deep breath when he tapped in the number. It was answered immediately. "Hello, Detective Palotti. How's it hanging?"

Mike chortled. "Wrong on both counts. No more detective, and it ain't."

"No shit? What's up?"

Mike leaned back, closed his eyes, and in five minutes gave a quick overview of his personal and professional life – both of them gone to hell in a hand-basket.

Eric listened in silence. Mike wasn't the first cop to fall on his face for a fling, and he wouldn't be the last. Nevertheless, they were friends and he knew what had to happen.

"Grab your toothbrush and get out of your pad, pronto. They'll be coming to serve you with termination papers and you don't need that. It'll screw up your retirement big time. Listen to me. Write this down and get the hell out now. You can go back for your stuff later, but first you've got to cover your ass. You know the Texas Plains Bank on Central Expressway?"

"Right. It's up by the Galleria."

"Correct. Go there. You need to go to the law office of Miner and Miner. They'll take care of you. I'll have things ready for you by the time you get there. Listen to them. Do what they tell you and then get out of town for a couple days. Come here to the ranch. They'll have the directions for you at the office."

"Is that where your wife works?"

"No. We'll go into that later. Right now, get your butt in gear. I know how the department works. They'll have some little shit banging on your door with the papers and then you're screwed. We're going to beat them to the punch, but we have to put you somewhere just to be safe. Got it?"

Mike looked at his watch. It was seven-thirty. "It's nighttime. The Personnel Department doesn't work nights."

"To hang your ass, they'll work 'til they've got you, so go!"

Mike took a quick look around. He didn't have much anyway, so there wasn't anything to lose. "Okay, I can be at the bank in about forty minutes."

"They'll have everything ready. Good luck."

#

Mike slipped his VW into the darkened parking lot near the front doors. He did as Eric directed and brought nothing with him, not even his toothbrush. He could pick up some essentials later.

He pushed the revolving door open and stepped into the nearly deserted lobby. A lone security guard sat behind the counter; a row of video surveillance screens behind him scanned the parking lot and the empty hallways of each of the eight floors in the building.

"Miner and Miner," Mike inquired as he stepped toward the counter.

"Sixth floor," the guard responded. "They told me to expect you, so the elevators are unlocked."

"Thanks," Mike replied. He stepped to the bank of elevators, paused, took a deep breath and pushed the button. He knew his life was taking a twist he'd never anticipated, but one he must take to survive.

#

The former Dallas Police Detective Michael Palotti, stepped into the hallway as the elevator doors opened. He turned to the right in the direction of footsteps coming down the hall. She was beautiful – blonde hair swept over her shoulders, a crisp white blouse and dark skirt, and long shapely legs. She stepped out like a model in her spike heels. She extended her hand. "Hi, I'm Ms. Miner. Glad to see you."

Before he could respond, she turned on her heels and retraced her steps. Mike caught himself flatfooted, then quickly fell in behind her. He did a quick double-step and caught up with her as she reached the office door. "Thanks for seeing me at such an odd hour. I really appreciate it."

She turned when she reached for the door and allowed him to open it, then stepped inside and nodded. "Thanks," she said as she pointed to a chair in the outer office. "If you'll have a seat, we'll be with you in a few minutes." She didn't wait for a response before she strode around the empty receptionist counter and disappeared into the inner office.

Mike looked around. It was a typical law office – an expensive glass-topped coffee table; a scattering of up-to-date magazines; a leather sofa and two overstuffed chairs. Soft light emanated from the lamps in the corners. Soothing music floated from the intercom system.

He grabbed a magazine and slouched down in a chair, not sure of what was happening. His skin tingled in anticipation; his ears strained for a sound beyond the music; he inhaled the aroma of the leather. Everything was so clean and orderly – a perfect disguise for the blurring of the lines and shadows of the justice system. He glanced at the magazine, then tossed it unceremoniously back on the table.

A digital clock on the receptionist's counter clicked over to eight o'clock. Nearly an hour had passed since he'd pulled out of his parking lot. He waited. The minutes ticked by and finally showed nine o'clock. He looked at the door she went through so long ago. He willed her or anyone else to come out for him, but he was as alone as he'd ever felt in his life.

Nine-fifteen. Finally, the office door opened. A tall man, roughly the same age as Ms. Miner, stood in the open door. He was dressed in a dark suit with a red and white striped tie. His dark hair was combed back. *A living GQ model*, Mike thought. The man stepped forward and extended his hand. "Sorry to keep you waiting so long, but we've got everything ready. I'm Jerry Miner."

The two men shook hands as Mike replied, "Nice to meet you, although I wish it was under different circumstances."

"Come on in," Jerry said. "Just a couple papers for you to sign, then we'll get you on your way and everything will be in good shape." He pointed to a desk in the inner office. Ms. Miner was seated in the executive chair behind the desk.

Mike inhaled her professional yet elegant magnificence. She looked as though she was the president herself. Tall, stately, professional, and completely in control. She nodded and smiled. "Have a seat, please. We need to go over these papers with you and get your signature."

Mike looked back as Jerry closed the office door and pulled up a chair alongside him.

She spoke first. "We understand the situation you're in, but we've taken care of it. You'll be okay, we guarantee."

Mike pulled back the chair and sat down, glancing back and forth between Miner and Miner. He let out a deep breath and spoke. "I'd like to say I understand, but truthfully, I don't. I just know I'm in a hell of a fix and ..."

She slipped a single typewritten paper across the desk. "Take your time and read it carefully. It's your intention to retire effective immediately. Sign it, and we'll have a staff member deliver it to the PD immediately." She sat back and crossed her legs. "That's what took us so long."

Jerry leaned forward and interjected, "We had to check, and sure as heck, they've got your termination papers ready, but they don't know where you are to serve them. Basically, we beat them to the punch." He shook his head and looked into Mike's eyes. "We can't save your job, but we can save your retirement and your resume. Professionally speaking, you'll retire before any disciplinary process is implemented. That means you can still find meaningful work."

Mike nodded his approval, picked up the paper, leaned forward on the desk and read it – slowly. He bit his lip and felt drops of perspiration on his forehead. He read it a second time, then sat back and offered a weak chortle. "Yeah, you're right. It's all I can do now, and it's my own fault."

Jerry took a fountain pen from his shirt pocket, removed the cap and handed it to Mike. The former detective looked at the pen like it held his life in its bladder, and it did. With a quick stroke, he signed the document and sat back. Tears formed in his eyes, but he held them back. It was over.

"Just one other document," she said as she placed another paper in front of Mike. "It is a statement of services and it's already paid. We just need your signature to satisfy our accountant and auditor, but you don't have to pay anything. It's all taken care of."

"By whom?"

"The people we work for," Jerry replied. "Trust us. Everything is on the up-and-up. However, it's not appropriate at the moment to divulge any more information than what we already have."

Mrs. Miner offered a soft and delicate laugh. "We understand your confusion, but things will work out fine for you." She uncrossed her legs and rose as she extended her hand. "My apologies. I didn't thoroughly introduce myself."

Mike rose to take her hand.

"Rhonda Miner, Jerry's wife, and I'll tell you this much." She cocked her head and put her hands on her hips. "You've got a good friend who speaks highly of you, and something tells me we'll meet again."

Mike accepted her remark and smiled. "Good friends are better than gold."

"You've got a goldmine in that case. Anyhow," she said as she pulled a hand-drawn map from her desk drawer, "here's the map to his ranch. You've got his cell number if you can't find the place, but you need to go now. It'll be after midnight by the time you get there. He'll be waiting for you. In the meantime, we'll have your papers downtown within the hour."

Jerry stepped forward and took Mike by the shoulder. "Come on. I'll walk out with you."

CHAPTER TWENTY-SEVEN

MIKE LEANED FORWARD IN THE darkness and held his watch under the dim green light of the instrument panel. The Miners were right. He was almost there. It was nearly one o'clock.

His glazed eyes followed the white outline of the narrow winding highway. Its dotted center line became a blur. It had been almost forty-eight hours since he'd last slept. A twinge of a headache pranced on his temples; his lips were dry; the steering wheel held his fingertips, not visa-versa. Sleep crept up on him, demanded his time, and was unrelenting in pursuit of his whole being.

Suddenly, it was there on the left. The stone arch overhanging the dirt road – Mule Creek Ranch. He'd done it. He was safe. The VW braked hard and made the turn; its headlights swept across the tall grass and mesquite trees. A doe and a fawn froze in the glare of the lights, then bolted into the darkness, their white tails flashing *adios* as they disappeared into the trees and brambles.

Adrenalin pumped through his veins when he saw the lights of the house near the hilltop. His mind raced over the last two days – from Dallas to John's house; finding Emily there; John dead in his bed; his late-night incursion and arrest; Lt. Hauk; the drive home; the attorney's office; and now, a secure haven and a friend. Indeed, he'd found a goldmine. Mrs. Miner knew exactly what she was talking about.

He slipped the car into the curved driveway in front of the house, killed the engine and let out a sigh of relief. Safe!

The ranch house was just as he'd imagined. Burnt adobe to match the southwest décor; half-a-dozen steps from the driveway to the front porch; lights in all the windows serving as beacons for lost souls; and most of all, a port in the storm.

He looked up as the massive double front doors opened. Eric, in all his considerable size, filled the entryway. He hadn't changed since they'd last seen each other four years ago – a mountain of a man; salt and pepper hair brushed back; trim and muscular at the same time. He was a man among men, but most of all, a true friend in the face of trouble.

His powerful voice broke the night stillness. "Michael, my good friend, welcome home. Come on now, times a-wastin'. You need to eat and rest up. We've got lots to do."

Mike bounded up the steps and took his friend's outstretched hand. He grimaced as he felt the powerful grip. "Damn it, Eric, you haven't lost your touch."

The big man chuckled and led Mike into the front room. An unlit fireplace was across the back wall, a pronghorn antelope mounted above it. To the left, an arrangement of heavy leather chairs and couches were gathered around a rough wooden coffee table. To the right was a combination work station, bar, and recreation area replete with a pool table and poker table.

Mike followed him past the living room and into the kitchen. "Sit there," Eric said as he gestured to a breakfast nook, reminiscent of Emily's, nestled into a corner by the window. "My wife is working tonight, but I've got some venison chili and biscuits ready for you. I reckon you've got to be hungry."

Mike lowered himself into a chair, stretched his legs and let out a past-due yawn. "Tired and hungry is an understatement, but I can't tell you how much I appreciate your help. If it wasn't for you, I'd be fired by now and probably thinking about eating my gun instead of your chili."

Eric laughed. "You haven't tried it yet. The gun might be the cooler of the two." They laughed at his humor, then downed the chili, biscuits and beer. The night grew late. A grandfather clock chimed two o'clock. Yet unspoken among the laughter and grab-ass of days long gone was the knowledge there were still miles to go before the mystery of Emily Morgan was solved, but that could wait.

#

Mike rolled over and lifted his watch off the night stand. He could barely read it through his bleary eyes – one o'clock. He'd slept almost eleven hours. He lay back and listened. The house was quiet. He closed his eyes and waited. It was pure luxury. The smell of fresh sheets; a clean house; well fed and eager to take on the new day, albeit a late start. He kicked back the sheets, sat on the edge of the bed and looked out the window. The azure sky went on forever; the tall buffalo grass swayed in the soft breeze. A hawk floated effortlessly among the treetops. All was well with the world.

"Well, almost," he mumbled.

He went to the adjoining bathroom and found a razor, soap and towels laid out on the countertop. Minutes later he was absorbed in the hot spray of the shower, his lathered body regaling in the sumptuousness of everyday life, at least for the time being, without the worries of a betrayed love and serial murder. This moment was his to enjoy.

He stepped out, wrapped a towel around himself and looked in the mirror. Not only did he feel better, he looked better. He had life again, not without challenges, but a life nevertheless.

The sound of an engine drew his attention to the window. It was Eric getting out of his big diesel pickup truck, carrying half-a-dozen bags. He glanced up at the window, raised the bags over his head and shouted. "Clothes!"

Mike slipped quickly back into yesterday's clothes before his host came in.

"Couldn't let you run around smelling like a wet dog. I came in a couple hours ago and you were zonked out. I checked your sizes and made a quick trip to the mall. Here you go," he commented as he dumped them out on the bed. "Some Levis, a couple shirts and underwear. That ought to hold you until you can get home and pack."

"Am I going somewhere?"

Eric smiled as he sat on the edge of the bed and began pulling price tags off the clothes. "Probably so, but we need to talk first." He looked up at Mike. His forehead was furrowed. He wet his lips and continued, "I think you're into a life-changing event, as the psychologist say. Big time!"

Mike nodded approval and responded. "Thanks for the clothes. Give me five minutes and I'll be out."

Eric nodded, then strode out of the room and closed the door behind him, leaving Mike alone to conjure his future. It was here, now.

#

The smell of bacon and coffee drifted through the house. Mike found Eric seated at the table, a plate of eggs, bacon and toast laid out for him.

"Eat," his host commanded. "Then we need to talk."

Mike gobbled the food while Eric sipped his coffee. They ate in silence. Eric was deep in thought. He stirred the coffee, added more cream and sugar, sipped, and stirred some more. Finally, he looked across the table and spoke.

"You won't be the first and certainly not the last cop to take a fall like this, but you'll come out okay, relatively speaking."

Mike started to respond, but was cut off. "Hear me out," Eric said. "While you were asleep I did a little digging around." He nodded self-approval and continued, "I work with some special people. We work quietly and accomplish what most people will never dream about, but we get it done and the whole world is better for it. I travel. My wife travels. We know people, and we know people who know other people." He looked deep into his cup, but his eyes had the thousand-yard stare of a sniper. "We gather intelligence and then do whatever has to be done. Sometimes we hit a home run; sometimes we strike out. Whichever way it goes, we see a world beneath the world of cops and robbers. We see the darkest recesses of the world. Michael, my friend, you walked right into one."

Mike leaned forward. "What the hell? You mean Emily?"

Eric nodded. "In a way, but more so, Andre Ilin. I know him."

Mike was puzzled. "You're losing me. How do you know him?"

Eric got up, poured himself another cup of coffee and returned to the table. "Sit back and I'll tell you the story. Plus, I think we have a job for you."

Mike sat back, wiped the plate clean with the final bite of toast and nodded. "I'm all ears."

"There are a lot of us – contract workers. We go everywhere in the world. We teach every topic that ever existed on counter-intelligence, firearms, explosives, listening devices – you name it – we do it."

Mike fired back. "Assassinate someone?"

"I won't play word games with you. We contract to do a job and do it – period. We're well paid and on our own. The government has complete right of denial. On paper, they don't know we exist."

"So how do I fit in all of this?"

"For starters, you're a hell of a good cop. You were a tough son-of-a-bitch when you were in Tactical Operations, and for the bit of time you were in SWAT you showed you knew how to handle guns. Plus, you had firearms discipline. You were a Hostage Negotiator and had a couple successes." He looked into his cup and gave a self-deprecating chuckle. "Except that time the crazy fucker killed his mom and then himself because you sent in Kentucky Fried Chicken for him to eat and you didn't know the nut was a vegetarian." Eric laughed again. "What the hell, the world isn't perfect. If it was, we wouldn't have jobs. Anyhow, we can teach you what you need to know and you can make a lot more money than the DPD could ever come up with. You'll get a passport under a new name; all new identity papers; you'll be trained and ready to go in five or six months. Afghanistan, Iraq, Bosnia. You'll work with the best people in the business, but you have to watch your ass. People like your sweet little Emily can be your downfall. Spies and sex are a dangerous mix."

"Is she one of you?"

Eric laughed heartily. His whole body shook. "Hell no! It was Andre. It rang a bell the minute I heard his name. I ran him while you were crapped out and sure as hell, he was who I thought he was. I've never worked with him, but heard about him. You know, the rumor mill – he was one of those crazy bastards who got his thrills whacking people." Eric looked out the window and gathered his thoughts. "He liked it too much, so the company had to terminate him. He was a loose cannon, and that's putting it mildly." He paused again and continued, "Sex, liquor and killing. That's what he lived for – and of course, the money. He was too uncontrollable, so we couldn't keep him."

Mike jumped in. "Eric, I appreciate what you did for me, but I'm a bit apprehensive. Who is this 'we' you're talking about?"

"It's a private company, more or less a branch of the CIA, but not a part of the government. That's so Uncle Sam can have deniability. They can legally say they don't know us, so we're not their problem."

"What about Andre?"

"He was recruited in Moscow about ten years ago and was a valuable resource, but then he got too head-strong. He was too wild. He couldn't be controlled, so as part of his separation package, he got U.S. passport, some new identity papers, and viola, he lands in bed with your girlfriend."

"It can't be that simple," Mike retorted. "There's got to be more to it."

"You're probably right, but if there is, I don't know it. All I can tell you is your guy Delmonico is Andre Ilin. That's fact number one. Number two, he gets murdered in Durant and your favorite fuck is caught on a security camera in the same Podunk berg the very same night." Eric paused, leaned back, and like a dog ready to devour a raw steak, licked his lips. "And last but not least, wherever Emily goes, people die; her husband, John, Delmonico, all the people of her supposed research paper, and then of course, there's you."

"You think she murdered her husband?"

"Why not? Take a look around. The doctor who treated him and called it asthma got whacked. Why shouldn't I think that fine-looking broad wasn't fucking the doctor and got him to snuff her husband? She collected the insurance and whatever other assets they had and the doctor got beaten to death, not totally unlike Andre himself bought the farm. Is there any other conclusion we can draw from this?" He didn't wait for a response before he continued, "Plus, as the Tulsa dicks saw, somebody was the director of photography when you had your little – well, whatever. Anyhow, Andre and Emily are a pair and that's a fact. Now there's only one person left, and that's you."

Mike leaned back and slowly nodded his head in acknowledgement. "Yeah, I know it, but damn, it's just not coming out the way I wanted it."

Eric chuckled. "That's an understatement."

Mike picked up his dishes, walked to the sink and began to rinse them. He spoke as he worked. "Tell me about the job. I need some advice on what I need to do now."

"First things first," Eric replied. "I'll download some documents on a secure file, you'll fill them out, and we'll submit them and see what happens. Frankly, I don't have any doubts. You'll get the job. Your record is clean. You retired in good standing, so that's not a problem. It'll take a few days, and in the meantime we'll get your apartment closed down and move you somewhere else. It'll be far away from her, and we'll close out your cell phone so she can't call you."

"What about her? What are your thoughts?"

"She's got to kill you. That's my first thought, so you need to play it cool. Frankly," he said, then took a long pause, "she needs to go."

"You mean kill her?"

"Listen, my friend. I can get you a good-paying job, but if you get back with her, I have no doubt she'll do you. Plus, she has proven to be very enterprising. If she can find you, she'll get someone to snuff you. It's that simple." He nodded self-approval and continued, "As long as she's alive, you've got a price on your head. It's that simple."

Mike walked slowly to the table and sat down. He stared hard at Eric. "You really think that?"

"No, I don't think it. I know it. You're a dead man. It's just a matter of time. So, either she buys the farm or you do. Short, sweet, and to the point."

Chapter Twenty-Eight

FORTY-EIGHT HOURS LATER, MIKE'S APARTMENT was emptied by Eric's compatriots. He was officially employed by GovCorps and was enroute to his training assignment. He caught a Southwest Airlines flight from San Antonio to El Paso. After a two-hour wait, a burger and beer, he boarded a Southwest flight to Las Vegas, Nevada.

The bright lights of the strip painted a kaleidoscope of colors across the darkening sky when they flew over the Grand Canyon, still thirty minutes flying time from McCarren Field. Mike sipped the last drops of his Jack Daniels, passed the cup to the flight attendant, tightened his seat belt and with a touch of finality, put his tray in a closed and upright position. His new life was about to begin.

The dazzling lights came sharply into view as the aircraft banked and made its final approach, literally into the heart of the gambling mecca. The Boeing 737 flared and touched down softly, then braked and turned toward the gate. Minutes later, Mike was enmeshed in the mob of Vegas weekenders finding their way to the baggage carousel. He wormed and jostled his way through the horde, grabbed his three suitcases, tossed them on a baggage cart and backtracked toward the counter marked, "Janet Air." A stylish, forty-something black woman stood behind the counter, her bright smile his reward for an otherwise long and tiring day.

Mike shoved his bags off the baggage cart and into the luggage bay, pulled out his passport and handed it to her. She flipped it open, took a glance at his picture and handed it back to him.

"Good evening, Mr. Reich," she commented as she tugged at his bags and pitched them onto the luggage belt. He chuckled softly at his new persona: Richard Reich. He smiled in return, then looked in the direction in which she pointed. "Gate seven in the Haven Street

Terminal, but hurry. You're the last one and they're holding the plane for you."

Mike nodded, turned and hurried toward the terminal. He was winded by the time he reached the concourse. His plane was on the tarmac, one engine running; the ramp down waiting for the last man on the last flight of the night – a flight into the unknown.

He flashed a boarding pass to the gate agent and jogged across the pavement to the plane, another step on the journey into his new life. He paused for a moment at the first step. It was a familiar aircraft, a Beech 1900C, similar to one the DEA agents he'd worked with over the years flew back and forth around the southwest chasing dopers and, in general, doing the best they could to stem the tide of the ever-flowing river of drugs crossing the border.

He boarded and found a seat in the sparsely filled plane. It was just him, four other men about his age, two women in their thirties, and who he thought was a flight attendant, but turned out to be a one-woman greeting committee from GovCorps. She was a forty-something beauty queen dressed in sharply creased tan slacks and a white blouse. Her blond hair flowed over her broad shoulders. She flashed a beautiful smile at her last passenger and offered a simple greeting, "Welcome, Mr. Reisch." She closed the hatch, took a seat, and at the same time grabbed the microphone from a hook and gave the prefunctionary airline message about seat belts and cell phones.

Moments later, the turbo-prop raced down the runway, lifted off, tilted away from Sin City and headed into the blackness of the Nevada desert.

Mike peered out the window at the rapidly disappearing lights of the strip, then turned his attention to the sound of her melodic voice as she started moving down the aisle with a handful of brown manila envelopes. She paused by his seat, shuffled the envelopes, then handed one to him. "Mr. Reisch," she stated. He nodded as she handed it to him, then she moved on toward the rear of the aircraft.

Mike leaned back in his seat, flipped on the overhead light and looked at the envelope – a standard business size with the Gov-Corps logo emblazoned in the upper left corner and his name neatly inscribed in calligraphy on its face. He flicked it open, scanned the bureaucratic mumbo-jumbo, new employee introduction to Gov-Corps, filled out the W-2, signed it, and had it ready for her as she returned to the front of the aircraft.

The next two pages provided a broad outline of his and his fellow newcomers' itinerary for the next twenty-two weeks: Coping in Dehydrated Condition; Physical Fitness and Endurance; Advanced

First Aid; Insects and Snakes of the Desert; Firearms and Explosives; Improvised Explosive Devices (Making and Defusing); Self-Defense; Interview Techniques; Customs and Traditions; English as a Second Language in the Middle East; Political Reality in the Middle East; Installation and Removal of Listening Devices; and, a course on general words and phrases of Arabic/English words and statements. He scanned the multi-page attachment:

What is your name?	-	Ismack eh?
You	-	Inta
Well done	-	Kowayes
Thank God	-	Alhandullellah

He flicked to the back: twenty pages to be memorized before completion of the training program. Mike closed his eyes, took a deep breath and exhaled slowly. There was a lot of work to be done.

The sound of the landing gear being dropped roused him from his catnap. The plane rotated left, lowered its nose, and seconds later made a perfectly smooth landing. Mike looked out the window into the inky blackness, a total reverse from the bright lights of Las Vegas. His new life was upon him.

#

Mike sat on the edge of his Vietnam era cot and gazed out the window of his Spartan eight-by-ten room. He and the other "newbies" were housed in one of the world's most secret training bases in the middle of the Nevada desert. They came from diverse backgrounds, each with his or her inner secrets, each looking to kick-start their lives in a unique environment. They were preparing for their new careers in the service of – he paused and deliberated for a moment. Who were they in the service of? GovCorps? In a way, but not really. GovCorps was simply the company who signed the paycheck. In fact, he was in the service of his country in a conflict with complete deniability. Some might call them mercenaries. To others, they were contract employees of the CIA. Nevertheless, it didn't make any difference. There was work to be done. It paid well, was not taxable, and gave him time to think – not just about his own life, but about her.

In his heart, he knew what must be done. The facts were inescapable. She killed with impunity, and whether he was still a cop or not didn't make any difference. One way or the other, she would be held accountable. Not today. Not tomorrow, but someday soon.

#

The days and nights became a blur. They went non-stop. The instructors were half tortuous drill instructors and half a good friend who showed the lost souls how to survive in their new and strange world. The trainees were about to embark into a world without rules, yet will be required to know and follow international law.

His bloodshot eyes peered out the window at the vast, silent desert as it reflected the last golden rays of the sun. Not more than an occasional sage brush poked its scrawny branches through the arid wasteland. If God invented lonesomeness, then Mike sat on the king's throne.

#

Five months had slipped away since his escape from Dallas, but it just as well could have been a lifetime. His entire life had changed – no more Dallas Police Department; no more family; no more recognizable haunts; and, no more Emily. Not yet, anyway.

He stood, shed his dust-covered boots and dungarees, and stepped out of his shorts. He slipped on his sandals, wrapped a fresh white towel around his waist and made his way down the hall to the shower.

He stood beneath the lukewarm spray of water, tilted his head, listened and smiled. A touch of reality. Someone was playing a radio or cd. Patsy Cline music floated throughout the building. He recognized it as one of his favorites: "Faded Love."

Memories swept over him – driving his pickup truck down the Stemmons Freeway to meet his friends; going with Annalisa to the bookstores in Archer City; easing his old truck over the ruts in the road on a deer hunting lease north of Albany, Texas. It was good music and good memories. Those were the days.

The shower was first-rate as it bathed away the grime of another grueling day. The music made it even better, but those days were history. That was then; this is now. There was more than one job to be done. First, he must earn a living; second, he had to see Emily one last time.

Five months down and one more to go. Then, two weeks' vacation as an interlude to his assignment imbedded with the Kurdish militia in Northern Iraq. If he didn't see her now, there was no way of knowing when he could possibly have another opportunity. Plus, there was the question: Will she strike again?

#

The newbies and the training staff woofed their Friday night dinners in the mess hall – steaks and baked potatoes, followed by hot apple pie and ice cream, and a cup of steaming hot coffee. Then everyone got their singular occasion in the work week to relax and do whatever they wanted: a movie in the theater; beer and drinks in the slop shoot; cards and billiards; or, in Mike's case, take advantage of his GovCorps cell phone and put his play into motion. The time was at hand.

The cell phones were issued to each of the trainees at the end of the Friday training session. They had been the only means of contact with the outside world since the day he stepped off the plane and looked at his new home, referred to by some as Area 51, but more accurately, Groom Lake, Nevada. Mail and email were prohibited.

Eric told him the training would take place in near isolation, and he wasn't kidding. They were disconnected from any form of civilization, so the opportunity to call outside was nothing less than a joy, even if the purpose was less than honorable. Plus, the cell phones were untraceable – a vital quality in this line of work.

Mike checked out a Hummer from the garage, exited the parking lot and headed up Trail 7A in the moonless night, a fairly smooth dirt path up the side of Gossamer Hill, the highest point of land on the base. The trail was little more than a blur in the non-descript featureless terrain. He guided it over a few small boulders and ruts in the road, slowed, then eased it around one of the notable high points on the base, a greenish-yellow, leafless greasewood tree, the only green life he'd seen since he arrived – except, of course, for the stories of little green men.

Mike pushed in the clutch, shifted down into first gear, then pressed firmly but gently on the gas pedal. He guided the vehicle up the last two-hundred steep yards to the knoll, a smooth asphalt-like mound perched over the nothingness of Groom Lake and the secrets it held.

With a flick of the wrist, the engine stopped and he turned off the headlights. The deathly quiet and inky darkness of the desert bathed him into a black hole, physically and metaphysically. Not a light was to be seen. Las Vegas and Reno were too distant, and the barracks and support buildings were too close to the foot of the hill. He was alone. Only Emily stirred his thoughts.

There was no factual need for the privacy of the mountaintop, but it was merely a comfortable thing to do. The loss of one you love is difficult at best. Solitude provides an essential comfort zone, if indeed such a place can exist at all.

He pulled the cell phone from his pocket and with the effortlessness touch of practiced fingers, punched in her number. She picked it up on the third ring.

"Morgan residence."

"Hi beautiful," he replied.

"Michael," she shouted. Her voice strained with excitement. "Michael, where are you? I've been worried sick."

"I took a sudden trip out of town. They were going to fire me and I went undercover, so to speak. I got a lawyer and turned in my retirement before they could take it away from me."

"But, Mike. It's been months. Where have you been? In fact, where are you now? My caller ID shows all zeros."

"Idaho," he lied. "The city had ninety days to challenge my retirement, but they had to serve me, which of course, they couldn't."

"What about me?' she replied. "You could have at least told me where you were or given me a call. You didn't have to hide from me."

"Yeah, I really did. They were so pissed ..." He related to her the story of his arrest and later punching Hauk in the face.

"Mike, you didn't."

He chuckled. "Sure did. Dumb as hell, but it felt good at the time. Anyhow, they were bound and determined to dump me, so I hit the road. I couldn't take the chance of calling you or even sending a letter. The bastards would've placed you under surveillance just to get to me, so I did what I had to do."

He paused and gazed at the firmament. Peace and solitude abounded. "Lover," he said, "that's behind us. I'm free and clear, and they can't touch me. I'm ready to live again. What about you?"

"More ready than you can ever believe. I've been a basket case without you, and not knowing anything was pure hell." She paused, then added a soft inflection to her voice. "So what are you doing in Idaho? I never heard you mention anything about that."

"His name is Dennis Miller," he continued with his lie. "He was a guy I knew years ago. We fished together a couple times, but I hadn't talked to him in a few years. I knew he owned a place up here, so I gave it a shot and found him. Good news, though. I've been working with him getting his property ready and we're going into partnership on a fishing lodge. I've got to get you up here to see the place. You'll love it."

"Me? Trout fishing in Idaho?"

"Okay, so maybe that isn't exactly the kind of future we thought about, but at least it gave me a little psychological life and financial footing for the time being."

"Are you coming home? I want to see you, Michael. I want to hold you and *fuck* you," she emphasized.

"I love it when you talk dirty," he joked. "Yeah, let's make a plan to get together and restart our lives." His voice softened. "I mean that sincerely. I want us to start a new life together – forever. You and me!"

"I love you," she whispered.

"I love you, too, Emily. Forever and ever," He paused and continued, "Dennis has a plane and we're flying down to Pueblo, Colorado in a couple weeks. His ex and kids live there, so he wants to spend a few days with them. I can fly there with him, rent a car and we can meet. We can do something, just the two of us."

She chuckled softly. "Umm hmm. I can handle that."

"What about this. You've heard of my favorite place just north of Chama. The Second Meadow. The weather will be perfect by then and we can have two or three days of privacy. It'll be just the two of us and the mountains. You'll love it."

"Wouldn't you rather have some time in a luxurious hotel or resort, and let some slave wait on us hand and foot?"

He laughed. "You know me. I'm an outdoors guy, but I'll make you a deal. Go with me to the mountains, then when we get married I'll take you wherever your little heart so desires."

"Is that a proposal, Detective Palotti?"

"Yes and no. Yes, it's a proposal, but no, it's not from any detective." He paused and the phone was silent. "That was another life. It's over. Now, it's Mike Palotti and his fiancé." He paused, inhaled deeply and set the plan in motion. "Why don't you catch a plane to Albuquerque, rent a car and head north. It'll take you three hours, maybe a little more, and we can meet at the café in Conejos, Colorado. We'll put together a couple packs and head up the mountain. You'll love it."

"I love you, Mike. I'll be there. Give me the dates and what I need to bring. You know how much I love you. I'd follow you to the gates of hell just to be with you."

Mike leaned back and put his boots up on the dashboard. She was reeled in! "Two weeks from tomorrow we're flying down. I'll call you and we'll coordinate our schedules. Until then, just to be on the safe side since I still don't trust those Dallas bastards, let's keep our business to ourselves. Just you and me."

"Love you, big guy. When you're ready, give me a whistle. I'll be there."

"I'll get loose and call you in a week, but for right now let's target June 24th. That should be about right."

"Okay," she replied. "I'll check some flights. Call me, though. I can't wait to hear your voice."

"I love you, Mrs. Palotti."

"And I love you, Mr. Palotti."

He heard her take a deep breath and then her whispered voice. "Until death do us part."

#

He snapped his phone off, laid his head across the back of the seat and looked up at the stars – millions of them in the blackness of the Nevada sky. As sure as there is a heaven and a hell, he was going to kill her.

The soothing warmth of the desert evening caressed the whole of his being. His muscles, taut from the week's training, were now completely relaxed; his heartbeat smooth and steady. He held his hand out, palm down. The twitch in his fingers was gone – solid as a rock. He flicked the phone open again and punched in Eric's number.

His friend caught it on the first ring. "Right on time, *amigo*. I've been waiting. How'd it go?"

Mike fell back on his training and avoided the obvious. "Fishing was great. I tossed a dry fly in the stream and a big trout hit it on the first cast."

"Did you reel it in?"

"Oh yeah, easy money. She bit hard and I set the hook, then pulled her right into my net. She's as good as cleaned and cooked."

Eric replied. "I knew you'd enjoy the fishing lodge. Why don't you give me a buzz when you're about ready to break camp and we'll plan a little get-together?"

Mike chuckled. "We're about there. I'll miss this place, but I've got to get to work and earn a living."

"That you do, my good man. Give me a call and I'll have everything ready – frying pan and corn meal. We'll cook up a good mess of fish."

"See ya, good buddy," Mike replied as he clicked the "end" button on his cell phone.

#

It was three days before graduation. Mike packed most of his belongings, setting aside the few incidentals he would need until Friday. Then, Part One of his new life would begin. Part Two would be exactly as he planned, but not with her. She'd never see Second Meadow. She would be dead.

He picked up another cell phone from the duty-officer, wandered nonchalantly outside to the park bench alongside the basketball court, sat down and called her for one last time.

"Hi lover boy. I've been holding my breath for your call."

He chuckled. "I've been holding more than that just thinking about you, but we're about there. You ready?"

"Sure am," she replied. "I get to Albuquerque at ten o'clock on Continental. By the time I pick up my luggage and car rental, I'm thinking I need a few hours to get to Conejos." She paused for a moment. "Mike, I'm looking at the map and the place looks pretty small. Are you sure this is where we should meet?"

"Sure, since there is only one café. You'll see it on the curve after you cross the river. I'll be there. Just pull in the parking lot. We can't miss each other." He blew her a kiss over the phone. "I can't wait to touch you, to kiss you and call you my wife."

"Oh, Michael, I love you so much. I'll be there. I promise, and I'll take you as my husband all the days of my life – Mr. and Mrs. Michael Palotti."

"Love you, babe. Have a good flight and drive safely so I can give you a good squeeze." He didn't wait for a reply before he flicked his phone off and tapped in Eric's number. Once again, he caught it on the first ring.

"We've got a problem with this fish," Mike said immediately.

"No details," Eric retorted. "Just a fact or two, and I'll take it from there."

"Continental Airlines getting to Albuquerque is the long way around."

"Yep, you're right about that, but I'll take care of it. No sweat. Enjoy what's left of your fishing trip."

Mike looked at the phone. The conversation was over. The deed was in motion. Whatever game she had in mind was too little too late. She was already dead, but didn't know it.

#

Eric sat his desk and turned on his computer. Her schedule came on the screen a few seconds later. Continental from Dallas to Houston, then a quick transfer and into Albuquerque at ten o'clock.

Another phone call to an indebted colleague at the CIA and he got what he needed. She'd bought two tickets – one from Dallas; two from Houston. There was a friend.

"Hope you get a good lay, dude," Eric mumbled when he hung up, "because it's going to be the last piece you get from her."

#

Eric joined the line at Houston's Intercontinental Airport, wormed his way through the crowd and took his place with the other passengers. Only two people were in front of him. Emily and her friend, an indescribably gorgeous thirty-something goddess – long slender legs slipped into her tight jeans; a silver and turquoise grommet holding her long blond hair back; a white blouse seductively unbuttoned to the top of her cleavage; and, a pair of Lucchese snake-skin boots. *A class act*, he thought, *but looks can be deceiving*, and in her case that was a certainty.

His mind wandered. *What the hell is going on?*

Tucked comfortably into his seat, Eric accepted a Bloody Mary from the flight attendant. He sat back and observed the women two rows in front of him and across the aisle. Their conversation appeared to be casual chit-chat – the early morning flight, parking at the airport, getting comfortable in their seats and accepting their Bloody Marys. They toasted each other with a tap of the glasses and spoke softly, words he could not understand, but their gesture was overwhelming – they kissed. Not once, but twice. First on the cheek, then softly and directly on the lips.

A cold chill ran the length of his body. Emily had an accomplice; or, she was on the prowl and there was another victim ready for the taking. Either way did not spell good news. He'd anticipated an accomplice, but thought it would be a man – another Andre Ilin, and he would be easy enough to handle. This threw a wrench into the works. If he was to go through with the car wreck he'd already planned it would kill whomever was in the car, but if this gorgeous thing was another of Emily's victims being set up for the kill, he would be doing the killing for her.

He looked at his watch. His co-worker should already have stolen the truck from the mountainside logging area. It would be loaded with timber and on the way down the road toward the highway. The plan was simple enough. Time it to meet her from the opposite direction immediately after she topped the 10,230 foot La Manga Pass. The curve in the road would place her on the outside where it was nearly straight down for almost 1,000 feet. The truck would slip over the centerline at the last moment, leaving her without time to respond. Literally, she would run out of road and life. Her car would be no match for the heavily loaded truck. It would catapult her over the edge and pulverize her and whoever else was with her – accomplice or her lover for the moment.

Eric and his second colleague would come upon the "accident" almost immediately, feign a cell phone call to the Highway Patrol and help the truck driver, who would be suffering shock, into their car. In the chaos and excitement that followed, the Good Samaritans would take the driver to the hospital in Espanola where they would disappear into a well-practiced oblivion, a scheme they'd pulled many times around the world.

Eric ordered another Bloody Mary, then sat back and relaxed. There was nothing he could do. The plan was underway. There was no pulling back.

#

The two women made their way to the baggage carousel, found their items, loaded them on a cart and made their way to the Avis counter. Eric followed at a discreet distance, fumbled with his keys, then found his associate standing near the exit. He was a big but suave Mexican, in his forties, and looked as though he could handle anything or anybody. He was dressed straight out of an advertisement in the Sunday paper, but nonetheless, a professional killer. He wore a white Guayabera, tan denims, his standard Cole Han loafers, a gold chain and medallion around his thick neck, and his dark hair was oiled and combed back. Their eyes touched in acknowledgement. Everything was in motion precisely as planned.

Eric followed his associate to the curb, tossed his carry-on bag into the back seat of the SUV, slipped into the passenger seat and spoke softly to his accomplice. "A bit of a twist, but nothing we can do about it."

The men shook hands. "Antonio, thanks for scoping this thing out for me on such short notice, but it looks like we'll get it done one way or the other. I sure as hell hadn't figured on that good-looking bitch. It would be a lot easier if it was some big gorilla who we'd like to see flushed from the DNA pool."

The two laughed. "That's life," Antonio replied.

They watched the women board the shuttle to the car rental. Minutes later they left the car lot in their Lexus, found the northbound I-25, and were enroute to their demise.

"I don't know what the deal is with the gorgeous thing, but she's a fish in the skillet and there's nothing we can do about it. Let's just get it over with," Eric commented dryly.

#

They followed Emily and her friend north where they took a surprising exit from the Interstate and drove onto the square in Santa Fe. The men followed in silence. *That's the trouble with every plan*, Eric thought. *You never know what your adversary has in mind.*

The Lexus pulled into the guest driveway at the upscale Inn of the Mountains and stopped at the front door. Antonio pulled his SUV around to the side, but positioned them in a location to maintain the eyeball on their target.

Emily hopped out and grabbed a suitcase from the rear seat while her radiant passenger exited and walked around the vehicle. They paused face-to-face for a moment, then embraced before exchanging a tender kiss. The blond picked up her suitcase as Emily jumped back behind the wheel, lowered the window, and gave a brisk wave good-bye as she pulled away and headed back to the Interstate.

Eric offered a soft chuckle. "She'll never know how close she came to being dead meat."

Antonio tossed him a sidelong glance. "From her or from us?"

"You've got a point there," Eric replied as they swung back onto the Interstate. He looked at his watch. "Maybe two hours." He slid down in the seat and rested his head on the headrest. "Tell me about getting the truck."

Antonio cracked his window, pulled a cigar from his pocket and lit up. "Maduro. Want one?"

"No thanks, I'll die fast enough just getting my share of your smoke. So, tell me about getting the truck."

"No big deal," the Mexican replied as he accelerated. They whipped past a couple trailer trucks and fell in comfortably several hundred yards behind their prey. "There're lots of small independents up there. We got it early this morning, slapped a magnetic sign on the doors, changed the license plates, and tucked it away just north of the state line by five o'clock. Mejia has a fake driver's license just in case, plus both of us have satellite cell phones so we can coordinate as we get closer."

He looked over at Eric. His eyes were closed. "Remind you of the deal we did in Kazakhstan?"

Eric nodded his agreement and mumbled, "Yep. Sure does. Let's just get it over with and get on with life." He sat up straight, stretched and yawned. "Glad you guys could get free for a few days.

I was a little worried a couple weeks ago whether or not I could get you out here on such short notice."

Antonio chuckled. "This is what we do for a living, Mejia and me. We've got this down to an art form." He paused and looked at Eric. "So what did this woman do to earn your wrath?"

Eric shrugged. "Just a bitch who deserves it."

"Gotcha," Antonio replied. "I'll mind my own business."

#

Eric checked his watch – twelve-forty and they were at the foot of La Manga Pass. He tossed a quick glance at his cohort. "Okay, let's roll."

Antonio flicked on his cell phone, paused while it made contact, then punched in the number. Eric listened to their brief conversation. "We're about a quarter mile back. Traffic is light. It's the Green Lexus. Driver only. Speed holding at fifty-three miles per hour. ETA seventeen minutes on contact."

He flicked the phone off and stuffed it back into his shirt pocket. "We'll stay in touch as we get closer, but right now I'd say we're right on schedule." He laughed softly. "Good thing for that other chick she didn't take a ride in the mountains today."

The men rode in silence. A light shower began to fall. Eric nodded. It would only help to serve the story – slick highway, no guardrail, big truck. It had all the ingredients for another traffic fatality.

The tall evergreens swayed in the breeze and rain. The setting was perfect. The road glazed with a touch of ice at the high elevation. Antonio slowed as they approached the summit, tapped in the phone numbers and gave a brief comment. "Summit. Two minutes to go." He pulled over to the scenic overlook, paused and looked at his watch, counted out thirty seconds, then pulled back onto the highway. Moments later they swung around the curve of the quickly descending road and saw it in front of them. The lumber truck sprawled across both lanes. Its front end was heavily damaged. The driver was climbing out, screaming unintelligibly at the horror of the accident. A car that was following the truck pulled up, its driver and passengers bailing out to offer their assistance.

Antonio pulled the SUV to the side, jumped out and ran to the edge. The Lexus was at the bottom of the cliff, upside down, partially submerged in the river. The car itself was a mangled heap of scrap metal. No one could have survived the wreck and the fall. The river was just a stroke of good luck in case she somehow survived everything else. He ran back to the SUV and hollering over his shoulder to the other Good Samaritans that he was calling the Highway Patrol. He feigned the call, then walked toward the "distraught" Mejia, who was sitting on a rock on the roadside crying helplessly.

"Come with me, my friend. We'll get you some help."

Once again, Antonio called out to the others. "I'm taking him to the hospital in Espanola. Tell the cops when they get here. I'll wait there for them," he lied.

The three men buckled their seat belts and when they were safely out of view, offered their congratulations to each other. "Any trouble?" Eric asked Mejia.

"Nope. Not a bit. Went like clockwork. Say, that was a nice ride we dumped into the canyon. Too bad."

"Yeah," Eric responded. "Too damn bad."

Epilogue

MIKE TOOK THE JANET AIRLINES Friday morning shuttle from Groom Lake to Las Vegas, transferred to U.S. Airlines and found himself at the base of the Rocky Mountains in Colorado Springs by early afternoon. He rented a car, tossed his bags in the trunk, and three hours later was at the café in Conejos. Of course, she would not be there, but it was important to carry out the ruse to be on the safe side. That was the way they'd planned it, and it was a standard part of the training exercises – always follow through. Always cover your bets. There is no room for slipups.

By four o'clock the news reached the café – a horrible accident on the highway and a woman was killed. A timber truck knocked her over the edge and down into the creek. When rescuers reached her car, they found her body strapped in with the seat belt and under four feet of water.

Mike sucked the last drops from his coffee cup, scanned the little group of customers spread out around the tables, each with his and her own version of what had happened. He slipped his money to the cashier and left.

It was a long and lonesome drive in the darkness back to Colorado Springs. He wept. All those he loved were gone – Annalisa, Samanta, and Emily – Sweet Emily.

*****

CPSIA information can be obtained at www.ICGtesting.com
Printed in the USA
LVOW092311040612

284646LV00001B/23/P